PRAISE FOR BARRY EISLER

"Eisler combines the insouciance of Ian Fleming, the realistic detail of Tom Clancy, the ennui of Graham Greene, and the prose power of John le Carré."

—News-Press

"Furious and creative . . . Rain's combination of quirks and proficiency is the stuff great characters are made of."

—Entertainment Weekly

"No one is writing a better thriller series today than Barry Eisler. He has quickly jumped into my top ten best American mystery/ thriller writers, along with Michael Connelly, Lee Child, Walter Mosley, and Harlan Coben. . . . Rating: A."

—Deadly Pleasures

"Written with a delightfully soft touch and a powerful blend of excitement, exotica, and what (ever since John le Carré) readers have known to call tradecraft."

—The Economist

THE
GOD'S EYE
VIEW

ALSO BY BARRY EISLER

A Clean Kill in Tokyo (previously published as *Rain Fall*)
A Lonely Resurrection (previously published as *Hard Rain*)
Winner Take All (previously published as *Rain Storm*)
Redemption Games (previously published as *Killing Rain*)
Extremis (previously published as *The Last Assassin*)
The Killer Ascendant (previously published as *Requiem for an Assassin*)
Fault Line
Inside Out
The Detachment
Graveyard of Memories

SHORT WORKS

The Lost Coast
Paris Is a Bitch
The Khmer Kill
London Twist

ESSAYS

The Ass Is a Poor Receptacle for the Head: Why Democrats Suck at Communication, and How They Could Improve
Be the Monkey: A Conversation about the New World of Publishing (with J. A. Konrath)

THE GOD'S EYE VIEW

BARRY EISLER

Text copyright © 2016 Barry Eisler

Published by Thomas & Mercer, Seattle

www.apub.com

Amazon, the Amazon logo, and Thomas & Mercer are trademarks of Amazon.com, Inc., or its affiliates.

Hardcover ISBN-13: 9781503951518
Hardcover ISBN-10: 1503951510

ISBN-13: 9781503949614
ISBN-10: 1503949613

Cover design by Rex Bonomelli

Printed in the United States of America

For the whistleblowers

The Panopticon must not be understood as a dream building: it is the diagram of a mechanism of power reduced to its ideal form.

—Michel Foucault

Knowledge has always flowed upwards, to bishops and kings, not down to serfs and slaves. The principle remains the same in the present era . . . governments dare to aspire, through their intelligence agencies, to a god-like knowledge of every one of us.

—Julian Assange

Comrades, I must tell you again: we must collect everything! Nothing can be missed!

—Erich Mielke, leader of East Germany's Stasi

PROLOGUE........

. . . .

General Theodore Anders was dreaming of marlin fishing when the secure phone rang on the bed stand next to him. He sat up immediately, concerned but not unduly so. He'd been awakened plenty of times over the course of his career, and by much worse than a telephone.

He blinked and reflexively scanned the room by the dim light of the bedside digital alarm clock. His wife, Debbie, continued snoring softly beside him. She'd learned to tune out NSA's intrusions almost immediately after he'd been appointed director. If it were an internal problem, he wouldn't be able to tell her. If the problem were external, she'd see it on the news soon enough. Either way, she didn't want to know, or at least not before she had to. She was a good woman.

He cleared his throat and picked up the handset before the unit could ring a second time. In the army, he'd learned to impress his superiors with an image of constant readiness. The habit had stayed with him long since his superiors had become his subordinates.

"Go ahead," he said quietly. It was his standard greeting—a crisp, efficient command. He also liked responding to a knock with a single word: *Come.* The implication being that the extra syllable of the standard *Come in* was wasteful and unnecessary. Debbie hated it and had trained him not to do it at home. She told him it was how someone talked to a dog—*come, sit, stay.* Which, he had to admit, was probably part of the appeal.

He was expecting an immediate, succinct briefing on whatever situation had necessitated the call. So he was surprised to hear his executive officer instead say, "This is General Remar. Your access protocol, please."

Anders was momentarily so surprised he said, "Mike, it's me."

"I'm sorry, Ted. I need your access protocol before proceeding."

The access protocol was an additional layer of security for use of the secure phone, a way of determining the bona fides of the person on the other end of the line. In all the years they had worked together, Remar had never asked for it when calling Anders at home. Either something exceptionally bad was afoot, or his XO was taking extra care to cover his ass by following strict procedure. Which, Anders knew, amounted to the same thing. He felt a shot of warmth in his gut as adrenaline spread through his system.

He thought for a moment. What was the last protocol he'd been issued? "Romeo Bravo Foxtrot. Seven, three, niner."

"Victor Delta Golf. Eight, one, four."

"All right, what is it?"

"Data breach. Potentially huge."

The warmth in his gut got hotter. "Define *huge.*"

"We don't even know yet. Tens of thousands of documents. Maybe more. This guy had access to everything. PRISM. XKeyscore. Policy Directive 20. Boundless Informant. Upstream. Everything."

The heat in his stomach was suddenly a frozen knot. This was bad. Unbelievably bad.

"Who?"

"We're 80 percent sure it's a contractor named Snowden. Edward Snowden. Former CIA infrastructure analyst, DIA counterintel trainer, full administrator privileges."

Full administrator privileges. For a moment, Anders actually couldn't breathe.

"Wait," he said. He got out of bed, picked up the base unit, and padded silently across the soft carpet into the bathroom, the long phone cable snaking along behind him. He left the light off because the darkness was suddenly comforting, a hiding place, a cocoon. He cradled the handset between his cheek and shoulder, closed and locked the door, turned on the sink faucet to mask sound, and stepped inside the glassed-in shower stall. Only then did he close his eyes and say, "Tell me he didn't have access to God's Eye."

"He didn't have permissions."

"I know he didn't have permissions. That's not what I asked." He realized his tone was sharper than he'd intended.

"There's no evidence of a breach there. But Snowden . . . this guy is extremely capable. We're interviewing his colleagues. The word *genius* is coming up a lot."

"We need to know if God's Eye is secure. I don't care what else has been compromised. That is the absolute top priority."

"I'm working on it. But it's slow going because I can't bring in an ordinary forensics team."

No, of course not. In the history of the US government, there had never been a program as compartmented and prejudiced as God's Eye. Though he was suddenly terrified none of it had been enough.

He opened his eyes and blew out a long breath, working to calm himself. "Where is Snowden now?"

"We believe he's in Hong Kong."

"No. He's working with MSS?"

The Ministry of State Security was the Chinese intelligence agency, a kind of combination CIA and FBI. If Snowden was an MSS agent, maybe this could be contained. A rival intelligence service, true, but that didn't mean certain protocols didn't exist, certain understandings couldn't be reached.

"We don't think so. Greenwald and Poitras are there, too. We think he's giving the documents to them."

He blinked. Was he having a nightmare? Glenn Greenwald and Laura Poitras . . . this was far worse than MSS. Unimaginably worse.

A long, silent moment went by. He'd been in Santiago in 2010, when Chile had been hit by the 8.8 quake. For three long minutes, what he'd always known to be solid ground had bucked and roiled beneath him. This was like that. Only more surreal.

He forced himself to focus. "Has the *Guardian* contacted us yet?"

The *Guardian* was where Greenwald worked. Before its management published anything, they would reach out to NSA for comment.

"Not yet."

He felt an iota of desperate hope. They still had a chance. A slim chance, probably, but . . .

"How fast can we get a team into Hong Kong?"

"There are contractors dealing with Abu Sayyaf in Mindanao right now. We could have them on the ground in Hong Kong in six hours. Maybe less."

"Do it. Right now. OBL rules, you understand?"

The SEALs who had taken out Osama bin Laden had understood that under no circumstances was he to be captured.

"Ted, we're talking about . . . these people are Americans."

Remar was a good XO, and as loyal a man as Anders had ever known. As he should be. Anders had pulled him from a burning Humvee in the early days of Desert Storm, saving his life if not the right side of his face. After which Remar had hitched himself to Anders's rising star and relentlessly watched Anders's back. But no one was perfect, and Remar's weakness was a streak of squeamishness. Anders wasn't sure where it came from—some innate wiring in his personality? Childhood environment? The experience of multiple reconstructive and plastic surgeries that had fostered too much empathy with other people's pain? Some combination, probably.

And while Remar's different worldview often functioned as a useful pressure check on Anders's somewhat more ruthless instincts, now was absolutely not the time.

"Just take them out," Anders said. "All three of them. Is that clear? We'll blame it on MSS."

"It's not going to look like MSS."

"Why would MSS do something and make it look like their own work?"

There was a pause. Then: "There's another *Guardian* reporter with them. A Scotsman, Ewen MacAskill."

"Then take out all four. Do we know where they're meeting? Where they're staying?"

"Not yet."

Okay, probably that was too much to hope. "Put eyes and ears on them. Mobile phones, Internet access, hotel reservation systems, security cameras, satellite imagery, everything."

"It's already in motion."

That sensation of the ground roiling hit him again, this time with an accompanying wave of dizziness and nausea. He willed it all back and made himself focus. What was he missing? What else did they need? What would be their fallback? If they were forced to tell a story, they would need a narrative. And that would be . . .

"Put together briefing papers. If we can't silence Snowden, we're going to have to undermine his credibility, and we'll need our friends in the press for that. Make sure the word *narcissist* is prominent in our talking points. Be subtle. 'I'm not saying he's got outright narcissistic personality disorder' . . . that kind of thing. All of it on background."

"We already used the narcissist thing with Julian Assange."

"Yes, and it worked. Use it again."

"Understood."

"Also . . . make sure to emphasize that Snowden 'violated his oath of secrecy.' We want that phrase picked up, too."

There was no "oath of secrecy," of course. The only oath government employees took was the oath to defend the Constitution. But that was just meaningless nuance. The main thing was, you could always count on the establishment media to adopt whatever nomenclature the government fed it.

"All right," Remar said. "Who do you want spearheading the press campaign?"

"Ernest is the best in the business. Wake him up."

"Ernest?"

"The guy who got everyone in the media to describe that Gulf of Mexico undersea oil eruption as a 'leak.'"

"You mean the guy who came up with 'enhanced interrogation techniques'?"

"Actually, the Gestapo invented that phrase—*Verschärfte Vernehmung*, I think it's called in German. But Ernest was smart to borrow it. You think Snowden is a genius? Wait 'til he gets a load of Ernest. The media will have him armchair-psychoanalyzed as a narcissist and tried and convicted of treason in a day."

"I'll make sure he's on it."

"I'll see you at headquarters in a half hour."

He ended the call, opened the shower door, turned off the sink faucet, and went back into the bedroom. He paused for a moment, gazing at Debbie, still soundly asleep. He couldn't say he loved her anymore, if he ever did. But there was always something satisfying about knowing he was protecting her. And protecting what was yours . . . that was a form of love, too, wasn't it? Maybe the highest form.

He went into the closet and started getting dressed. He knew he probably couldn't stop the *Guardian*. And he didn't even care that much about the extent to which he could inhibit them.

All he really cared about, all that really frightened him now, was God's Eye. In the end, everything else was negotiable.

CHAPTER........
........1

Evelyn Gallagher sat in an upholstered chair outside the director's Fort Meade corner office, knees pressed together, skirt smoothed, fingers intertwined across her lap. As always when she waited in this chair, she wondered whether the pose was too stiff, too self-consciously formal. But it was better than fidgeting. She didn't want anyone to think the director made her nervous. Well, amend that— she didn't want anyone to *know*.

Not that anyone would notice. No one else was waiting in the outer office, and the director's executive officer, General Remar, hadn't so much as glanced at her from behind his monitor since ushering her inside. Of course, Remar, with his eye patch and ruined profile, the left side of his scalp salt-and-pepper crew cut and the right an irregular mass of Silly Putty pink, always made her feel nervous, too. It was hard not to stare at the scar tissue, or wonder what horror lay hidden behind the patch. His wounds and his recovery were legendary at NSA, his suffering conferring a kind of sanctification not just on him, but on his battlefield rescuer, the director, as well. They were like a unit, a left and a right hand, and no matter what secrets she might be privy to, in the presence of their bond she always felt like an outsider.

She glanced discreetly at her watch. How long it would be, she never knew—it could be a minute, it could be two hours. The uncertainty might have been demeaning, but on the other hand, how many people had not just an invitation, but outright instructions to come to the director immediately whenever their system threw up a red flag?

So she waited, hearing nothing but the muted clack of Remar's keyboard and the quiet hum of the HVAC air-conditioning the room. No, she couldn't deny that she liked that there were no layers between her and the director—liked how special it made her feel, liked how the direct line gave her an aura of power and importance within the organization. On the other hand, the relationship left her isolated. Even within the standard compartmentalized NSA environment, the walls around her work were extreme. So far as she knew, no one other than the director himself was aware of her function, and the director had made it clear in a variety of unmistakable ways that the privilege of direct access wasn't free, that there would be severe penalties for any osmosis, accidental or otherwise.

Which, right this moment, felt particularly inconvenient. She had something on her mind, and no colleagues she felt comfortable running it by. She wanted to ask the director but was reluctant. Because what would bringing it up with him accomplish? It was so far-fetched it would just get her flagged as untrustworthy, even paranoid. And for what? She had too much to risk. The job was right for her, the work was important, the pay was decent, and the benefits were great. The health insurance especially, without which she wouldn't have been able to enroll Dash in the special school. Her ex-husband was a deadbeat, and she was afraid to sue him lest he retaliate by enforcing his custody rights; her mother was gone; and her father was in a nearby senior center with advancing Alzheimer's. So she needed her job, and it was enormously reassuring to know the job seemed to need her. As for her doubts . . . well, didn't everyone have doubts they simply learned to keep to themselves?

She'd been sitting for close to twenty minutes, and was just thinking maybe she should have stopped at the restroom before coming and that she definitely should have thrown on a sweater because as usual the outer office was freezing, when Remar paused in his typing, glanced over from his monitor, and said, "You can go in now."

She always wondered how the director signaled him. Some kind of text message, presumably, the same way Remar had alerted the director she was waiting. That, or they'd become psychic, working together so closely for so long. She stood, hesitated for just a second, and opened the door.

The director was sitting behind his L-shaped wooden desk. The wall to his left was festooned with photographs of various luminaries—presidents, prime ministers, generals, captains of industry—all shoulder to shoulder with the director or shaking his hand. The wall to his right was devoted to bookcases filled with serious-looking tomes on military strategy, business management, and philosophy. In one corner was a coffee table, a couch, and two upholstered chairs—the space for longer and perhaps more casual meetings, though she had never been invited to join the director there.

She closed the door behind her and stood silently while he scribbled notes in the margins of some papers. After a moment he glanced at her over his reading glasses, his eyebrows arching at . . . what? Was he annoyed at the intrusion? Did he welcome it? As usual, she found him impossible to read. He was a slight man of about sixty, with thinning hair and sallow skin. She'd been working with him for over a year, and had yet to see him display any real emotion beyond a periodic intense narrowing of his pale blue eyes. She'd never even caught him ogling her breasts, which had gone from a

C to a D when Dash had been born and then decided to stay put even after she'd gotten back to exercising and lost her pregnancy weight. She didn't mind the extra size—in fact, as a single mother, she welcomed the attention brought by her new dimensions—but the director's failure ever to even sneak a glance was a little weird. Was he gay? She knew he was married, with four grown daughters, but that was no guarantee; even in the twenty-first century there were plenty of closeted people in the military, especially among the higher-ups. She'd wondered from time to time what he would do if she ever showed up with an extra button undone and leaned across his desk to point something out . . . would he be unable to resist a look? But she'd never tried. He wasn't the kind of man you'd want thinking you were messing with him.

He gestured to one of the chairs in front of his desk and said, "What is it?" The question was a kind of challenge, a suggestion that if she was taking advantage of the direct access, of course she would have something important to bring to his attention. That she'd *better* have something important.

She sat, her feet pressed firmly against the carpet. Like the waiting area, his office was over-air-conditioned, but she could feel a slight slick of perspiration under her arms and was glad she'd worn deodorant.

"Sir, my system threw up a flag—a match for two faces on the watch list. A reporter with the *Intercept* named Ryan Hamilton. And the SUSLA in Ankara. Daniel Perkins."

The Special US Liaison Advisor was NSA's senior representative in Turkey, reporting directly to the director. There were only five others in the world—in Germany, Italy, Thailand, Japan, and Korea. If a SUSLA had gone rogue, it was a major breach, and she watched the director closely, curious about his reaction.

But there was nothing beyond that slight narrowing of the eyes. "What did you observe?"

"Well, as you know, sir, we're tapped into CCTV networks all over the world. The feeds run through a facial recognition system and a Convolutional Neural Network analyzing other biometrics like height, stride length, and walking speed, and when certain people are observed together, the system sends out an alert. There are a lot of false positives that have to be screened out, but this one is confirmed. I'm pretty sure Hamilton and Perkins met in Istanbul."

The director's expression was so impassive it looked momentarily as masklike as Remar's burned profile.

"You have them face-to-face?"

"No, sir, not face-to-face. But I'm pretty sure I know where they met—a Bosphorus commuter ferry. I was able to go back and track them taking separate routes, though there's no camera on the ferry itself."

The director leaned back in his chair, the casualness of the pose, like his initial *What is it?* question, a kind of challenge. "How do you know it's not a coincidence?"

"Well, sir, I can't prove it's not. But the ferry feels like tradecraft to me. And you told me to err on the side of inclusiveness, especially when one of the principals is NSA."

If her statement came across like an admonition, he did nothing to show it. "When did this possible meeting occur?"

"Two hours ago."

"And they're still in Istanbul?"

"Presumably. I'm guessing . . ." She paused, thinking better of it.

"Yes?"

"Well, I know that as SUSLA Turkey, Perkins is your direct report. I'm guessing . . . you didn't know he's in Istanbul."

The director raised his eyebrows. "Why do you guess that?"

"Because of the way you just asked if they were still there, sir. If Perkins were traveling on official business, I'd guess you would know."

The director looked at her silently, and she wondered whether

11

she had said too much. But she wanted him to know she could do more than just hack networks and create monitoring systems. She wanted him to know she had good instincts, too, and that she deserved more responsibility.

"Anyway," she went on, "I'd recommend checking customs records to determine when Hamilton arrived, and I'd look at their mobile phones, too. If the phones were turned off, or left behind somewhere else, it sure would look as though they're trying not to be tracked. XKeyscore could tell us a lot, too. I would have looked into it myself, sir, but I'm not authorized."

It was a subtle hint that she could do her job better, more efficiently, if she had more tools.

But he ignored it. "That's good thinking. Send me the raw data. I want to know exactly where and at what time they were picked up by the cameras."

"Yes, sir."

He removed the reading glasses and placed them on his desk, then looked at her closely. "Tell me, Evie, you designed the camera system, didn't you?"

She blinked, surprised he had used her name. Surprised he remembered it.

"Uh, yes, sir. Well, I mean, we already knew that these days most CCTV cameras are wired into networks, meaning remotely exploitable by us."

"Yes, but you were the one who led the team that got us into the networks and tied them together. You were the one who automated the system, exploiting new networks as they went online, like that one Harvard secretly installed in its classrooms ostensibly as part of a study on attendance at lectures. You were the one who proposed using the access not just for directed tasking, but for passive surveillance, too, by tying it all together with the facial recognition technology and the Convolutional Neural Network."

"That's correct, sir."

He nodded. "If this Perkins thing does turn out to be a breach, it's exactly the kind of problem we would have overlooked if it hadn't been for you. Very good work."

She recognized she was being dismissed. If she was going to bring up what had been bothering her, it was now or never.

Just do it, she thought. *Or it's never going to stop bugging you.*

"Sir, can I . . . there's one other thing I wanted to ask about, if that's all right."

He raised his eyebrows and said nothing.

"Sir, remember last month, the CIA sysadmin I discovered was in contact with Marcy Wheeler, the journalist at *Emptywheel*?"

"Scott Stiles, of course."

"Yes, Stiles. Well, as usual, all I can do is confirm by access to the network that a meeting took place. I'm not supposed to otherwise task anything. So . . . I never know what the follow-up reveals."

She waited, hoping again that maybe he would take the hint, agree that she could do her job better without the blinders. But he said nothing. Just that unnervingly neutral expression and the penetrating stare. She almost decided to drop it. But she'd come this far. The hell with it.

"So, well, just a few days after I flagged the Stiles/Wheeler connection, I came across a news item in the *Post*. Stiles had been found hanged in his McLean apartment."

"Yes, I'm aware of it. Very sad."

"Yes, sir, it was. And I was just . . ."

She couldn't finish the sentence. What the hell was she doing?

The director offered her the trace of a smile. "Are you asking, was that a coincidence?"

"Uh, well, yes, sir, I guess that is what I'm asking. It just seemed—"

"You want to know whether we had anything to do with Stiles's death."

She swallowed. She couldn't deny that, yes, that was precisely what she wanted to know. But she couldn't say it out loud, either. Even just having suggested it seemed suddenly crazy. The idea itself, and mentioning it besides.

A silent moment spun out. Then the director chuckled. "The answer is no."

She looked at him, but his gaze was inscrutable. After another awkward, silent moment, she nodded and stood. "Thank you, sir. I . . . I feel silly that I asked."

He shook his head. "I'm glad you asked. It's exactly the kind of question, the kind of connection, each of us should be trying to make. It just happens that in this case, the connection was a coincidence."

"So . . . Stiles wasn't involved with anything . . . untoward with Marcy Wheeler?"

There was a pause. "I didn't say that."

"No, sir, but you said Stiles's death was sad."

There was the slightest furrowing of his brows. "As it was. Whatever he may or may not have intended in his contacts with irresponsible bloggers, he served his country for many years. By my lights, that makes his unfortunate, unnecessary, and untimely death very sad indeed, as I said."

She nodded and stood, recognizing she had hit a dead end and wishing she hadn't gone down the street that led to it. When she got to the door, he said, "Evie."

She turned and looked at him.

He nodded as though in appreciation, or appraisal. "Very good work."

"Thank you, sir."

She headed back to her office, mentally kicking herself. She'd felt she had to ask, but why? What point had she been trying to prove, and to whom? If she'd been watching a movie, she'd be angry at the heroine for having thoughtlessly tipped her hand. She'd learned nothing, and in doing so had probably caused the director to question . . . she didn't know what. Her loyalty, or something.

All of which was bad enough. But there was something worse, something she sensed was the real reason she wished she hadn't asked about Stiles.

She thought the director was lying.

CHAPTER . . . .
. . . . 2

The moment Gallagher left, Anders was on the phone scrambling the geolocation and customs records units. Gallagher had good instincts, which worried him somewhat at the moment, but he would deal with that presently. For now, what mattered was Hamilton and Perkins, and whether NSA had a new Snowden operating out of Turkey.

He decided not to contact anyone in Ankara. Not yet. He expected he would be able to find out all he needed from the geolocation and customs records people. And from a system set up by a computer network exploitation unit, one that had penetrated just about every hotel and other travel system in the world. If Perkins needed to be dealt with, it was better that as few people as possible knew of the underlying problem, especially with Gallagher expressing suspicions about what had happened to Stiles. The whole purpose of the compartmentalized security program—cell phone geolocation, customs, law enforcement, CCTV monitoring, satellite imagery, license plate reading, and several others, in addition to the more widely available and less walled-off metadata programs—was to ensure that no one without the appropriate clearance would have more than the most fragmented sense of who was being looked at, or why. Or what was being done about it.

Well, not the whole purpose. There was another benefit: no one but Remar and Anders himself understood all the means of monitoring NSA could bring to bear on a problem. He had a gut-level feeling it was precisely this compartmentalization, which he himself had designed following the Snowden breach, that had tripped up Perkins. If Perkins had gone traitor, the man would have known to be ultracautious about his cell phone, the sites he visited online, and a variety of other security tells. But Perkins didn't know about the facial recognition or other biometrics analysis. A mole could only avoid and evade the monitoring systems of which he was aware. Which made it crucial that almost no one be permitted to see the whole picture.

Within ten minutes, he'd received confirmation that Hamilton had arrived that afternoon on a BA flight from London. He had checked in at the Rasha Hotel two hours after that. And his cell phone had remained at the hotel since then. Why would a reporter leave his cell phone in his hotel room while he was out, if not as an attempt to fool anyone tracking him into believing he, too, had remained in his room? And worse, Perkins had done the same: his cell phone left in his Ankara apartment while Perkins was traveling in Istanbul.

And Gallagher had been right. It was unthinkable Perkins would travel to Istanbul without first informing Anders. Snowden slipping off to Hong Kong had been what had killed them in 2013. Since then, all travel, like all foreign and media contacts, had to be strictly accounted for in advance. That Perkins had violated the protocol looked bad. Very bad. But Anders needed more to be certain—certain enough to do what he sensed was going to be required.

He called Gallagher. "Evie, how many camera networks are you into in Ankara and Istanbul?"

"Virtually all of them, sir. There are a few banks with especially heavily encrypted systems, but—"

"And the footage is stored for how long—three months?"

"At least, sir. If necessary, we can often retrieve earlier material that's been overwritten."

"I want you to run your system and see if you can place Perkins in or around Ankara Internet cafés over whatever time frame is available to you."

"Sir, I think if you focus on his mobile phone—"

"I sincerely doubt he would have had it with him during the visits I'm imagining."

There was a pause. "Understood, sir."

"If you find anything, I want the dates, times, and locations."

"Yes, sir."

He clicked off and considered. Why would Hamilton and Perkins risk meeting face-to-face? If this were a simple leak of documents, no matter how massive, it could all have been handled remotely. Electronically.

But that was the answer right there, wasn't it? Signals intelligence was NSA's bread and butter. Perkins knew that. So he was more afraid of an electronic intercept than he was of being compromised through a meeting. It was the same reasoning bin Laden had employed in eschewing phones and the Internet and relying on human couriers, instead.

But he sensed there was more than simply that. Maybe they didn't just need to meet face-to-face; they wanted to. Why? He thought of Snowden again. The material Snowden had leaked was recondite, practically a foreign language to outsiders. He'd spent a week walking Greenwald, Poitras, and MacAskill through it, providing background, explanations, crucial context. If all Perkins wanted was a leak, he could have just uploaded his information to *WikiLeaks*. No, what he wanted was a known journalist's imprimatur—a way of laundering a leak into something newsworthy. Otherwise, the damage control would be too easy. The government could dismiss the revelations as vandalism, or deny them entirely.

A message alert popped up on his monitor. Gallagher had come through. Perkins favored at least four Internet cafés in Ankara. Presumably there were others, involving a kind of shell-game effect, but he'd been picked up only at the four so far. Still, that was more than enough.

He called a PRISM analyst and told her he wanted to know if any of the Internet activity at the Ankara cafés in question was suspicious. With the dates and times, it took less than three minutes for the analyst to confirm that someone was using those cafés to read the *Intercept* and *WikiLeaks* and various other radical websites. Worse, that someone was focusing on the bios of activists that read like a who's-who of international subversives: Barrett Brown, Sarah Harrison, Murtaza Hussain, Angela Keaton, that FOIA terrorist Jason Leopold, Janet Reitman, Trevor Timm . . . and that damn Marcy Wheeler again. With the attention gradually narrowing to one name in particular: Ryan Hamilton.

The beauty of the security system was that the analyst had no idea who was being tasked. She would never connect Anders's query today with the unpleasant news about Perkins tomorrow.

A call to a geolocation analyst confirmed that on each occasion Perkins had been using an Internet café, his mobile phone had remained in his apartment. He thought doing so would disguise his movements, and therefore his activity. And he would have been right—except for the camera network. He didn't know about that.

For a moment, Anders was irritated at all the trouble he had to go through just to confirm a single person's location. It would be so much easier, and better, if everyone were fitted with a microchip. He'd read an article somewhere about how a dog had slipped away from its home in Pennsylvania, and how it had been discovered months later in Oregon—all because a shelter technician had read the microchip her owners had implanted in her. There might be some resistance to the notion of doing something like this to people, of course, but he imagined if it were billed as insurance against kidnapping . . . and if a high-profile kidnapping could be arranged to be foiled—a child saved from the worst depravity, its parents from bottomless horror and grief, solely because the child's loving parents had possessed the foresight to implant a chip while the child was an infant—it wouldn't be long before all parents would feel criminally negligent for failing to implant their children. He wondered if a law could be passed, the way there had been for car seats and bicycle helmets. But no, it probably wouldn't even be necessary. The fear of a kidnapping coupled with a *Why, why did we not have the microchip done?* would be more than sufficient.

He shook off the daydream, knowing he had to work with the tools available to him today. Tomorrow was another matter.

Istanbul, he wondered. Why Istanbul for the meeting? Close enough to Ankara for Perkins to be able to slip away and travel by train or by car. No cell phone, no credit cards, no electronic breadcrumbs. Ankara would have been more convenient, but if Hamilton were on any kind of watch list—and he was—his presence in Ankara might have drawn suspicion onto Perkins once the *Intercept* published whatever Perkins was handing over.

All of which meant there might still be a chance to contain the damage. If this was the first meeting . . . if nothing had been transferred electronically yet, or, even if it had, if no one else had the encryption keys . . . if they were planning on spending at least a little time together so Perkins could bring Hamilton up to speed . . .

He had to be careful, though. Gallagher was suspicious. Not so suspicious she was afraid to share the suspicions with him, he was glad to see. But suspicious enough. On top of which, she was smart, and observant. Another suicide—or worse, two suicides—of problems Gallagher herself had flagged would likely worsen her concern. He needed something even more deniable.

But no matter how deniable, Gallagher would have to be watched. In his experience, suspicion was like flu. Many people caught it, but only a relatively few succumbed. Given time and proper treatment, most got better. But the illness still had to be monitored. You couldn't let a fever reach a point where it threatened the health of the body.

Most of all, you couldn't take a chance on contagion.

He thought about Hamilton. For a moment, he felt . . . not bad, exactly. But sorrowful. Some of his colleagues looked at the world through a cartoon prism in which their domestic enemies hated America and loved the terrorists and other such comforting absurdities. Anders understood human nature to be generally more subtle than that, and assumed Hamilton loved his country in his distorted way, no matter how much his activities were likely to harm it. Well, there was a sort of solemn pride in knowing the reporter's death wouldn't be in vain. That the manner of his dying would actually serve to unite Americans, to bring them together in strength and common purpose. Hamilton would never know, and even if he could, would never understand, but in an odd way, Anders respected him. If the man had to die—and he did—wouldn't he want his organs to be harvested, for example, that he might give the gift of life to others? Of course he would. As would any decent person. And there was some solace in the knowledge that Anders was honoring Hamilton by making his death the occasion for an equivalent bestowal. That he was mitigating Hamilton's loss, not magnifying its tragedy.

He called in Remar, who sat ramrod-straight facing the director's desk during the briefing—the posture he tended to adopt, Anders knew, when he was resisting difficult conclusions. And indeed, predictably, Remar remonstrated about what clearly needed to be done. But also predictably, in the end, he reluctantly agreed there was no other way. Only after they had agreed on a plan did Remar ask, "Why do you think he did it?"

Anders leaned back in his desk chair, relieved the difficult part of the conversation was done. "Who knows? He had a strained relationship with his family, which I know he attributed to the demands of the job and how it took him away from them. Maybe this was his way of showing them he was one of the good guys. Or maybe it was some misplaced sense of conscience, growing like a tumor as he got older and more aware of his own mortality. I knew some of this might have presented a vulnerability. I should have taken it more seriously."

"You can't know everything."

"Our *job* is to know everything."

Remar's expression remained frozen. Sometimes it was hard to know whether the impassivity was the result of his injuries, or whether he was trying to hide his thoughts.

After a moment he said, "This couldn't have been . . . there's no way Perkins could have known anything about God's Eye, right?"

Anders shook his head at the absurdity of the thought. But he felt a tightness in his gut that was like a flashback to the night Remar had awakened him with the news about Snowden.

"It's impossible that Perkins could have known anything," he said after a moment. "You and I are the only ones who have full access. The only ones who even know it exists, at least on a big-picture level. But . . . let's conduct an audit. Personally conduct it, obviously."

Remar nodded. "Of course. But . . . would you agree that now would be a good time to call it something else?"

"You've never come up with anything better."

"I know, but—"

"God's Eye fits. It's perfectly descriptive."

"What I'm saying is, The Patriot Act and The Freedom Act . . . those were effective names. They made surveillance sound good. Carnivore, Total Information Awareness . . . those programs came under fire because the names sounded scary."

"The Eye of Providence is already ubiquitous. It's on the reverse of the Great Seal of the United States, and the back of every one-dollar bill. It's familiar. Comforting. But none of this is even relevant. Because God's Eye is not going to get out."

"Of course not, but—"

"What we're talking about now is just a precaution. No more than looking under the bed to make sure the bogeyman isn't hiding there. Confirming what we already know."

"Fine, but—"

"Look, God's Eye was secure even before Snowden, yes? We know this for a certainty. Because—"

"—because if Snowden had access to God's Eye, he would have revealed it."

"Exactly. Just like if al-Qaeda had access to nukes before 9/11, New York and Washington would have been vaporized. In both cases, the absence of evidence—"

"—was evidence of absence."

"Correct. And even so, out of an abundance of caution, we had Chambers increase all the security protocols."

Remar looked at him, the old disapproval in his eyes. "Aerial was an amazing talent. And loyal."

Anders didn't like Remar referring to Chambers by her first name. Well, her nickname—her real name was Nicole—but that was even worse. It made what was purely a national security decision seem more personal. Worse, he didn't like the probe. He looked into Remar's eye. "Are you questioning my decision, General Remar?"

Remar dropped his gaze. "What's done is done. But if you're not worried Perkins might have accessed God's Eye, why such extreme measures?"

"Just because there's no way Perkins could create Armageddon doesn't mean he doesn't represent catastrophe. You want another Snowden? The costs of all that publicity, the distractions? That damn Greenwald, mocking NSA for being the only organization to lose the data we've been trying to get back?"

"No, of course not."

"Not to mention how it's going to make us look personally if it happens again."

Remar nodded.

Anders sighed. "We don't know what Perkins was up to. But we can assume if the SUSLA Turkey, of all people, thought it was newsworthy, it was going to be damaging. Exceptionally damaging."

Remar nodded again, seemingly mollified. "Who do you want on it?"

"I'm thinking Delgado for Perkins. Manus for the journalist."

"Perkins is the finesse job, the journalist is brute force?"

Anders shook his head. "Don't misjudge Manus. Just because he can't hear doesn't mean he's incapable of finesse."

"I don't know about that guy, Ted. I can never tell what's he thinking."

Anders looked at Remar's ruined face, and refrained from noting that the same could be said for his XO.

"It's not what he's thinking, Mike. It's what he does."

"He doesn't make you nervous?"

"I know how to handle him."

"That's not what I asked."

"It's what matters."

"I know he's loyal to you. Like a . . . I don't know, an abused dog you rescued, or something. But a dog like that is damaged, you know? Down deep. You can never really trust it."

"It's not a question of trust. It's a question of utility."

It came out a little more bluntly than he'd intended, but on the other hand, could anyone deny the statement's essential truth?

Remar stood. "All right. What else?"

Had he taken Anders's words as commentary on their own relationship? The director hadn't meant it that way.

24

No, Remar was all right. As loyal as Manus—though sometimes with too many questions. But at least he always knew when it was time to swallow his objections and carry out his orders.

"We'll need a Turkish cutout," Anders said. "Contact our guy. Manus will deliver the journalist to the Ergenekon people. They'll smuggle him into Syria."

"A second cutout."

"Correct. Tell our guy Ergenekon gets paid in three tranches—when they take delivery, when they deliver to the Syrians, and when the Syrians complete the transaction."

"What Syrians are we talking about?"

"Does it matter? We'll describe them as ISIS."

"The ISIS brand is pretty well known at this point. Might be better to use something new."

Anders considered. "Well, we could attribute it to the Khorasan Group. You know, 'too radical even for al-Qaeda.'"

"I don't know. We claimed to have killed the group's leader once the bombing in Syria began. Plus, the name never really caught on. Too much like 'Kardashian.' I've told you, names matter."

Anders ignored the gambit. God's Eye was a perfect name, and he wasn't inclined to change it—or anything else—to something less than perfect. "Keep it vague, then. But attach it to ISIS. 'An ISIS splinter group,' something like that. And as far as the Turks, start at twenty thousand US per tranche, but be prepared to go up to a hundred overall."

"They want hardware more than cash these days."

"Tell our guy if this goes well, next time we can talk about multiple grenade launchers. They're hot for those. But don't let him get greedy."

Remar headed to the door. "I'll get Delgado. And your human dog."

CHAPTER ....
.... 3

Twenty minutes later, there were two firm knocks on the door. Anders looked up and said, "Come."

Thomas Delgado entered and closed the door behind him. Five-five and fit as a ferret, he was wearing an immaculately tailored gray suit and white shirt, the absence of a tie his only stylistic concession to Maryland's late August heat. As if in recompense, a half inch of white linen emerged from the breast pocket of his jacket. The outfit was ostentatiously stylish in the corridors of NSA, especially during shirtsleeves summer, but Anders supposed the look had its merits—chiefly that it at least partly disguised the fact that once upon a time, Delgado had earned a reputation as a technology-savvy killer for various East Coast crime organizations, foreign and domestic.

That had been ten years ago, when Anders had warned him about and ran interference with an FBI task force looking to put him behind bars. The warning had of course been part of a quid pro quo, and Delgado had proven enormously capable—imaginative, discreet, decisive. You told him who, you told him where, you gave him parameters about how. He never asked for anything beyond that, and he never failed to take care of the problem. If he had a shortcoming, it was that he enjoyed aspects of his work a little more than might be considered . . . desirable. But no one was perfect.

Delgado sat. His breathing was regular, but there was some perspiration along a row of hair plugs that seemed to be struggling to take root.

"You come from outside?" Anders asked.

Delgado nodded. "Fucking murder out there. Like a hundred degrees. Remar said you wanted to see me right away."

Anders steepled his fingers. "We have a problem in Ankara. You'll be leaving on a military flight from Andrews immediately. This one can't be a suicide. Can you make it look like a car crash?"

Delgado smiled. "You know I can, especially if it's a newer model."

There was something about Delgado's smile that always looked like a sneer. Well, the man wasn't employed for his charm.

Anders thought of the fancy European car he knew Perkins drove in Ankara. "New enough. If you can't get inside yourself, I'll have a Tailored Access Operations team as backup."

"I won't need them."

"Probably true, but they'll be available in case."

The TAO people were magicians. One team had been tasked with developing access to the checked baggage computer networks of every major airline. Now it was child's play to cause a bag, or better yet a whole planeful of bags, to be temporarily "misplaced," and, while the bags were missing, to replace a wheel or a handle or the heel of a shoe with a listening or tracking device. After a few hours, perhaps a day, the airline would discover its error, apologize, and send the bags on to their proper destinations. Airline incompetence was so universal that no one ever thought to question whether sometimes something else might be at work. Snowden had revealed a lot of these capabilities, but not all. Thank God.

Delgado wiped a bead of sweat from his scalp. "The particulars?"

"General Remar will provide you with an encrypted file on your way out. You can read it when you're airborne." He paused, then added, "You won't be able to liaise with the local field office. The problem is the head of that office."

If Delgado was surprised by that, he didn't show it. He simply nodded and said, "Well, now I know why you want a car crash. Are you going to stick me with the freak, or do I get to operate alone this time?"

"You'll be on a plane together. It's already waiting at Andrews. Manus will be in the region, but on something else."

As if on cue, there were three soft knocks on the door. Anders waited. If it was someone else, the person would leave. If it was Manus, he wouldn't hear Anders's command to enter.

The door opened, the office beyond it briefly blotted out. Then Marvin Manus was inside, the door closed behind him. Delgado turned so that Manus could read his lips and enunciated extra loudly and clearly, "Well, don't just stand there, genius. Sit."

Not for the first time, Anders wondered at Delgado's animus. The smaller man had a mean streak, that much was clear. But did he also have a death wish? Delgado was formidable, yes. But Manus . . . Manus was something else, something elemental. Anders had rescued him fifteen years earlier, when Manus had just turned eighteen and was about to graduate from the juvenile correctional center in St. Charles, Illinois, to the maximum-security adult facility in Pontiac. It said a lot that Remar was nervous about him. Because Remar, who had fought his way back from wounds and endured pain that would have killed most other men, wasn't nervous about anyone.

Manus ignored the taunt and looked to Anders for his cue. Anders glanced at Delgado and said, "Go."

Delgado hesitated, then stood and sauntered past Manus, eyeing the larger man up and down as he moved. He paused so Manus could see his lips, then said loudly, "Glad we'll be traveling together. I'd miss your scintillating conversation."

Manus watched him leave, saying not a word. Anders knew how to handle Manus, of course, but even so he sometimes found his stillness . . . disquieting. Especially when it was in response to something that would have produced some evidence of anger in an ordinary person.

Anders gestured to a chair, then simultaneously signed and said, "Marvin. Thank you for coming." The courtesy was deliberate. With Manus, it was powerful currency. And though he knew Manus was an excellent lip-reader, whenever he could he still tried to add some of the bits of American Sign Language he had learned, because he knew how much Manus appreciated his efforts.

Manus nodded an acknowledgment and lowered himself onto one of the chairs, gripping the arms gingerly as though concerned he might inadvertently snap them off.

"You're going to Istanbul," Anders said. "Same military plane as Delgado, different assignment when you get there. General Remar will give you an encrypted file with all the particulars. This is only a snatch. A journalist, presumably not security conscious, presumably unarmed. It doesn't matter if he sustains some damage when you take him, as long as he's alive and basically intact."

"What do I do with him?" Manus's voice was low and sonorous, the pronunciation slightly off because he couldn't hear himself talking. Overall, his tone offered no more clue to the thoughts behind it than did the more customary silence.

"You're going to turn him over to a group of Turkish middlemen who have contacts on the other side of the Syrian border. General Remar is arranging the logistics now, and I'll brief you in the air as soon as I have details. Any questions?"

Manus offered a single shake of his head.

Not a surprise. If there were more Manus needed to know, Anders would have told him.

Anders looked at him. "How are things with Delgado?"

There was a pause. "How do you mean?"

29

The tone was as neutral as a flat-lined heart monitor.

"He's got a lot of hate," Anders went on. "But he's useful to me."

Manus nodded.

Anders sighed. "I appreciate . . . what you sometimes put up with."

Another nod. But Anders sensed the loyalty behind it. The response to what might have been the only kindness this man had ever really known.

"When you're back," Anders went on, "I have something else for you. An employee about whom I have some . . . doubts. I want you to keep an eye on her."

Manus frowned slightly, perhaps dubious. It wasn't the type of task for which Anders ordinarily employed him.

"Her little boy is deaf," Anders said. "It might provide an opening for you, a way in."

The frown smoothed out. "All right."

"Of course she'll be monitored electronically, but she's smart, she'll be sensitive to that. I'm looking for something else."

"What?"

Anders drummed his fingers along the desk. "I'm concerned what's about to happen in Turkey might upset her. And I want to know . . . is she satisfied? Settled? Content? Or is her conscience troubling her? Is she a team player? Or is she starting to think of herself as an outsider? We learn a tremendous amount from SIGINT, yes, but there are people who forget the human aspect, the unquantifiable, the ghost in the machine. I don't want to leave that out. I don't want to leave *anything* out. Your firsthand impressions will be useful in that regard."

For a moment, Manus looked at his huge hands, as though he might find some answer in them. Then he said, "You want to know everything."

Anders only nodded. Didn't everyone?

CHAPTER........
........4

Manus spent the entire flight to Istanbul in silence. Some of the time he slept; some of the time he reviewed the updates the director sent him; all of the time he ignored Delgado. The man's smell was always unpleasant—a cologne Manus didn't recognize from anywhere else, a too-strong floral soap, and some kind of hair gel, all combined with an underlying, slightly acrid odor that was uniquely Delgado's. Delgado had once caught him wrinkling his nose, and asked what his problem was. Manus had told him he didn't like Delgado's cologne. Delgado had looked surprised—Manus had been standing almost twenty feet away—and had asked how Manus could smell it from all the way over there. Manus had merely shrugged. He had an unusually keen nose—lose one sense, and the others converge to pick up the slack—and he accepted that Delgado's stink was one of the downsides.

He knew Delgado hated him, though he didn't know why. He didn't know why anyone ever hated him. People just sometimes did. The hate didn't bother him. It was only a problem if it made someone try to hurt him. That was what he watched for. When he saw it coming, he would hurt the person first. He hoped that wouldn't happen with Delgado. The director seemed to need Delgado, to value him, and Manus didn't ever want to do anything bad to the director.

The part of his life that had happened before the director was vague to him now, dreamlike, disjointed. His father had been the first person to hurt him. Usually it happened when his father had been drinking. His father came from nothing in Granite City, Illinois, got a football scholarship to Ohio State, blew out a knee his first season, lost the scholarship, lost everything. Came back to Granite City to a job in the steel mill, knocked up a girl he knew from high school, married her. The baby had been Manus.

His father didn't like Manus. He was too small. He was too quiet. He was stupid. Well, it was true Manus had been small; his size hadn't kicked in until he was sixteen. And of course he was quiet. When his father drank, anything could set him off. So Manus learned not just to be quiet but to be *still*, to be like a table or a rug or a wall, when his father was in a hating mood. It didn't always work, but he knew it wasn't stupid. Quiet was smart. Quiet was survival.

When Manus was four, his father had hit him so hard in the head that Manus blacked out. When he'd awakened, he was in a hospital. His mother was sitting next to the bed, and her mouth had formed an enormous O of joy and relief when he'd opened his eyes and looked at her. He thought she had shouted, but he couldn't hear her. In fact, everything was so quiet. It was as though he was under water.

People in white jackets did tests. He could hear a little, but only when people were talking very loudly directly in front of him. They told him his hearing might come back, that it was impossible to say. And that he had to be more careful near the stairs, because he had hurt himself falling down them. That seemed strange. He remembered his father yelling at him—in fact, his father yelling was the last thing he remembered hearing ever—but had he also fallen down the stairs? He wanted to ask, but it was hard to make himself understood. And anyway, what did it matter?

After that, his father didn't drink for a long time, and he left Manus alone. A teacher came to the house and taught him and his mother something called American Sign Language. Manus liked it—a way to talk without making any sound. His mother worked hard to help him with it, but she also insisted that he watch her talk because most people didn't know sign and he had to learn to read lips.

Manus went to the public school. It was hard. Some of the teachers remembered to face the class when they were talking so Manus, who always sat in front, could read their lips. But others didn't remember, or didn't care. There was a speech therapist who was nice, but Manus hated meeting with her. The drills she made him do were boring, and he didn't understand the point. Why did he even need to talk? Early on, when the other kids made fun of him, he'd answered, and something about his voice only made them laugh harder. Silence was better. His mother told him he had to practice his speaking as much as he did lip-reading or he wouldn't be able to make friends. But no one wanted to be friends with the deaf kid, the kid they called *idiot* and *doofus* and *retard*.

When he was ten, his father broke a hand at the mill and got something called disability. He started drinking again. And hurting Manus again. His mother tried to protect him, taking the hurt so he wouldn't have to. Afterward, when his father was passed out, she would sign to Manus that it was all right, it hurt less than it seemed, less than seeing anything happen to her beautiful boy. He remembered she liked to call him that. And the smell of her perfume.

One night when Manus was fourteen, his father came home very drunk. Manus was doing homework at the kitchen table. His mother was cooking dinner, spaghetti and garlic bread, the sauce with mushrooms and sausage simmering in a big pot on the electric stove. Enough for lots of leftovers.

He could smell the alcohol the moment his father walked in. He looked up and watched his mother say, with a falsely cheery expression, that his father's timing was great, the sauce was perfect now, it had been simmering all afternoon. His father said he wasn't hungry. He looked around. Then he said the food stank. The whole place stank.

Manus thought the food smelled good. Spaghetti was his favorite. And his mother had worked hard to make dinner. For one tiny second, he forgot to be smart, to be a table or rug or wall. He glanced at his father. Only for that tiny second. But a second was enough.

"Don't you fucking look at me like that!" his father had shouted, so loudly Manus could faintly hear it. "Who do you think puts the food on the table in this house? Who?"

It was bad when his father asked questions. Manus had learned there were no satisfactory answers. And once his father was asking questions, it was hard to be like furniture. Once his father had noticed you, not answering could make him feel like he was being ignored. Which he didn't like. Manus didn't know why. Manus preferred to be ignored.

So he did the best he could. He glanced down at the homework in front of him and kept very still.

"You look at me when I'm talking to you!" his father roared. He strode over to where Manus sat. "Look at me!"

His mother jumped between them. Manus craned his head to see her face. "He's just doing his homework, Dom," she'd said, her expression frightened. "How about some garlic bread?"

It was horrible when she intervened. Manus was always grateful for it, relieved to have his father's rage diverted. But with the relief came shame, more and more so as he was getting older. And suddenly, instead of feeling afraid, he felt something else. He felt . . . angry. Which instantly frightened him more. What if his father noticed? He had to be still, really still, like always. Until his father was tired and went away.

But his father was looking for something, and he'd found it in that tiny flash of anger. He shoved Manus's mother out of the way and swatted Manus open-handed across the head, blasting him and the chair he sat in to the floor. Manus saw stars. He saw his mother scream, "Dom, stop!" Manus looked up and saw his father cuff his mother across the face, saw her stagger back into the wall with a *boom* he could feel through the floor. His father moving toward her, bellowing, his fists clenched. And the anger he'd felt flare a moment earlier—an anger he realized years later had been building and building beneath his efforts to suppress it—suddenly detonated.

He lurched to his feet and leaped onto his father's back, yelling something, not words, just yelling. His father tore him off like a scab and shoved him two-handed so hard that Manus actually flew through the air and slammed into the wall next to the stove. He saw stars again. Things became fragmentary. His mother screaming, "You leave him alone!" His father advancing on him. His mother, yelling something, picking up a chair and raising it, stepping in and bringing the chair down hard on his father's head. A loud *crack*. A shiver running through his father's body. Then his eyes narrowing to slits, his head rotating like a reptile's, the huge body swinging around behind it.

"You little cunt," Manus had seen him say as he turned, and though he couldn't hear it, it felt like a whisper, which was so much worse than any shouting, so much scarier. His mother tried to raise the chair again and his father snatched it from her hands like it was a child's toy and flung it across the room, then grabbed the edge of the table and upended it out of the way. His mother was terrified now, Manus could see that; she was backpedaling, her eyes wide, her mouth aghast. His father moved in like a dog on a cornered squirrel. He grabbed the back of her neck with one hand and drove his fist into her face with the other. Blood burst from her nose and she staggered. His father grabbed her shoulders, not letting her fall, and smashed her backward into the wall, pulling her into him and then

smashing her into the wall again, the back of her head slamming into the plaster and ricocheting off each time.

Everything seemed to slow down. Manus looked at the stove. The fat cook pot of spaghetti sauce, the bubbles rising through the viscous red amid mushrooms and chunks of meat. He felt hate blossom inside him. It was a supremely beautiful feeling, enormous and clean and focused.

He took hold of both handles of the pot and pulled it off the stove as he advanced on his father, aware the metal was burning his palms but hardly feeling it. *"Hey!"* he roared in a voice he had never used before, never imagined. A voice his father had never heard. It startled him. He released Manus's mother's shoulders, and as she slid to the floor, he started turning toward Manus, flinching as he did so, his head turtling in, his arms coming up, something in Manus's new voice having reached past the drunkenness and warning a primitive, animal part of his mind of danger.

But too late. Manus was only a few feet away, and as his father's head continued to come around, he flung the pot violently forward, keeping his grip on the handles so the pot stopped at the limit of his reach. An enormous red blob emerged like a dragon from its lair, seeming to float through the air as his father kept turning, turning toward him in slow motion . . .

The boiling sauce caught his father directly in the face and neck, smothering his features. He shrieked and collapsed to his knees, his body shaking, his hands clawing at his eyes. For a moment, Manus thought his father was wiping away mushrooms, and then realized what he was seeing instead was melting skin.

Manus ran past him and knelt next to his mother, who was lying on her back, her legs folded weirdly underneath her. Her eyes were open but rolled up in her head. He shook her and patted her cheek, whispering "Mommy, Mommy, wake up" again and again through a constricted throat. It had been *Mom* for years at that point, but his terror at her unresponsiveness was childlike and she was suddenly *Mommy* again.

He kept shaking her and patting her face. He could faintly hear his father howling, but soon there was no sound at all, and when he looked up, his father was lying still. He realized he should have called 911, how could he not have thought of that? He ran to the phone and dialed. He couldn't hear if anyone picked up or what they were saying so he just kept repeating that he was deaf and needed help, his mother was hurt, please, he needed help.

An ambulance came. Police. Everyone went to the hospital. His mother was dead. Something called a subdural hematoma, a doctor explained. Bleeding inside the head. His father was unconscious. They bandaged his face like a mummy and doctors said he wouldn't be able to see again even if he woke up. But he didn't. He got pneumonia and died two weeks later.

The police brought in an interpreter who knew sign, and they asked Manus a lot of questions. He didn't want to talk about it, but he told them the truth. Someone who called himself the district attorney explained that Manus wasn't going to be prosecuted. But his grandparents didn't want him. His deafness had always been a barrier between them, and now it was only worse—his father's parents didn't believe his story, while his mother's wanted to know why he hadn't done something sooner. Manus didn't have an answer for that. He'd been too afraid, and look what had happened.

They put him in a special school. He got in a lot of fights. He had teeth knocked out, his nose was broken, he fractured knuckles. No matter what happened, he always learned. What parts of the body to hit with. What parts to hit. How to read people's intentions, to know when it was coming and how. When to attack beforehand, when to attack back.

The other boys spit threats and cursed and shouted when they fought. But Manus never said anything, never made a sound. When someone was trying to hurt him, hurting them back came to feel like a job, just work to be done. The thing he found best was to get the other boy on the ground and then stomp his pelvis or face or neck as though he were crushing a can or breaking a log. But it was also good to bite, and attack the eyes. Even the toughest boys forgot everything except trying to get away when Manus dug a finger into an eye socket.

The people who administered the school made him take a lot of tests. They told him he was intelligent but that he was wasting it. He didn't care. They told him if he didn't stop fighting, they would have to send him to another special school, one "for boys like him." But people kept trying to hurt him, and he kept going to work on them in return, so eventually they sent him to the other school, which was actually more like a prison.

One night during his first week there, he was awakened by a weight on his back. He tried to get up but couldn't—someone was pinning him to his cot. He struggled and the somebody held something cold and sharp against his throat. He realized it was a knife. Two pairs of strong hands pulled at his pants. He knew what was happening and struggled, but the knife pressed harder. He froze. The hands stripped off his pants, then gripped his legs and spread them. He wondered why none of the other boys in the dorm were doing anything, then realized: they were just glad that this time it wasn't them.

Three of them, and a knife—there was nothing he could do. So he relaxed. He wasn't submitting. He was waiting. They were going to hurt him and he had to let them. Until he could go to work.

As his body relaxed, the one on top of him began to shake with laughter. The hands on his legs gripped less tightly.

It hurt. The boy who was doing it was trying to make it hurt, too. It wasn't as bad as some of his father's beatings, but it was worse, too, because it was inside him, inside his body. Manus gritted his teeth, tears spilling from his eyes, and waited.

The boy shuddered and Manus could feel him finishing. Manus hadn't resisted. They were holding him only loosely now, thinking he wouldn't fight, thinking he just wanted it to be over.

The hands came off his legs. The knife started to come away from his throat.

He grabbed the blade with his left hand, his right hand seizing the wrist of the boy holding it. The edge cut deeply into his palm, but he didn't let go. He thought the boy might have yelled, but he wasn't sure and anyway it didn't matter. Manus pushed hard on the blade and the leverage broke the boy's grip. Manus grabbed the handle with his right hand. The boy tried to grab it back. Manus got his mouth around the boy's thumb pad and bit down on the meat there.

The boy howled and tried to pull away. His hand came loose, something remaining in Manus's mouth. Manus spat it out and twisted toward them. They tried to pin him, but he was slashing with the knife and they couldn't get hold of him.

One of them had fallen to the floor and was getting to his knees. Manus stomped the back of his neck and flattened him. He stomped the same spot again and felt something shatter under his heel.

The second one started to run, but tripped over something in the weak light. Manus tried to grab the boy's hair, but his hand was bleeding and the fingers wouldn't close. He shoved the boy's face onto the concrete floor and stabbed the knife into his neck. Blood erupted from the cut. The boy screamed and thrashed.

The third boy, the one who had hurt him, had made it to the locked dormitory door. He was pounding on it, screaming for someone to help. Manus moved in. The boy glanced back and saw him coming. Manus could see a guard through the thick glass in the center of the door, fumbling with his keys.

He didn't know how long it took the guards to get inside. Long enough. Manus went to work on the boy. By the time the guards had used their batons and dragged Manus off, the boy's face was mostly gone and he looked like a giant rag doll soaked in blood.

Two of the boys died. The one whose neck Manus had stomped lived, but he couldn't move his arms or legs, and they sent him somewhere that knew how to take care of him. They made Manus take more tests. There was a hearing, and Manus was transferred to what they called the Special Ward. The boys there were scary, but there were no gangs like the one that had attacked him. And people heard about what he had done. Killing two boys and paralyzing a third inspired respect.

A few times, other boys tried to hurt him. When that happened, he would go to work. It wasn't long before nobody wanted to try to hurt him anymore.

There were a few other boys like him in the Special Ward—quiet boys who left other people alone, and who other people had learned were better left alone themselves. Those boys knew ways of hurting people that Manus hadn't figured out yet. They exchanged information. Manus learned a lot.

There were some classes on math and English, but Manus didn't pay much attention. There was one class he enjoyed—carpentry. He liked working with his hands, even the bad one, the one he had used to grab the knife blade. He was good with tools. Everything was a tool, really, if you knew how to use it.

When Manus turned eighteen, he knew they were going to send him to a real prison because of the boys he'd killed. He didn't care. He didn't think it would be any different.

But something else happened. A soldier came to see him. The soldier told him he understood what Manus had been through. The soldier even knew a little sign, and though his efforts were almost comically clumsy, Manus sensed he had learned it because he thought Manus was important. He'd never felt important before. He didn't know what to make of it.

The soldier told him he thought Manus had ability, that he was destined to do something special, and that it was his misfortune to be stuck with all these ordinary people who couldn't recognize the extraordinary talent in their midst, who didn't know how to harness that talent and put it to its proper use. He offered Manus a deal: he'd get Manus out of prison if Manus would train with the army.

Manus explained he couldn't join the army because he was deaf. Surely the soldier knew that. Besides, he'd hurt too many people and had a criminal record. The soldier told him not to worry about the deafness, he knew doctors who could help with that. And that those records could go away. Manus showed the soldier the hand he'd used to grab the knife from the boy who had hurt him. The hand was frozen into a claw—how could he join the army with that?

The soldier had looked at him and said, "I didn't say join the army. I said train with it. And some other training, too. If I can get that hand fixed so it works again, will you follow my lead?"

Manus said yes. They flew him to Walter Reed Army Medical Center, where there were doctors who knew how to repair injuries like his. There was surgery, then a lot of physical therapy, and his hand got better. They fixed some of his other injuries, too—the missing teeth, the messed-up nose. They fitted him with hearing aids, which made some things audible but which he never really liked. He'd become accustomed to a silent world, and preferred it to the noisy one.

And then he went through the training the soldier had spoken of: short- and long-range weapons; edged weapons and unarmed combat; demolitions and improvised explosives; surveillance, counter-surveillance, counter-terrorism. Sometimes he worked with civilians who were themselves obviously former military; sometimes with elite military units. There was a course called SERE, for Survival,

Evasion, Resistance, Escape; and another called MOTC, the Military Operations Training Course, taught by the CIA at a place known as the Farm. The soldier, who had been a colonel, became a general. He used Manus for special assignments, assignments that Manus, grateful to the point of awe for all the general had done for him, always did well. Eventually, the general became the director. Manus continued to work for him. The director was the only person he'd ever known who seemed to truly appreciate Manus, to value him, to use him for what he was good at.

He didn't know what this journalist had done to make the director assign him to Manus, but he didn't care, either. That the director wanted it was enough. Manus would make sure it got done.

CHAPTER . . . .
. . . . 5

Daniel Perkins jerked awake as the bus lurched to a stop. He looked out the window, and through the spatter of gray rain saw the concrete and glass of AŞTİ Station, crowds lined up under umbrellas to board the dozen or so buses in the terminal parking area.

He cleared his throat and checked his watch. Almost noon. Christ, he'd slept practically the whole way from Istanbul. He hadn't even heard the announcements the driver must have made about their imminent arrival in Ankara.

He waited while the other passengers—a few European backpackers, but mostly Turks without the money to fly from Istanbul or to take the high-speed train—stood to collect their bags from the overhead racks. His own bag had remained nestled on his lap during the entire five-hour drive, except during his one trip to the bus's restroom, when of course the bag had accompanied him.

He scrubbed his eyes, feeling almost drugged. When was the last time he'd really slept? Not since he'd first contacted Hamilton, which meant . . . almost three weeks. In all his preparations before that, he'd never been worried. He knew NSA's capabilities as well as anyone, which meant he knew how to avoid them. But once he'd made contact, he was only as secure as Hamilton's precautions. And though the kid had been security savvy to begin with, and was even more so now that Perkins had briefed him, the contact itself was still a risk, a new vulnerability. Electronic countermeasures were the same as physical ones: you could run the best countersurveillance route in the world, but if the asset you were meeting was less careful and got himself tailed, you were as fucked as he was.

A wave of anxiety coursed through him, and he worked to will it away. Hamilton had the information. By now, he'd be flying to Frankfurt, and from there back to DC. If Perkins was going to get caught, it would have happened already. And if it happened now . . . well, at least the information would come out. At least it wouldn't have all been for nothing.

He thought of his ex-wife, Caryn, and how many times she had told him his career was eating him like cancer, estranging him from their children, estranging him from her. What she hadn't known was, he'd already been estranged. His obsessive devotion to the job was as much consequence of that as it was cause. He'd married young, and by the time he had known better, there were children, and expectations that had hardened like concrete, and responsibilities he couldn't ignore. He was trapped in a life he didn't want with a woman he didn't love, not the way he could love, not the way he needed to.

And then he'd met Aerial, a systems administrator marooned in her own unhappy marriage. Well, Nicole was her real name, Nicole Chambers, but she'd been going by Aerial, or Aer, since acquiring the nickname as a surfer growing up in Santa Cruz. He'd see her in the same headquarters cafeteria, getting to work early, staying late, just like him. Small talk became a friendship. Friendship became an affair. The affair blossomed into love. They'd planned to wait until all their kids were in college, and then they'd divorce their spouses and finally be able to have a relationship in the open instead of just stolen moments in a series of out-of-the-way hotels.

Not that those stolen moments weren't wonderful. Sometimes he thought they were all that kept him going, all he really lived for.

One night, Aerial had told him about a program she had devised on orders from the director, something the director had dubbed God's Eye. It was supposed to have filters that would keep it focused on terrorists and deny access to domestic traffic. But Aerial had created a backdoor for herself, and when she'd checked, the filters had all been turned off. She was horrified to see how the program was being used, she'd confided to him, and she felt like she had to do something. But she was terrified at the prospect—look how they'd tried to ruin Bill Binney and Thomas Drake, to name just two—and for a long time, Aerial did nothing more than talk, as though confessing guilt about her inaction could somehow expiate it. And Perkins, at least as terrified as she was, made no attempt to encourage her.

But eventually, she started siphoning off information from and about the program, encrypting it and storing it on a Darknet site she had created in such a way she was confident even God's Eye couldn't see it. She showed Perkins how to access the information in case anything happened to her. He had told her she was being ridiculous, that nothing was going to happen, that they weren't living in a spy novel.

After Snowden, the director had Aerial reengineer all the God's Eye security protocols. In retrospect, Perkins knew, that was the moment to go public with the information if she was ever going to. But Aerial said the new protocols wouldn't prevent her from creating a new backdoor, so she would be able to continue to gather the proof she needed. Perkins didn't push. In fact, he secretly hoped she would continue to use her need for more proof as a kind of excuse to not act.

The night she finished architecting the new system, she was supposed to meet Perkins at a hotel near Baltimore/Washington International Airport. But she never showed up. Perkins, guessing something had come up at home and that she couldn't contact him about it in real time, was no more than disappointed. But the next morning, it was all over the news: area woman raped and murdered.

Initially, his denial had been so profound that he'd actually believed the reports. Aerial's body had been found behind a strip mall in Laurel. Her car was in the parking lot of her gym, which made sense—if you could call it that—because her habit was to do an abbreviated workout before meeting Perkins so she could be seen at the gym and have a kind of alibi. The police had speculated that she'd been forced into a car or van and driven to a secondary location. The footage from nearby traffic cameras had been scrutinized, to no avail. Semen was recovered, and matched what had been found in five similar attacks. The same serial rapist who had struck up and down the I-95 corridor over the last several years.

But eventually, denial had given way to doubt, doubt to determination. What better way to guarantee the integrity of the new security protocols than to kill the very person who had designed them? Hadn't the pharaohs done just that with the architects of the pyramids, the better to ensure that no one unauthorized could ever discover their riches? And what were the chances of a "random" murder mere hours after her redesign went live?

He'd been initially terrified that whoever had killed Aerial would come after him next, knowing they had been lovers, seeking to tie off all loose ends. But then he realized—if they had known, he would have been dead already. He was safe. He and Aerial had been careful. Maybe not as careful as they should have been, in retrospect, but careful enough, thank God.

Six months after Aerial had died, Perkins was moved to Ankara. It was a scheduled posting, and he'd been fighting it so he could remain at Fort Meade with Aerial. But now it was an excuse to be away from his family, to not have to hide his grief from the people around him.

For a long time, he steered clear of Aerial's archived files, superstitiously afraid that going to the site she had established would somehow render him a target. But eventually, his rage at what had been done to her, his determination to do right by her, and his caustic shame at his own cowardice impelled him to act. The backdoor was closed, and he didn't know whatever new one she had established. But her trove of explosive files was intact. He considered anonymously uploading everything to multiple news sources, but then decided that in the end, he would be safer, and the release more effective, if he could find the right journalist to use as a conduit. Gellman, Greenwald, Poitras . . . all were obvious choices, but they'd already made their bones and had gone on to other journalistic endeavors. Assange had been bottled up by the UK government, with *WikiLeaks* successfully positioned in the public mind as some sort of reckless espionage outfit. He wanted someone with courage and integrity, but with an organization the government hadn't yet managed to vilify with propaganda. A young *Intercept* reporter would make sense—the Greenwald-Poitras lineage, and an outfit with the right reputation and resources. There were several possibilities, but he had settled on Hamilton because the kid had a computer science background that would enable him to understand the material and equip him to keep it safe.

God, he hoped he'd made the right choice. For himself. And for Aerial, too.

He stood and filed off the bus with everyone else, a few fat drops of rain spattering on his head and shoulders as he ducked under the overhang. It was unseasonably cold, and between that and the wet he was suddenly shivering.

He pushed through the crowds, found a restroom inside, and took a long, much-needed piss. As he shook off, he told himself again it was okay, the worst of the danger had passed. Still, he was afraid, badly afraid, of what would happen to him if he were caught.

Chelsea Manning had been kept naked in solitary for almost a year and awakened every five minutes by guards to check that she was "okay." And Snowden . . . Christ, he couldn't imagine what they would do if they ever got their hands on him. But no matter what, at least now, the program he'd uncovered would be public. At least whatever might happen to him if he were caught wouldn't be for nothing.

He headed back into the station, the noise of the bustling crowds and arrival and departure announcements headache-loud against the granite floor and high, vaulted ceilings. He realized he was starving, and stopped at a kiosk for a coffee and sandwich. He watched while the barista mixed and then heated the coffee powder, sugar, and water in a *cezve*, eager for the jolt the strong Turkish brew would provide, but glad the young man was taking the time to prepare it properly, heating it slowly, ready to pour it carefully down the side of a waiting demitasse the moment the coffee came to a boil. After that, it would need to sit for a few moments so the grounds could settle. He smiled, thinking that whatever happened next, he would miss Turkish coffee.

CNN International was playing on a television monitor mounted on the wall at the back of the kiosk. The White House spokesman was disputing Yemeni claims that a drone strike had killed twelve members of a wedding party. The spokesman was explaining, "There must be near certainty that no civilians will be killed or injured—the highest standard we can set," and claimed the victims were "militants." Perkins shook his head disgustedly at the lies, tired of it, tired of it all.

The chyron changed to *Breaking News* and a blow-dried talking head came on. "This just in," the talking head recited in the grave tones of a trained news actor. "An American journalist is feared kidnapped by ISIS."

Perkins watched, thinking it was going to be a busy day and that he'd gotten back just in time to avoid being missed. And then the announcer went on. "*Intercept* reporter Ryan Hamilton was apparently vacationing in Turkey when he disappeared somewhere near the Syrian border. Authorities fear the young man may have gotten too close to trafficking routes used by ISIS and related terrorist groups, perhaps hoping to cover a topic that has proven a source of contention between Ankara and the White House."

Perkins felt the blood drain from his face. He'd left Hamilton not six hours earlier, in Istanbul, nowhere near the Syrian border. What the fuck was this about? Was he blown?

He dropped twenty lira on the counter and hurried through the terminal to the taxi stand. He had a backup phone and was desperate to turn it on, but didn't want to risk it until he was away from the terminal. Because how the hell would he explain what he was doing at the bus station? He was supposed to have driven to Cappadocia, and yes, he'd already prepared cover for action in case he was spotted doing anything inconsistent, but he didn't want to have his story tested, not ever, and especially not now.

The line for taxis was monumental. Everyone seemed to have an umbrella but him. He hunched his shoulders against the rain and tried to think.

It was almost certainly bad. He rated the chances of coincidence at about 4 percent. Meaning a 96 percent chance that this ISIS story was bullshit. He realized with a nauseous wave of terror that if they'd gotten to Hamilton before he left Istanbul, they might even have contained the information. Hamilton had wanted to transmit the files using the *Intercept*'s SecureDrop system, but Perkins had been so paranoid he'd prevailed on Hamilton not to do anything over the Internet. He could snail-mail a backup to himself if he had an anonymous means of doing so, Perkins had told him, but other than that the safest thing would be to just carry on his own person the encrypted thumb drive Perkins had prepared. The kid hadn't wanted to keep the thumb drive on him—*Look what the Brits did to David Miranda*, he'd argued—and eventually Perkins had just told him, *Fine, do what you think is best and it's better if I don't know anyway.*

But now what? Would the kid give him up? James Risen had been prepared to go to jail rather than reveal his sources, but if they'd disappeared Hamilton, the kid was facing far worse than prison. And even if they couldn't get Hamilton to talk, how long would it be before they started interviewing everyone he might have met in Turkey? Thank God he'd told the kid they had to do the meetings in Istanbul, not Ankara; that gave him at least a little cover, but not much. For a moment, he was ashamed that all he was thinking of was himself when the kid was facing who knew what. But Jesus, this must have been the kid's fault. Perkins had briefed him on every goddamned possible vulnerability, but somehow the kid must have screwed up anyway.

He finally made it to the front of the line and ducked into a cab, his arms broken out in goose bumps. He had the driver take him to the nearby Gazi Park Hotel, where he'd left his car. He hadn't wanted to park it too near the station and the hotel had seemed like a good compromise, but he realized now he hadn't been seeing things as they would look if Hamilton were compromised. He'd been too optimistic. On the other hand, shit, if he'd allowed himself to be anything else, he never would have had the balls to do what he'd done. But now everything in his story was going to be checked, every inconsistency exposed and exploited. What the hell should he do? Probably he needed a lawyer, but contacting a lawyer now would be like sending up a giant beacon confessing his guilt. No. No, he needed to stay calm. Get back to the office, play it cool, check the cable traffic. Use the same backdoors that had allowed him to discover the program in the first place and get a better idea of what he was up against. And then decide what to do.

It took less than ten minutes to get to the hotel. Another ten for a valet to retrieve his car. And then he was off, heading to the office, fighting his fear, the heat blasting and the seat warmer a godsend against his shivering back.

He made a right on Beştepe and followed it until it became Alparslan Türkeş. The freeway would be crowded, so he went under it, following Bahriye Üçok and then going right onto Mareşal Fevzi Çakmak. He had just passed the Anittepe sports complex when he heard the door locks click. He glanced over, recognizing the sound but not sure what to make of it—had he pressed something by mistake? Maybe some electronic glitch?

And then, to his astonishment and horror, he felt the gas pedal press itself to the floor under his foot. The engine roared and his head smacked into the headrest as the car shot forward, the speedometer surging to the right.

He yelped in terror and stomped the brake. Nothing, no resistance. He overtook the car ahead of him and was about to plow into it when the steering wheel twisted left, then right, passing the car and rocketing past two others in front of it. He fought for control but couldn't move the wheel. Terrified, he glanced at the speedometer and saw the needle surge past 150 kilometers per hour.

He stomped the brake again. Nothing. The car was still accelerating. He scrabbled at the electronic parking brake, ripping loose a nail and barely feeling it. Nothing.

Suddenly he understood. Understood everything. For one second, he felt overwhelming sadness, a tidal wave of regret. Then it vanished. He closed his eyes, took his hands off the wheel, and hugged himself. "Acrial," he whispered. "I love you."

. . . .

Thomas Delgado used a finger to direct the car left, then watched as the screen of his iPad was consumed by the grille of a tractor trailer, the blare of its horn filling his ears through the headphones . . . and then, nothing. No sound. Dead screen.

He smiled, removed the headphones, and eased back in the desk chair. A good chance a head-on impact like that would have resulted in fire, but Delgado, not the kind of man to leave things to chance, had been sure to attach incendiary devices to the gas tank and alongside the camera he had mounted behind the car's grille. The camera was the only possible evidence of any sort of foul play—the rest he had accomplished by hacking the car's Bluetooth-accessible diagnostic system, and from there taking over whatever in the car was microprocessor controlled, otherwise known as everything. The antilock brakes and door locks were integrated with the accident-avoidance system; there was an omnidirectional microphone for hands-free cell phone use; even the steering wheel was controllable through the self-parking system. A lot of the newer models were incorporating front-facing cameras, too, and Hertz was even installing cameras in its vehicle interiors, so soon he'd be able to take full remote control of a car without having to install any of his own hardware.

He loved this kind of progress. Just a few years before, more often than not, causing an accident meant an exceptionally delicate black-bag job involving replacing the mark's car with the identical make and model, customized for an exact match: idiosyncratic scratches and other signs of wear; gas level; odometer; swapped personal items; programmed radio stations; faked Vehicle Identification Numbers . . . everything. It took time; it cost money; it required a team rather than an individual. Worst of all, it left evidence, in the form of the additional mechanics that had to be installed to allow the necessary remote control, evidence that could be reliably obscured only through fires so intense they themselves could cause suspicion. But now? Christ, the carmakers were practically doing his job for him.

He cut the satellite link and shut down the application, then checked his watch. Past noon, but he'd called the front desk and arranged for a late checkout. Door double-locked, Do Not Disturb sign . . . everything was fine.

Jesus, that fear sound the guy had made had given him a hard-on. He didn't usually get that from a man, or when he wasn't working up close and personal, but yeah, that had been a really sweet sound. So . . . pure, or something. And what was the other thing the guy had said? "Ariel, I love you," that was it. His wife? Didn't matter.

Although . . . he could pay a visit to the grieving widow. A little risky, sure, but the thought of it was causing renewed stirrings down south. *Hey, I worked with your husband. Such a good man. Wanted to express my condolences. All right if I come in?* She'd be all fucked up with grief, not thinking clearly, vulnerable. Wouldn't realize her mistake until the door was closed and locked behind him and he was pressing her up against the wall with a blade at her throat. And probably so ashamed and traumatized afterward she wouldn't even report anything.

Fuck, that was actually pretty hot. He got up and went to the bathroom to jerk off to it.

CHAPTER . . . .
. . . . 6

Manus drove steadily along Highway E90, the landscape an undifferentiated series of dry hills and cracked lake beds. It had been
raining when he'd set out from Istanbul before dawn, but the sun
was high overhead now, harsh, glaring, bleaching the surrounding
terrain white as old bones.

Hamilton had been easy. The hotel room's lock had opened
in just over thirty seconds—longer, ironically, than had the hotel
employed the sort of state-of-the-art electronic locks NSA could
bypass remotely. Manus had waited until Hamilton came in, con-
cussed him from behind with a single bearlike swat, and injected
him with Diazepam. Hamilton had barely struggled, losing consciousness almost immediately. After that, it was easy for Manus to
cut off his clothes, zip-tie his wrists, duct-tape his mouth, insert a
Diazepam suppository, diaper him, and zip him and his belongings
into a wheeled canvas cargo bag Manus knew from Hamilton's medical records and driver's license would be more than roomy enough
for the man's five-foot-seven, 130-pound frame.

He had been told Hamilton was staying at the hotel under a
pseudonym and paying cash, so no one would ever even know what
had become of the mysterious guest who had left without any word.

If by any chance Manus had been picked up by cameras or was seen by any witnesses, the baseball cap, nonprescription eyeglasses, and fake beard would be more than adequate protection. The room safe would be found drilled and opened, true, but it wasn't likely the hotel would want to advertise that. Manus had taken the passport he had found inside it, but Hamilton had been carrying everything else: wallet, phone, thumb drive. A specialist would examine the phone and the thumb drive. Manus didn't know what would come of all that, but he knew the director would be happy.

It was a long drive, and Manus would have preferred the people taking delivery of Hamilton to come to him. They were Turkish, after all; they knew the territory better and could blend in better. But unsurprisingly, they preferred to offload as much risk as possible, and the director seemed all right with that. Which meant Manus was all right, too. He'd packed food and a thermos of coffee, so all he needed to stop for was gas and bathroom breaks. That, and inserting fresh suppositories.

The first time he pulled over to a deserted spot and opened the trunk, Hamilton struggled and tried desperately to speak through the duct tape. It meant nothing to Manus. He said to Hamilton, "I don't want to talk to you. But I'll give you some water. Do you want water?"

Hamilton nodded his head vigorously. It was hot in the trunk, the interior gamey with the man's sweat.

"If you try to talk to me, I'll refasten the duct tape and you won't get any water. Do you understand?"

Hamilton nodded again.

Manus pulled free the duct tape and let Hamilton have a long drink. Predictably, the moment Manus took the bottle away, Hamilton started begging him to explain what was going on, to listen, to just please listen. Manus refastened the duct tape, pushed Hamilton down, stripped off the diaper, injected him again, inserted a suppository, and then held the man in place until his struggles had faded.

The used diaper went into a plastic bag, which also went into the trunk, and he was back on the road, following the GPS nav system, in under three minutes.

The next time they pulled over, Manus told him any more talking and he'd get no more water for the rest of the trip. After that, during water breaks Hamilton kept quiet.

The rendezvous point was a town on the Syrian border called Kilis, which Manus supposed was ironic given Hamilton's likely fate. But none of that was his concern. His job was to deliver Hamilton, and that was all that mattered to him. If he encountered a problem along the way, he was carrying fifty thousand lira to buy his way out of it. If that wasn't persuasive, there was the SIG MPX-K machine pistol under a road map on the passenger seat. If all else failed, a panic button on a transmitter would instantly call in the spec ops personnel who were shadowing him, cleared to engage but ignorant of his mission.

He nodded, the radio blaring Turkish music he didn't know but the vibrations of which he enjoyed. By the time the nav system indicated he was almost there, the sun was low in the sky. Manus pulled over and hung the SIG from a custom harness at the bottom of the steering wheel. Hard to spot through the window at a distance, instantly accessible if there were a problem. He opened the glove compartment, pulled out the Tanfoglio Force Pro F in nine millimeter, and eased it into the elastic holster in the back of his waistband. Then he double-checked the Cold Steel Espada folder clipped to his front pocket—a monster knife almost seventeen inches long when deployed, destructive as hell but unsuitable for everyday carry except by someone of Manus's size. Of course, if things got to the point where he was stabbing people rather than shooting them, a lot would have had to go wrong, but it was better to have it and not need it. Finally, he slid the RMJ Tactical Berserker tomahawk from under the seat and placed it across his lap. Then he drove on.

A half mile later, he reached his destination—an abandoned gas station in the hills outside the city. He turned into the lot. A dusty white van was already parked there, three men with dark mustaches standing alongside it under the long shadow of a sagging portico. They were smoking, and other than the cigarettes, their hands were empty. That was a good sign. The director had told him they knew they were getting only a third of the payment on delivery, so if they didn't follow the plan, they'd be leaving a lot on the table, and that was good, too. But maybe the upfront money was all they hoped to collect. And he didn't know what might be concealed under their loose shirts, or whether there were others inside the van. So he watched them carefully, both hands on the wheel where the men could see them, the SIG just a six-inch reach away. They were hard-looking men, and he'd been told they were experienced, so they'd know to keep their hands in sight as he was keeping his. They'd understand he'd read anything else as an attack, and that he'd respond accordingly.

The man in the center, the tallest of the three, waved. Manus nodded and scanned the area. There was a rectangular concrete structure, paint peeling, graffiti-covered, the windows all blown out. Decent concealment and cover. A lot of scrub to the rear of the structure, but too far off for anyone but a sniper to meaningfully engage.

He swung around and parked a ways off, not close as they would have been expecting. He was facing the structure, the van between them, the rusting gas pumps behind the van. This way they couldn't flank him, and if they tried to engage, they'd be stacked up and he'd have a clear field of fire. And the sun was at his back and in their faces, too. A small thing, but he'd make sure it was working to his advantage, not theirs.

They started walking toward him. He swung open the door and stepped out, staying behind it for cover and letting them see his hands but keeping within reach of the SIG.

"Hello," the tall one called out. "You are here for the Kilis Kebabi?"

It was a little hard to read his lips—English was his second language, and he formed the words differently. And facial hair never made things easier, either. "No," Manus responded with his half of the bona fides. "For the baklava."

"Oh, the baklava is also excellent," the man said with a big smile, his teeth white against the dark skin and mustache. "You are Miller, yes? You have something for us?"

Miller was the pseudo the man had been given. Manus stepped to the left, reached slowly into his pocket, and pulled free a thick envelope. He tossed it underhand and the tall man caught it smoothly. With barely a glance, he passed it to the man on his left, who opened it and started counting. Another good sign. If they'd been intent on killing him, they wouldn't be focused on the money. Not yet.

Manus reached down and popped the trunk release, took hold of the Berserker, then closed and locked the door. The men's eyes bulged slightly at the sight of the weapon—over three pounds of black 4140 chrome-moly steel, five inches of razor-sharp cutting edge, and an aggressively curved handle, the kind of axe a Viking or Mongol might have carried to sack a city. The men pulled up short, but no one reached for a weapon.

"What is this?" the tall man said, eyeing the Berserker as though it was a cobra.

"A tool," Manus said. He moved to the trunk, not turning his back, reached inside with one hand, and pulled Hamilton up. He helped the small man get his shaky legs out and onto the ground, then helped him stand.

The tall man pointed. "He is wearing a diaper?"

Manus nodded, not really understanding the question. It had been a twelve-hour drive, and Hamilton had been in the trunk. Of course he was wearing a diaper.

The tall man said something to the others. Manus couldn't make it out and figured it was Turkish. They all started laughing.

Manus stripped the duct tape away. "Please," Hamilton said. "Please tell me where we're going. Tell me what's happening."

Manus reached into the trunk and took out a water. He uncapped it with his teeth and held the bottle until Hamilton had drained it.

One of the men was saying something in Turkish, pointing through the window at the SIG. The tall man came over and looked. "Yes, what is that on your steering wheel?" he said.

A slight breeze picked up and carried the men's scent to him—sweat and tobacco and garlic. Manus wrinkled his nose and tossed the empty bottle in the trunk. "A tool," he said. There was a moment of tension, and then the tall man laughed. The other two laughed also.

Manus smelled shit. He said, "You need to change his diaper."

The laughter stopped. The tall man said, "What's wrong with your voice? You talk funny."

Manus said, "You need to change his diaper."

The tall man said, "You don't tell me what to do."

Manus looked at Hamilton. "Please," Hamilton was saying, and Manus realized he'd been saying it all along. "Who are you? Who are these people? What the fuck is happening?"

Manus looked at the Turks. He didn't like them. It would have been easy to kill them. But that wasn't what the director wanted.

He pulled Hamilton roughly around to the trunk, set the Berserker down inside it, and, keeping the Turks in view, bent Hamilton over and changed the idiot's diaper. Manus didn't like the way the Turks watched. Their expressions reminded him of what had happened in the juvenile prison.

"I don't know where you're going," Manus said when he was finished. "My job was to deliver you."

Hamilton's eyes were wide, desperate. "Look, you're American, right? Don't leave me with these guys. Please!"

Manus didn't know why he'd said anything. What had been the point? He picked up the Berserker and walked Hamilton to the three men. One of the Turks yanked him over by the arm.

"We are done, yes?" the tall one said.

Hamilton looked back at Manus. "Please!" he said again, and Manus realized he should have retaped his mouth.

The Turks laughed. One of them swatted Hamilton on the ass and squeezed. The other swiveled and shot an uppercut into Hamilton's liver. Hamilton cried out and crumpled to the ground, moaning and writhing.

The tall one smiled at Manus. "Are you worried we won't take good care of him?"

Manus said nothing. He could have taken the man's head off with the Berserker. And dropped the other two with the Force Pro before the blood had finished jetting from the stump. But the director didn't want that.

The tall one barked a command in Turkish. One of the others answered, then helped Hamilton to his feet. His sweat had mixed with the dust he had rolled in and it looked like he was covered in mud. The Turks didn't seem to mind. They were eyeing Hamilton up and down. One of them said something. Manus didn't know the words, but he knew what they meant.

"What did he say?" Manus asked, his voice once again surprising him. It didn't matter what the man had said, so why had he asked?

"He says you have underpaid us," the tall one said, looking at Manus. "He says this is not the money we agreed upon."

Manus shifted the Berserker to his left hand and placed his right on his hip, inches from the butt of the Force Pro. He realized he was glad the conversation had taken this turn. He also realized he shouldn't be. It wasn't what the director wanted.

"I gave you what I was told to give you," he said.

The tall man shook his head. "It isn't enough."

"You mean you've changed your mind?"

A long moment ticked by. The three Turks were tense. Manus knew they were on the verge of going for weapons. He felt his lips stretching into a grin at the prospect, his right hand feeling light, quick, the weight of the Berserker good in his left.

The grin made the men flinch, an effect Manus was accustomed to. The tall man laughed. "No, of course not. I'm only joking. Don't Americans like to joke? Aren't you such a funny people?"

Manus said nothing. He watched as they bundled Hamilton into the van, opening his door for cover and to regain access to the SIG as they drove off. The last thing he saw was Hamilton looking back at him, his eyes terrified, one of the men leering and holding him close with an arm around his neck.

Manus got in his car and drove off, the SIG across his lap, watchful in case the Turks decided to try to ambush him on his way back to Istanbul. After an hour, the sun long since set, he started to relax.

He hadn't liked those men. He knew what they were going to do to Hamilton. He was concerned he'd been happy when it looked like they were going to give him a reason to kill them.

He shook his head and reminded himself that whatever the director wanted, it was more important.

The director had said he wanted him to watch that woman, too—the employee the director was worried about. It sounded like an easy enough job, and Manus would be glad to ease the director's concerns. By watching, if no more than that was required. Or by more than watching. His job was to protect the director. That was all that mattered. It wasn't his fault what happened to anyone who got in the way of it.

CHAPTER . . . .
. . . . 7

Evie left work at five and headed back to the apartment in Columbia. Digne was on the clock for another hour, but Evie always tried to relieve her early when possible. Her time with Dash was precious—it was hard to believe he was already in fourth grade, and she was acutely aware of how fast the time was passing. Soon it would be sports, and girls, and he'd be embarrassed by his mother, and she wouldn't even see him anymore. Okay, well, not that she wouldn't *see* him anymore, but it would be different. He wouldn't need her the way he did now, he'd be independent, he'd have so many other interests and connections. And of course that was all wonderful, but the time they had together now, the bond they shared, was so special, and when he wasn't her little boy anymore she didn't want to ever feel that she'd wasted a minute.

Dash had been her ex-husband's idea—the name, not the child. The child had been unexpected, a word she preferred to *accident*, while she and Sean had been in their fourth year of the graduate computer science program at Cornell and their second year of dating. They'd talked casually about getting married after graduating, and when she told him she was pregnant, they just decided to speed things up a bit. Her mom moved to Ithaca to help with the baby, and they managed.

For a while, being a father seemed good for Sean. He went out less with his buddies, and, when he did go out, he came home earlier and a little less wasted. She never begrudged him his boys' nights. He was a gregarious guy with easy good looks and a ready laugh, and his high spirits made him popular with everyone in the program. In fact, she'd been surprised when he'd first asked her out. She'd never thought of herself as especially attractive, and she'd been flattered by his attention. She realized in retrospect that for a while she'd grown dependent on that flattery, on the boost the reflected glory of his looks and popularity provided to her own self-esteem, and that her dependency had come to occlude her own clear judgment.

They'd both been recruited heavily by NSA—programs like Cornell's were a magnet for the government—and they were excited about careers there. But less than six months before graduation, they got some bad news: Sean had failed the background test. No, no explanation was ever given, they were told. No, no second chances, either. Evie was still welcome, but Sean was out.

To his credit, Sean had refused even to consider a change in plans. He'd taken a job teaching math at a high school in Laurel, her mom had gone home to Spokane . . . and again, for a while, they'd managed. She liked her job, and her career was blossoming. But Sean had drifted back to partying. She tried to overlook it because, yes, he was home from teaching and taking care of the baby hours earlier than she was, and okay, he needed to get out of the house, needed a little fun. But the fun was happening more often, and going on until later, and there were mornings Sean was so hungover he had to call in sick. A few times, when she got home for dinner, she could smell that he'd been drinking already. She would mention it, and he would get angry—did she think he had planned on becoming a high school teacher, a househusband, moving to the place where she had a real job and supporting her career? She might have pointed out that salary-wise, she was doing more of the supporting than he was, but she recognized that, too, was a sore spot, and she didn't push.

When Dash was three, he'd come home from day care looking under the weather. The next morning, he was worse. There was a fever; light and sound were bothering him; and her normally loving boy was uncharacteristically irritable. Evie was worried, and wanted to take him to the doctor. Sean told her she was being ridiculous, the kid just had the flu. She stayed home with him anyway, and Sean went to work.

By noon, they were in the emergency room. Dash was having seizures. The doctors drew fluid from his spine. Then they uttered the most terrifying word Evie had ever heard: *meningitis*.

For three days, Dash was in and out of consciousness while they treated him with antibiotics. The doctors told them his prognosis was good. Evie thought that was the optimistic way of acknowledging he might very well die. Sean went home at night, but Evie refused to leave Dash's side. She didn't sleep or eat or even take her eyes off him. All she did was whisper over and over, *Mommy's here, baby. Mommy's here. Mommy's here. Please come back. Please come back. Please come back.*

On the third day, he did. The fever broke, and he was able to eat; he was weak but smiling. They took him home, her beautiful boy.

Her beautiful deaf boy.

They didn't notice it right away. The changes were subtle. He just seemed . . . slower than he had been. Less responsive. More in his own world. She was worried, no, *terrified*, that the meningitis had affected his brain. Sean, predictably, told her she was overreacting, that Dash was just tired from his ordeal and that he'd bounce back and be fine.

For a while, she allowed herself to be persuaded. But then she took Dash to a pediatrician. The pediatrician did some tests and referred her to a specialist. The specialist did more tests. And informed her that cognitively, Dash was fine, absolutely nothing to worry about. But that his hearing was gravely impaired, a not-uncommon result of meningitis. It might come back. It might not. But they had to assume the worst and start aggressively intervening right away. They had to make decisions about where Dash should go to school, how they would communicate with him, whether they should consider cochlear implants. It was overwhelming. Sean wanted the implants. Evie was against them. Sean wanted Dash to go to regular school. Evie thought he would do better surrounded by other deaf kids. Sean didn't want to learn to sign. Evie took to it like a fanatic. In the end, Sean acceded to everything she wanted. But it cost them. Dash's condition seemed to clarify something she had always sensed but hadn't wanted to face: that she loved their son more, was more devoted to him, was more willing to sacrifice for him, than Sean was. What happened to Dash affected Sean, yes, but it wasn't going to define him. She wasn't built that way. And she didn't want to be, either.

She realized her devotion to Dash's needs was driving Sean away. Or was giving him the excuse he wanted. Though ultimately it was a distinction without a difference. His drinking and his drift from them both worsened, and when they finally separated, it was a relief more than anything else. The divorce was reasonably amicable. When the dust settled, Sean got Dash Monday and Tuesday evenings and alternate weekends. In practice, he saw Dash more like once a month. He had found a girlfriend, a fake blonde named Tina, and apparently Tina wasn't interested in being a babysitter to a deaf kid. Which suited Evie just fine.

She remembered something her mother had told her when she was a teenager: "The boy you date is different from the boy you're engaged to, the boy you're engaged to is different from the man you marry, the man you marry is different from the father of your children." She might have added, "And your ex-husband is going to be different than all of them, too."

But he wasn't that bad, actually. Beyond flaking out from time to time when he was supposed to take Dash, he didn't cause any trouble. He was going to meetings and seemed to have gotten the drinking under control. She had to nag him for support payments, and more than once she thought about going to court and having his salary garnished, but she just didn't have the energy. That, and she didn't want to rock the boat. On paper, he had rights to Dash. In practice, Dash was all hers. She didn't want to do anything to jeopardize that.

Eventually, she learned from a friend in personnel that the reason Sean hadn't gotten into the program was a problem with the polygraph—evidence of deception regarding alcohol and controlled substances. Which, she could see now, made perfect sense. She felt like a fool for not having recognized it earlier. Somehow it made her feel sorry for him. What terrible unhappiness plagued him that he would carry around a secret like that? Even after it had cost him the career he wanted? And though Tina, who had some trampy eye-candy appeal, might have seemed a salve, Evie knew better. Tina hadn't been at the front of the line when whoever was in charge was handing out brains. Sean looked unhappy, and though they never spoke of it, she knew he regretted how things had turned out and wished he could do it over.

Which should have given her some satisfaction, she supposed. A feeling of vindication. Victory. Or something.

Instead, it just made her sad.

She pulled into the parking lot in front of the senior-care facility where her father stayed and tried to shake off the feeling. She knew there were stories out there ten times worse than hers, a hundred times worse. But still, sometimes it all just seemed so hard. So . . . perilous.

She got out of the car and looked at the building for a moment. It might have been anything. A low-slung medical center surrounded by a few afterthought shrubs; an office building filled with accountants and actuaries. So plain. So interchangeable. So soulless. Although she supposed if it were in any way lively or distinctive, she'd find it annoyingly false.

She sighed and went in, past the pretty receptionist, down the antiseptic-smelling corridor. The door to her father's room was open, and she could see him propped up on the adjustable bed. He was wearing a bathrobe, not regular clothes, and she knew instantly he was having a bad day. She knocked on the jamb to get his attention, and when he looked up at her, the resentment she saw in his eyes made her want to cry.

"Hey, Dad," she said with false cheeriness. She walked over and kissed his thinning hair, making sure to not wrinkle her nose at the old-man smell.

He looked past her into the corridor. "What are you doing here?"

It was the same time she usually came by. Either he'd forgotten, or he was being passive-aggressive.

"I snuck out of work a little early. I wanted to say hi."

"Where's Dash?"

She didn't bring Dash anymore; it was too upsetting to him when her father didn't recognize him.

"He's at school, Dad."

"Pretty late in the day for school."

"You know Dash. Baseball practice. I'll bring him next time, okay?"

By next time, she reminded herself, her father would forget having asked, so her promise would cause no hurt. She wondered when her own visits would become superfluous. Her father wasn't that far gone yet, but the doctors had warned her it was mostly a matter of time. Sometimes he talked about her mother as though she were still alive—was she back from the store yet?—that kind of thing. But on the other hand, they'd had a happy marriage. Maybe it was a blessing, the way his wife had crept back from the realm of his memory and into his waking life.

There was a moment of awkward silence. She searched for a way to break it.

"It's sunny out, Dad, you want me to open the curtains?"

"I like the dark."

"You don't feel like bingo today, with any of your friends?"

"They're not my friends."

And so on. She stayed only twenty minutes, pausing to kiss him again when she left. That smell was getting worse, wasn't it? Like the other symptoms. She promised him she'd be back soon, maybe even tomorrow, knowing the promise would be broken, this time not even rationalizing that it didn't matter because he wouldn't remember.

She stopped at the adjacent Safeway and picked up some fried chicken for dinner and ice cream for dessert. Digne often cooked for them, but Safeway fried chicken was Dash's favorite, and sometimes Evie just liked to surprise him with it. Especially when she'd just come from visiting her father and needed something to make herself happy. She reminded herself the ice cream was for Dash, not for her. And to peel the skin off the chicken. She exercised regularly and was pleased with the results, but no one exercised that much.

She pulled into her apartment lot and cut the engine, her Prius at home among the Ford Fusions, Honda Accords, and Suburu Outbacks. Practical cars for practical people. People who couldn't afford to be otherwise. And suddenly she was fighting back tears.

How had it come to this? The drift and the divorce. Her mother, eaten alive by melanoma that had spread to the lymph nodes. Her father, still recognizing her and appreciating her visits, but slowly sliding into darkness and dementia. And no one else. No one to fall back on if anything really bad ever happened. She looked around at all the empty cars. Did the people who drove them feel as scared and isolated as she did? Did *they* wonder how they had arrived here, what they were doing, why they bothered, who would miss them if they were gone?

She thought of Dash, the auburn hair he got from his father, the freckles he got from her, the gap-toothed grin for which she couldn't afford braces, not right now. Dash would miss her. Wasn't he waiting for her right now, in their little apartment? She loved the way he always instantly dropped whatever he was doing when she got home and ran over to give her a hug, the way Digne would nod in recognition at the bond they shared. And how he wasn't embarrassed to hug her even in front of his friends. How could she ever feel sorry for herself, with a son like that?

She smiled and went inside to see him.

CHAPTER . . . .
. . . . 8

The video was posted on YouTube at seven in the morning Washington time—perfectly timed for morning coverage on the major news websites and hysterical follow-on commentary on the evening shows. Hamilton kneeling, dressed in an orange jumpsuit similar to the ones made infamous as the official uniform of prisoners at Guantanamo, his wrists bound behind him, an undifferentiated desert landscape all around. Beside him, a masked jihadist holding a long Bedouin dagger, explaining with calm confidence that soon the man would be beheaded as a lesson to America.

Anders called Remar into his office the moment the video went live. He knew the White House would be on the line any minute and they didn't have much time.

"What the hell is this?" he said, standing behind his desk and gesturing at the monitor. "They were supposed to *kill* him on camera, not just threaten it."

Remar came around, moving crisply in his blue army service uniform, and nodded. "I know. I just saw it."

"So what happened?"

Remar moved respectfully back to the other side of the desk. "I'm guessing they decided to squeeze some extra propaganda value out of the exercise. Milk it a little while longer before collecting their reward."

"How much longer?"

Remar looked at him. He didn't have to answer. They were both thinking the same thing: *Long enough for US Spec Ops to mount some sort of rescue operation?*

Anders looked at the image on his monitor again. "This isn't good."

"You want me to contact Ergenekon? Suggest a completion bonus if the work is finished in the next twenty-four hours?"

Anders moved out from behind his desk and started pacing. "You could, but it's as likely they'll smell blood in the water as it is they'd go for the money. Or maybe they don't care about the money at all at this point. We don't even know if whoever is holding Hamilton is really ISIS affiliated. More likely, Ergenekon gave him to some wannabe group willing to spend a little more cash, and the game for them is notoriety. Right now, ISIS is the brand to beat, so these idiots are probably going to milk their new captive for a good long time. They can only kill him once. But they can display him again and again and again."

Remar moved to the door and paused, as though ready to leave the moment Anders ordered him into action. "The more they display him, the more intel it's going to produce."

"Correct. And the more likely the president will order a rescue operation."

"We could obstruct it. JSOC would need our SIGINT to carry out a rescue."

Anders stopped pacing, realizing Remar was missing a crucial change in the way the Pentagon's Joint Special Operations Command ordinarily had to rely on NSA's Signals Intelligence.

"You're not seeing it," he said, holding up his hands in a *stop* gesture. "Any rescue will be carried out from Turkey. Which would have ideally positioned us—if we had a live SUSLA there. But Perkins just died in a car accident, remember?"

There was a long pause. Remar said, "Jesus."

"Jesus has nothing to do with it. Without someone on the ground for liaison, JSOC will have a pretext to use their own operators and their own intel. We won't have a chance to muddy the waters."

"Okay, but this is all assuming the president even orders a rescue."

Anders laughed. "His ratings are down. If he could pull off the rescue of an American journalist from an evil jihadist group, it would be a political wet dream. The longer Hamilton is alive and suffering on YouTube, the more the president's opponents will try to flank him by screeching he's not being tough enough. Hell, Senator McQueen's going to be ecstatic over this. The president could order the nuclear destruction of Russia, and McQueen would still be trying to make him out to be some kind of eunuch."

"McQueen's white noise. No one takes him seriously."

"No? He's on the Homeland Security Committee, the Finance Committee, and the Intelligence Committee; and the networks love putting him on because they can always count on him to say something incendiary in that Alabama drawl of his."

"You really think the president is going to respond to that bozo?"

"Not respond. React. If he sees a chance to shore up his national security credentials, he'll take it. That means the longer this goes on, the more he'll be tempted to do something dramatic. Can you imagine how it'll play on the news if the president sends in Delta or DEVGRU and they bring Hamilton safely home?"

"Yes, and I can imagine how it'll play if the raid is botched and Hamilton gets killed."

Anders waved a hand as though fanning away some minor flatulence. "They'll say they had intel that Hamilton was about to be killed anyway. At least they sent some jihadists to hell with him. The president will make the announcement surrounded by brass. He'll look tough either way. 'We don't negotiate with terrorists,' that kind of thing. I'm telling you, if this goes on for more than another day, two at the most, he's going in."

They were both silent for a moment. Remar said, "How do you want to handle it?"

Anders considered for a moment. "That talking-head interview I have later this morning."

"You want me to cancel?"

"No, I want to exploit it. Use it to give the president a little breathing room. What do we have on McQueen?"

Remar squinted with his good eye. "We don't have a file. He's always been on-side, we've never needed anything on him before."

"Well, we do now. Use God's Eye. You'll find something."

"How heavy-handed do you want me to be?"

"No more so than necessary. But make sure the job gets done."

"Roger that."

The secure line buzzed. Anders glanced at the monitor. "The White House. Go. Get McQueen on board. We might not have much time."

CHAPTER . . . .
. . . . 9

It turned out to be worse than Anders was expecting. The White House chief of staff told him the president was convening the National Security Council to consider "all options," including a rescue. They needed to know what NSA could deliver based on everything in the video: topography, angle of the sun, quality of light, vegetation. Every electronic communication in the region was to be scoured. If they could identify Hamilton's location, JSOC wanted to go in. And the president was inclined to let them.

He assured the chief of staff that NSA was collating all available intelligence and would have it ready for the NSC's consideration later that morning. And then he headed over to his interview.

The original plan was for a general-interest discussion, with the talking head softened up by the sight of Anders in his full fruit-salad army service uniform. The venue would also be seductive: an otherwise useless room called the Information Dominance Center that had been designed to look like the deck of the starship *Enterprise*, with arrays of giant flat-panel screens, ellipses of LED lighting, and banks of computer monitors. The NSA advance team knew to instruct the camera crew to film only from certain angles, lest the top-secret nature of the room be revealed to America's enemies, and the crew would naturally comply, grateful for the opportunity to behold one of NSA's mysteries, with the desired subservience thereby established before even a word of the interview had been conducted.

Anders arrived on schedule, a tablet-toting aide in tow. The aide held the tablet while Anders scanned and signed something on it, and then the aide made a show of scurrying off, as though the fate of the free world rode on the timely delivery of Anders's signature. Of course the aide could have just transmitted the signature rather than hand-carrying it, but where was the drama, the importance, in that?

"Brian," Anders said, extending his hand. "Good to see you."

"A pleasure, General," the talking head replied, pumping Anders's hand. "I really appreciate your taking the time. Especially with the new terrorist video this morning. Is it all right if I ask about that? I know the interview parameters have already been agreed upon, but I think the American people would want to hear your thoughts on so important a matter."

Anders smiled at the man's attempt at flattery. Was he really so dim he didn't know Anders would *want* to discuss that video, that he wouldn't have to be cajoled into doing it?

"Of course, Brian. I'm happy to discuss what I can. I'm afraid we might have to cut things short, though. Obviously there's a lot going on just now."

"Of course, sir, absolutely. If the way we've positioned the camera is acceptable, we can get started right away."

Anders nodded. *Sir* and *General* and *If that would be acceptable.* He would never get over the supposed watchdog press's instinctive deference to power. Not that he minded, of course.

With the camera rolling, the talking head introduced himself and explained in breathless tones that he was conducting this interview from NSA's own Information Dominance Center, which they weren't permitted to film because it was all so secret.

"Good morning, General."

"Good morning, Brian."

"Sir, I know your schedule is particularly tight today and I appreciate your taking the time. This morning we all woke to another horrifying video: an American journalist, bound and on his knees, threatened by a masked terrorist."

They'd be sure to overlay the appropriate image when they aired the interview. That was good.

"Yes," Anders said in his most sober tone.

"I guess what I and every other member of the civilized world is wondering now, sir, is what response the government is planning."

"Obviously, Brian, I'm not in a position to discuss what we may or may not be thinking in terms of a response."

"Fair enough, sir, but what about your capabilities? For better or worse, and many would say worse, we all know a great deal more today about NSA capabilities than we did not so very long ago. And yet here we have another journalist kidnapped. Is there anything the government could have done to prevent this?"

That, Anders knew, would strike viewers as a tough question, which was why the talking head had asked it. Appearances had to be maintained.

"Well, Brian, what I'd say is this: There's a lot NSA can lawfully do, and within that legal framework, we are as aggressive as we can be. And, of course, there are always additional tools we'd like to have to keep Americans safe. But whether we should have those tools is a question for the legislature, not for NSA."

"Not even an opinion, sir?"

He badly wanted to float the notion of implanting people with chips, but sensed it would be too much at this point. But wait, what about what the Pakistani government was doing . . . cutting off cell phone service to anyone who hadn't agreed to have his or her fingerprints matched to a phone SIM card? If Pakistan could do that, why couldn't America? And in fact, wouldn't that be a great sound bite? *Why is Pakistan doing more to keep its citizens safe than we are?*

But he rejected that temptation, too. This wasn't the occasion. And certainly there would be other opportunities.

"Not one that would be relevant or appropriate, no," Anders said, after a moment. "As for our response to the latest outrage, that is of course the president's purview."

The talking head seized on that, as Anders had hoped he would. "If—hypothetically—the president were to order a rescue, what would be NSA's role?"

Anders adjusted his glasses thoughtfully. "Our role is to support the president with all available resources. And while those resources are considerable, Brian, I do want to caution any hotheads among us. We know Ryan Hamilton is in a grave position. Exceptionally grave. And as desirous as all of us are to see him return safely to the Homeland, we also want to make sure we don't do anything that worsens his situation or the possible outcomes. There are many, many moving parts right now, and they need time to work properly. Anyone demanding immediate action, without a comprehensive understanding of Hamilton's circumstances, could easily be hastening the worst for the young man. So I would urge everyone to be patient, to give the president space to use all the sources and methods available to us to ensure Hamilton's ultimate safety."

The rest of the interview was the usual awestruck network suck job. Not that Anders minded. It was just that this time, burnishing his brand wasn't a particular priority. He had to clear up this Hamilton situation. It would be very bad if the journalist somehow were to make it home.

CHAPTER........
........10

Remar sat in the waiting area outside Senator McQueen's office in the Hart Senate Office Building. He'd been told to arrive at two o'clock and it was now a quarter past. Remar suspected the man was keeping him waiting on purpose. If you wanted to understand the mentality of most Washington insiders, all you had to do was put yourself in the mind of an insecure teenager, at which point it all began to make sense. Even the director liked to play these little power games from time to time. Remar had little patience for it. He considered himself a straight shooter and preferred to deal with people like himself. He smiled, thinking not for the first time that, given his preferences, he was definitely living in the wrong city.

He thought about the audit the director had ordered him to carry out on God's Eye. He hadn't found any way Perkins could have had access, which was the main thing. But he'd discovered something else, as well. The most sensitive uses to which the program had been put had been walled off. What remained . . . well, if the worst were to happen, if the program were to be revealed, it would all pose less of a problem for Remar than it would for the director, who had conceived God's Eye in the first place as part of his "collect it all" mantra.

The thought made him feel guilty, and he half-consciously rubbed the plasticized scar tissue below the eye patch. He'd been the director's man ever since waking in agony while being tended by a forward surgical team, unable to see through the dressing covering his face, the director himself, then a colonel, holding his hand through his own bandages and telling him he was all right, he was going to be all right.

And he *had* been all right, eventually, after a half-dozen reconstructive surgeries, extensive rehabilitation, and a yearlong addiction to painkillers that would have led to a formal reprimand had the director not intervened to have the problem expunged from his record. He'd told the director Manus was like a dog, but he hadn't meant it as an insult. He admired that kind of loyalty, valued it. And, when it came to the director, shared it. He owed his life to the director, his career, his position. He didn't approve of all the director's decisions, and if it were up to him, things would be run differently. But it wasn't up to him, that wasn't how fate had played out, and what he owed the director, he sometimes just had to borrow against his own conscience.

So it didn't matter that his audit had revealed a possible . . . divergence in their potential exposure, and therefore in their interests. And besides, any divergence was only theoretical anyway. Because Perkins didn't have the access. He couldn't.

At just past two thirty, two frightfully young and bright-eyed staffers emerged from the inner sanctum and closed the door behind them. *Yes, I get it*, Remar thought. *You were keeping me waiting just for a conversation with a couple of interns.*

A few minutes later, a secretary ushered him in. McQueen stood from behind his massive desk and hurried around to shake Remar's hand, his jowls bouncing. "General Remar! So good to see you. Thanks for coming and apologies for keeping you waiting."

"Senator," Remar said, wanting to get the whole thing over with as quickly as possible. The man's hand was moist, and Remar resisted the urge to wipe his palm on his trousers after they shook.

"Please," McQueen said, circling back behind his desk as though afraid he might shrivel if too long away from it. "Have a seat. What can I do for a genuine war hero?"

Remar didn't mind the bullshit, but he hated when these idiots felt compelled to attach it to some notion of his heroism. He'd been in a Humvee when a mortar round had struck the area. If there was a hero involved, it had been the director, not him. He wondered sometimes if the McQueens of the world, who had probably never even handled a rifle, much less served, really meant it when they laid it on about the glory of soldiers, or if it was just another DC con job. He supposed it didn't matter either way.

He set his attaché case on the floor, opened it, and took out a bug detector. He turned it on and quickly swept the office. It was clean.

"I recommend we power down our phones, Senator. And place them in my attaché case, which is soundproofed and jams all electronic signals."

McQueen eased himself into his enormous leather chair and touched an imaginary imperfection in his gray bouffant. "Are you serious?"

The guy's ignorance was breathtaking. Did he think that because he was on the Homeland Security Committee and the Intelligence Committee, he was somehow immune to surveillance? Did he not understand that his positions in fact *made* him a target? But knowing all this would be clarified in just a moment, Remar simply said, "Do I look like I'm joking?"

McQueen chuckled. "Well, you're the national security expert. Whatever you say." He turned off his mobile and handed it to Remar. Remar powered off his own, and placed both in the attaché. Then he took out an acoustic noise generator and set it on McQueen's desk.

McQueen eyed it suspiciously. "And that is . . . ?"

"Speech protection system. Just being extra careful. And Senator, if I could trouble you to disconnect the power cord from your desk phone and from your computer."

"Come on, Remar, this is ridiculous."

"Senator, I assure you that when you've received my briefing you will thank me copiously for taking precautions."

McQueen rolled his eyes and smiled. He shut off the surge protector to the desk phone and computer, and ostentatiously checked his watch. Then he pointed to the watch and said, his tone mock-serious, "Oh, do you need me to take this off, too?"

McQueen was peeved that someone was telling him what to do in his own office, and had to show he wasn't cowed in response. Remar was accustomed to the juvenile bullshit, of course, but still found it vaguely pathetic.

"You know what they say," Remar said, taking a seat and closing the attaché. "Just because you're paranoid doesn't mean they're not out to get you."

"Sure, and just because they're out to get you doesn't mean you're not being paranoid. Come on, Remar. I've seen more than my share of NSA razzle-dazzle. Bow down to the high priests of info security. You should save it for the youngsters in these corridors. I've been to the show too many times to be impressed by it."

Remar nodded as though in understanding, then shifted into character. "Senator, I won't deny there's some theater involved in what we do. How could there not be, in this town? But that's not why I'm here. I'm here because we have evidence the Chinese have put together a sensitive dossier on you, which we believe they intend to use in an attempt to influence your votes."

McQueen's eyes widened and he looked genuinely surprised. "What?"

Remar did nothing to reveal his satisfaction with the stimulus/

response effect. The director had taught him that with a certain class of national security fetishist, attributing something bad to the Chinese, or Russians, or Iranians was the equivalent of blaming domestic crimes on angry black men. Prepping people to believe something was the hard part. Once the framework was established, they became eager to fill in the details themselves, and could be counted on to do so even if those details made little sense.

Remar leaned forward and lowered his voice. "It seems the Chinese have managed to track your cell phone and correlate its movements with that of a second cell phone—a prepaid model purchased for cash in a Walmart two years ago. They have further tracked the movements of both phones to an apartment here on Capitol Hill. The lease on this apartment is being paid by a dummy corporation set up by your personal attorney. And the inhabitant of this apartment is a young woman named Natalia Robart, the movements of whose own cell phone have been correlated to yours on numerous business trips you've taken, on none of which has your wife's cell phone indicated your wife was present."

McQueen had gradually paled as Remar briefed him, and his mouth was now agape. Remar waited while it all sank in.

"I don't . . . I don't see how . . ." McQueen stammered, and then was silent, shaking his head, apparently unable to find words.

"Obviously, this is all just metadata. But also obviously, it's more than enough to cause a scandal—and that's assuming the Chinese haven't penetrated Ms. Robart's apartment and installed hidden cameras. That is something we could discreetly rule out, if you'd like."

"I don't . . . I don't understand . . ."

"Let me assure you, Senator, this information is being held in the strictest confidence and in the tightest circle possible at NSA. None of us wants to see you hurt."

"Yes, but . . . Jesus Christ, how is this even possible?"

Remar permitted himself a sympathetic smile. "Do you still feel I'm being paranoid?"

McQueen looked as though he'd been gut-punched. "Christ, no. Is there anything that can be done?"

"In fact, there is. The system we've uncovered seems to be automated. We've tracked its uploads to a dedicated server, which we've covertly penetrated. We're in a position now where we should be able to permanently destroy the data on that server."

"Well, that's great news!"

"Yes. We're holding off to first confirm there isn't a backup server. If there is, we want to trace back to it and destroy it simultaneously. If we act too quickly, we could tip off the Chinese and lose the chance to wipe out the problematic records completely."

All at once, McQueen's shocked expression transmuted into a more canny one. He leaned back in his chair and looked Remar up and down as though evaluating him. Then he nodded and smiled.

"All right, Remar. What's your game?"

"Game, Senator?"

"Why are you really telling me all this? What do you want from me?"

Remar realized the man had figured out the situation was less scary than he'd first thought. He'd seen that it was a business transaction, not a random threat, and therefore that presumably there was no reason the parties couldn't arrive at a mutually acceptable price.

Remar effected a puzzled look. "I don't want anything from you, Senator. Well, I'd like you to be more careful, but of course in the end that's up to you."

McQueen's smile broadened. "Oh, really? There's no quid pro quo here?"

Remar shrugged. "No, but if there were, I'd say you've already delivered through all your support of the intelligence community. So if anything, this is a thank-you, not a quid pro quo."

They were quiet for a moment. McQueen looked confused. Could it really be that simple—his friends paying off a debt by protecting him?

"All right, then," McQueen said, his tone cautious. "You'll just . . . keep me posted on your efforts against that Chinese server?"

Remar retrieved the attaché from the floor. "Of course. We're making every effort, and I'm cautiously optimistic we'll be able to contain it."

McQueen nodded, as though afraid to speak.

Remar stood and placed the attaché on the desk. "Well, I've taken enough of your time today, Senator. Please do be more careful about the phones—we downplay it to the public, but the metadata really does reveal a lot. As the saying goes, 'We kill people based on metadata.'"

McQueen nodded again. "Yes, I can see that."

"Oh, and one other thing. You know that journalist who's been kidnapped in Syria?"

"Hamilton? Of course."

"Yes, Hamilton. There's a pretty decent chance we can get him out. But it's going to have to be done quietly and will require a little patience. Naturally, the president wants to send in Delta or whoever and make political hay out of a rescue."

McQueen cocked his head. "The president *wants* to send in the military?"

"Unfortunately, yes. He thinks it's a guaranteed political win— either Hamilton gets rescued, or Hamilton gets killed while Spec Ops mows down a bunch of jihadists and the president gets to crow about how he'll never negotiate with terrorists. We've told him the right way to get Hamilton out is something low-key that won't offer him a big political payoff. You can imagine how that advice is going over."

"Yes, I can."

"Anyway. I know you and every other responsible person affiliated with the intelligence community wants the same thing we do—
to get that young man out of there alive. Now, I don't have to tell
you, your national security credentials are unimpeachable. People
listen to you. Even the president listens to you, despite himself. So
when the networks bring you on to talk about Hamilton, it would
be great if you could speak up about the virtues of patience and
stealth, and the vices of hot-headed military showboating that's more
likely to get Hamilton killed than anything else. Can we count on
you for that, Senator?"

McQueen came to his feet and all but saluted. "You know you
can, General. I'm glad you asked and I'm pleased to help."

It was fascinating, how people could be so reluctant to recognize
blackmail, how eager they could be to convince themselves it was
something else, even something fundamentally mutually coopera-
tive. And sometimes it seemed the more powerful the individual, the
greater the capacity for self-deception.

He shook the senator's hand again and left. Out in the corridor,
he wiped his palm on his trousers. There was a time, he knew, when
the kind of thing he had just done would have horrified him. He
tried, but couldn't remember when that had been.

It didn't matter. What mattered was that they had bought themselves some time.

And owned another senator.

CHAPTER.......
.......II

Anders sat with the other principals of the National Security Council in the White House Situation Room. The atmosphere was claustrophobic, and the small, low-ceilinged room, dominated by a wooden table large enough for twelve, exacerbated the feeling. Small talk was minimal, and the participants radiated all the warmth one might expect of a gathering of jealous warlords, or of scorpions shoved together into a bottle. Everyone in the room looked at everyone else as an enemy or, at best, as a potential ally of convenience. Every one of them thought he or she would make a better president than the guy running the meeting. And a few of them might even have been right.

The president, exercising his prerogatives and indulging a habit, showed up a half hour late. He sat, waited while an aide poured his coffee, took a sip, and said, "We all know why we're here. What are our options?"

Anders noted the use of the plural pronoun. Hamilton wasn't the president's problem. He was everyone's problem. Of course, if things went well, only the president would get the credit. It was good to be the king.

The question hadn't been directed at anyone in particular. Anders had long ago noted that the president liked to run his meetings like little Rorschach tests. Who would speak up first? Who was bold, who was canny? Anders knew the technique because he liked to employ it himself.

Vernon Jones, the chairman of the Joint Chiefs, glanced at the secretary of defense, who nodded his assent. "Mr. President, DEVGRU and Delta are already in position and ready to go. All we need are intel and orders."

Anders didn't like Jones, a tall black man with an appealing Southern baritone Anders thought was an unfair advantage—the American equivalent of Oxford British, something that conferred a gravitas the substance of the person's remarks couldn't alone achieve. And even beyond his native antipathy, Anders hated the way Jones had framed the issue. He was as much as saying, "Assuming you have the balls, sir, the only question is whether the intel community is worth a damn."

Everyone turned and looked at Anders. They knew better than to expect anything from the director of National Intelligence, Anders's nominal superior and, by statute, a required attendee at meetings of the National Security Council. If there was one thing each of these people understood, one thing their shark minds were tuned for, it was where real power lay.

The DNI gave Anders his most serious look, a pantomime of authority. "Well, Ted, what have you got in the region?"

Ah, the *you*, not the *we*. Anders didn't even look at him. "Mr. President, we are focusing all appropriate resources. SIGINT teams are scouring the area. A geomapping team is attempting to precisely locate the spot where the video was filmed. Voice analysis could give us the actual identity of the terrorist in the video."

The president looked unimpressed. "How long is this going to take?"

"It's difficult to say, sir. Sometimes we can get a break quickly. Other times—"

"I don't want to wait. I understand the risks. But you need to understand, James Foley was waterboarded by these animals. Every hour we wait could be another hour they're torturing Hamilton."

Anders glanced around, noting the discomfited looks on some of the faces in the room. Describing waterboarding as torture produced a fair amount of doublethink these days.

"Yes, sir. I am personally monitoring—"

"I understand there's been a tragedy in Istanbul. Your SUSLA was in a car accident."

Anders didn't hesitate. "Yes, sir, that is correct."

How did the president already know that? And how did he even know what a SUSLA was? Then he realized: Jones told him. The man had seen his opportunity and had been quick to exploit it. Of course, Anders had played the same sort of games before being appointed to run NSA. But intel was his fiefdom now, and he knew from experience how rapaciously other players within the Defense Department wanted to encroach on it.

Anders quietly seethed. He'd been trying for years to assemble a file he could use to manage Jones. The problem was, either Jones really was an exceptionally God-fearing man with no indiscretions that might be unearthed, documented, and used against him; or he was exceptionally savvy in the way he conducted those indiscretions. And, naturally, he was also the person who was positioned, and inclined, to make the most trouble.

"Well?" the president said, looking at Anders. "Does this degrade your capabilities in the region?"

This was a difficult question. A *no* would lead to a question: *What the hell does your SUSLA even do, then?* But a *yes* would create an opening for the Pentagon to move in for the kill.

Finessing it, Anders said, "Sir, for a position this vital to the regional war effort, of course we have built-in redundancies. So while Perkins's loss is indeed tragic, it will not impede our ability to carry out our mission."

The president nodded as though this was what he'd been expecting. "All right. Keep on it. In the meantime, I'm formally tasking the Pentagon with the development of its own intel regarding Hamilton's whereabouts and condition. As you've noted, redundancy is important. And this is America—we know competition is good."

Anders nodded crisply, allowing nothing to betray his actual feelings. But this was a bad development. Worse than he had feared.

"We'll convene again in twenty-four hours," the president said. "By then, I want us to have the necessary intel, I want us to have a plan, and I want us to be in a position to immediately execute that plan."

Out of the corner of his eye, Anders saw Jones nod, obviously pleased at how the meeting had gone. The president wanted a rescue; he had made that plain. And the Pentagon brass saw an opportunity to make him happy and more reliant on the military. They'd get him the intel. Even if they had to distort a few things in the process.

Well, Anders could distort a few things, too.

CHAPTER . . . .
. . . . 12

Evie sat in a restroom stall—a different floor, a different part of the building from the one near her office. She didn't want to see anyone likely to recognize her. She just needed a few minutes alone, a few minutes to compose herself, where no one could be watching.

Everyone was talking about the Hamilton kidnapping. There were rumors of a rescue operation, and it was all hands on deck. If anyone had heard about Perkins and his car accident, it wasn't being much discussed. Maybe Hamilton had eclipsed that news; maybe no one really knew the SUSLA Turkey or particularly cared. Either way, no one was making the connection. She was the only one who knew anything about that.

Not *knew*, she corrected herself. *Suspected.*

Because what did she really know? Yes, it looked like Perkins had been feeding classified information to Hamilton. Yes, she had alerted the director just a day before he died. But car accidents happened. And Hamilton . . . well, if the reporter had gone to the Syrian border in pursuit of a story, he might have just been unlucky. He'd hardly be the first. And anyway, Hamilton wasn't dead; he was kidnapped. Why would anyone have engineered something like that?

Not anyone. The director.

She realized she didn't want to believe any of this was other than coincidence, and that her mind was offering up a kind of double-think as a shield against unwelcome insights.

But still. Even if the director wanted Hamilton dead, then why wasn't the journalist just dead? Why engineer a kidnapping?

Because he's supposed to die. Or was supposed to. Or something. The kidnapping was all intended to obscure what's really going on.

All right. That was logical, in a manner of speaking. But then . . . why have Perkins and Hamilton killed? Why not just have them prosecuted? She knew enough about the Espionage Act to know the government had no compunction about invoking it.

Against whistleblowers. It hasn't been used yet to stop a mainstream journalist from reporting.

So . . . what then? The director knew, or suspected, that Perkins had turned over to Hamilton something so sensitive that ensuring silence warranted having him killed? She was privy to a tremendous amount of top-secret, sensitive, compartmented information, but she didn't know anything that would justify murder. There had been leaks before. Whole books written about NSA. God, they'd even survived Snowden. Why would the director risk murder rather than just riding out the revelations the way they'd always been ridden out before?

Because these revelations implicate him.

But in what?

Something . . . criminal.

She had to laugh at that. Criminality so bad it was worse than murder, or justified the risks of murder?

What about blackmail?

She considered. It was true people joked that the higher-ups must have had some kind of dirt on Feinstein and Rogers and the rest of the legislative committees, because "oversight" had really become a euphemism for "rubber stamp." Not to mention the secret

FISA "court," which offered something like a 99.97% approval rate for government surveillance requests.

Still, those were just jokes. There was no real evidence. And despite the public relations hit they'd all taken post-Snowden, she'd always felt her colleagues were good people with good intentions. In all her years with NSA, she'd never seen anything remotely like the skulduggery portrayed in movies.

All right. Maybe it all really was a coincidence. She knew she wanted to believe that, but that didn't mean it wasn't so, either.

She stood and went to flush the toilet in case anyone had come into the bathroom while she was in the stall. It would have seemed odd for someone to use a stall and not flush. But she paused, her hand halfway to the handle.

She was being ridiculous. Who would notice, or care, whether or not they'd heard a toilet flush? And anyway, she'd deliberately used a restroom in another part of the building, somewhere it was unlikely anyone would even recognize or remember her. And while there were cameras all over the corridors at NSA, what was someone going to report, *Alert, Evelyn Gallagher, suspicious bathroom choice?* And sure, she'd just sat in the stall, she hadn't even needed to pee or anything, but it wasn't like there were cameras in the damn bathrooms. That would be completely insane.

Of course, if you really *wanted to get into people's heads, you'd want cameras in the bathrooms. The moments people think they have the most privacy are exactly what you'd want to be able to watch. The more people are trying to hide their behavior, the more revealing it's apt to be.*

She looked up at the plaster ceiling and around at the metal partitions, feeling she'd had some sort of epiphany, and then stifled a chuckle. *Sure, Evie. NSA has installed a massive camera network so it can watch all the employees pee.*

She flushed the toilet and went out.

CHAPTER . . . .
. . . . 13

It was nearly midnight and Anders was still at the office, as he expected to be more or less continuously until the Hamilton thing was resolved. Debbie had called to let him know she was going to bed. It was nice that she maintained the custom even after so many years of late nights at the office, so many canceled plans. Keeping her disappointments hidden was a sign of her love for him, and he would always be grateful to her for that.

There was a knock, and Manus came in. He closed the door behind him, strode directly to Anders's desk, and handed over the thumb drive and mobile phone he'd briefed Anders on before leaving Turkey.

"Continuous custody?" Anders said, holding up the items for scrutiny and aware that his tone and manner were unusually peremptory.

If Manus noticed any lack of the courtesy Anders usually extended him, he didn't show it. "I personally took them from Hamilton's pockets. They haven't been out of my possession since then."

"And the phone—"

"Faraday cage since I took it from Hamilton. No way to track its movements."

Anders nodded. "Of course. I just need to be certain. And I'm sorry. It's been a very long day."

Manus gave no sign that the explanation had meant anything to him. No wonder the man put Remar on edge.

Anders plugged the thumb drive into a special unit, then placed a finger on the biometric pad and typed in his passphrase—standard two-factor authentication. A moment later, he had accessed the Cray massively parallel supercomputers NSA ran in the belly of Fort Meade. If he was very lucky, Hamilton would have used either weak encryption, or one of the commercial applications NSA had long since infected with backdoors. He waited a moment while the drive was scanned at nearly one hundred petaflops, his screen unable to keep up with the speed of the Crays. But the encryption held. Damn it. Hamilton must have been using something solid, probably open source. NSA had been so successful in weakening international encryption standards, in persuading companies to install backdoors . . . it was always frustrating to encounter one of the programs that hadn't yet been subverted.

He wondered just how much information was on the drive. Ten thousand documents? Fifty thousand? The computer couldn't break the encryption, but it could tell him how many gigabytes of information was stored on the drive. Not a particularly useful thing to know, but it was something, and he was morbidly curious. He keyed in a query. The response came instantly: eight kilobytes.

He blinked. Eight kilobytes? That was just a wrapper. The drive itself was empty—there was nothing on it. His stomach lurched as he realized the drive Hamilton had been carrying was a decoy.

He plugged in the phone. It wasn't even encrypted, just protected by a four-digit passcode. The Crays cracked and scanned it in under a second. There was nothing on it beyond the usual address book, calendar, and other data.

He looked at Manus, who was still standing motionless, watching him.

"He didn't have anything else with him?"

"I told you, wallet and passport. I destroyed them."

"No laptop?"

"No."

"No tablet?"

"No."

"No other portable media?"

"I searched his room, including the safe. And his bag, his clothes, and his shoes. There was nothing."

Anders scrubbed a hand across his mouth, fighting the panic he felt closing in on him.

"Okay," he said, working it like a puzzle. "Okay."

He knew Perkins must have handed off something to Hamilton. Even if there were a backup cached somewhere on the Darknet, he would have given Hamilton *something* he could have walked him through. Otherwise, why bring in a journalist at all? If all Perkins had wanted to do was upload whatever he had stolen to a dozen subversive websites, he could have. But he didn't. He must have wanted a journalist's imprimatur, the fig leaf afforded by the First Amendment. Anders knew in his bones that Perkins had given Hamilton something, something big, something that involved enormous risk. The question was, what had Hamilton done with it?

"Okay," he said again. "You never saw Hamilton go into a post office, say, or a FedEx facility while you were tailing him, anything like that? Or an Internet café?"

"The only time I saw him was in his hotel room."

Anders nodded, having anticipated the answer. He didn't really think Hamilton would have risked electronically transmitting whatever Perkins had given him. The public's understanding of NSA's prodigious electronic surveillance abilities was pretty advanced. What they didn't know was how much was monitored in other ways. Hamilton might have transmitted something, and Anders would have a team follow any footprints left by any such transaction. But more likely, the reporter would have put his faith in something more primitive. Like terrorists, journalists had figured out all their electronic communications could be compromised. It was why Greenwald and Poitras had been caught using Greenwald's partner, David Miranda, as a courier. And that *Guardian* editor, Alan Rusbridger, had acknowledged his Snowden reporters were taking a huge number of flights because they didn't trust anything other than face-to-face meetings. Why would Hamilton be different?

Damn it, he needed to wrap this up quickly. At least Senator McQueen had come through, stunning various talking heads with his appeal for calm and patience, his expression of support for the president's deliberative style. But all that would do was buy some time. It wouldn't solve the underlying problem.

All right, he'd have a team scour everything that had gone out of Istanbul by FedEx or other private carrier from the moment Hamilton had arrived. They'd be able to track it in the air, to whatever sorting facility, even to the truck it went out on for delivery. If Hamilton had used the postal service, it would be trickier, but not impossible. It wasn't widely known, but the US Postal Service photographed every piece of mail it handled. The system was primitive and labor intensive, but if they had an indication Hamilton had mailed something from Istanbul, they'd mobilize enough people to track, and with just a little luck, maybe even preempt it. But hopefully it wouldn't come to that. Hopefully Hamilton would have placed his confidence in one of the private courier services, instead.

Gallagher, he realized. She could help with this. He'd have her use the camera system to do a block-by-block search of every move Hamilton had made in Istanbul. Backup for the other systems he would deploy to track whether anything had been sent.

The thought wasn't a happy one. Following their conversation, and her doubts about the death of the last whistleblower her network had uncovered, she was likely agitated about Perkins's death and Hamilton's kidnapping. Involving her further could only increase the fever of her suspicions. Well, so be it. All that mattered for the moment was Hamilton and whatever Perkins had given him. Anders would use every resource available to button that up. When the crisis was resolved and those resources were no longer essential, they could be . . . disposed of.

He looked at Manus and decided he would be perfect for the task.

CHAPTER........
........14

Remar ushered Evie into the director's office the instant she arrived the next morning. She'd received a text at midnight telling her to be there at seven sharp. Something to do with Hamilton, she'd guessed, and her heart had kicked up a nervous notch at the thought. Luckily, Digne had been able to come early to take care of Dash and get him to the bus stop. Evie loved the Salvadoran woman and didn't know what she would do without her.

She'd closed the door behind her, taken a seat per the director's gesture to do so, and then fought the urge to shift in the chair while he looked at her closely, his hands clasped in front of his chin. As though expecting her to speak, or confess, or whatever—she didn't know.

Finally, he sighed, leaned back in his chair, and said, "Given your concerns about Scott Stiles's suicide, I find myself more than a little interested in what you must make of Dan Perkins's car accident. And the journalist Hamilton's kidnapping."

Whatever she'd been expecting, it wasn't something so direct. Which was probably the reason for his gambit. Somehow she sensed that denying any concern at all would be the wrong response. Staying closer to the truth would be better. But not too close.

"Well, sir, honestly, it does look pretty weird immediately after the flag my system threw up. And I won't deny I've turned it over in my mind. But I can't imagine why anyone would go to such lengths against an insider threat. And even if someone had, why not do the same against the journalist? Why a kidnapping, which is so much less clean?"

She waited, glad she'd remembered to use the preferred nomenclature *insider threat* rather than the inflammatory *whistleblower*.

A long moment went by. She had the sense he was trying to draw her out with his silence. She'd never received interrogation training, but the technique certainly worked with Dash when he'd done something he shouldn't have.

He chuckled and waved his hands palms up as though dismissing the absurdity of it all. "It is all quite a coincidence, I'll give you that. I wouldn't blame you, or anyone else who knew of the connection between Perkins and Hamilton, for wondering."

She nodded, sensing she had passed a test, if only barely. But what kind of test? For what purpose?

"I believe there's going to be a rescue operation," he went on after a moment. "That's strictly my opinion for the moment, and is to go no further. And while it's probably a long shot, I want to know if there could be any connection between Perkins, on the one hand, and Hamilton's abduction by terrorists, on the other. Did the terrorists have some knowledge of what Hamilton was up to? Did they take him in the hope of acquiring the very information he had received from Perkins? Needless to say, if Perkins passed Hamilton classified information involving NSA sources and methods, and that information wound up in the hands of ISIS, it would be a grave threat to national security. I want you to confirm that didn't happen."

It sounded logical enough. Why was it making her nervous?

"How, sir?"

"I want you to go through every inch of footage you have on Hamilton's movements from the moment he arrived in Istanbul and particularly from the moment he first met Perkins there. Did he visit any store, or post office, or kiosk, or anywhere at all he might have mailed a parcel?"

"Because if he mailed something—"

"Yes, while it wouldn't be proof, it would at least leave open the possibility he didn't have any sensitive information on his person when he was taken. But if he didn't send a package—"

"You're concerned it would suggest he was carrying something when he was taken—a thumb drive, something like that."

"Precisely."

"Couldn't he have uploaded whatever he received from Perkins?"

"He could have. But my gut tells me he was relying on something low-tech. If so, and if he didn't put it in transit, he had it on his person. That would be quite bad."

Bad enough to call in a drone strike on his position? she thought. The idea seemed crazy, but . . . not quite as crazy as she wanted.

"Our coverage of Istanbul isn't great," she said, hoping she didn't sound as reluctant as she felt. "If I don't come up with anything, it doesn't mean he didn't send a package."

"Yes, in a sense I'm asking you to try to prove a negative. But we might get lucky. If we don't get a positive, then I need to be able to report to the president that we tried, and what we did and didn't find."

"Yes, sir."

"I doubt I need to say it, but this requires your full and immediate attention. A young man's life might depend on the work you do today."

She spent the rest of the day scrutinizing the footage from Istanbul. The facial recognition system and biometrics program made the job possible—without it, she would have needed an army to manually search through the tens of thousands of hours of video in search of an image of Hamilton—but it was still laborious. Every automated positive required extrapolation based on the direction Hamilton was traveling, whether by car or bus or taxi, because he passed plenty of cameras that didn't pick up his face or other useable details. She realized this was something she could and should have thought to automate sooner. There was no reason she couldn't tie the cameras and the biometrics recognition together with mapping software so the system could extrapolate a subject's movements even when his face or movement was obscured—even when he passed through an area without a camera network. Well, at least the tedious, manual work she was doing today wouldn't be totally wasted. The experience would help her conceive the most elegant way to automate the system for next time.

She had a sudden, queasy thought. What if the director really had been behind Perkins's death and Hamilton's kidnapping? Of course it was far-fetched, but still . . . she'd already given him the tools that would have enabled him, and now she was optimizing those tools. Why? Because it was just satisfying to come up with an improvement?

She paused and massaged her temples. She didn't want to have these doubts. She wanted to do a good job, to be appreciated, to have the kind of security Dash needed. And a little advancement in the ranks wouldn't hurt. But being this close to something . . . bad was making her aware of concerns she'd been trying to suppress since Snowden. People tended not to talk about it—nobody wanted to be flagged as weak or a potential traitor, and it didn't take much to get reported as such under the Insider Threat Program—but she was pretty sure her feelings weren't atypical. So many engineers and mathematicians continually expanding NSA's capabilities, finding personal satisfaction and corporate advancement in every cool new hack they came up with. But losing sight of the big picture along the way, ignoring the risks, ignoring the reality, of what all those hacks could and would be used for. Until Snowden made it all impossible to deny.

For a moment, she thought about the data sets behind her biometrics system: top-secret clearances on one side; journalists, activists, and other radicals and subversives on the other. She wondered who had put together the lists. Security clearances would be pretty easy: true, there were over 1.5 million top-secret clearances, but you could still hack together a database. But who put together the list of subversives? That would require judgment calls rather than a binary, bright-line approach. What were the criteria? What was the review process, if any? The list was just given to her. And just as she could use only one set of tools to analyze red flags, similarly she didn't know what happened with the information she passed on to the director. Presumably, he gave it to another compartmented person who didn't know where or whom it came from or what it was being used for.

The program had always struck her as pretty fragmented, but that had never particularly bothered her. Just the usual unwieldy result of too much paranoia, she had assumed, too little planning, too many fiefdoms. And not something someone at her level could, or should, try to address. But now, the fragmentation felt . . . deliberate. Less accident, more design.

But what could she do, really? This was her job. And she needed that job badly. She'd looked into her private-sector options, and they weren't good—everything involved less important and interesting work; decreased flexibility; lesser benefits; and a relocation that would mean pulling Dash from the school he loved, not to mention renewed custody battles with Sean. She wasn't a hero, and she didn't want to be. She wouldn't even know how. She was just a bit player, totally dispensable if it came to that. More than anything else, she was a mom fearful for her son's future and trying to make that future as secure as possible.

Focus, Evie. Just focus. All you have are suspicions. No actual evidence, no proof, just a couple of crazy coincidences. Do your job. You're good at it.

It was painstaking work. And strange, to rewind the last days of a life that had veered so suddenly and spectacularly into horror. She knew there were many other people, many other systems, that were in motion, trying to uncover his movements, his motives, his whereabouts. And that was good. But—

She paused. If Hamilton had sent something by FedEx or other private carrier, it would be trivial for even the greenest NSA technician to zero in on it. And something handled by the postal service wouldn't be that much harder.

So why was the director having her do something that was both inefficient and redundant?

Backup. Covering all the bases.

Maybe. But then why hadn't he said as much?

Because it didn't even occur to him. He's focused on a dozen other things.

Again, maybe. But—

He's testing you. He already knows the answer, and wants to see if you try to hide something. That's an interrogator's trick, isn't it? And didn't it feel like he was interrogating you in his office? That he's suspicious? You should never have asked him about Scott Stiles hanging himself. Never. Stupid, stupid, stupid.

Was she just getting paranoid? She felt like these sorts of thoughts were dangerous, and wanted to push them away. But she couldn't shake off the thoughts any more than she could shake off the feeling that was feeding them.

After four hours, she got her first break: Hamilton, going into a post office. Her heart kicked up a notch. Had he mailed something? A moment later, he came out—but wait, he was holding an envelope, an envelope with postage affixed. He'd bought postage, but hadn't mailed the letter he was holding? Weird. And therefore interesting.

Earlier she'd watched him go into a supermarket and come out with a small bag, but hadn't thought much of it at that point. He'd been carrying the bag with him when he went into the post office, but was carrying only the single letter when he came out. Suggesting he'd thrown away the bag inside the post office. Her heart kicked harder. Had he bought envelopes in the supermarket, and postage in the post office? Okay, but then why not mail the stamped letter from the post office? He'd used one envelope, tossed the rest, affixed the proper postage . . . and then left to mail the letter somewhere else. Why?

He wanted to make sure he had the correct postage, but didn't want to mail the letter from somewhere he'd been seen.

Okay, then now he would be looking for a mailbox. She tracked his movements from one camera network to the next. In one sequence, the envelope started to come into view. She slowed down the footage—

There—an address. She backed up, slowed to frame-by-frame, and zoomed in. Too blurry. She enhanced, and got a partial. She enhanced again, and . . . *Yes.* The remainder of the address. She looked it up—a shipping and packaging place in Rockville, a Maryland suburb. Presumably a mailbox Hamilton had rented. She accessed his tax returns and found his home address: Potomac, one town over. Gut call: he had mailed the envelope to himself, avoiding his home and work addresses out of exceptional caution.

There was a return address, too, something in Istanbul. She looked it up—a cheap hotel in Sultanahmet, not where Hamilton had been staying. A dummy, unconnected with Hamilton, something to make a letter to the States look normal so it wouldn't attract unnecessary attention.

She went through frame by frame. There was a slight bulge inside the envelope. Either a lot of folded paper, or, say, a thumb drive secured in cardboard. This had to be it.

She tracked Hamilton further. For a while, she lost him, but when he'd reappeared, the envelope was gone. A safe bet he'd simply dropped it in a mailbox and kept moving. An ordinary letter wouldn't require any customs forms. He could have mailed it anywhere, and it looked as though that was exactly what he had done.

The letter was a significant find, a huge find, and she was gratified at the thought that the system she'd designed had uncovered something so important. But the director would want to know if there had been anything else. So she kept watching. And was rewarded with footage of Hamilton ducking into a FedEx facility in Beyoğlu. This time he carried nothing in or out. But then he wouldn't need to—he could have dropped a thumb drive into a mailer, and that would have been the end of it.

Two packages, then—the primary and the backup. The FedEx package they could track through FedEx's own system. The letter, though, would be unknown to anyone but her. No one else had access to the camera network, or the expertise to use it.

She drummed her fingers along her desk, suddenly intrigued.

What if she simply failed to mention the mailed letter? Even if the director somehow knew of it, and she couldn't imagine how he could, it would have been an easy enough thing for her to overlook amid all the footage she had to manually review. She didn't like the idea of appearing less than competent, but it was hard to see how anyone could infer something suspicious from her oversight. Especially when she had turned over the FedEx find. The director would focus on that, be excited about that. She doubted he would even consider whether there had been a second package. And even if he did, he had no way to know.

For a moment, she considered deleting the incriminating footage, but then decided against it. It would be one thing to cop to an oversight. Explaining deleted footage, if it came to that, would be something else entirely.

She took a deep breath and considered. What was she really going to do about the letter Hamilton had sent to the Rockville mail drop? Maybe nothing. Or maybe she was telling herself she would do nothing because the alternatives were crazy and she didn't want to acknowledge them. The main thing was, she didn't have to do anything. She'd tell the director about the FedEx package and pretend, even to herself, that there was nothing else to report. And then she could just . . . wait. Wait and see. Yes, that was it. Wait and see.

She logged out and went to brief the director.

CHAPTER . . . .
. . . . 15

Evie was at the Camden Yards Orioles game with Dash when they met the strange man.

They were sitting in the highest section of the ballpark, overlooking left field—too far to make out the numbers on the various players' uniforms, though Dash knew all their positions by heart anyway. Dash had explained this was a *really important game*, because it was against the Orioles' rivals the Yankees, and because if the Orioles won, it meant they were the division champions. Evie didn't really care what it all meant, but if Dash was excited, then so was she.

And indeed, it was hard not to get caught up in the fervor of the day. The ballpark was packed and raucous, the cheering crowds throwing up delirious wave after wave after wave, and the score was close all the way to the top of the ninth, when the Yankees had pulled ahead by two runs. Now the Orioles were at bat, with runners on second and third, two outs, and a guy named Manny something at the plate. He had three balls and two strikes, and the entire ballpark was on its collective feet, pumping its fists and chanting his name. Dash was signing to her furiously that Manny was under pressure now, because if he got another strike the game was over and the Orioles would lose. But if he was walked or got a hit, it could set up an actual grand slam, something Dash had never seen before. And if Manny himself hit a home run, it would be a walk-off and the Orioles would have won. His expression was so earnest and his signing so passionate that she could have swooned from love for him. She nodded as he regaled her with statistics and history, understanding only some of it, showing him with her tightly crossed fingers that she knew how important it all was.

The Yankee pitcher shook his head, shook it again, and finally nodded at whatever the catcher had signaled him. The crowd was suddenly quiet, everyone leaning forward, fists clenched, hands held over mouths, the collective focus electrifying, galvanizing. Then the pitcher brought his lead knee up, twisted, and exploded forward, his arm trailing behind his body and then whipping past him like a flail, and the ball rocketed toward the plate and Manny swung, and there was a *CRACK!* Evie could hear like thunder all the way in the stands, and the ball shot skyward, taking off like a rocket, like a missile, and the crowd screamed, and the ball sailed over the shortstop and the left fielder and it was still ascending, and the crowd's scream became a roar of ecstasy, and the people around them scrambled onto their seats to get even higher, higher, because the ball was still coming, flying over the first tier, the second, and it was heading right toward them.

A man in front of her shoved the guy to his left and the guy fell, cursing. She watched the ball and her heart leaped—was it really coming straight for Dash? Dash was watching, too, his gloved hand held as high as his arm could stretch. But then she saw that no, the ball was too high, and she wished she could have thrown Dash in the air to catch it. A man actually dove from one of the higher seats to try to get a better position; there was a scream, a scuffle broke out. Someone spilled beer on her from behind and someone else nearly knocked Dash over. He grabbed her arm and they managed to stay on their feet.

She turned, and in the midst of the tumult, she saw a man just behind them, a big, solid-looking man in jeans, a dark flannel shirt, and an Orioles cap, watching the ball descend with a quiet intensity. Someone shoulder-checked the man from the left to try to displace him, but it had no more effect than if the man had been a tree. Someone on his right held up a gloved hand and tried to force himself into the space in front of the man, but the man simply moved forward slightly and the interloper fell back. Then there was a firm *smack* as the man caught the ball in an enormous, outstretched hand. The force of the impact drove the man's arm back, but somehow he held on to the ball. Evie, amazed, thought, *Ouch!* The people behind the man and to his sides all began grabbing at his arm, heedless of the fact that he had clearly caught the ball and it was his, it was over, but the man simply extended his arm beyond their reach and pushed them away left and right with his free hand as easily as if he were brushing off flies. His expression never changed and he was unnervingly calm, even when someone pulled so hard at his shirt that the sleeve tore at the shoulder.

After a few seconds, a semblance of reason seemed to restore itself. The people who had been so frenzied a moment before went back to their seats and returned their focus to the field, where Manny was jogging the bases to the delirious roar of the cheering, stamping crowd.

Evie glanced at Dash to make sure he was all right. Dash was smiling at the man, a bright, generous, innocent smile, and Evie knew it meant *Congratulations, you caught the ball.* And she loved him for it, because he didn't have a selfish bone in his body, he was actually happy for this stranger in the Orioles cap, even though just a moment earlier he had so badly wanted that ball for himself.

The man was looking down at Dash with a strange expression— Recognition? Sympathy? Puzzlement? She wasn't sure. And then the man squatted, extended his arm, and held out the ball to Dash.

Dash's eyes widened and his mouth dropped open. Then he shook his head as though afraid to believe the man was serious. The man extended his arm further and pointed to Dash with his free hand, then to the ball, indicating, *Here, it's yours.* It was the oddest thing—it was as though the man knew Dash was deaf. Well, of course, he must have seen them signing. But it felt like more than that, some deeper level of understanding.

Dash looked to her, his eyes beseeching. She badly wanted to accept the stranger's kindness, but it was too much—she didn't know baseball the way Dash did, but that ball was going to be worth a lot on eBay. She shook her head and with a reluctant smile said to the man, "It's so nice of you, but really, we couldn't."

But the man didn't retract his arm. He simply glanced at Dash and raised his eyebrows, the expression conveying, *Are you sure?*

Dash looked at her again, his eyes such a torment of longing she couldn't have said no for all the politeness in the world. She hesitated for a second more, then nodded and said, "Okay."

Dash was so happy he clenched his fists and jumped up and down. He took the ball reverently from the man's outstretched hand and said in his slightly slurred voice, "Thank you thank you thank you!"

The man nodded. And then signed, *You're welcome.*

Dash was so flabbergasted that for a moment he forgot he was holding the ball and tried to sign back. He hooted and shoved the ball off to Evie, who herself was so surprised she almost dropped it.

You know sign? Dash signed.

Yes, the man signed back. *I'm deaf.*

So am I!

I know. I saw you signing with your mother. You sign better than she does.

Dash laughed. *Yes, I always tell her that.*

The man smiled. There was something . . . wistful about it, as though his face was unaccustomed to the expression, as though he distrusted the feeling behind it.

Dash signed, *Why did you give me the ball?*

You looked like you wanted it.

But don't you want it, too?

Not as much as you do.

Evie was watching the exchange, dumbfounded. Then, remembering herself, she placed the ball in her bag and signed, *Thank you. That was really nice of you.*

The man shook his head, as though embarrassed by their gratitude, and stood.

Evie had to admit, she liked his looks. About forty, she guessed. With sandy brown hair and a darker stubble of beard. She stole a glance at his left hand and noted the absence of a ring. There was something intriguing, and appealing, about how calm he'd been while all those people tried to get the ball away from him. She liked his smile—and that odd reluctance, or sadness, she sensed behind it. And of course it was hard not to be blown away by how nice he'd just been to Dash, and by how Dash had responded. She was always nervous about dating because she'd heard so many horror stories about pedophiles using single mothers to get to their children. But everything in life involved some risk, right? And besides, she had ways of checking up on dates most people could only dream about.

Without thinking it through any further and before she lost her nerve, she signed, *We were going to get a hot dog on Eutaw Street. Would you like to join us?*

It's nice of you, the man signed, *but I don't want to intrude.*

Are you sure? It's no intrusion.

The man glanced down for a moment, his expression conflicted. She sensed he wanted to accept her invitation, and tried to figure out what could be behind his reluctance. Was he just being polite? Did he sense her attraction, but not share it?

Dash touched the man's knee, and when the man looked at him, signed, *Don't you like hot dogs?*

The man looked momentarily perplexed. *Everyone likes hot dogs,* he signed.

Then why don't you come with us?

The man's hands floated for a moment, seemingly stuck. He looked at Evie as though for help.

Come on, she signed, smiling. *Let me buy you a hot dog. Just a small thank-you for being so nice.*

CHAPTER . . . .
. . . . 16

M anus went along with the woman and her son, aware he had handled things badly, confused about what to do next. The baseball
meant nothing to him; he should have just let it drop. Why had he
caught it? He hadn't thought, he just saw it coming and stuck up his
hand. And then giving it to the boy . . . even stupider. It had made
people notice him. Worse, it had made the woman and boy notice
him. So much so that he was now in the surreal position of being
on his way with them to get a hot dog.

But . . . the director wanted him to watch the woman, didn't he?
And he hadn't specified the degree to which Manus was supposed
to be surreptitious about it. He'd mentioned the boy's deafness as a
possible entry route, which meant he didn't object to some level of
interaction, and might even welcome it. Yes, that was all true. Maybe
that was why Manus had given the boy the ball.

He tried to convince himself, but he knew better. Because there
had been no thought at all behind the decision. Instead, he'd been
watching them for hours, and something about the way the woman
looked at the boy, and signed with him, and tousled his hair had
all made Manus feel . . . something. Something from a long time
before, from another little boy's life, a life so distant he was no longer

even aware of its absence. And yet it existed still, stirred to consciousness by this woman and her son.

Or was there more? He didn't think the woman's face was what most people would call beautiful, but there was something about her smile, something warm and inviting and genuine, that made him want to look at her. And her body, he had to admit. It had such a . . . ripeness to it. So soft and curvy and full. She was wearing a V-neck cotton sweater, and Manus had to force himself not to glance at the area at the lowest part of the collar, the smooth skin there, the swell of her breasts, the hint of cleavage.

Fortunately, Eutaw Street was adjacent to the ballpark, because the walk over was somewhat awkward. The crowds were thick, which made it hard to watch the woman while she talked and signed. The boy made things more comfortable, darting in and out of the people around them so he could briefly pause, turn to Manus, and sign him all sorts of questions about Manus's favorite Orioles players. Manus didn't care about baseball, but it would have been hard to live in the area and not know the names of at least a few of the most famous players. So he mentioned what he knew, and otherwise covered for his ignorance by asking the boy about his own favorites, and how many games he'd been to, and other such nonsense.

Evie ordered them hot dogs at a stand on Eutaw. One of the advantages of being deaf was that you could talk with your mouth full, and Manus carried on his animated conversation with the boy while they munched on foot-longers covered in mustard and relish. The woman spelled out her name—*Evelyn, but please call me Evie*—and Manus did the same, *Marvin.*

My name's Dash, the boy signed. *Because I'm fast.*

Your parents must have known you were fast early on.

They could tell.

Evie smiled, and Manus had a feeling she'd heard this exchange before.

What do you do, Marvin? she signed.

I'm a contractor.

She glanced at his work boots. *Construction?*

Yes. And what do you do?

I work at NSA. Computer stuff.

Thousands of people in the area worked at the giant intelligence organization, so the acknowledgment itself was unremarkable. But to add *computer stuff* was as informative as if Manus had followed the news that he was in construction with a mention of hammers and nails. The redundancy was just an indication that she couldn't discuss her job beyond the bare fact of her employment. That was fine with Manus. The director hadn't shared anything specific about the woman's work, which meant for Manus it wasn't relevant.

They chatted more, the crowds gradually dissipating, the light fading from the sky. The boy went to a special school in the area. He was on the baseball team, and wanted one day to play shortstop for the Orioles. His signing was voluble, enthusiastic, unselfconscious. He didn't seem at all afraid of or uncomfortable with Manus, which for Manus was an unfamiliar thing. The woman, too, seemed intrigued by her son's ease with this stranger, smiling indulgently while the boy regaled him with information about his school and statistics about baseball and complaints about homework. He asked Manus whether he had been born deaf, and Manus told him he had, a lie so long-standing and consistent it now felt like the truth. *Not me,* the boy told him. *I had meningitis.* He conveyed it simply as a bit of interesting information, the same way he might have shared the breed of his dog or color of his bike or where his grandparents lived. Manus thought he detected the tiniest wince in the woman's expression at the mention of the disease, but also pride at how unaffected her son was in the telling of it.

A few times, Manus saw someone looking at him a bit closely, which he didn't like, and then realized why: they were wondering if this was the guy they'd seen catch the ball on the giant screen behind center field. Probably the cameras had switched to the hitter's victory lap immediately after, and Manus hadn't been filmed actually handing the ball to the boy. Otherwise, he would have been getting a lot more attention now, maybe even from news crews. He'd been lucky. He reproached himself again for having done something so impulsive and stupid.

He asked the woman where she had parked, though he already knew, having followed the movements of her cell phone with a portable StingRay tracking device. She told him a parking garage, and he offered to walk them. She seemed pleased by that, which Manus found surprising and somewhat discomfiting.

At their car, she signed, *It was nice meeting you, Marvin. I really don't know how to thank you for what you did for Dash.*

It's nothing.

It most certainly is not *nothing,* she signed, her hands moving aggressively to contradict him, the sentiment so gentle and the expression of it so fierce that for the second time since he'd begun watching them, he felt something stir inside him, something familiar and yet forgotten. For a moment he only looked at her, unsure of how to respond.

The boy pulled on his sleeve and he looked down. The boy pointed to his mother's purse, where she had put the ball, and then, his expression solemn to the point of graveness, signed, *Can I really keep it?*

It's yours.

But you caught it.

It's yours now.

The solemn expression persisted for another moment, then dissolved into a grin of pure joy. The boy leaped forward and hugged Manus tightly, his face pressed against Manus's belly. Manus looked down at him, stunned, and somehow managed to pat the boy awkwardly on the shoulder. After a moment, the boy stepped back, still grinning.

The woman looked at her son with an expression Manus didn't understand, something both joyful and aching. Then she signed, *Hey good-looking, don't forget to say it, too.*

The boy looked at Manus and signed, *Thank you thank you thank you!*

Manus signed back a slightly solemn *You're welcome.*

Do you have a card, Marvin? the woman signed. *It's just Dash and me, and I'm not very handy. I mean, if you ever do small jobs.*

Regardless of what the director might want, it didn't feel like a good idea. But Manus was concerned it would seem odd if he said no. He hesitated for an instant, then handed her a card. Of course it was all backstopped. He even had Yelp and other job references: work done by a contractor the director had set up with Marvin Manus credentials. And a carpentry cover worked well for him. He was good with all sorts of tools.

She looked at the card, then placed it in her purse. *It would be nice to see you again,* she signed, smiling. *A hot dog doesn't seem like an adequate thank-you.*

He smiled back, a little uncertainly. He didn't know why it felt like he was doing something illicit. The director wanted him watching the woman. What had he said he wanted to know? *The human aspect, the unquantifiable, the ghost in the machine.* Well, how could Manus report on any of that from a distance? Getting close to the woman was simply a way to watch her better.

Still, he hoped the director wasn't going to ask him to do more than just watch.

CHAPTER........
........17

Anders sat at his desk, waiting for Delgado, trying not to be impatient. It hadn't been difficult to create some "intel" about a letter bomb en route from Istanbul to Washington, DC. In exchange for the promise of a half dozen M32A1 Multi-Shot Grenade Launchers plus ordnance, his contacts in Turkey simply phoned each other on some prepaid mobile units, using English and words like *bomb* and *explosion* and *Allahu Akbar*, along with a mention of FedEx and Washington, DC. NSA's AURORAGOLD eavesdropping network flagged the cellular traffic; a Tailored Access Operations team tapped into FedEx's computer network to track the package; and Thomas Delgado, credentialed as an army Explosive Ordnance Disposal expert, was sent to meet the plane carrying the "letter bomb" when it touched down at Washington Dulles. Discreet calls were placed to corporate officials; instructions conveyed to field personnel; employees directed to offer complete cooperation. Nothing left to chance, and nothing left now but to wait.

Remar opened the door and leaned his head in. "The president is convening the National Security Council again. He wants you back in the Situation Room in two hours."

Anders swore under his breath. "What's your take?"

"I think he's going in."

"Wasn't McQueen supposed to give us breathing room on that?"

"He did what he could. But the advice of a general versus the advice of a senator . . . not much of a contest."

"You think this is blowback? The president taking advantage of McQueen's urge for patience to make himself look tough by comparison?"

"Could be. Impossible to say. I still think it was the right call at the time."

Anders checked his watch and rubbed his hands together. "All right, I'll need the car ready to go in an hour. Delgado should be in before then."

On cue, there was a brash knock on the outer door. Remar went out. A moment later, he returned with Delgado, who marched in, this time in a digitally camouflaged army combat uniform rather than the customary natty suit, strode directly to the desk, and handed over a FedEx package. Remar eased out, closing the door behind him.

Anders looked at Delgado for a moment, resisting the urge to immediately tear open the package. No need for the man to see how important this was. "Any problems?" he asked, keeping his tone casual.

"Nope. The minimum-wage guy loading packages onto the truck was very happy to show me where I could find what I was looking for. And to move off to a safe distance until I'd retrieved it. Guess the word had gone out."

Anders pulled the cord on the mailer, reached inside, and retrieved a thumb drive. He inserted it into a USB port and ran a decrypt program. A minute went by, and then another, but it seemed that not even the supercomputers the special desktop unit was tied into were going to be able to crack it, at least not immediately as he had hoped. There were multiple gigabytes of information on the drive, though—the real deal, presumably, not another decoy. Well, even if the encryption held, the main thing was that he had it. Perkins was gone. Now all he had to do was tie off Hamilton and the whole breach would be rectified.

For a moment, he wondered what Perkins had turned over. Well, it seemed he might never find out. He supposed he could live with that. The main thing was that it wasn't God's Eye. It couldn't have been.

Delgado nodded toward the package. "You want me to check out the address it was going to?"

Anders had already sent Manus to do a little sniffing there—a mailbox facility in Adams Morgan, a neighborhood in downtown DC—but he'd found nothing. Still, a variety of systems had confirmed that Hamilton had rented a box there two weeks earlier. Almost certainly a one-off he'd established before leaving for Istanbul, and therefore almost certainly, at this point, a dead end.

"No," Anders said. "No need."

Delgado nodded and turned as though to go. Then he turned back. "Hey, I meant to ask you something earlier. It's probably nothing, so it slipped my mind."

Anders raised his eyebrows.

Delgado touched the hair plugs as though to ensure they were still there. "Do you know an Ariel?"

Alarm bells went off in Anders's mind but he maintained his neutral expression. "I don't know. Aerial who?"

"I'm not sure. Perkins said something about an Ariel. In the car, before he died. I think that was the name."

The alarm bells got louder. "What did he say?"

"Ah, forget it, it was nothing."

Anders suppressed his irritation at what was obviously a gambit intended to tease out the real level of Anders's interest. He fixed Delgado with an even stare. "I'd always rather you share too much,

Thomas, and let me decide whether something is really nothing. Does that make sense?"

Delgado glanced away like a schoolchild embarrassed by a reprimand. "He said, 'I love you, Ariel.' And I was just wondering . . . I don't know. Was that his wife?"

Anders knew perfectly well Delgado could have looked into that question himself. Presumably he'd already tried, but found nothing. Anders didn't know why the man was curious, and he had to be careful about revealing his own growing concern.

"No, I believe his wife's name was Caryn."

"Maybe a daughter, then."

Another thing Delgado could have, and probably had, already checked. But why?

"Doubtful. Perkins had two sons, but no daughters, so far as I'm aware."

Delgado looked faintly disappointed. "Oh. It's just interesting, the places people's minds sometimes go when they realize it's the end."

"Well, whoever she might have been, at least Perkins felt the presence of someone he loved when he died. A small grace, but something."

Delgado cracked a knuckle. "Anyway, like I said, probably nothing, but like you said, better to mention it than not."

"Indeed."

The moment Delgado was out the door, Anders called in Remar and briefed him. That feeling he'd had with Snowden—of being in Chile again, the ground shaking, sidewalks disintegrating—was back, and he had to place his hands on the desk to maintain his equilibrium.

"Aerial?" Remar said. "You don't think—"

"What else *can* we think? 'Aerial, I love you'? If Chambers had a relationship with Perkins, who knows what she might have told him on the pillow? Without a doubt she would have told him about the new God's Eye security protocols we had her implement. The protocols she took live the very night she died. If she confided in Perkins, he'd know what happened to her wasn't random. And whatever she confided, he'd have a powerful motive to reveal it. Why else would a twenty-five-year-veteran on the verge of a full pension and honorable retirement turn traitor? Nothing else makes sense."

There was a long pause. Remar said, "Jesus Christ."

"Look into it. I want to know if they were together."

"The data's going to be over a year old."

"I want to know if they were together. If Hamilton knows about God's Eye, we have got to short-circuit this rescue. More so now than ever."

Remar's expression was grim—whether over the possibility of God's Eye being exposed, or over what might be required to prevent exposure, or both, Anders didn't know. Or care.

"Do you understand?" he said. "Hamilton needs to be stopped. No matter what it takes."

CHAPTER . . . .
. . . . 18

Two hours later, Anders was back in the Situation Room with the other principals of the National Security Council. The president convened the meeting and immediately turned it over to the secretary of defense—a bad sign. The secretary then gestured to Jones. That was even worse.

"We've intercepted the following cellular traffic in Turkey and Syria," Jones said. He nodded at a uniformed flunky, who fired up a laptop. On the screen at the front of the room, a map of the Turkey-Syria border appeared. Jones stood and approached it, highlighting areas with a laser pointer. The subdued lighting glinted against his fruit salad of medals.

"What we've pieced together," he said, "is that these geolocated units"—he gestured with the laser pointer to a set of coordinates on the Turkish side of the border—"were engaged in moderate and then increasing contact with these two units"—he directed the laser pointer to a set of coordinates on the Syrian side—"culminating in a flurry of chatter at the exact time we estimate Hamilton was taken. The Turkish units are associated with a criminal group called Ergenekon that's of concern primarily for heroin trafficking. But the two Syrian units are numbers associated with a jihadist group loosely affiliated with ISIS, but also a rival to it. A competitor, if you will."

If you will. Anders hated that self-indulgent, patronizing expression. But there was nothing he could do but sit and do a slow burn while the Pentagon stole his thunder. At least he could find a little solace in knowing the "loosely affiliated with ISIS, but also a rival to it" part came from NSA. Though he was beginning to sense that planting that piece of "intel" might be on its way to some unintended consequences.

"We believe Hamilton was spirited by the Turkish group, perhaps in a kidnapping-for-cash operation, across the border here, at Demirışık"—God, but the man loved his laser pointer—"and taken to Azaz, about twenty miles northwest of Aleppo. Fighting between rebel and government forces in Aleppo has been fierce; the entire area is chaotic; opportunities for concealing a high-value target, considerable. That said, we believe we know where Hamilton is being held. Here."

The screen changed to an image of a bombed-out concrete house on a rubble-strewn street.

"This is a composite image," Jones explained. "A computer rendering based on satellite and Unmanned Aerial Vehicle photographs. We also have satellites and UAVs equipped with variations of something called SHARAD—Shallow Subsurface Radar—developed by NASA for the Mars Rover to scan the surface of Mars for water or ice."

The screen helpfully changed to an artist's rendering of the Mars Reconnaissance Orbiter shooting radar from space to look for water on the red planet's surface. Anders had to admit that as much as he hated it, Jones gave a good presentation. Well, you didn't rise to chairman of the Joint Chiefs without that much, at least.

"We've also done high-altitude fly-bys using infrared imaging," Jones continued, the screen now showing examples of drones outfitted with infrared imaging systems. "The upshot is, we know the composition and thickness of the walls of this structure, of its doors—"

The screen flashed rotating, computer-generated, three-dimensional images of the structure. Jones paused for dramatic effect, and the screen changed again, this time to a grainy, infrared image of a man, his arms above his head, presumably shackled to the ceiling.

"—and the precise location within the structure of this person, who we believe is the American journalist Ryan Hamilton. Ladies and gentlemen, let's bring this young man home."

Lord. For a moment, it seemed this room full of grizzled, self-serving cynics was going to burst into applause. But the moment passed, Jones returned to his seat, and all eyes moved to the president.

The president looked at Jones. "Vernon, you're confident in the accuracy of the technology behind these findings?"

"Mr. President, had we possessed this technology during the Iranian hostage crisis, Operation Eagle Claw might have ended very differently."

Anders seethed. Eagle Claw was botched because of helicopter malfunctions. It had nothing to do with intel about the location of the hostages. And what the hell did "might have" mean, anyway?

But he said nothing. Jones clearly had the advantage, and there was nothing Anders could do to change that.

For the moment.

His mobile phone vibrated. He glanced down and saw a text from Remar:

Cannot obtain definitive match of two individuals of interest. However, records indicate both powered down their mobile phones at the same time after work and on weekends on dozens of occasions.

He'd already known in his gut from what Delgado had told him, but this was proof: Daniel Perkins and Aerial Chambers had been intimate. They were cautious enough about their infidelities to turn off their phones before meeting. But the simultaneous blackouts were their own form of confirmation. Perkins knew about God's Eye. Which meant that Hamilton knew. Which meant that Hamilton absolutely had to be silenced.

"How soon can you be ready?" the president said to Jones.

"We have a team building mock-ups of the structure as we speak," Jones responded, his chest swelling slightly at the chance to say so. "Forty-eight hours would be adequate to coordinate logistics and for the team to train on a replica of the very structure they'll be breaching in Azaz. We can move faster if necessary, but if we think Hamilton has at least forty-eight hours, I recommend we wait that long. We don't want to go in half-assed."

All eyes turned to Anders. The president said, "Do we know anything about Hamilton's circumstances?"

The humiliation felt calculated, but there was nothing to do but endure it. "No, Mr. President, we have no indication of how much time Hamilton might have. Beyond the fact that this group seems intent on milking his capture for propaganda value. In which case, at least forty-eight hours seems a safe bet."

The president nodded, probably thinking he could have gotten a similar analysis from an intelligent high school student, and might have hoped for something more substantial from the director of NSA.

"Comments? Criticisms?" the president asked, looking around the room. "No? All right then, I've decided. Barring an unforeseen development, in forty-eight hours we go in and bring this young man home."

An unforeseen development, Anders thought. *You have no idea.*

CHAPTER . . . .
. . . . 19

Manus was back in Turkey, ostensibly to deliver grenade launchers to the Ergenekon crew that had taken the journalist. In fact, the director had told Manus, he was to kill the Ergenekon men, and it was imperative Manus collect their phones. Why the director wanted their phones, Manus neither knew nor cared. But the killing part was good. He'd wanted to kill them last time. Now he'd be able to do it.

The meeting was on the eastern shore of Tuz Gölü, an immense salt lake about ninety miles southeast of Ankara. He drove along the shore, the sun bright overhead, the dry lake bed an oval of pale blue fringed by iridescent white. All around was nothing but parched grass and stunted shrubs. He passed some tourist restaurants and souvenir shops, a few travelers venturing out to photograph mineral deposits. The paved road began to give way to gravel, then gravel to dirt. Soon there were no more buildings, and no more people.

Ahead he saw a small structure, not much more than a foundation and a few cinder block walls, standing derelict amid the surrounding brown scrub. Next to it was the dusty white van he remembered from the last meeting, the same three men smoking cigarettes alongside it. They squinted as he approached, then recognized him and waved, their hands empty. He nodded and eased forward until he was a few feet from the front of the van, the vehicles kitty-corner, the driver's side of each on the outside. The men might find his behavior odd because it would have been easier and more discreet to transfer the grenade launchers if he had parked adjacent and tail to tail. Or they might understand he was being careful. Manus didn't really care. The only place for concealment in the area was the van itself, and he wanted to be able to open his own trunk while keeping the van completely in view, and to give himself some cover and reaction time if anyone emerged from the van's rear doors.

He looked around and detected no problems. Across the vast dry bed of the lake, rippling through heat shimmers, were the towers and tubing of a mining plant. A short distance away, a single truck tire lay black and baking against the salt around it. Manus cut the engine and rolled down the driver-side window. He couldn't know, but he sensed the area was silent.

Keeping his eyes on the men and a grip on the Berserker, he got out of the car and closed the door. In addition to the tomahawk, he was armed as he had been before, but with one small difference: this time, the SIG MPX-K suspended from the steering wheel was unloaded. He had a feeling about these men, and he thought he saw a way to exploit it.

"Hello, Miller," the tall one said, with the smile Manus distrusted. No need for bona fides this time. They all knew each other. "You have toys for us, yes? We will take them from you."

Manus nodded and went around to the trunk. He opened it and waited. The tall man walked over along the passenger's side of the sedan. The other two went the other way, along the driver's side, eyeing the vehicle's interior as they moved. They saw the SIG. One man stopped at the door. The other kept coming. They were boxing him in, denying him access to his weapon. They thought.

Manus stepped back from the trunk and gestured for the two men to have a look. There were three duffel bags inside.

The tall man held back while the other guy reached inside and unzipped the bags one by one. After opening the third, he looked back and nodded. Manus could have dropped them all right then with the Force Pro concealed in the waistband holster, but he wasn't sure how far the sounds of the shots would carry over the flat terrain, and the tourist shacks he had passed weren't that far away. He'd shoot them if he had to, but he thought he'd have an opportunity for something quieter. And more satisfying.

The guy who'd checked out the hardware reached inside, extracted one of the M32A1s, and handed it to the tall man, who hefted it, then pointed it at Manus and laughed.

"You can show us how to use, yes?" the man said.

Even without orders to do so, Manus would have been happy to kill the man for pointing a weapon at him, especially without even checking first to see if it was loaded. In this case, the move felt like a feint, and sure enough, out of the corner of his eye, Manus saw the third man reach inside the driver's door and pull the SIG free from its harness. Manus pretended not to notice.

"What do you need to know?" Manus asked.

The third man walked over, pointing the SIG at Manus's chest. Manus glanced at him and effected a surprised expression.

"I want to know why you talk funny," the tall man said.

Manus glanced from one to the other as though in fear. In fact, he was measuring distance. "What are you doing?" he said, injecting a little nervousness into his tone.

"Give me the gun in the back of your pants," the tall man said, holding out his hand but eyeing the Berserker warily. "And put down the axe."

They thought they had the drop on him, but still they were uncertain of themselves. Otherwise the tall man would have reached into Manus's pants and taken the gun himself.

Manus took a step back to prevent them from surrounding him, and dangled the Berserker alongside his leg as though ambivalent about complying. "If you kill me, you get no more toys."

The tall man's mouth twisted into a cruel smile. It reminded Manus of some of the boys at the juvenile prison. "We're not going to kill you. Only . . . have fun with you. Give us the gun."

They were just a little farther away than ideal. Manus wanted one of them to step in closer.

"I'll tell my people."

The tall man laughed. "What man would ever tell of something like this? Even a woman wouldn't tell."

The man with the SIG was flushed and breathing heavily. He gestured with the muzzle toward the trunk. "Reach inside the trunk," he said. "All the way in back."

Manus merely looked at him.

The man's face darkened. "I said, reach inside the trunk."

Again, Manus said nothing. He knew the man wouldn't just pull the trigger. He would look for one more way to threaten first.

The man pointed the muzzle at Manus's face and stepped closer. "I said—"

Manus stepped in, swatted the SIG out of the way, and swung the Berserker underhand, arcing its five-inch razor-sharp head up into the man's genitals. The blade sliced through cloth and flesh with equal ease, shattering the pubic bone and burying itself in the man's sacrum with such force the impact carried the man's feet off the ground. The man's eyes bulged in shock and agony, but if he screamed, it wasn't loud enough for Manus to hear.

Manus pivoted to his right, wrenched loose the Berserker as the first man crumbled to the ground, and swung it backhand toward the second man's face. The man flinched and started to turn away, instinctively throwing a hand up for protection. The Berserker sheared off his fingers, blasted through teeth and jaw, and erupted from the left side of his head along with a geyser of blood. The man shuddered, took two spasmodic steps, and collapsed.

The tall man's eyes were so wide it looked like they could pop out of his head. He took a step back and fumbled desperately at his waistband, presumably for a gun. Manus dropped the Berserker and instantly had the Force Pro pointed at the man's head in a two-handed grip. The man's arms froze where they were.

"Raise your hands," Manus said. The man didn't move, and Manus said, "If I wanted to kill you, you'd already be dead. But don't make me tell you again."

Slowly, warily, the man raised his hands. Manus could see he was breathing rapidly.

"Now face away from me and lace your fingers tightly behind your neck."

The man complied.

Manus tugged one of his sleeves past his fingers, stepped forward, pulled free the man's gun, using the sleeve to ensure he didn't touch it, and stepped back again. He tossed the gun away, adjusted his sleeve, and retrieved the Berserker. "Now reach inside the trunk. The way you wanted me to."

The man turned to him. "What? No."

Manus pointed the Force Pro at his face. "Your choice."

The man grimaced, his respiration terror-fast now. He glanced at his comrades. The first one was fetaled up and shaking—maybe crying, Manus couldn't be sure. The second was lying still. The ground around them was saturated with blood.

Trembling now, the man approached the car. He leaned into the trunk. Manus knew that unless the man could instantly figure out how to load one of the grenade launchers, there was nothing inside he could use as a weapon. Still, he hadn't searched the man for a knife or backup pistol, so for the moment, he maintained some distance.

"Reach further inside," Manus said. "And spread your legs."

The man complied. Manus had the sense the man was talking now, probably begging, but of course he couldn't know and anyway it didn't matter. Manus switched the Force Pro to his left hand and the Berserker to his right. He paused for an instant to watch the man, then raised his arm, swiveled his hips, and blasted the blade down directly into the man's spine. The edge cleaved vertebrae and spinal cord and would have blown right through the man's abdomen had Manus not pulled back at the last instant. The man's body collapsed, his legs spasmed, and his scream echoed inside the trunk loudly enough that Manus could just hear it.

Manus grabbed the back of the man's waistband, hauled him out of the trunk, and dumped him on the ground. The man flopped on his back like a fish on the deck, his hands groping at the gaping wound, his legs motionless. He was saying something, but Manus couldn't read his lips—either the man had reverted to Turkish, or in his terror and agony he was no longer able to form words clearly enough for Manus to make out.

"You want to know why I talk funny?" Manus said. He scanned the area quickly for danger, saw none, and returned his gaze to the man. "It's because I can't hear anything. Even screams." He raised a leg and smashed his foot down into the man's throat, obliterating his trachea.

He walked over to the first man, who was the only one who might still be a threat. But no, he was still fetaled up and shuddering. Even if he had been carrying a weapon, he was obviously too overcome by his injuries to do anything with it. Manus stomped the man's neck into the dirt.

He went over to the second man, who was lying still. Manus saw brains amid the blood and knew there was no need to do anything further. He wiped the blade of the Berserker on the man's shirt, then set it down on the passenger seat of his car.

He paused for a moment, watching the van. He doubted there

was anyone inside, but better to be sure. He circled quickly, the Force Pro in a two-handed grip, darting in and out for a peek through the passenger-side window, then the windshield, then the driver-side window. He saw nothing.

He gripped the side-door handle through the tail of his shirt, threw it open, and leaped to the right, ready to lay down fire if he needed to. But again, there was nothing.

No, not nothing. There was someone inside, curled up on the floor. Manus blinked, checked his surroundings, and looked again. He saw a frilly dress, a pair of hairy arms emerging from its sleeves, a glint of metal—handcuffs, the wrists secured behind the back.

He moved in, the Force Pro up, scanning the interior of the van. There was nothing else. Just a man, a small man, handcuffed, in a dress. The man seemed to be shivering.

Keeping the Force Pro just below his chin with his right hand, Manus reached out with his left and shook the man's leg. The man flinched, but that was all. Maybe he said something or made some sound, but Manus couldn't know.

Manus shook him again, harder this time. The man brought his shoulders up as though in anticipation of a blow and looked back over his shoulder. It took Manus a moment because the man's face was so damaged—the eyes bruised and puffed, nearly closed; the lips swollen and split. There were cigarette burns on his cheeks and all along his arms and shoulders.

It was Hamilton.

Manus was so stunned that for nearly a second he forgot to check his surroundings. Then instinct honed by experience kicked in, and he did a quick sweep of the area. Nothing. When he came back to Hamilton, he saw the man was saying, "Please. Please help me. Please."

Manus tried to process it. What had happened? He'd seen the news reports, the video, of Hamilton being held in Syria by some ISIS splinter group, and had assumed the director had used the Turks as a cutout to deliver Hamilton. Well, that seemed to have been the plan, anyway. But what had happened instead? Had the Turks made their own video, hiring an Arabic speaker for the role of knife-wielding terrorist? Had they delivered someone else to the Syrian group? If so, who? And why? Maybe to keep the man so they could use him until they grew bored, then resell him?

He glanced out at the bodies and wished he hadn't finished the men so quickly. Wished he could go to work on them again.

He looked back at Hamilton. "Please," the man was still saying. "Please, help me."

Manus considered. What would the director want? Probably for the man to die. Why else have him kidnapped in the first place, if not to have him killed, ostensibly at the hands of some jihadists?

And the truth was, it would be a mercy. The man was fucked up, fucked up in a way Manus knew he might never recover from. Step into the van, pull the door closed to muffle the sound, a single quick shot to the back of the head. End the man's pain, end his horror.

"Please," the man said again, and tears spilled from his puffed-shut eyes. "I want to go home. I just want to go home."

Manus looked around again. The area was still quiet.

Just do it, he thought. *Make it quick. He won't feel anything.*

He started to step into the van, then hesitated.

He realized he didn't want to kill the man.

He tried to persuade himself again it would be a mercy. He couldn't. Instead, it felt like an extension of the cruelty he had already delivered the man into.

Fuck.

This was taking too long. He had to focus on what he had come for. Hamilton wasn't his problem.

He walked over to the bodies and found a mobile phone in the pants pocket of each. He removed the batteries, tossed them all into the trunk of his car, retrieved the SIG, popped in a full magazine, charged it, and placed it on the passenger seat. He glanced at himself in the visor mirror, and was unsurprised to see a fair amount of blood splatter on his face. He walked around to the trunk, grabbed a wet towel he had placed there for this very eventuality, and cleaned off. There was some blood spray on the car, as well. He wiped it down, threw the towel inside, and closed the trunk.

He paused for a moment, watching the van, wishing he had never looked inside it. Then he thought, *Well, maybe you didn't.*

There was something to that. Because even if Hamilton made it out of here, who would he tell? Manus doubted the man could even see through those blackened eyes. The fact that he'd begged, *Please help me*, rather than, say, *Please don't hurt me*, suggested he didn't recognize Manus as his abductor. And even if he could see, what would he describe? Manus had been wearing his light disguise of beard, glasses, and hat the first time, and he was wearing it now. He supposed Hamilton might have picked up on the strangeness of Manus's voice and on his deafness the first time, but this time Manus had said nothing.

Besides, the man was badly fucked up, that was clear. He would probably die here, alone, weak, helpless in the van.

Just kill him, then. You'd be doing him a favor.

Maybe. Yeah, maybe that was right. But it didn't feel right.

Or . . . you could just take off the handcuffs. After that, it's up to him.

That felt a little better. Because if Hamilton were smart enough to figure out that one of the dead Turks would have the keys to the van, and that they probably had money he could take, too, and if he were tough enough to drive himself out of here, and resourceful enough to find a place to recover, then didn't he deserve a chance? And if he wanted to lie down and die, then that was what he deserved, instead. Either way, it would be on him.

Manus went to the bodies and dug around in their pockets until he found a handcuff key. He got back in the van and stepped behind

Hamilton. The man began to struggle feebly—a reflex, Manus knew, from the things he'd endured. Manus also knew the man wouldn't listen to words, no matter how reassuring. So he simply pushed him down firmly, put a knee in his back, and removed the cuffs. He wiped them with the tail of his shirt and let them drop to the floor of the van. He looked around. There were some work clothes in back— a dirty tee shirt and coveralls. That was good. The clothes the Turks were wearing were soaked in blood, and Hamilton wouldn't make it far in that dress without getting a lot of attention. Assuming he could make it at all.

He stepped out of the van, took one last look around, got in his car, and drove off. When he was safely away, he'd get rid of the towel and bleach down the Berserker. But first, distance.

He drove and considered. He was sorry for what the Turks had done to Hamilton. He was glad he'd killed them, and hoped the man would find some solace in the sight of their broken bodies.

He wondered what he should tell the director, and decided he would tell him nothing. After all, was he even sure the director would want Hamilton dead? The director was smart, and playing at a level Manus probably couldn't really understand. Maybe there were other plans for Hamilton. Maybe there were other factors Manus wasn't aware of. What had they taught him in the CIA course? "You don't know, you don't go." Well, the maxim certainly applied here.

All right. He had killed the men and taken their phones and left, and that was all. That's all he had been sent to do, so it made sense. A van? Yes, there had been a van, but he had never looked inside it. Why would he?

And probably there would be nothing to tell, anyway. Hamilton would die in the van, or the director would find him again and he would die that way. That Manus had encountered him again would, in the end, make no difference. And wasn't that the same as if Manus *hadn't* encountered him again?

He put Hamilton out of his mind—because there *was* no Hamilton—and thought of the phones in the trunk, instead. The director would be happy. Then he thought of the woman and her son. He wondered if the director had someone watching them while Manus was away. The thought made him uneasy, though he didn't know why.

CHAPTER . . . .
. . . . 20

Thomas Delgado emerged from the Washington, DC Metro at Farragut West and headed south on Seventeenth Street NW, the area a kaleidoscope of streetlamps and office windows and car head-lights. The worst of rush hour was past, but there were still plenty of cabs jockeying for position as they trolled for evening fares; office workers heading off for a bite with their cronies or a drink by themselves; Metro buses hissing and squealing as they absorbed and disgorged the nightly worker-bee effluent. More pedestrians would have been a plus, but daylight would have made for clearer footage on surveillance cameras. This was the right compromise.

He turned left on H Street, pulling the wheeled carry-on bag behind him, just another cubicle denizen returning to the office after arriving at Washington National or Union Station, still casually dressed in jeans and a button-down shirt, comfortable travel attire. A pair of nonprescription horn-rimmed glasses fit the overall office geek vibe, and though his Orioles cap might have been a little out of keeping, well, who in DC would begrudge a fan for flying the team's colors? The main thing was to look enough like a local not to be noticed, while obscuring the features enough not to be recognized. The glasses and cap weren't much, but in the low light, he was confident they would do.

He passed Lafayette Square, where a few lonely protestors stood facing the White House, holding vigil amid the buzz of insects in the trees and the surrounding sounds of traffic. Stop the war, stop the fracking, stop killing black men, stop, stop, stop. Perennial shit. He wondered why these losers bothered, why they didn't just give up and get a life.

He powered up one of the phones the director had given him and used it to call the cell phones of a few members of a local mosque, along with the numbers of the two other phones the director had provided him. Then he powered down the unit and kept moving.

A few blocks from the White House, he saw what he was looking for: a catering truck, parked in front of one of the area's innumerable monolithic office buildings, its driver doubtless delivering dinner inside to keep late-working drones nourished and productive into the night. He unzipped the carry-on bag and checked his surroundings, then ducked down, removed the device, and attached it via its magnetic fastenings to the truck's undercarriage, no more obtrusive than a man tying his shoe. Seconds later, he was on his way.

He zigzagged over to Pennsylvania Avenue and headed southeast, losing the carry-on in a Dumpster along the way after wiping down the handles and zippers. Maybe someone would find and appropriate it; maybe it would molder in a landfill. Either way, there would be no way to connect it with him.

He paused in front of the Capitol Reflecting Pool, where he repeated the phone operation with the second of the units the director had given him and another set of numbers. Finally, he looped around the Capitol grounds to the Supreme Court, where he went through the procedure once more with the last of the three phones. Then he continued southeast until he reached the Seventeenth Street

SE side of the Congressional Cemetery. He slipped over the low brick wall, into the comforting gloom, and padded across the soft grass toward the interior, the light growing dimmer and the sounds of traffic more muted with each step.

He came to a row of mausoleums, faintly outlined against the glow of the adjacent Anacostia River. He paused with his back to one, letting his eyes adjust, listening. The director had warned him there would be intense coverage of the cell phones he was carrying, and that he needed to begin and end his route in what the director called "cataracts"—blind spots in NSA's pervasive coverage. The Congressional Cemetery was one such. No cameras, no sensors, no IMSI-catcher phone trackers. Going in one end of a cataract and coming out the other was akin to crossing a river to throw off pursuit. Not a perfect solution, but with enough such crossings, a pretty effective way of ensuring no one would be able to follow your tracks.

He unbuttoned his shirt, exposing a tee shirt and belly bag beneath. Into the belly bag went the outer shirt, the glasses, the baseball cap, and the phones; out came a bandana, which he wrapped around his head. An office worker had entered the cemetery; a hipster in a do-rag would leave it.

He had zipped up the bag and was about to move out when he saw a pair of faintly glowing eyes looking up at him from the ground—eyes and a human figure. He leaped back, one hand going up in a protective gesture, the other clearing and opening the Zero Tolerance 0300 folding knife he kept clipped to his front pocket. "What the fuck?" he said in a loud whisper.

"Oh . . . sorry, man," the person said. "Didn't mean to startle you. I thought you'd seen me. This is my spot."

Delgado squinted, trying to make out who he was talking to, then reminded himself to look around. He didn't see anyone or anything else, but then again he'd missed this guy. Christ, he'd been so sure he was alone, he hadn't been paying adequate attention.

He looked back to the man and could faintly make out bushy hair and a long beard. "What do you mean, your spot?"

"This is where I sleep, man. Find your own spot."

"You're homeless?" It was so ridiculous it was almost funny. All this care avoiding advanced NSA capabilities . . . and busted by some skell sleeping it off in the cemetery.

"No, man, the Waldorf Astoria was full tonight, so I decided to sleep under the stars, instead."

The guy was funny. "The Waldorf Astoria is in New York. Maybe you mean the Willard."

"Whatever, man. Look, I'm not looking for company, you know what I mean?"

"There are other people sleeping in this cemetery?"

"What am I, the fucking census taker? Yeah, people sleep here. But we respect each other's privacy, too, if you catch my drift. Hey man, what's with the costume change?"

Shit. "Costume change?"

"Yeah, the shirt and the bandana. What are you, like, on your way to an ultimate Frisbee game?

Oh, well. "Actually, I'm up to no good."

The man chuckled. "Ain't we all, man, ain't we all."

"If I give you fifty bucks, will you forget you saw me?"

The man's eyes grew wide in the dark. "For fifty bucks, man, I'll forget my own name."

Delgado smiled. "All right, it's a deal. Where are you, though? I can barely see you."

The man sat up and extended his hand. "I'm right here, bro. Lay it on me. And this conversation never happened."

Delgado stepped to the side of the man's outstretched arm, pivoted behind him, dragged his head back by the hair with one hand, and slit his throat with the other. The man's hands flew to his neck and Delgado kicked him away to avoid the spray. The man fell to his side, managed to get to his knees, then collapsed again, all the while making a series of low burbling sounds. Delgado looked around. He saw no one, which suggested no one was close enough to see him, either.

After a moment, the man lay still. Delgado wiped the blade on the grass, then closed and pocketed it. He moved off in the direction of Stadium Armory Metro Station.

Bad luck, running into someone. But no harm done. These bums seemed uppity about their little sleeping spots. He doubted this was the first time an argument about who the ground belonged to had escalated to bloodshed. And he doubted the police would give the matter any attention beyond that obvious explanation.

He wondered again who Ariel was. He wished he knew. Killing the bum had made him horny.

CHAPTER . . . .
. . . . 21

Manus spent his Sunday afternoon at the woman's apartment. She had called and asked if he could build a loft for Dash. Like a bunk bed, but with a dresser underneath, so her son's small room would be less cluttered. She couldn't be there except on the weekend, she'd told him, and though Manus didn't doubt it was true, he was aware also that she might *want* to be there when he was. And was disturbed at how pleasing he found that thought.

He was happy to build a loft for the boy—a simple job, and a good way to get close to the woman, as the director wanted. But he sensed his own motivations were less straightforward than they should have been. He'd been thinking about the woman a lot. About her smile. Her face. Her shape. About that hint of cleavage he could see, just above the V-neck of her sweater.

He'd never been in a relationship. Deafness was repellant to a lot of hearing people. And the wall he felt between himself and the civilian world because of the things he'd done, the things that had been done to him, was thicker and higher still. He knew he made people uncomfortable, and he'd long since stopped trying not to. So when he needed sex, he would email a service, and a woman would come to the hotel he designated, take his money, remove her clothes, and allow Manus to use her body as he needed to. If these women were turned off by his deafness, they were usually too professional to let on, and afterward, Manus would feel relieved, if sometimes a little sad. He'd never aspired to anything else, or been at risk of it. But now this woman, so comfortable around the deaf, and apparently so comfortable around him, was inviting him into her home on what he knew might be a pretext. It was intriguing, and exciting, and disturbing, and he didn't know what to do about it.

In the end, he had placated his conflicted feelings by telling the director she had contacted him. The director had been characteristically blunt. "Is she interested in you?" he asked.

"I'm not sure."

"You think she really just wants you to build a bed for her son?"

"I think it's like you said. They don't meet many deaf people."

He didn't know whether the director bought that, or whether he had noticed Manus hadn't really answered the question.

"Well," the director said after a moment spent stroking his chin, "on balance, I think it's good she seems comfortable with you and . . . receptive to you. If you have the opportunity, engage her about her work. I doubt she'd open up very much to a stranger—certainly she shouldn't—but I'd like to know if she seems troubled or conflicted. Whether she's happy. Whether she's considering a change of career. Anything like that. She's doing some quite sensitive work right now, and she's at a delicate stage in terms of her feelings about her role here. Anything you can provide might be important."

Manus nodded, relieved that to the director it all seemed so uncomplicated.

"But please," the director continued, "no more stunts like that thing with the baseball, all right? I've had six teams out scrubbing the footage from YouTube and the phones and computers of the people who uploaded it. And we had to call in a few favors from the media, too. You're lucky you don't have all the networks chasing you, wanting to interview the Samaritan who gave the winning ball to the deaf boy. My God, Marvin, you might have made yourself a celebrity."

Manus knew the director was only half serious. But the comment embarrassed him regardless. He still wasn't sure exactly why he'd given the ball to the boy. It had just happened. Though he supposed some good had come out of it. At least the director had seemed pleased.

He bought the lumber he needed at a local Home Depot, and showed up at the woman's apartment at one in the afternoon, as she'd requested. She was wearing jeans and an oversized button-down shirt, and Manus was intensely aware of the warmth of her palm as she shook his hand in greeting, and of the shape of her body beneath her clothes. He made sure he didn't look at that spot above the top button of the shirt, though preventing himself wasn't easy.

The woman and the boy were barefoot, and the woman asked Manus if he wouldn't mind taking off his boots, as well. Manus liked that they didn't wear shoes inside, though he wasn't sure why. It made the small apartment feel separate from the world, somehow, more a personal space for the woman and the boy, more a home.

The boy told Manus he wanted to help with everything, and they started by carrying in the lumber from the pickup. The boy seemed so eager about the whole project that Manus wondered if maybe the woman's call had been aboveboard after all. The baseball, Manus was weirdly touched to see, occupied pride of place in the center of the dresser in the boy's room, surrounded like a shrine by other, lesser baseball totems.

Manus explained the basic design—how the legs would each be stabilized on the short ends by a strut attached to the frame, which would leave the front end open for easy access; why a two-by-four was stronger turned on its side than it was lying flat; why they were depending more on bolts than on nails. He showed Dash how to use the basic tools of carpentry: tape measure, combination square, bubble level; marking pen and utility knife; hammer, screwdriver, crosscut saw, power drill. The boy wanted to choke up on the hammer and tap nails down in increments, but Manus showed him that no, if he held the handle low and flexed his wrist on the downswing, he could blast a nail into place with a single blow. And the handsaw—no, not a short, vibrating motion, but rather a long, end-to-end stroke, pushing down at the beginning, drawing up at the finish. The boy wanted to know where Manus had learned all this. Manus told him he'd been taught by his father, which was not entirely a lie, though for the most part the skills had come from years in the juvenile facility's woodshop.

The job would have gone more quickly without a novice doing so much of it, but Manus didn't mind. It was strangely satisfying to teach the boy, who was a fast and enthusiastic learner. Periodically, the woman would poke her head in to ask if they needed anything, or to bring them a snack or soda, and Manus was struck repeatedly by that way she looked at her son, the pleasure in her expression, the pride, the protectiveness.

At a little past seven, the woman asked Manus if he'd like to stay for dinner—just pizza, nothing fancy. The loft was nearly done, and Manus reflexively signed that he didn't want to be a bother. To which Dash immediately insisted that he *had* to stay, it was La Pizza Banca, his favorite, and did Marvin like Italian sausage? Because La Pizza Banca had the *best*. Manus hesitated, thinking he hadn't had a chance to talk to the woman alone, the way the director wanted, and that maybe it would be good to stay after all. The thought made him feel both pleased and concerned, though he wasn't sure where to assign either emotion, and while he grappled with his conflicted feelings, the woman smiled and signed that it was no bother at all, the least they could do was provide him with a little nourishment after he'd spent most of the day teaching Dash carpentry. So Manus relented, glad and guilty at the same time.

The pizza was as good as the boy had promised, the sausage especially, the sweet and spicy taste of which stirred memories from a long time before. Or maybe it was just the environment, the feeling of being in someone's home, welcome in someone's home, with people who seemed comfortable with him and unafraid of him. The woman opened a bottle of wine, and though Manus didn't drink much wine, he enjoyed it. The boy seemed especially energized by the work they'd done and carried a lot of the conversation, but it was fine talking with the woman, too, who asked a lot of questions about where Manus grew up and who had taught him carpentry and how he enjoyed living in the area. The answers were all second nature to him; he'd been living the legend so long it felt like the truth. Which was good, because the protectiveness he sensed in the woman made Manus suspect she'd already done her research on the Internet, and probably via some unauthorized searches of NSA databases, as well.

After dinner, they finished bolting together the loft and built a ladder. Manus put the boy's mattress, which had been on the floor with no bed frame, on top of the structure, and helped them rearrange the rest of the furniture in the room. They both thanked him profusely, the boy's delight focused primarily on having his bed so high up, the woman's on how much space they had created in the small room. The boy attached a clip-on lamp to one of the railings so he could read in bed; Manus collected wood scraps and his tools; and the woman vacuumed up the sawdust they'd created. The boy wanted to hang towels and turn the loft into a fort, but the woman insisted no, it was a school night and already past bedtime, the boy needed to go to sleep. The fort could wait until tomorrow. The simultaneous firmness and gentleness in her manner gave Manus that strange feeling again, a recollection, a longing, another life.

They stepped outside and closed the door so the boy could get ready for bed. A moment later, he emerged wearing pajamas and headed to the bathroom to brush his teeth. The woman ruffled his hair as he passed, then signed to Manus, *What do I owe you for the work?*

The thought of having her pay him when he was supposed to be spying on her made him feel uneasy, though of course that was ridiculous. He had a cover and he had to live it.

I don't know, he signed. *How about two hundred dollars?*

Two hundred dollars? You've been here all afternoon! And what about all that lumber?

Don't forget, you fed me.

She laughed. *I fed you pizza. Plus you spent so much time teaching Dash. Two hundred isn't enough.*

Okay. Two fifty.

She smiled and shook her head as though exasperated, and Manus wondered with both unease and excitement if she was pleased at the low price as much for what it might indicate about his intentions as she was about receiving such a good deal.

All right, you drive a hard bargain. I accept—on condition that you help me finish the wine. No sense wasting it, right?

His ambivalence worsened, and he hesitated. Then he reminded himself this was what the director wanted.

That would be nice. Thank you.

The boy returned. He signed, *Thank you for building me a loft, Mr. Manus. And for letting me help.*

You're a good helper, Manus signed. *Remember, don't choke up when you're using a hammer.*

I know, the boy signed back, and pantomimed a solid hammer swing.

And keep your free hand out of the way.

The boy smiled and nodded, then signed, *We have tickets to the Os' last regular season home games. Want to come?*

Manus hesitated, not knowing how to respond. The woman saved him by laughing and signing, *Mr. Manus has a busy schedule, hon. And so do you—bedtime!*

Can I read?

It's really late, so just ten minutes, okay? Then lights out. Need the bathroom?

The boy shook his head, then stepped close and gave Manus a hug. It made Manus feel strange, as it had at the baseball game, but he patted the boy on the shoulder again and that seemed okay. The boy stepped back and hugged the woman, who kissed him on top of the head.

Ten minutes for real, Dash. No flashlight.

The boy gave her a small *busted* smile, went into his room, and climbed up into his loft. The woman closed the door, and they went back to the kitchen. A moment later, the boy walked in. *Bathroom?* The woman signed. The boy nodded a little sheepishly and went off. The woman smiled and shook her head. *That's my son. Either he doesn't need the bathroom at all, or he needs it right away. Nothing in between.*

I was like that, too. Too many interesting things going on. It's easy to forget the everyday ones.

Manus sat while the woman filled two glasses. She leaned forward a bit as she poured, and before he could stop it, Manus's gaze went to that area, that maddening area with its swells and shadows and contrasts. He looked away, trying to concentrate. The director wanted to know if she was happy at work, or stressed, or thinking of leaving. He didn't know how to ask about any of that without being obvious. All he had really noticed was that she seemed happy. Though maybe there was something a little sad behind the happiness. But who wasn't that true for?

The woman sat and took a sip of wine. *It was really nice of you to come out here on a Sunday,* she signed. *And for such a small job.*

Manus shook his head. *It was nothing. He's a good kid.*

The woman beamed. *The best.*

How old was he when he lost his hearing?

Three.

That's why he signs so well.

Yes.

You learned for him?

Of course. And you? Were your parents deaf?

No.

Did they learn sign?

My mother did.

Not your father?

The legend was that Manus's father had died when Manus was an infant. Manus's hands came up to tell her that, and instead wound up shaping the unfamiliar words, *My father wasn't a good guy.*

What do you mean?

Manus didn't know why he had said what he'd said. Instead, he took a sip of wine, then signed, *It's a long story.*

I'm not in a hurry.

It was strange, the way he wanted to tell her things. He almost felt she would understand. But he reminded himself he needed her to talk to him.

So what do you do at the NSA? he signed, careful to use the outsider's *the. Can you talk about it, or is it all secret?*

It is pretty secret, actually. But also nothing all that interesting.

You like it?

She sipped her wine. *It's technically challenging. I have a computer science background, and there aren't that many fields where I could apply it the way I do in my job. So there's that. But it's not such a practical skill set, is it? I mean, I wish I could build a loft for Dash.*

He recognized she might have been steering the conversation away from herself. Still, he signed, *You're happy, then?*

She looked at him closely, so closely Manus had to look away. Then she got up and walked off. Manus wondered if he'd said something wrong, and tried to figure out what it could be. But she returned a moment later and signed, *He's out cold. You must have worn him out.*

Manus was relieved—she had only been going to check on the boy. He signed, *I didn't mean to.*

No, it's good. I'm glad you were teaching him. His father was never very good with tools.

Was?

Divorced. We don't see him that often.

They were quiet for a moment. Manus drank more wine. It tasted good. He realized he was a little buzzed.

He could feel her watching him. When he looked up, she signed, *You're not married, are you?*

Her cheeks were slightly flushed and he realized she must have been as buzzed from the wine as he was. The realization produced a little adrenaline hit, and he could feel his heart rate and respiration increase in response.

You mean you work at the NSA and you couldn't find that out?

She laughed. *Maybe I just want confirmation.*

Why?

I'm not sure. Are you?

No.

Divorced?

No. Never married.

Why not?

He finished his wine and looked into the empty glass. *I don't know. Never met anyone.*

She laughed. *Me, neither. But I got married anyway.*

Manus hesitated, then signed, *I like the way you are with your boy. I can tell you're a good mother.*

How?

The way you look at him.

They were quiet again. Manus didn't feel like he was doing a good job for the director. Worse, he didn't care.

When he finally glanced up, the woman had finished her wine

and was looking at him with a frankness that gave him another adrenaline hit.

Do I make you nervous? she signed.

What? he signed, his heart beating faster. *No.*

Because I feel like you keep looking away from me.

Flustered, he looked away. Then caught himself and looked back.

Do you want *to look at me?* she signed.

Manus could feel himself stiffening. He sensed he was losing a game he hadn't even realized he was playing. He swallowed and tried to think.

Do you? she signed again.

Breathing hard, Manus nodded.

Where?

Manus glanced at the skin above her top button, then back to her eyes.

She touched the spot and raised her eyebrows. *Here?*

His heart pounding, his head spinning, again Manus nodded.

Still watching him, she closed her fingers around the top button, undid it, and then, with her fingertips, spread the material to each side, exposing the edges of a lacy white bra, the curve of her breasts insanely smooth and full inside it.

Manus couldn't believe what he was seeing. It was unreal, like something happening to someone else.

She reached across the table and took him gently by the hand, the feeling of her fingers against his intense, almost electric. Manus couldn't find words. He couldn't think. All he knew was that he wanted, he *needed*, to touch her.

She stood, and he allowed her to lead him to a utility room adjacent to the entrance. It was a small space devoted mostly to a washing machine and dryer. The light was on a rheostat. She dimmed it, closed the door, put her hands on Manus's chest, and eased him back against the door. Manus's heart was beating combat fast.

He stood there, his hands curled into fists at his sides, wanting, craving her, but at the same time terrified, unsure of what to do. She glanced down, and he could tell from a slight pressure from her hands that she'd seen how hard he was, and the realization was both exciting and horrifying.

She looked up at him again, then took his hands and placed them on her breasts. Manus felt himself moan. He squeezed, careful to be gentle, afraid of how out of control he felt, how confused. Her mouth parted and he could tell she was breathing fast, as fast as he was, and she put her hands over his and she squeezed, too, harder than he had, telling him it was all right, she wanted him to, it was good.

His hands shaking, Manus began to unbutton her shirt. He sensed her watching him but he couldn't look back. He felt too out of his mind, and he needed to see what he was doing anyway, because suddenly a few shirt buttons seemed to require all his fragmenting concentration. He worked his trembling way down, and when he finally bested the last one, his hands pulled back and floated aimlessly for a moment, trying to say something, ask her something, though he had no idea what.

For a long moment, she just looked at him. Then she reached slowly back with both hands and undid her bra. Manus watched her, his mouth agape, the blood pounding in his head, and then the bra was open and she took his hands and put them under it, and the feel of her breasts, so full and ripe and smooth, was so overwhelming that he could feel tears wanting to well up. She reached for the back of his neck, her palm hot against his skin, and brought his head down. Manus pushed the bra out of the way, closed his mouth over a hard, pink nipple, and sucked. He felt her gasp and he dropped to his knees, his hands and mouth still on her. The shirt fell to the floor beside him, followed a moment later by the bra. He moved to her other breast and she knotted her fingers in his hair and pulled his head closer. He sucked harder, cupping her breasts, squeezing her ass, running his hands along her waist and up her sides, feeling her, wanting her, needing her.

She got on her knees, too, and suddenly he was kissing her, his mouth open, her tongue inside it, and he felt her unbuttoning his shirt and pulling it down over his arms. And then her hands were on his shoulders, his torso, his chest, moving, pressing, and he realized she was exploring his body the way he was hers, and the thought caused a cascade of renewed excitement inside him. She broke the kiss, pushed him back by a shoulder, leaned forward, and closed a mouth over one of his nipples, something no one had ever done to Manus, something he had never even considered, and he was shocked to feel an explosion of pleasure from it. He couldn't think anymore and didn't want to, he just needed to be naked, against her, all the way inside her. He pulled her to her feet and fumbled with the button on her pants, but she was faster and got his open first, and pulled them down, his pants and boxers both. Manus stepped out of them and even as he realized what a relief, what a joy it was to be naked, she curled a hand around his cock and squeezed, and the feeling of that obliterated everything else and made his head swim anew. She pulled something from her back pocket and he saw it was a condom, and she opened it and with some difficulty rolled it onto him, and then she pulled off her own pants and her panties and Manus drank in the sight of her body, even smoother, softer than he had imagined, and realizing how much she wanted him was the headiest thing he'd ever known.

He put his hands under her arms and lifted her, carrying her back until her ass bumped against the edge of the washing machine, her feet a few inches off the floor. He held her perched that way for a moment, panting, so engorged it hurt. She curled a hand around his cock again and nodded, and she licked her lips, and she moved him close, and she guided him in.

For a moment, the pleasure was so stunning that Manus didn't move. He closed his eyes and just felt it, his chest brushing against her breasts, her hands on his back, his cock inside her body. Then she kissed him again and he kissed her back, and then he was moving without even meaning to, he was fucking her and God it was good, and she leaned back and put her elbows on the surface of the machine and slid her hips forward, and Manus lifted her ass and pulled her closer and drove into her, his eyes on her belly, her breasts, her face. She gripped the edge of the machine and pushed back into him in time with his thrusts, her mouth open as though in shock or wonder, and Manus fucked her more deeply, as deeply as he could go, and her mouth opened wider and her eyes squeezed shut and her body shook and Manus could feel her muscles clenching and rippling as he moved back and forth inside her and he realized she was coming, coming because of him, and the thought was obliterated by an explosion of pleasure and he was coming, too, coming inside her and feeling her and watching her and taking her, all of her, her, her, her.

And then the world came back, and she opened her eyes and looked at him, and he could see from the rise and fall of her chest that she was still panting, and he realized so was he. He set her ass gently back on the machine and sagged against her. She crossed her legs around his lower back and held him like that, one hand around his shoulders, the other caressing the back of his head, the fingers running through his hair, her breasts pushing against his chest in time with her decelerating breathing.

When he'd caught his own breath, he pulled back a few inches. She kissed him again, long and tenderly, holding his face in her hands. Then she unwound her legs and gripped the end of the condom as Manus eased back, and when he was out she slid it off and dropped it on the washing machine. Manus put his hands around her waist and lifted her back to the floor.

He stood before her, looking at her body, then her face, shaking his head slowly in amazement. She smiled and glanced at his subsiding cock, then signed, *I thought you were going to kill me.*

He didn't understand and felt horrified at the thought. *What?*

She pointed, then signed, *You're big. Very big.*

He felt himself redden. *Oh.*

She laughed. *Don't worry. I liked it.*

He hesitated, then signed, *I'm glad.*

Has it been . . . a long time for you?

He wasn't sure how to respond. *A long time for what?*

Since you've made love.

He sensed a simple yes would have been the safe answer. Instead, he found himself telling her the truth again.

Never. Not like that.

She raised her eyebrows. *You mean on a washing machine?*

He shook his head. *Just . . . like that.*

That's nice.

It's true.

So it was good?

Yes. For you?

She laughed again. *Could you not tell?*

He tried to find words, but nothing came, and his hands drifted aimlessly for a moment. Finally, he managed, *Really?*

She stroked his cheek and nodded. *Yes. It's been a long time for me.*

Why?

I don't know. I don't meet that many people. And it's hard with Dash. There are a lot of creeps out there. But . . . he really likes you. And he has good instincts for people. I think that made me trust you.

Manus looked down, ashamed. She touched his chin gently, and when he looked up, she signed, *Am I embarrassing you?*

He shook his head.

She smiled. *You're shy, aren't you?*

I'm not sure.

That was just . . . good. So good. I'm sorry if I took advantage of you. I've been thinking about it since we met you at the baseball game.

You have?

Why are you surprised? You're a good-looking guy. And that was so nice, what you did for Dash. At the game. And letting him help you today, too.

He shook his head, her gratitude again making him ashamed.

She touched his cheek. *I know I should be a little more coy, but . . . I don't have time for games. I'd like to see you again. And if that scares you away, or if you've already gotten what you wanted, that's okay, I'd rather know now.*

He reached out and touched her face the way she had touched his. And then his hands trailed down her neck, and along her shoulders, and across her breasts. When his fingertips brushed against her nipples, she shivered, and he was instantly hard again.

She glanced down and smiled. *I could go get another condom. Or . . . we could do other things.*

They wound up doing the other things. For Manus, it was an ongoing revelation.

⋅ ⋅ ⋅ ⋅ ⋅ ⋅ ⋅ ⋅ ⋅ ⋅ ⋅ ⋅ ⋅ ⋅ ⋅ ⋅

Anders closed down his monitor, having seen and heard enough. He had of course previously sent a team to black-bag Gallagher's apartment, a precaution he only wished he had thought to take with Perkins, and naturally had said nothing about it to Manus, who had no need to know. Not that Anders had expected anything like what he had just witnessed. The truth was, he hadn't realized Manus was even capable of anything like that. Contrary to Remar's impression, the man was no simple brute, true, but this? Well, maybe he had been watching too many James Bond movies, and had concluded the best way to assess a subject was to take her to bed. Or to a washing machine, as the case may be. Regardless, Anders supposed it was probably all to the good. Gallagher had seemed quite . . . tender with Manus, as well as passionate. If she had developed feelings for the man, and Manus could exploit them, they might well learn more about her state of mind than would otherwise have been possible. He decided it really was a good piece of luck that she had a deaf son. As he had hoped, it was probably part of what had made her open up to Manus in the first place.

For just one moment, he considered the possibility that Manus might actually have developed feelings for Gallagher, but then dismissed the thought. The man was human, yes, and presumably had human physical needs. In fact, Anders knew from spot checks of Manus's cell phone metadata and geolocation records that from time to time the man availed himself of the services of prostitutes. But actual feelings? Anders tried to imagine it, and couldn't. The truth was, he had never known anyone who seemed to have *less* feeling than Manus. It was part of what made Remar so uneasy around him. And of course, it was also part of what made Manus so useful. There was nothing the man couldn't do, nothing he wouldn't do, out of loyalty to Anders, the man who had rescued him, raised him, practically *created* him. What had Remar said? That Manus was like an abused dog, that was it. Devoted to serving his master in whatever his master required.

And that would never change. Anders would never allow it. Because any dog that turned on its master simply needed to be put down.

CHAPTER . . . .
. . . . 22

Anders was in his office at eight o'clock the following morning when he got a call from the Secret Service about an explosion near the White House. He called Remar and told him to have the appropriate units begin scouring recent cell phone activity in the area. Then he called Barbara Stirr, a reliable CNN Pentagon correspondent he regularly used to launder talking points into what people digested as news.

"Barbara," he said. "General Anders here."

"General, is this about the explosion? I'm on my way right now. Anything you'd like to share with me on background?"

Anders smiled. He couldn't remember the last time a reporter had even attempted to ask for something on the record. The understanding was as clear as it was unspoken: *You give me the access; I'll give you the anonymous news reports.*

"Nothing formal right now, Barbara, but I can tell you this. Cell phone activity in the area over the last twenty-four hours indicates a jihadist connection."

"My God. Another ISIS splinter group?"

It was amazing, and gratifying, the longevity of the talking points he fed the press. "Possibly. Or an affiliate, yes."

"And you were able to identify them by their cell phones?"

That was his opening. "Not as precisely as we'd like. You have to remember, Barbara, people are able to purchase and use cell phones with a great deal of anonymity in this country. By contrast, look at what the government of Pakistan is doing to crack down on terrorism—requiring that everyone who uses a cell phone has registered a fingerprint as a way of denying the terrorists the ability to communicate clandestinely."

"I didn't know that."

"Yes, look it up. Very effective program. Well, we do what we can, even with one arm tied behind our back."

"Anything else you can share?"

"Not at present. But things are moving quickly. I may have more later today."

"Thank you, sir. And thank you for what you're doing to keep our country safe."

He ended the call and turned on CNN, where there was a story about a drone strike in Pakistan—stock footage of a Reaper Unmanned Aerial Vehicle accompanied by a voiceover so neutral it made a weather report sound urgent by comparison. Two minutes later, the drone story was interrupted by a live report—Barbara Stirr, on the street, smoke billowing from the wreckage behind her, sirens wailing in the background and military helicopters circling noisily overhead, the chyron proclaiming dramatically *Explosion Near the White House*. Anders watched as Stirr got into character, a few area residents doing their bit as extras by standing around with their hands pressed over their mouths in telegenic shock and grief.

"This is Barbara Stirr, CNN Pentagon correspondent, at the scene of an explosion just blocks from the White House. We don't have reports of casualties yet, though as you can see paramedics are on hand and it's hard to imagine no one was injured by such a huge blast at morning rush hour. In fact, you can't help but wonder whether whoever was behind this didn't time the attack to coincide with rush hour, and administration officials do believe this was the work of ISIS or an affiliated terror group."

Anders nodded in appreciation of her slight deviation from script—the point about rush hour was nicely done. In fact, he should have thought of it himself.

The sounds of nearby sirens got louder, then stopped, and the camera swung around to track an Asian woman in a paramedic's uniform racing toward the scene. "Excuse me," Stirr called out. "I'm Barbara Stirr, with CNN—can you tell us whether there are casualties?"

The paramedic glanced at Stirr and didn't even break stride, but for an instant her expression was so pristinely disgusted at the question that Anders couldn't help but wince. Stirr's recovery was impressive. She turned to the camera and said, "The paramedics are understandably busy. It looks bad. We'll all keep hoping for the best and reporting whatever we learn. Barbara Stirr, Pentagon correspondent, CNN."

Remar came in. He closed the door behind him and strode to Anders's desk. "Who the hell told Stirr ISIS was behind this?"

Anders leaned back in his chair and patted his stomach. "She said ISIS or an affiliated group."

"That's not a difference, Ted. Where's she getting that?"

"It's the expected speculation. She could have gotten it anywhere. She could have made it up herself."

Remar nodded, looking unpersuaded. Anders trusted Remar, of course, trusted him as much as he trusted anyone. But he also sensed there were things Remar . . . might not understand. And that he therefore didn't need to know.

"The president is convening the National Security Council," Remar said after a moment. "Situation Room. One hour."

"Anything from the mobile phone analysis?"

"Yes. Three units in the area, all on watch lists."

Anders sensed Remar was hoping for some reaction. He saw no need to oblige him. "What else?"

"Several suspicious calls. A mosque in the area. And it looks like one of the units was used to call a prepaid unit attached to the bomb as a detonator. Significant electronic trail to follow. Some pretty sloppy jihadists, I'd say. It's almost like they want to get caught."

"Maybe it's just their way of letting us know it's them. Some of these groups aren't exactly publicity shy, Mike."

"On the other hand, the attack was fairly sophisticated. It looks like they attached the device to the bottom of a food service delivery truck, tracked it via GPS, and detonated when it was maximally close to the White House."

"You see? Anything other than a direct hit, it would take a nuke to damage the White House. It's the publicity they're after."

Remar didn't respond. Anders waited, not comfortable with the man's newfound reticence. Ordinarily he could tell what Remar was thinking. Not today.

After a moment, he gave up and said, "I need to get to the White House. Brief me on any further developments en route."

Remar nodded, then said, "Ted."

Anders raised his eyebrows.

"Those phones . . . they're the same ones associated with that 'letter bomb' Delgado intercepted from FedEx."

Anders didn't blink. "Is that a problem?"

"I told you, those units are on several watch lists. They're affiliated with Ergenekon. Up until now, a DEA narcotics thing, not terrorism, but still."

Anders said nothing, not liking where Remar seemed to want to take this.

"So even if this is a coincidence, it's a bad coincidence. We don't need anyone looking into our relationship with those guys. Into what we use them for."

"Nobody knows about that relationship except you and me."

"How much do I really know? What are you not telling me?"

So that's what was bothering him. Well, no one liked not knowing. Anders looked at his hands while he picked at a cuticle.

After a moment, Remar started to move toward the door, then turned back. "There has to be a limit, Ted."

"Of course there does."

"But do you know where it is?"

The intercom buzzed.

"That's going to be Manus," Anders said. "Give me a minute with him. And make sure I'm prepped with a set of razzle-dazzle slides on everything we've got regarding these jihadist mobile phones. Today is our show, not the Pentagon's."

Remar brought in the big man and then left, eyeing him warily before closing the door on his way out.

"Marvin," Anders said, and gestured to one of the chairs in front of his desk. "Please. Have a seat. I'm afraid I have only a minute—a meeting at the White House."

Manus sat.

Anders waited a moment, but Manus offered nothing. First Remar, now Manus. Maybe there was something in the air today that was making everyone taciturn. Finally, Anders said, "Well? How did your loft-building go with Ms. Gallagher and her son?"

"It was fine."

Anders's instinct was to draw the man out by waiting for more, but he didn't have time. Worse, he doubted it would work. So he simply said, "And? What are your impressions about her state of mind?"

"I think she's okay."

The response was anodyne to the point of being useless. Anders said, "Based on . . . ?"

"She invited me to stay for dinner. Pizza and wine. We talked for a while after the boy went to bed. She seemed happy to me."

I'll bet she did, after the washing machine, Anders thought. And then realized: *He's not going to tell you about that.*

The realization was so astonishing it required confirmation. Anders said, "You just talked? Anything else?"

"I saw her interacting with her son. He helped me build the loft, which made the job take longer. So I was there for a while."

Not only was Manus holding back about the details of his evening, and not only was he offering Gallagher at least a qualified clean bill of health, he was doing what he could to give his diagnosis greater credence by emphasizing the extent of his interaction and observation.

All at once, Anders realized he'd been wrong about Manus. The man *was* capable of feeling.

And right now, he was feeling infatuated.

Maybe Anders should have foreseen the possibility. After all, there was something . . . womanly about Gallagher. Her body, certainly, and her demeanor. But it had never occurred to him that she, or anyone else, could be interested in Manus, whose chief effect on people seemed to be to make them nervous, if not outright afraid.

It didn't matter. The man was obviously compromised. Not fatally. But enough so that he had to be pulled off Gallagher—figuratively and literally—and assigned to something else.

"Well," Anders said, standing. "That's helpful information, Marvin, and I'm glad to hear it. As I mentioned, Gallagher is doing important work for us and it's a relief to know she's as reliable as I had hoped. If she needs further monitoring, I may turn to you again. In the meantime, I'd like you to steer clear of her. We wouldn't want to take any unnecessary risks with your cover. Thank you, as always."

Manus nodded and left immediately, perhaps relieved Anders hadn't pressed him more closely for details.

Yes, the man was clearly smitten. Best to keep him as far as possible from Gallagher until the Hamilton situation was resolved. Of course, the woman would still need to be monitored. She might even need to be . . . neutralized, if the fever of her suspicions grew any hotter. Of course, if it came to that, Manus would now be completely unsuitable to handle the thing itself.

Well, there was always Delgado. He almost felt sorry for Gallagher when he imagined how Delgado would go about it. On the other hand, there was never any danger of Delgado falling for a subject. He loved his work too much for that.

CHAPTER . . . .
. . . . 23

A t the National Security Council meeting in the White House Situation Room, it was Anders's turn to shine.

When the president asked, in a tone indicating he was expecting nothing but bromides, what Anders had managed to uncover about the perpetrators of the bombing, Anders waited a long beat before responding in his gravest, most confident tone, "Quite a bit, Mr. President."

The president raised his eyebrows. Anders indulged just the briefest of satisfied glances at Jones, then stood and nodded to the aide he'd brought with him. The aide fired up the laptop he was manning, and the wall screen displayed the faces of the three men Manus had disposed of in Turkey—all looking suitably sinister with their dark complexions, mustaches, and stubble, and each with a graphic of a mobile phone and phone number alongside his profile.

"You'll see these numbers," Anders said, indicating each with a laser pointer, "are the very same geolocated units the Pentagon managed to identify in Turkey and to confirm as being in contact with jihadist units on the Syrian side of the border—the jihadists believed to be holding Ryan Hamilton." He turned to Jones. "Vernon, nice work on that."

Jones glared at him, recognizing the deliberate condescension behind the ostensible compliment.

"These units are now active in the DC metro area. Each has made several suspicious calls, information regarding which we have of course provided to the FBI and to the relevant section chiefs at the Department of Homeland Security, and on which we are otherwise following up."

The attorney general and the secretary of homeland security nodded, the prerogatives of their agencies having been respected. In fact, both organizations depended on NSA for SIGINT analysis, so providing them mobile numbers was mostly pro forma. The only role of their FBI or HSI agents would be to carry out arrests once proper suspects had been identified. That identification, naturally, would come from NSA's own intelligence.

A White House flunky knocked and entered the room, carrying a sheaf of photos. "Nine confirmed dead, sir," the flunky said. "Fifteen more hospitalized, seven in critical condition." He handed the photos to the president and left, closing the door behind him.

The president leafed through the photos, then passed them to the secretary of state, who was to his left. Anders judged the timing of the casualty report propitious. "Of particular note," he continued, "is that one of the phones"—he paused and circled the number with the laser, then looked meaningfully at each of the people seated at the table, stopping at the president—"is the unit that was used to detonate the very device that went off this morning."

There was a long, silent pause. "What does this mean?" the president said.

Anders clicked off the laser pointer and crisply returned it to his jacket pocket. "It means that groups affiliated with ISIS are moving out of the Syrian kidnapping business, and into the American mass-casualty bombing business."

"Who, exactly?" the president said.

Anders was waiting for that. "Sir, if we had a biometric cell phone program like Pakistan's, we'd probably be interrogating the bastard who did this in a black site right now. As it is, our information is unavoidably more general. But I can tell you this. The calculus we've been using to determine whether and how to rescue the journalist Ryan Hamilton has changed."

Jones said, "Changed how, exactly?"

Anders didn't even look at him. It was the president he was talking to, and the president was listening. "Sir, prior to this morning's attack, we had the luxury of telling ourselves we could attempt a surgical rescue of a single journalist being held in Syria without increasing the danger to American citizens here in the homeland, on American soil."

Anders knew that even with a crowd as cynical as this one, it was important to use the proper buzzwords, if only so the president could more easily imagine how his own subsequent speeches and interviews would sound. And he knew the president was a particular fan of the word "homeland," derived by the government after 9/11 from the German *Heimat*. He even knew, through his access to God's Eye, that the White House had discreetly employed a private polling company to gauge the word's emotional resonance with the public, and had found that resonance very appealing indeed.

The president's eyes narrowed slightly. "You're not answering my question, Ted."

Oh, but I am, sir. "Sir, the Syrians the Pentagon believes are holding Ryan Hamilton have now been proven to be connected to a mass casualty attack on American soil."

The Pentagon merely believes; NSA offers proof. He wondered whether anyone would seize on that sleight of hand. No one did.

"An attack that took place just blocks from the White House," he went on, "the real and symbolic seat of American power and world leadership. In my opinion, sir, this group has demonstrated a global reach and a fanatical zeal that requires a response more robust than a mere rescue. For strategic reasons as well as symbolic, we have no choice but to eliminate the individuals behind this attack. And fortunately, we have the opportunity to do so. Right now. Today."

Anders had smoothly transitioned from "connected to" an attack to "behind" the attack, but if anyone noticed, nothing was said.

Anders turned to Jones. "Vernon, you have a UAV base in İncirlik. Not far from the Syrian border. On the president's command, how quickly could you have Reapers hit Azaz and take out the group behind this morning's attack?"

Jones looked at him for a long moment, obviously trying to figure out what he was up to. Why was Anders dealing him in, when a moment earlier he seemed intent on dealing him out?

Jones looked at the president. "Sir, we're ready for that rescue. But yes, if you decide to emulsify these bastards instead, we can have Hellfire missiles pounding Azaz in three hours."

Anders was pleased. He had recognized he was coming dangerously close to usurping the president's prerogatives in proposing the new course of action. The "on the president's command" had been intended to mitigate any chafing he had caused. Jones's attempt to save face by responding not to him but directly to the president could only help in that regard, by demonstrating that everyone recognized the only person in the room, indeed, the only person in the world, with the authority to make these decisions was the commander in chief. On top of which, that "emulsify these bastards" flourish suggested Jones had decided to accept Anders's peace offering. He was signaling he was okay with Anders changing the destination, as long as the Pentagon could still own the glory when they got there.

Again the room was silent. The president leaned back in his chair, crossed his arms, and stroked his chin. He looked first at Jones, then at Anders. "Are you certain the people behind this morning's attack are at that location?"

"This kind of intel is inherently uncertain, sir, but our confidence is as high as it gets in such matters." Much further out on a limb than he would ordinarily be willing to go, but today certain risks had to be taken.

The president nodded and turned to Jones.

"Vernon, if you send in those Reapers, what are the chances—hypothetically—of a hostage making it out alive?"

Jones paused, clearly uncertain of what the president wanted to hear. "I would call those chances low, sir."

The president sighed. "And therein lies the problem."

Damn. "If I may, sir?"

The president extended a hand, palm up, in a *go ahead* gesture.

"Sir, first, with all respect to Vernon's very impressive collection efforts, we can't be certain the person we think is being held in Azaz even is Hamilton."

"Respectfully, Ted," Jones shot back, "you yourself just said this kind of intel is uncertain."

"Respectfully, Vernon, you advised that the Turks you believe delivered Hamilton to the Syrians were simply drug runners. Yet this morning, they set off a bomb a few blocks from the White House."

Jones had no answer to that other than to seethe, and Anders immediately regretted the riposte, which had been ego driven, unrelated to the goal he was trying to achieve. He held up his open hands in supplication. "What I'm saying is, what if we're both wrong? It's not Hamilton in Azaz, and it's not our jihadists."

Jones shrugged. "Then we have some collateral damage on our hands."

"*Unattributable* collateral damage, yes. Which, while certainly unfortunate, is neither new nor particularly costly. Now, what if we're both right?"

Jones watched him as though wary of being tricked. "We take out the jihadists," he said slowly, "but we also take out Hamilton."

"Agreed. Now, what I'm asking—what we all need to be clear-eyed about—is this: Are we willing to lose the opportunity to take out the people behind this morning's attack because there's a risk of a potential American casualty? How do we explain that kind of squeamishness to the American people if there's another attack and this group turns out to be behind it?"

The president looked at Jones. "Are we certain the person being held in Azaz is Hamilton?"

Anders watched Jones and could almost feel the man's calculations. Everyone had just agreed certainty was impossible. Which meant the president knew the answer would be no. And if he was asking the question anyway, it meant he *wanted* the answer to be no. Presumably because he had already decided the political risks and rewards of an immediate, simple drone strike were preferable to those of a slower, more complicated rescue attempt. The success of a rescue attempt was easy to grade: Was Hamilton really rescued? While the success of a drone strike was easy to fudge: If the bodies were military-age males and Muslim, and the government claimed they were terrorists, how could anyone prove otherwise?

Jones shook his head. "Not certain, sir, no."

The president gazed at the ceiling for a moment, then said to no one in particular, "And is it possible the group behind this morning's attack wants us to believe they're holding Hamilton, even though they're not, as a way of staying our hand?"

It was so obvious what the president wanted to hear that it was inconceivable anyone would argue with him. Still, it was an effort for Anders to wait. He wanted it to come from Jones. It would be the signal that Jones was in.

"It's possible, sir," Jones said after a moment. "We know they're terrified of our UAVs. Pretending to be holding an American hostage—a kind of fictitious human shield—would be one way of dissuading us from pressing our technological advantage."

The president smiled slightly, perhaps pleased to have demonstrated that, in the end, he was always the smartest guy in the room.

"Vernon, you're friendly with Mike Rogers at CNN, correct? The former congressman?"

"Yes, sir."

"If the worst should happen, could we give him our version of events on background, and count on him to explain why this was a difficult call, and why it was of paramount importance that we seize this opportunity to keep the American people safe?"

"I have no doubt of it, sir."

The president nodded. "Make sure he's properly briefed, then. And what about Declan Walsh at the *New York Times*? Didn't he publish what our 'counterterrorism officials and analysts' fed him the last time an American hostage was killed? How valuable and successful the UAV program has been overall, that sort of thing?"

"Yes, sir, that was Walsh. Really helped us get out our version of the story."

"Make sure to reach out to him, as well."

"Yes, sir."

"All right," the president said, "here's the official narrative. If it's not Hamilton, we carried out a successful reprisal against the terrorists behind this morning's barbaric attack on our nation's capital."

The president paused for the assembled players to murmur their assent, then continued. "If, on the other hand, in the unfortunate event Hamilton loses his life in the course of the operation, the narrative is that the terrorists fear our UAV program so much they're trying everything they can, including deliberately placing hostages in the line of fire, to get us to dismantle it. To deliver to them that sort of victory would itself reward the very terrorism with which we are at war. That the terrorists would do to a hostage what they did to Hamilton is, in a sense, proof of just how well the UAV program has been working, and criticizing the program would itself be a perverse reward for the terrorist propaganda strategy. Are we all clear on that?"

The president paused again while everyone nodded, probably enjoying the drama of making his national security team wait for their commander in chief to issue his decision. Then he said, "I took an oath to protect the American people. Today, that oath requires a difficult call. We can't let this morning's attack go unanswered. We can't take a chance on the people behind it acting again. Vernon, how did you put it? 'Emulsify these bastards.' Without delay."

Jones nodded crisply, then remembered for form's sake to glance over at the secretary of defense. The necessary and inevitable nod procured, Jones said, "Yes, sir, Mr. President."

Anders maintained a poker face, but inside he was awash with relief. The meeting could have gone either way. He'd played it well, but he knew to some degree he'd been lucky. It didn't hurt that the president seemed to be under the misapprehension that his constitutional oath was to protect the American people, rather than to protect the Constitution. Anders certainly wasn't going to be the one to correct him.

In the corridor on the way out, Jones caught up to Anders and took him by the arm. "Hey. What the hell were you pulling in there?"

Anders glanced at Jones's hand and waited until it had been removed. "I don't know what you're talking about."

"Why are you so intent on a drone strike? Why don't you want us to rescue this guy?"

"Personally, I wish we could rescue him. As the president said, it was a tough call."

"Don't bullshit a bullshitter, Ted."

"I'm not bullshitting anyone. Do you want to be the one to explain after the next bombing why we didn't hit these bastards when we had a chance?"

Jones eyed him for a moment, clearly unconvinced. It didn't matter. The president had made the call. And it was the right call.

In the car on the way back to Fort Meade, Anders thought of the images he'd seen on CNN that morning. It was unfortunate, but on balance he believed it would be beneficial. In so many ways, a country was like a person—which made sense, after all, because a country was in the end just a collection of people. And people were always concerned about their health, and rightly so, but not always properly solicitous of it. A man might therefore visit the dentist and be warned he needed to floss more often to prevent gum disease, and the man, in the immediate aftermath of his run-in with the pick and the drill, would promise himself that this time, he would be more diligent about his dental hygiene. And he might even follow through, brushing more conscientiously, flossing more regularly, for a few days, perhaps even for a week. But inevitably, as the dentist's warning and the discomfort induced by her instruments receded into the distance, the man would revert to laziness, complacency, denial. The simple truth was, twice a year just wasn't enough to make the average person take better care of his teeth. And similarly, the occasional random terror attack demonstrably wasn't enough to keep the citizenry properly vigilant. An occasional supplement might be required, and while that supplement might involve some unpleasant inherent side effects, surely those side effects were nothing compared to the actual disease they were required to protect against?

He wished the supplements weren't necessary. He wished the country could grasp the nature of the threat, as he did, and give him without question the tools he needed to combat it. But he supposed he couldn't blame them. They didn't have access to the information he did, they didn't understand just how dangerous the world was, they didn't know what was needed to keep that danger at bay.

Well, they knew slightly better today than they had the day before. And that was something, anyway.

CHAPTER . . . .
. . . . 24

E vie was in her office, reviewing camera network footage. The director had told her to task the biometrics system with queries on
every jihadist in the database, but she had received no meaningful positives. And though the prospect of manually reviewing the
amount of footage her system scraped up from DC was daunting,
she thought it was at least worth a try.

The working theory was that the terrorists had planted the
device on the chassis of the food truck while it was out making
deliveries, then had monitored the truck's movements via a GPS-
equipped phone attached to the device, detonating it when it was
close to the White House. She had tried a few XKeyscore searches of
various Internet and email parameters—anyone searching for food
delivery routes, things like that—but got nothing useful. The detonator was likely the key. Which meant that somewhere in the building, teams of technicians were scrutinizing mobile phone metadata,
trying to track whatever phone had made the call that triggered the
device. She wished as always she could have access to that data; it
would have helped her focus her own efforts. But of course everything was too compartmentalized for that.

The FBI had obtained the truck's route from the day and week before, so she worked backward, going on the reasonably safe assumption that the bomb had been planted as recently as possible as a way of minimizing the chance of discovery. The work was tedious. So much footage, so many possibilities she had to zero in on, only to abandon them upon closer inspection. All the while knowing that her efforts would probably be useless, that no matter how diligent she was, the terrorists might have planted the device earlier, or from an angle she couldn't see, or in a place where there was no camera coverage.

She tried not to let thoughts of the other night intrude, but it wasn't easy. God, it had been so long. And while a vibrator was certainly better than nothing, she hadn't realized just how much she must have been craving real human contact. Because . . . lord, she had really seduced poor Marvin. She felt herself blushing as she remembered. Was it the wine? She wasn't sure where she had gotten the courage to talk to him like that. To . . . be with him like that. It wasn't like her. She'd always let the man make the first move. Or at least she thought she had—before Sean, it had been so long she wasn't even sure anymore. But something about the way Marvin kept trying not to look at her, and when he did, the hunger she saw in his expression, the longing . . . it was just such a turn-on, to be looked at that way. She remembered how easily he had lifted her and set her on the washing machine, how strong he was, and at the same time gentle. Well, not *that* gentle. She closed her eyes and remembered that moment when he had really started to fuck her, when she could feel him still trying to hold back but no longer able to, and she felt herself get wet. She couldn't remember the last time she'd been fucked like that. Never, was the truth. She'd ached the next day, wonderfully so. She wanted to ache like that again.

She smiled and thought, *Slut.*

He had texted her the next morning. Just one word: *Wow.* Such a perfect text. Not too much, not too little. She had texted back,

Yeah? And had waited an awful few minutes before getting something even better than the first one: *Can't stop thinking about it.*

Not *Can't stop thinking about you.* That would have been too much, at this point. She didn't want that. *Can't stop thinking about it* felt honest. It felt right. It felt like . . . exactly what she was thinking.

He'd told her he had to be out of town for two days—a work thing. But that it would be good to see her again when he got back, if she wanted. She'd told him yes, she wanted. *Wanted*, there was a word. Right now, she didn't even know what would happen when they saw each other. She couldn't imagine having dinner with him, or a conversation, or anything like that. All she wanted was for him to put his hands on her again, and his mouth, and set her on that washing machine and do everything he'd done last time, everything and more.

She hadn't heard from him since, but she wasn't worried. If she'd been him, she'd be concerned about coming on too strong, and she would have waited a bit. Two days was nothing, and anyway that meant today, or tonight. Tonight was a nice thought. If he texted her after Dash was asleep, she'd invite him over for a drink. The thought made her shift in her seat and blow out a long breath.

She shook it off and focused again, tracking the truck's positions through every available network of cameras. The mind-numbing hours crept by. And just as she had reached the point where she was convinced the whole exercise was useless, she saw a man, in glasses and an Orioles cap and pulling a wheeled carry-on bag, leave the sidewalk to cut behind the food truck where it was parked near Farragut West Metro Station. For about ten seconds, she couldn't see him. Then he emerged and stepped back to the sidewalk. He was smiling slightly, the smile almost a sneer.

What the hell was that?

Feeling her heart rate kick up a notch, she backtracked and watched the footage again. Damn it, she couldn't get the correct angle. She couldn't see what the man was doing behind the truck—only that he stepped behind it, then out, and then was back on his way. Why would someone do that? Confusion over which way he was going, a street he was looking for, something along those lines? Maybe. He was carrying a bag, after all, and there were numerous hotels in the area. It was possible he was from out of town. But he was keeping his head down in a way she didn't like. If he was a traveler and unsure of where he was going, he wasn't going to pick up any clues looking at the sidewalk.

She tracked the man southeast and picked him up again near the Capitol. He was no longer carrying the bag.

Her heart kicked harder. What had happened to the bag? Had he checked into a hotel and kept walking? She examined the time lines and saw there was no way, he must have been walking steadily southeast, with no detours. He'd discarded the bag. He must have.

She was able to stay with him all the way to the Congressional Cemetery, where her coverage went dark. Frustrated, she expanded her search to the cemetery's periphery. She could find no sign of the man. She examined the footage of every network all the way up until she was looking at things in real time. Still no sign of the man. She had a crazy thought: *Could he still be in there?* She'd have to apprise the director of the possibility.

But in fact, it felt like . . . something else. Like the man had known the cemetery was a blind spot. That he'd gone there deliberately, understanding that if anyone were tracking him through the camera network, in the cemetery the trail would go dark.

No, that didn't make sense. How could anyone know something like that? Probably just a coincidence. Lucky for the man; unlucky for her.

She reversed to the moment she had first seen him step behind the truck, and followed him backward from there. She got him emerging from Farragut West. Coverage inside the Metro system was excellent, and she had no trouble tracking him backward on the

Orange Line to West Falls Church, where he had approached the station walking southwest on Idylwood Road . . .

And then he was gone again. Disappeared into a hole in her coverage. She tried every network he might have crossed into before walking into that blind spot, and got nothing. He had appeared and then vanished and damn it, it *couldn't* have been a coincidence. This guy *knew* where she could watch him and where she couldn't. Where she could see him and where she was blind. *He knew.* And he had exploited that knowledge.

She looked at her monitor, shaking her head, trying to get her mind around it.

As far as she knew, there was only one person besides her who understood the capabilities and limits of her camera monitoring system. Only one person who had access to it. Only one person who even knew it existed.

The director.

Well, the director and maybe his XO Remar, though she wasn't sure that was really a difference. They were so close it was unlikely they would be working other than in tandem, and even if they were, what was she going to do, go to them and say, *Hi, which one of you tipped off the guy who planted that delivery truck bomb?*

And then she thought, *Why? Why would anyone do this?*

She couldn't see it. Nothing made sense. A provocation? A false flag? For what? NSA and the rest of the community already had a blank check from Congress. And the FBI was continually creating, and then taking credit for dismantling, Potemkin terror plots that could never have existed without the FBI's assistance. What had that senator once told Harry Truman . . . that the only way to get what he wanted was to "scare hell" out of the American people? Well, that had already been done. What was to be gained by scaring them further?

A thought popped into her head: *Hamilton. Something with Hamilton.*

She tried to make sense of that, but couldn't. Even if there were something . . . untoward going on, even if, in some way she couldn't quite imagine, the director had been involved in Hamilton's kidnapping, what could setting off a bomb in Washington have to do with it?

She was suddenly uncomfortably aware of just how much the director restricted her ability to see, of how limited her vision of things really was. She had a tiny peephole others didn't know about, true, but how much could you really see through a peephole? One part of one room. There could be all sorts of things, all sorts of connections, she would be blind to. And in fact, now that she was really thinking about it, she understood for the first time that she was blind to far more than she could see.

And all those times she was watching other people through her peephole . . . had she ever paused to think about who might be watching her?

She needed to figure out what to tell the director about what she'd just seen. He'd only told her to task the system with data from the jihadist database. That had turned up nothing, and she didn't need to volunteer that she'd done more. If he wanted more, he would ask. In fact, that he *hadn't* asked seemed to suggest he didn't *want* her to find anything, didn't it? Because he'd certainly been eager for her to manually review whatever footage her system could scrape from Istanbul, when he had wanted her to determine whether Hamilton had mailed anything. Why then, but not now?

Okay, then. Tell him you found nothing.

She reached for her mouse to purge the history of the search she had just done. How should she break the news? She would just tell him—

"Any progress, Evie?"

She almost jumped out of her seat. "Jesus!" She turned and saw the director, leaning forward with his hands on his knees, peering at her monitor. She hadn't even heard him come in.

"I'm sorry," he said. "I didn't mean to startle you."

"No, no, sir. I was just . . . really immersed."

"Yes? And have you found anything?"

He could see from her monitor what she was doing—a manual search, not the automated matching. Improvising, she said, "Well, the facial recognition and biometrics were negative, so I decided to try what I did in Istanbul—going through the footage manually."

His expression was inscrutable. "Really?"

"Yes, sir. But . . . I'm not really getting anywhere. It's not like Istanbul. There are a lot of camera networks in metro DC. More than most cities in the world, in fact. So I'm really just searching for a needle in a haystack."

The director nodded, still peering at her monitor. "We need that big haystack, Evie, otherwise how are we going to find the needle?"

"Yes, sir."

He looked at her. "Well? Any sign of it?"

"Sir?"

"The needle."

She almost said no, then realized there might be a way to test him. "I think so, sir, yes."

The inscrutable expression didn't change, but she thought she saw his pupils dilate. He moved his hands from his knees and began massaging his thighs. "Show me."

She backtracked to one of the false positives she'd reviewed. "Well, sir, you see this guy, standing along the truck, lighting a cigarette?"

"Yes, I see him." His tone was just a little curt.

"Well, I didn't like the way he stood there, smoking. It seemed strange. I mean, why not keep walking? And look at how he keeps looking around. It's as though he's watching for someone, maybe waiting for a signal. I know it's thin, but it's just a feeling I had."

"Perhaps," he said, and she could swear he looked almost relieved, "but we know your intuition has been good before. Maybe it'll lead us to a break this time, as well. Did you track him?"

"I did, sir. After the cigarette, he walked east and into this office building, 1700 L Street. So . . . I don't know. Probably it was nothing."

He straightened. "No, no, we don't know that. This is good work. Log the times of his movements and I'll get them to the geolocation people. I doubt we'll get more than a handful of cell phones that were in the spot where he had his cigarette and in that office building at the same times he was. We'll pull his records—Internet browsing history, telephone calls, travel, cell phone movements, everything—and if it turns out he was a nobody, we can at least screen him out and get some peace of mind. Good work."

Yes, he was relieved. She could see it in his face. Relieved the "needle" she had mentioned was anything but, that what she was offering instead was nothing but a distracting piece of hay.

"If it's helpful, sir, I'm glad. Do you want me to keep going? Of course I will if you think it's worthwhile, but I have to say, I've been at this for hours and that's the only thing I've seen that struck me as possibly helpful. There's just so much footage." She had another thought, another way of testing him, and added, "Unless you think it's worth getting some more eyes on this. Creating a grid and dividing the labor."

There was a pause. Was he considering her proposal, or looking for a reason to reject it?

"It's an interesting idea," he said after a moment, "but no. I think the chances of success are too small. And besides, I suspect the case is going to be broken another way, so to speak."

She looked at him, not sure what he meant, and he continued. "Just between us, we've tracked the phones involved with the attack. Phone calls to an area mosque that was already under surveillance. In fact, the FBI has been running a confidential informant from within the mosque's congregation. They're interviewing various members as we speak. Several of them, we've determined, have a history of quite suspicious web-browsing behavior. I expect arrests will be announced in short order."

She nodded, sensing the arrests were what he wanted. That they were *all* he wanted. "That's great news, sir."

"It is indeed. So no need for you to burn the midnight oil. I think on this one, the glory will go to the FBI."

She watched him stroll away. God, that was creepy. The way he'd appeared like some kind of apparition. But maybe it had been good. An opportunity to assess him. And to assure him she'd found nothing.

Haystack, though. She hated that metaphor. How was piling more and more hay on a stack going to help anyone find a needle? What was needed was the equivalent of metal detectors, or magnets, or something. Which was what she'd always tried to do, to find elegant solutions, automated systems for cutting to the signal, not ways of adding ever more noise. And she'd been good at it. She had been. If it hadn't been for her, no one would ever even have known about Perkins and Hamilton, until it had been too late. It wouldn't be her problem now. She wouldn't be faced with . . . with whatever she was faced with.

Which was what, exactly?

Something. Something big and dangerous and involving the director. But beyond that, she didn't know. She was just scared, and felt like she wasn't thinking as clearly as she needed to.

It's okay. You told him you didn't find anything, right?

Right. And besides, how sure could she really be that the bombing had been an inside job? Yes, the director had the means. And, she supposed, the opportunity. But what would be the motive? *Something with Hamilton, maybe* wasn't exactly a motive that would stand up in court, or even to logic.

You told him you didn't find anything. And you're not going to tell him. It's okay. Nothing's going to happen.

She almost believed it. And at the moment, almost felt like enough.

CHAPTER........
........25

Traffic was light on the way from work that evening, many people having stayed home when the news of the bombing had broken that morning. Police cars were all over, though, along with huge black armored police vehicles procured from the military, many of them with gun turrets on top. Helicopters were everywhere, too, and beyond them, she suspected, lurking unseen, surveillance drones, and maybe armed ones, too. She had to pass through several checkpoints manned by soldiers in army combat uniforms, M16s at the ready. It all would have felt surreal in any event, but combined with what she had seen at work earlier it was dizzying, phantasmagoric, something from an exceptionally bad dream.

She had on the radio—local news about two shootings, a burglary, a fire in Anacostia police suspected was arson—but she was only half listening. She was still thinking about her encounter with the director, wondering if she'd assessed things accurately, wondering if she'd managed to give him what he wanted. And then she heard the announcer say, "And this shocking murder: a homeless man, in Congressional Cemetery, with his throat cut. Police suspect a dispute with another man who was sleeping in the cemetery and are questioning suspects."

Her hand flew to her mouth. It couldn't be a coincidence. It had to be him—the man who had stepped behind the truck, and presumably planted the device on it, who had disappeared through the cemetery . . . he had murdered someone there, too. She didn't know why. A chance encounter? Someone who could identify him, who therefore needed to be silenced?

This was important. An important lead. She had to tell someone. She was afraid, but she had to.

The announcer suddenly stopped and said, "This just in. American forces have attacked a terrorist training camp in Azaz, Syria, in retaliation for this morning's horrific bombing in downtown DC. We have reports of drones and cruise missiles. The president will be giving an address from the Oval Office in fifteen minutes. Stay with us and hear it live right here."

The news made her head spin. Hamilton was being held in Syria, right? Of course, he could be anywhere in the country—there was no reason to believe he was in Azaz in particular. Still, it all felt . . . connected. But the connections were so hazy. She could sense, but not see them.

And besides, how could this be the payoff for an inside job, even if the bombing *had* been an inside job? Okay, maybe someone was trying to draw America into Syria's civil war, but there were so many other ways to do it. Maybe if someone started floating the idea that the Syrian government had been behind the bombing that morning, she could accept that there was some kind of conspiracy at work here. But until then, attacking a training camp just wasn't a convincing purpose or motivation.

She was still in the car when the president's address was carried live on the radio. "As many of you have doubtless already heard," he said, "earlier this evening, on my command, the defense forces of the United States carried out drone and cruise missile strikes on a terrorist training compound in northern Syria. Within this compound, our intelligence agencies confirmed, were the terrorists who plotted and directed this morning's barbaric attack on the innocent residents of our nation's capital. These terrorists—now former terrorists—will never again have an opportunity to carry out their atrocities.

"In addition to our military response to this morning's tragedy, the FBI has just arrested several suspects here on American soil. We expect information from these suspects will aid us in preventing other plots, and in neutralizing other terrorists.

"As much as we wish it were otherwise, we must recognize that our intelligence, security, and military forces will never be able to prevent every single attack launched against our nation. But let me be clear. As our response today has shown, for anyone who manages such an attack, or who promotes, plans, or participates in one, you will face American justice. And make no mistake, that justice will be swift. It will be certain. And it will be severe. Thank you, and God bless America."

There was follow-up commentary, but she barely heard it. She didn't like any of it, didn't like it at all. But what did it mean? And anyway, what could she do about it?

At home, she made dinner for Dash, then helped him with his homework. Somehow the routine, being in their apartment, spending time with her beautiful boy, served to settle her. Something was going on, that much was clear, but it was all above her pay grade and there was no reason to believe any of it was going to affect her. She had given no one any reason to worry. Or at least, no *real* reason. She didn't need to decide tonight. She could figure it out in the morning.

Once Dash was in bed, she took a shower, keeping the phone close in case Marvin texted. But he didn't. Well, maybe it had been a bit much to hope he'd get in touch right after returning from his trip. She was worried that he was done, that he wouldn't call her at all. But that was stupid. She had no meaningful data, no way of really knowing.

After her shower, she changed into sweats and poured herself a glass of wine, then sat in the living room with the lights low, just trying to relax and unwind.

She looked at her phone. Maybe she was being stupid, waiting for him to contact her. She hadn't waited for him to make the first move last time, had she? And he certainly hadn't minded when she took the initiative.

The hell with it.

She texted him. *Hey, how was the trip?*

Her phone chimed less than a minute later and her heart leaped. *It was fine. Just got back.*

She stared at the phone, struggling with herself. It was pathetic, how turned on she was just to be texting with him, at the simple prospect of seeing him. The prospect of everything else.

She blew out a long breath. *Still can't stop thinking about it?*

An immediate response: *Yes.*

She shifted on the couch. *Tell me what you've been thinking.*

There was a long pause. She got worried, then remembered how shy he was.

Do you not want to tell me? she texted.

I want to.

But it's hard to say out loud?

I think so.

Her heart was pounding. *Would you rather show me?*

Yes.

Her heart beat harder. *Do you want to show me now?*

Yes.

She felt herself get wet. *How soon?*

Half an hour. Maybe faster.

Good. Hurry.

She finished her wine and stood, surprised at how jittery she felt. She went to the kitchen and put the wineglass in the sink, then started pacing. God, what was she going to do to kill the next thirty minutes?

She peeked in at Dash and was relieved to hear him softly snoring. Then she went to her bedroom and spent a few minutes trying to decide what to wear. The sweats were too casual. But she didn't want to look like she was trying too hard, either. Something she'd naturally be wearing alone in the house, on the one hand, but that would be sexy, on the other. In the end, she settled on a pair of white lace panties, a matching bra, faded jeans, and an old white tee shirt she rarely used for anything but sleeping. The cotton had thinned so much over the years that her bra and her body would be just visible through it. She smiled, wondering if Marvin would be able to look away as much this time as he had the last. She took two condoms from the drawer where she had hidden the pack and put them in a pocket of the jeans. *Don't know where this might happen*, she thought, and a little shiver went through her.

Back in the living room, she tried reading a novel she was enjoying—M. J. Rose's *The Witch of Painted Sorrows*—but had to keep paging back because she couldn't remember the words she had just read. She kept imagining Marvin, coming through the door, his eyes on her face, his hands on her body. Carrying her effortlessly to the couch or her bed and peeling off her clothes and fucking her again like a force of nature.

She went back to the kitchen and turned on the countertop television she liked to watch while preparing meals. More news on CNN about the raid in Syria. She'd had enough of that. She was about to change the channel when the announcer said, "We also have unconfirmed reports that American journalist Ryan Hamilton, kidnapped in Syria by an ISIS splinter group just days ago, has died in the raid."

Oh my fucking God.

She stared at the screen, her hands over her mouth, only partly comprehending. The White House spokesman was saying something about how the terrorists had used Hamilton as a human shield, how they obviously hoped to milk his death for propaganda value, how this was further proof that the terrorists cared nothing for human life. After all, had they not already threatened to decapitate Hamilton, a threat they had carried out on other captives? Implicit in that, some distant part of her mind was aware, was the argument *He was going to die anyway, and horribly. At least we spared him that. And avenged him, as well.*

This was it, then. The director's motive. He had Hamilton kidnapped as a way of concealing his own complicity in the man's death, and something had gone wrong. The kidnappers hadn't killed Hamilton as planned, a rescue had been set in motion, the director got scared and created a kind of casus belli in downtown DC to turn a rescue into an attack.

Why?

She didn't know. She didn't *want* to know. All she could surmise was that Perkins had revealed something to Hamilton so explosive the director had both of them killed.

Please, she thought. *I don't know anything. I haven't done anything. And I won't. Please.*

Immediately a wave of guilt and shame rushed through her. If she hadn't reported what she'd seen to the director, none of this ever would have happened. Hamilton would be alive. Perkins, too. She had caused this. And all she was worried about was herself.

Not yourself. Dash.

Was it true she hadn't done anything? She had lied to the director, and not once, but twice. First, by not telling him about the letter Hamilton had mailed from Istanbul. Second, by telling him she'd seen nothing suspicious in connection with the bombing that morning.

Sins of omission, true, and difficult to prove, but still. She felt she was boxing herself in, somehow, and into what, she didn't know.

So wait until morning. Go to him, tell him you kept looking and found something new. He won't know. Maybe he'll suspect you were holding back, but he won't know. And he'll know you're loyal now, that you're not hiding anything.

But would that solve her problems? Or make them worse?

Think, Evie. You're smart. It's why they hired you. Now think.

She nodded to herself, beginning to see things more clearly now. Going to the director would be a mistake. He obviously didn't want her to find anything—she had seen that when she had tested him earlier. So what was she supposed to do, go to him and effectively say, *Hey, guess what, I'm the only person in the world who has a lead on your inside job, your false flag operation, the one you ginned up to finish off Hamilton, but don't worry, I promise not to tell anyone?*

She thought of the letter she had seen Hamilton send himself from Istanbul. Could she do something with that? She wasn't even sure what was inside the envelope. A thumb drive, probably. And probably encrypted.

She thought of Scott Stiles, hanged in his apartment. Of Perkins, killed in a car crash. Of Hamilton, kidnapped the very day Perkins died. How hard would it be for someone to arrange the same for her?

And then she thought of Dash again, and her throat closed up. What would happen to him?

For years she'd been shielding herself from the knowledge of how little backup she had. Sean didn't want to take care of his deaf son. He couldn't even sign, had never bothered to learn. The idea of Dash being pulled out of the school he loved, the school he was thriving in, horrified her. Where would he go? Who would he live with? Her father, in the senior-care facility? Half the time he didn't even recognize his own grandson. And what would happen to her poor father, anyway? What would the facility do with him if there was no one to pay the bills? She thought of *Soylent Green* and covered her mouth, half wanting to laugh, half to cry.

She had to figure out a way out of this. But she didn't even know what she was *in*.

Her phone vibrated and she glanced at it: *I'm here.*

Marvin. She blew out a few quick breaths. She had to pull herself together.

She turned the lights low and buzzed him in. A minute later, there was a soft knock. She checked through the peephole, then opened the door, closing it behind him.

He didn't sign. He just stood there, looking at her, and the hunger she saw in his expression, the way his eyes went from her body to her face and back again, made her forget her panic. She pushed him back against the door, took his head in her hands, brought his face to hers, and started kissing him. She felt his tongue in her mouth, his hands on her breasts, and it was good, it was right, it was making everything else go away.

She ran her hand down over his crotch, and when she felt how hard he was it made her moan into his mouth. She undid his belt and started to unbutton his jeans, but before she got them open he spun her around and put her back against the door. He swept the tee shirt up and she lifted her arms over her head so he could get it off. But he left it tangled around her forearms, pushed her wrists up against the door with one hand, and with the other reached around and unclipped her bra. And then he was rubbing his thumb between her legs, and she writhed from the pleasure of it and tried to move her arms but he wouldn't let her, and then he was kissing her again and still touching her, and the way he was holding her like that and doing what he wanted and not letting her touch him was so hot she couldn't stand it, and she needed him inside her, needed it to push back everything else, everything that had happened, to make it all unreal. She whispered *Please . . . please* into his mouth, knowing he couldn't hear the words but hoping he could feel them. And maybe he did, because he released her arms and pulled off the tee shirt and bra, and she got out a condom just as he pushed her pants down past her knees, her panties coming with them, and she stripped off his shirt while he got off his own pants, and he pushed her back against the door again and slid a finger into her wetness and oh, yes, that was so good, and she struggled to get the condom open and she managed to slide it onto him, and she wrapped her fingers around his cock and squeezed and she felt him shudder, and she guided him forward and he pushed inside her, and it hurt but she was pinned against the door and she couldn't move away from it, and he thrust again, thrust hard, and again, and again, and it hurt so good, so good, this was what she needed, God yes, and there was a short set of drawers next to the door, and she lifted one leg and put her foot on top, and he pushed deeper into her and she moaned again, and he put a finger in her mouth and she sucked on it, and then his hands were on her ass, cupping her, gripping her, bringing her into him in time with his thrusts, and she was close, she was so close, and she fucked him back, and then she felt his wet finger slide into her ass and she gasped and she fucked him harder, and she felt his cock swell and jump and then she was coming, and coming, even as he came, too.

When it was done, she lowered her leg to the floor and sagged against him, and he put his arms around her and held her. His touch was gentle but she could feel his strength, and she sensed how conscious he was of it, how careful to hold it back. Except when he couldn't. And that was such a nice thought.

She looked up and realized what Dash was going to see if he woke to use the bathroom. The thought of him brought it all back, the craziness, the disbelief, the fear, and suddenly she was crying, crying hard. Marvin signed, *What is it?* But she just shook her head and pulled him close, needing to feel him holding her, needing to get it out.

After a minute, she had it under control again. She nodded toward Dash's room and signed, *We should get dressed.*

Marvin just looked at her. *Did I hurt you?*

The concern in the question, and in his expression, was lovely. She signed, *No. The opposite.*

Then what?

Let's get dressed first.

They pulled on their clothes and each used the bathroom. In the kitchen, she asked, *Can I get you something to drink?*

Just water. Thanks.

She poured them each a glass and they sat at the table.

He looked at her for a moment, then signed, *Is everything okay?*

She didn't even know what to say. Probably it was better to say nothing. But even in the midst of whatever she was dealing with, she didn't want him to think she was crazy. Or so weak that she cried at just anything. Or a sad fuck. Or whatever.

It's . . . a work thing. Hard to explain.

You can't talk because it's secret?

Right.

But it's bad?

I . . . saw something I don't think I was supposed to see. And I'm afraid of what they're going to do about it.

What could they do?

That's what I'm worried about.

Fire you?

She had to laugh at that. *Yes, you could put it that way.*

He furrowed his brow. *What, then?*

She shook her head. *I don't know. I'm just scared. I don't know what to do. Who to talk to.*

You can talk to me.

She looked at him, and realized she almost could have. But what could he do? He was from another world. *Thank you. I just need to think things through.*

Is there someone at work you could talk to?

In theory. But . . . it's complicated.

He nodded. *Okay, I'm sorry for pressing.*

No, it's okay. It feels good to talk about it just a little. I'm sorry I can't say more.

I'm sorry I can't help more.

You helped me by coming over tonight. A lot.

He smiled. *You helped me, too.*

They sat wordlessly for a few minutes. Then she signed, *I want to ask you to stay. And Dash really likes you, but I think that would be too much right now.*

I understand. Are you going to be okay?

I'll figure it out. She hoped the way she signed it showed more conviction than she felt.

She walked him to the door. He kissed her, the kiss oddly tentative after the passion of just a short while earlier. Then he signed, *I'm glad you texted me, Evie.*

She smiled. *I think that's the first time you've said my name, Marvin. I like your name.*

She looked at his handsome face, the strange sadness she sensed behind his eyes, the reluctance, and realized she could almost jump him again. But no. It would be too easy to have him stay over. And she wasn't ready to explain all that to Dash.

I'm glad. I could get used to you saying it.

There was a pause, then he signed, *Good night, Evie.*

CHAPTER....... 26

After he was gone, she fell into bed and surprised herself by passing out almost instantly. But she woke in a panic a short while later, the comfort and distraction of Marvin's visit gone, the reality of what she was facing fully upon her again.

But she'd told the director she'd seen nothing, hadn't she? And she'd tested him, but she hadn't pressed. She'd been subtle. She'd been clever. She'd figured out he *wanted* her to see nothing, and she'd told him what he wanted to hear.

Yeah? How sure are you that he didn't know *you were testing him? That he doesn't suspect the guy with the cigarette you showed him was a distraction? That your question about bringing in more manpower for a manual review of the footage was a feint? Given what he's already done, given the stakes he's playing for, how much can you count on his assuming you didn't see anything, you don't suspect, you don't fucking* know?

She focused on breathing again, trying to slow her staccato heartbeat.

Stop it. This is crazy. The director isn't going to kill you. There are no conspiracies. The Parallax View *was a movie. This is real life.*

She imagined Stiles, and Perkins, and Hamilton, all telling themselves the same thing. Downplaying the threat, embracing denial, believing the world was what they wanted it to be, refusing to see it for what it really was.

And then dying. Because they didn't know what the director knew. Couldn't see what he saw. And so couldn't anticipate the fate he decided for them.

No. She wasn't going to let that happen to her. She wasn't going to let it happen to Dash. How was sticking her head in the sand supposed to protect him?

But what could she do? Go to the inspector general? Congress? The media?

The first two, she knew, would be worse than useless. Everyone understood what happened to whistleblowers who tried to work through the system. All you had to do was ask Bill Binney, or Thomas Drake, or Chelsea Manning, or Diane Roark, or Coleen Rowley, or Jeffrey Sterling, or Thomas Tamm, or Russell Tice, or Kirk Wiebe. And look what they'd done to John Kiriakou—for exposing torture, for God's sake. Not to mention Snowden, whose concerns had been suppressed until he took them public. And Jesselyn Radack, the whistleblower lawyer who represented probably half of them.

Which left the media, maybe, but the thought of being prosecuted under the Espionage Act terrified her. How could she afford to fight something like that? Even if she didn't wind up in prison for life, they'd ruin her. And who would take care of Dash while she was being held incommunicado as some kind of enemy combatant? How would he cope with something like that?

And besides, even if she were prepared to go to the media, what did she have? She could document a meeting between Hamilton and Perkins, but so what? The rest could be dismissed as coincidence. She could reveal the existence of the camera networks and the facial recognition and biometrics system, but if none of the programs Snowden had leaked had been egregious enough to protect him, hers would be no better. And if she showed her footage of the suspicious man she had discovered in connection with that morning's attack, it would probably *bolster* support for her camera initiative, not undercut it. Beyond which, she would be crucified for revealing sources and methods related to an ongoing terrorism investigation, the terrorism in question being extremely fresh in people's minds. They'd bay for her blood.

God. She had nothing. And no one to take it to, either. The bombing was an inside job, the attack in response was a lie, and she was the only one who knew it. And if the director knew she knew . . .

She thought of the letter Hamilton had mailed from Istanbul. She'd been so freaked out at her own temerity in not telling the director about it that she'd half decided to just pretend it didn't exist, that she'd never seen the footage of Hamilton mailing it.

But she *had* seen it. And presumably it was sitting in that mail drop in Rockville right now. What was in it? Something that would give her some answers, some ammunition, some leverage?

Whatever was in that envelope, it scared the director so much he had killed to keep it secret. Which meant it was something explosive. *Really* explosive. Something connected with Hamilton. Whatever it was, if it were revealed, the director would no longer have any reason to come after her. His secret would be out.

But what if he knows it was you? You might just go from one motive—ensuring silence—to another—revenge.

Well, that was a chance worth taking. She had once seen a cartoon—a hawk swooping down on a mouse. The mouse was completely outmatched, obviously helpless, doomed. So it did the only thing it could: it extended its arm and gave the hawk the finger. A final expression of dignity and defiance.

Maybe she was that mouse. Up against something she could never hope to defeat. But she wouldn't just lay down. She would fight.

And besides, if she handled things right, how would the director, how would anyone, know it had been her? She couldn't use email, she knew—NSA monitored the accounts of every journalist it considered a threat, which meant every journalist worth contacting. But Hamilton's organization, the *Intercept*, used SecureDrop, an encrypted system NSA hadn't yet found a way to crack. She could upload details directly using Tails and Tor, an operating system and a browser NSA had so far found similarly impenetrable. No emails, no phone calls, no secret meetings, nothing. Whatever was in that envelope, Hamilton had sent it. Yes, presumably whatever Hamilton had learned from Perkins in their face-to-face meetings was intended to inform his reporting, and that benefit was now gone. But the information alone could still protect her. She would just be . . . forwarding it. Anonymously.

But what if, whatever it was, Hamilton had encrypted it?

One thing at a time, supersleuth.

Right. Okay. She was going to get that letter. Decrypt whatever Hamilton had sent, somehow, if she needed to. And get it to the *Intercept* anonymously after that.

Or at least try. She couldn't control those other things. But she wasn't going to live in denial. Or die in it.

She glanced at the clock on the nightstand. It was two in the morning, but she was way too wired to sleep. And besides, she had a lot of planning to do. She was about to become an insider threat, up against the world's best-funded and most paranoid intelligence organization. An organization that had destroyed the life of every whistleblower who had ever challenged it.

Except for Snowden.

Yes, Snowden. She'd long suspected plenty of people inside the organization admired what he'd done, and the courage he'd shown in doing it, though of course no one would ever acknowledge something like that out loud. And what was that expression of his, the one that made the brass crazy? *Courage is contagious.* She'd always thought it was a bit silly, but sitting alone in her bed in the wee hours of the morning, facing what was ahead of her, she realized it was true.

And thank God, too. Because at that moment, her own courage didn't feel like nearly enough.

CHAPTER . . . .
. . . . 27

Manus drove east toward Baltimore/Washington International Airport, severely disturbed. He couldn't understand what had just happened. The director had told him to stop seeing Evie because she had checked out, she wasn't a problem, there was nothing to worry about. Okay, fine. But none of it was true. The woman was obviously distraught, terrified, oppositional—all the things the director had tasked him with discovering. So why had the director pulled him off? What was going on?

He parked the truck in a motel complex near the airport and got out, needing to walk, to get some fresh air, to think. The periphery of a motel parking lot was a good place to leave a car at night—numerous transient vehicles, no registration, people coming and going at odd hours after arriving from or departing for a flight. He had a pair of stolen plates no one was going to report hidden in the truck's toolbox—you never knew when you might need a little privacy—but judged that kind of precaution unnecessary at the moment. No one was going to notice one more vehicle here, much less remember it, much less report it. Not that it mattered anyway—he was here for a walk, not on an op—but he liked to keep good habits, especially when he was feeling anxious.

There were some woods behind the parking lot and he headed into them, wanting the dark, the feeling of being enclosed and enveloped. The oppressive heat of the day had dissipated, and the air in the woods was cool and soothing, city smells momentarily eclipsed by leaves and bark and earth. He made his way by the diffused light of the nearby highway and office parks until he came to a thick stump. He sat on it, breathed deeply in and out, and tried to figure out what the hell was going on.

Why would he pull me off? It was going well. Better than he could have expected. The meeting at the baseball game, the invitation to her apartment . . . he should have wanted me to keep going. What happened?

All right, true, he hadn't told the director everything. The way the woman made him feel when he looked at her. The way her relationship with the boy somehow conjured a forgotten part of his own life. And what had happened that night after the boy had gone to sleep . . . no, he hadn't told the director any of that. But how could it have been relevant? If anything, it was all a way of getting closer, of finding out what the director wanted to know.

But it didn't feel that way to you.

No. The truth was, none of it felt like what he was supposed to be doing for the director. In fact, the director had told him to steer clear of the woman, and yet Manus had gone to see her anyway. He hadn't meant to. He'd thought about little other than contacting her since getting back from Turkey, but he didn't because he knew the director didn't want him to. But then, when she'd sent him that text, and asked him if he still couldn't stop thinking about it, he just . . . he couldn't help himself.

He closed his eyes, and remembered the way she'd looked at him just a couple of hours earlier, like she'd been . . . craving him, or something. The way she'd pushed him back against the door and kissed him. The way he'd kissed her back. The taste of her skin. How it had excited her when he'd touched her. The way he could feel her moaning into his mouth while he was moving inside her.

He was getting hard from the memory and shook the images away. It didn't matter what had happened. Because how would the director know any of it? After all, it wasn't as though he could have seen—

It hit him then. Hit him so hard that for a moment, he couldn't breathe.

The director had black-bagged her apartment. Sound, low-light video, everything. Of course he had. What had he said? *I don't want to leave anything out.* What did that mean? Was it even *conceivable* the director would be as concerned as he obviously was—so concerned he wanted Manus to spend time with the woman and personally assess her—and at the same time not make sure he knew every single thing that happened inside her apartment?

Stupid. Stupid. Stupid.

For one moment, the notion—the image—of the director watching what had happened between him and the woman filled him with rage. The director had no right. It wasn't his business.

He breathed deeply in and out, willing it away. Of course he had a right. He knew things Manus didn't. And wasn't the director the one who told Manus to watch the woman as part of an operation? What was the director supposed to do, look away if Manus forgot himself, forgot why he was with the woman, let his own stupidity jeopardize an operation Manus didn't even understand?

He realized the director would have watched everything tonight, too. All of it, from the moment Manus walked through the door. Again, the rage gripped him.

Calm down, calm down, calm down.

The woman. Why hadn't she just left him alone? He was only supposed to watch her. He wasn't going to hurt her. Or her son. But she had asked him to come over, and to stay for dinner, and he'd tried not to, but it would have looked strange, and he was supposed to get close to her anyway, wasn't he? And then she'd given him wine, and asked him why he wouldn't look at her, and she'd unbuttoned her shirt, and—

Why do you think I wouldn't look at you? Because of this! This! Look what you caused!

He was suddenly frightened. What was he going to do? The director knew he'd been dishonest. First, in not telling everything that had happened. And second, in disobeying, disobeying that very evening.

Could he know about Hamilton? That you saw him and didn't tell?

His heart started hammering in growing panic.

Calm down, calm down, calm down, CALM DOWN.

He took a deep breath and blew it slowly out. Again. And again.

Why did he pull you off?

Yes, that was the question. The heart of it.

Because he knew you were dishonest. He knew he couldn't trust you anymore.

He stood and started pacing. What had happened? When had he started lying to the director? When he'd seen Hamilton in the van, that was when. It had been a mistake. The man was so messed up, it would have been merciful to kill him. It would have been good for everyone. He imagined himself closing the van door, placing the muzzle firmly against the base of Hamilton's skull, pressing the trigger, the man's head jerking forward from the shot . . . and he groaned aloud at the terrible mistake he'd made, the opportunity he'd lost.

He'd fucked up. He'd let Hamilton live. And he'd never told the director. That was a lie. And one lie had led to another. And now he was just . . . he didn't know. Ashamed. Angry. Alone. Afraid. And he didn't know how to make things better.

He continued along through the woods and emerged into another parking lot, this one behind a 7-Eleven. A white pickup was parked in the far corner, its engine idling, tobacco smoke drifting from the open windows. Manus knew his presence here was completely random and he wasn't unduly concerned. Still, he glanced over as he crossed the parking lot and saw two men sitting inside. They both had long hair and were wearing baseball caps. They eyed him as he passed. He didn't like them.

Halfway across the lot, he glanced back at the truck. The men had gotten out. Tee shirts, jeans, heavy work boots. Truckers or day laborers, he guessed. They were coming toward him. Their hands were empty. One of them was saying something—*Hey, buddy*, maybe? The light was too dim for Manus to be sure.

Manus checked his surroundings. There was no one else around. He stopped and watched them. They didn't look like pros. More like opportunists. Just idling here in the 7-Eleven parking lot because the bars were closed, they had no money for girls, they needed more cigarettes. They were broke, they were bored, they saw an opportunity for quick cash or at least a little entertainment. Or both.

He watched them, waiting. Mostly, people left him alone because of his size, his demeanor. But sometimes he would run into someone who was too drunk, or too desperate, or too stupid to know better. And sometimes he would run into someone for whom a big man was a challenge, as though size itself was a personal insult that could be neither overlooked nor forgiven. Most of these people, when they came in for a closer look, he could warn off with a smile. People didn't like his smile. These men looked like that type. He felt himself wanting to smile, and decided not to.

They weren't even spreading out to make it more difficult to drop them. Probably they found nearness comforting, even two against one. He took note of the metal clip he saw in each of their right front pockets. Folding knives, and each man right-handed. Of course he was carrying the Espada himself, but thought he'd prefer the Force Pro tonight. He'd left it in the truck when he'd gone to see

Evie, but he was carrying it now. He stepped back with his right leg, bladed his body, and rested his right fist against his hip, inches from the grip of the gun. They didn't even notice the move, or understand what it might mean.

They stopped a few feet away from him. "Hey, man," the one to Manus's left said. His tee shirt had a big smiley face on it. "Why don't you answer when we call out to you?"

Manus looked at him, then at the other, whose tee shirt bore a large, faded print of an American flag, then back to Smiley. "I didn't hear you."

Smiley looked at Flag, then back to Manus. "What are you, deaf?"

One of Manus's instructors at the CIA's Military Operations Training Course had taught him there were five rules for avoiding impending street violence: *Don't challenge him, don't insult him, don't threaten him, don't deny it's happening, give him a face-saving exit.* Manus had learned the rules the hard way in the institutions he'd grown up in, but being more conscious of them helped him commit fewer violations. And only when he wanted to.

The way he did right now.

He looked Smiley up and down and said, "You must be the brains of the operation."

Smiley glanced at Flag again. Flag nodded. The nod said, *Yeah. Good to go.*

Their hands went to their pockets. Manus brought out the Force Pro, quick as a magic trick, simultaneously stepping offline to his right to line up the men more neatly while creating extra distance between their right hands and himself. He pointed the muzzle at Flag's face and said, "Anything comes out of those pockets and you're dead right there."

The men froze and stared at him. Their hands drifted away from their sides, the fingers splayed. From the way they complied, Manus had the sense they'd been rousted by cops before and knew the drill.

Smiley glanced at Flag, then back to Manus. "Hey, man, we were just—"

"You're under arrest. Use your left hands to take those knives out. I'd do it very slowly if I were you. Just ease them out and drop them."

"Under arrest?" Flag said. "Come on, man, we were just—"

"You can either comply," Manus said, "or I will shoot you."

Of course the situation was odd. A deaf cop? Alone, on foot, not calling for backup? And not producing a badge? But there were always anomalies. The trick was to maintain the pressure, to keep things moving too fast for someone's brain to catch up to his gut.

Smiley looked at Flag. When Flag reached across with his left hand, eased the knife out, and dropped it, Smiley did the same.

"Now step backward. Two long steps."

The men complied. Manus kicked the knives away.

"Now on your knees, hands laced behind your necks."

Flag laced his fingers together and got on his knees, and Smiley followed suit. Smiley was obviously the beta. Without Flag to show him the way, he'd hesitate, maybe even freeze. That suggested the proper order of operations.

Manus moved counterclockwise, going behind them. He switched the Force Pro to his left hand, and with his right removed a flashlight from his pocket—a SureFire Defender Ultra, close to six inches of mil-spec hard-anodized aluminum, with a sharp, crenelated bezel and tailcap. A great tool.

"Knees wide. Wider. Lace those fingers tight."

To men of their apparent experience, it would feel like the familiar dance steps of being handcuffed. So Flag was probably surprised, or would have been, anyway, when Manus stepped in, brought the Defender high, and hammer-fisted the crenelated bezel into the top of the man's head, caving his skull into his brain.

Flag pitched forward without a sound. Smiley turned his head and watched, his face aghast, trying to process what had just happened. Manus didn't give him time. He put his boot heel into the back of Smiley's laced fingers and stepped through hard, blasting Smiley's face into the pavement. Smiley gave a muffled cry and managed to unlace his hands. He got them on the ground to push himself up, but before he could, Manus stomped the back of his neck again, crushing it.

He looked around. The area was still deserted. He glanced down at the two men. Neither was moving, not even a twitch. He clicked the Defender's tail cap and the light came on. But there was tissue and hair around the lens. He'd have to replace it.

He would have liked to walk more, but obviously now he needed to leave. And besides, though his heart rate was up from adrenaline, his mind felt clearer. He was glad the men had wanted to hurt him. It was what he needed. He walked back across the parking lot and into the dark of the woods, where he wiped down and buried the Defender.

Back in his truck, he headed northwest toward his apartment in Ellicott City. Even at that hour, there were plenty of other cars on I-95, and there was nothing about his pickup or his driving that anyone would find memorable. He kept to the speed limit, just a workman getting an early start, on the way to a job in Baltimore or Frederick or Hagerstown. He saw no one and no one saw him.

He tried to think things through again. And realized there was only one chance. One hope. He had to do now what he should have done the first time. Go to the director, and tell him everything. Everything that had happened, everything he had done.

And pray the director would forgive him.

CHAPTER . . . .
. . . . 28

Evie arrived at the Walgreens on Twin Knolls Road at just before seven, a few minutes before they opened. She had called Digne at five, apologizing for waking her but could Digne come early and take care of Dash? An emergency at work.

The problem was that she didn't know what time the mailbox place in Rockville opened. Seven? Eight? Later? Later than eight and she wouldn't be able to get there before work, and she didn't want to try to go later because she thought it would be emptiest in the morning, and empty was going to be critical for what she had planned. She'd sat down at her computer to check, and realized a search would leave a trail. She might have called the store and gotten the information from the store's recorded message, but that would have created a trail, too. It was bizarre to be so stymied on something so basic, but she had become reliant on the Internet and her cell phone for almost everything. She considered the payphone at the mall, but she'd heard rumors that DEA monitored every public phone in the DC area. An Apple Store or an Internet café? Maybe, but that was a one-off. What if she needed a secure means for something after that?

What about a prepaid smartphone?

Right . . . what television drug dealers called a burner. Flexible and anonymous. She could pay cash, use the burner to access the Internet and make any calls she needed, and dispose of it when she was done. Nothing that could ever be traced back to her.

She was waiting outside the doors when a store employee unlocked them, and was back in her car less than ten minutes after that. She pulled the packaging off the prepaid and was about to activate it when she paused, horrified. She had her own cell phone with her—if she turned on the burner and then drove off, the two would move in sync and enable someone to determine who had just bought the "anonymous" phone.

Only if they're looking, Evie. Only if they're looking.

But she had to assume they *were* looking now. Security through obscurity was no longer an option.

She realized she should have turned off her own phone until she was done with everything she had to do. But . . . she could turn it off now, head toward Rockville, activate the burner when she was close, turn the burner off as soon as she had the information she needed, then turn on her own phone again when she was back on her normal route to the office. Not perfect, but still pretty good.

What if they track the burner back to its point of purchase?

She supposed that was possible. But so many things would have to go wrong for them to be looking for the burner. And even if they found it and tried to get a match, there must have been hundreds of phones in the vicinity of the Walgreens when the unit had been purchased. Maybe now that she'd thought the whole thing through properly, it would have been better to do it later, but with everything going on she didn't know when she'd get another chance.

A little weird, your phone just going dark and then coming back online, no?

Yeah, that would look a little weird.

She got out of the car and looked around. There was a gap between the parking lot curb and the grass. She switched her phone to silent and slid it into the gap. There. Unlikely it would be discovered in the next hour or so. Even if it were, someone might return it to the store's lost-and-found. And if not? She must have dropped it somewhere, and someone carried it off. It happened.

She turned back to the car, then hesitated.

Sure you don't want to wait until tomorrow morning? Better to do it right, no?

It was a seductive thought. Too seductive. It was the thought of someone in denial, someone who wanted to believe she had all the time in the world when in fact she might have very little.

What about the cameras? There would be store footage from when the phone was purchased.

She'd have to live with the risk. But she thought it was manageable. She was in charge of the system, after all. Any requests to query it would go through her. She could decide how to deal with it at that point.

She headed south. Once she turned onto Route 28, she felt she was far enough from where she'd left her phone to activate the burner. She turned it on, called the 800 number, read them the purchase code, and a minute later was Googling the shipping center in Rockville.

If Dash ever surfs while driving, I'll kill him. But she didn't have time to pull over.

The store opened at eight. Thank God. The morning rush-hour traffic wasn't great, but she had a good shot of getting there not much after that, and maybe earlier. With luck, she'd be the only customer, at least for a few minutes. She powered down the phone and fought the urge to go through every red light she hit.

The store was in a strip mall that occupied the first floor of an office building. She went past, pulled into an adjacent townhouse lot, and parked. She looked at herself in the rearview mirror.

Come on, Evie. You can do this.

She unbuttoned an extra button on her blouse and spread the collar wide. She checked the mirror again, nodded in satisfaction, and headed out. She was at the door even as the employee inside, a college-age guy in a brown company shirt, was unlocking it. She caught him stealing a glance at her cleavage from the other side of the glass and thought, *Okay, good.*

"Morning," the kid said as she strolled in past him. She sensed his eyes on her legs.

"Morning," she said, turning to give him an appreciative smile. He was actually kind of cute. Which was good. She didn't think she was much of an actress, and the less she had to strain for the right performance, the better.

The kid straightened and tried to return the keys to his pocket, but kept missing. He blushed, glanced down, got them in, and looked up at her. "Something to mail, or . . . ?"

She started walking toward the counter, her head sweeping back and forth. Mailboxes on the left wall; copying machine and shipping supplies on the right. Counter and cash register alongside the mailboxes. "Actually," she said over her shoulder, "I was thinking about renting a box."

He hurried to catch up with her. "Sure, of course. Well, as you can see, we have three sizes. All different prices, of course."

They paused in front of the mailboxes. She scanned them left to right, then down . . . there, 406, Hamilton's box. As far from the counter as possible, naturally. But still. It was right there.

The large boxes were at the bottom, and she leaned forward as though examining them. She noted the kid enjoying the view. "I think a big one would be best for me," she said, hoping the double entendre wouldn't be too over the top.

"Uh, sure. The big ones aren't as popular, so we have plenty. Are you looking for a month-to-month, or something longer term . . . ?"

She straightened and walked over to the counter. "Do you have any literature?"

"Sure, I can give you a brochure," he said, heading around to the other side of the counter. "Or, it's all on the Internet. Whatever you like."

"Oh, a brochure would be great. And you are . . . ?"

"Hugh," the kid said, with an automatic glance at the name badge on his shirt. She had already noticed it, but wanted to keep him talking.

She offered her hand. "Hugh, I'm Jane. Nice to meet you."

He smiled and shook her hand quickly, almost nervously. "Nice to meet you, too. Here, let me get you one of those brochures."

"Thanks. And Hugh, would you mind if I used your restroom?"

The kid glanced around as though she had offered to sell him drugs and federal agents might be watching. "Uh, it's not really for customers . . ."

She smiled. "Well, it's just the two of us in the store, right?"

"Yeah, but my boss will be here soon."

"If I promise to be fast? Less than a minute, honest."

He peered over at the entrance, then gestured to a door behind the counter on his left. "Um, okay. Right over there."

"Thanks. I promise not to tell."

She headed past him and closed the door behind her. Damn it, she really did need to pee. Well, all right, that would make it even more realistic. She pulled her skirt up and her panties down and sat. While she peed, she took all the paper from the dispenser to her right and rolled it up into a large ball. When she was done, she stood, fixed her clothes, dropped the rolled-up paper into the bowl, and flushed.

There was a loud rush of water, and the bolus of paper was instantly sucked away.

She blinked and looked at the toilet, dumbfounded at the power of the thing. That ball of paper would have choked the one in her apartment. *What the hell kind of plumbing is this? Rocket-powered?*

She glanced around the room. A few cleaning items, boxes of shipping supplies, a row of cabinets. She tried the cabinets. They were locked.

Oh my God, who locks restroom cabinets? Is someone going to steal the toilet paper?

She looked around again. She didn't see a spare roll.

You have got to be kidding me.

This was bad. She needed more paper to make this work.

You should have brought your own. You shouldn't have assumed. Stupid, stupid, stupid.

She looked behind the toilet. Nothing.

Come on, come on, think of something. Improvise.

She had a tampon in her purse. She pulled it out and got the wrapping off. It looked woefully inadequate—she figured this toilet could vacuum down three at least, maybe four.

She rifled through her purse and found one more, and a travel-size package of tissues, too. She balled it all together. Close, but it didn't look like a sure thing.

All right. She slid her panties down over her shoes, wrapped them around the tampons and the tissue, and jammed the entire mass into the mouth of the toilet bowl until it would absolutely go no further. Then she took a deep breath and flushed. A tremendous sound came from deep in the toilet, a vacuum, a roar, an angry dragon. But the blockage held. The bowl began to fill rapidly, and in seconds it was overflowing.

Evie shook the water off her hand and forearm and opened the door. "Oh, my goodness," she said, "I think your toilet is overflowing!"

For a second, the kid was paralyzed and did nothing but gape. Then he rushed to the bathroom.

The instant he was past her, she strode to the sorting area behind the mailboxes, her heart hammering. The back was numbered just like the front. Well, of course it was, how else would they know how to sort the mail? She scanned—404, 405, there it was, 406. With a single envelope inside, the very one she had watched Hamilton mail from Istanbul.

She heard the entrance door chime—someone was coming in. She grabbed the letter, shoved it in her purse, and raced back to the counter. She reached the area behind it, and saw a tall man with dark, Brylcreemed hair straight out of the fifties closing the door behind him. He was wearing a brown shirt identical to Hugh's—the boss, apparently. Her heart went into overdrive and she fought to keep her breathing steady.

"Hi there," she said with a bright smile.

The boss stared at her suspiciously. "What are you doing back there?"

Shit, had he seen her emerge from behind the mailboxes?

She said the first thing she could think of: "Oh, just looking for one of the brochures Hugh mentioned. About the mailboxes. He's in the bathroom. I think—"

On cue, the kid emerged from the bathroom, holding a damp pair of panties. "I think this is what—" he started to say, then saw his boss and froze.

The boss frowned. His eyes went from the panties to the generous amount of cleavage revealed above her additional undone blouse button. He shook his head in disdain and disbelief. "What the hell do you think you're doing, Hugh?"

The kid blinked. "I, I didn't, I just . . ."

Come on, Evie, you need to get out of here. Now.

She walked over, retrieved the panties, dropped them primly in her purse, and kissed the kid on the cheek. "Thank you, Hugh," she said. "You were great."

The kid stood there, stupefied. She walked past the boss, who was equally nonplussed.

"It wasn't his fault," she said. "I took advantage."

She was out the door before he could even respond, and back on the road only a minute later, breathing hard, giddy. She'd done it. She'd done it. She couldn't believe it. She'd just . . . done it. She'd gotten the letter. Right under their noses, she'd gone in and taken it. And with just a bit of luck on the traffic, she'd be at Fort Meade in less than an hour, no one the wiser. And didn't she deserve a little luck, after that beast of a toilet?

She got the giggles. And just as she wrestled them under control, she imagined herself whispering to the director, *Oh, and I'm not wearing panties, either*, and broke up again so hard she almost had to pull over.

Okay, girl. Okay. Take it easy now. The hard part's done.

At a red light, she opened the envelope. Inside were two strips of cardboard. In between them was a thumb drive. Almost certainly encrypted.

What was that about the hard part being done?

Well, she worked at NSA. If she couldn't figure out how to decrypt a damn thumb drive, she'd practically be a disgrace to the organization. She knew a few people. She'd find someone who could help her. Tell them it was a personal issue. A cheating boyfriend who was hiding things from her and who she was checking up on, something like that. The practice of illicitly using NSA tools to monitor romantic interests was widespread enough that employees even had a jokey word for it: LOVEINT. The thought of bringing the thumb drive directly into the belly of the beast was unnerving, but she'd never been searched before and there was no reason to think today would be the first time. And even if she were mistaken, so what? She'd found an encrypted thumb drive and wanted to see what was on it. Thin, okay, but better than nothing. The main thing, though, was that it was unlikely ever even to come up.

She drove back to the Walgreens to retrieve her phone, tearing up the envelope and letting the pieces fly out the window en route. She thought of the *Intercept*, of SecureDrop.

Something occurred to her, something she realized she should have thought of sooner.

Would Hamilton have shared the encryption passphrase with anyone at the Intercept?

Maybe, if he had an "in case something happens to me" mentality. Maybe not, if he had a more paranoid mentality.

But there was a chance. She'd have to find a way to ask someone who worked there, though, and she had no idea how she was going to do that quickly and securely. But it was something.

Someone at NSA, or someone at the *Intercept*. Ironic that the help would have to come from one or the other, but she couldn't think of anything else. It didn't matter. Whatever was on that thumb drive, she had to access it. She didn't know how much time she had. What she did know was that if the director got wind of what she was up to, she probably had no time at all.

CHAPTER . . . .
. . . . 29

Anders ushered Manus into his office with the usual courtesy. He'd received an odd text from Manus in the middle of the night: *Please can I see you. I did something wrong.* Anders had a good idea of what that something was, and if Manus felt the need to unburden himself, Anders would be pleased to take his confession.

"Marvin," he said, after they were both seated on opposite sides of Anders's desk. "What's on your mind?"

Manus looked down and twisted his hands in his lap, the picture of guilt. Then he said, "I saw the woman again. Even though you told me not to."

Yes, Anders knew very well that Manus had seen her again. He'd watched all of it, and indeed was already having a transcription prepared by someone fluent in American Sign Language.

"Why, Marvin?"

Manus reddened. "When I went to her apartment the first time, I stayed for dinner."

"Yes, you told me."

"But I didn't tell you about afterward. Her son went to sleep, and, and . . ."

There was a pause. Anders said, "Oh. I think I understand."

Manus looked at him, his expression an odd amalgam of dread and hope. "You do?"

"Are you telling me something happened between the two of you? Something . . . sexual?"

Manus looked down and nodded.

Anders steepled his fingers and waited. When Manus had looked up again, Anders said, "Why didn't you tell me at the time?"

"I didn't think it mattered."

"Well, it might not have. But it's better if I make those decisions, Marvin, not you."

Manus nodded again, his shoulders slumped. The man looked so forlorn, Anders almost wanted to comfort him.

"Especially in this instance," Anders said. "I asked you to get close to her, remember? And you exceeded my expectations! If you'd told me, I would have been proud of you. And in fact, I am proud of you. Other than that you felt you had to conceal something from me."

"I'm sorry. She texted me. Last night. And I went to her. Because . . . because . . ."

"Yes, I think I can understand why you went to her. She's an attractive woman."

"I didn't think it would matter because you told me she was all right, that you trusted her. But then, last night, she told me something."

Anders felt a surge of intense interest, along with goodwill and relief. This was what he needed. Information. And beyond that, Manus—not just confessing the relationship to get out of trouble, but truly demonstrating where his loyalties lay. He leaned forward. "And what was that?"

"She was upset. Crying. She said she saw something at work she wasn't supposed to and was scared about what was going to happen. So I don't think you were right about her. When you said you weren't worried anymore, I mean."

Anders nodded and considered. He had sensed Gallagher had learned something from her review of the camera coverage. That man with the cigarette . . . it was too thin. She shouldn't have wasted his time with it. It felt like a distraction, a red herring. And why would she be trying to distract him unless she had seen something suspicious—something that had enhanced the suspicions she already harbored?

First, her questions about Stiles. Then her knowledge of the connection between Hamilton and Perkins. Then her odd behavior regarding the camera footage, not to mention the very fact of the manual review she had decided to undertake on her own initiative. And God knew what she made of the news about the attack on Azaz, and of Hamilton's resulting death. Of course, Hamilton was gone, and that was a huge relief. But now this woman was potentially positioned to exhume him. It couldn't be allowed.

"Did she say what she was planning to do?" Anders asked, with a casual wave of the hand designed to obscure the urgency of the question. He would know the answer himself, of course, as soon as he received the transcript of the conversation. But he wanted to hear it from Manus now.

"She said she didn't know. But she was very upset."

"Upset enough to . . . pose a risk?"

Manus nodded, but more to himself than to Anders. Anders let him take his time. It wasn't an easy question for a man in Manus's position to answer, and he wanted Manus to be able to consider the implications of his response.

After a moment, Manus said, "I think so."

Anders was enormously pleased. Manus was human. He'd been tempted, and he'd made a mistake. But he had returned to himself. He had returned to Anders.

Anders leaned back and rested his clasped fingers on the desk. "All right, Marvin. Thank you. Thank you for being honest with me."

Manus shook his head as though he didn't deserve the praise. "I'm sorry."

"You have nothing to be sorry for. You made a small mistake and you corrected it. This is very helpful information. Extremely helpful. Thank you."

Manus stood as though to go, then said almost shyly, "If you need to stop her from doing something bad, I want to help."

Anders was actually touched. Could there have been a more eloquent expression of loyalty? Or of the desire to demonstrate it?

"In fact, Marvin," he said slowly, "I think that's possible at this point. But . . . are you sure? It's not necessary. The truth is, this is probably more a job for Delgado."

For a moment, Manus's expression was troubled. But only for a moment. "I understand. But . . . if I can help, I want to. If you'll let me."

Anders considered. Well, Gallagher was probably apt to be more watchful just now than Delgado's usual targets. It wouldn't hurt for the man to have Manus there as a possible distraction. And as backup. And certainly Manus deserved a chance to make amends, in the only way he really knew how. Which was, as it happened, the only way that really mattered.

"You tracked her with a StingRay earlier, correct?" Anders asked.

Manus nodded.

"Good. Get in touch with Delgado. Give him the access codes so he can track her, too. I'll let him know you'll be assisting."

Manus nodded quickly, his eagerness momentarily sneaking past the usual stoicism.

Anders watched him go. He was glad he was able to offer Manus the opportunity to help Delgado. But he thought it best that Manus be involved only for the setup. After what had happened between Manus and Gallagher, it would be unnecessarily cruel to make Manus witness the woman's actual demise. Especially given

Delgado's proclivities. Which, though an occasional and unfortunate necessity, Anders couldn't deny he also found . . . distasteful.

He pushed the thought aside. Evelyn Gallagher had to go, and she had to go in a deniable fashion. And what could be more deniable, and distracting, than a long-term serial rapist working the I-95 corridor? That Delgado enjoyed his work, to the point of sometimes doing it even as an out-of-town hobby, wasn't a comfortable thing to know. But on the other hand, his behavior introduced an element of randomness that obscured the occasionally more targeted nature of his activities. And doubtless his predilections were also part of why he was so good at what he did, why he always achieved the proper results. Right now, those results were the only thing that mattered. In fact, the results were the only thing that *ever* mattered.

It was important to remember that. Even if other people couldn't understand.

CHAPTER........
........30

Remar looked at the closed door of the director's office. Manus had been in there for about ten minutes. Remar didn't trust the big deaf man, who he found about as readable as a statue. The kind of man who was capable of anything, anything the director asked of him. Remar wondered what the director was asking of Manus right that very moment.

There was a time when he didn't mind not knowing. But . . . this Hamilton thing. It felt loose. Out of control. In his own way, the director was as unreadable as Manus, but Remar had known him for much longer. So he could tell when the director was uncertain and trying not to show it—by closing people out, for example, or hoarding information, or otherwise being even more secretive than usual. And of course, that would all happen at the precise moment the director most needed another perspective, another set of eyes, a way of pressure-checking the decisions he was making under stress.

An Insider Threat alert popped up on his monitor. Gallagher. His stomach clenched. This was bad. Very bad.

He worked the keyboard to find out more, the whole while thinking, *Shit, shit, shit.* This thing was going to blow, he could tell. How much worse did it have to get before he could no longer deny that? And the director didn't know how to contain it. His instincts were always to double down—on the secrecy, on the machinations, on . . . everything.

You know he was behind that bombing. Either through Manus or Delgado. You know it.

Yes, he did know it, though he found it so horrifying he was trying to *not* know it. It fit the facts in every way . . . every way except his lingering desire to believe the director would never go that far.

Everything he'd done, he'd done out of loyalty to the director. And with the understanding—no, with the rationalization—that it was about protecting America. Saving lives. But bombing a DC neighborhood to save lives? That rationalization was more than he could muster. And the fact that the director apparently could was . . . horrifying. A person who could rationalize that could rationalize anything.

He thought again of the audit the director had ordered him to carry out on God's Eye. He'd been thinking about it more lately, especially after the bombing. About how, if the program were ever exposed, it would land much more at the director's feet than at Remar's. Not that Remar would be standing entirely outside the backlash blast radius, but with the right tactics, he could shield himself from the worst of it, possibly even divert the force of the blast toward . . .

He rubbed the unfeeling skin on the right side of his face. What was he thinking? He didn't know what to do. But not betrayal. Not that.

He forwarded the necessary information on the Gallagher alert to the appropriate team and told them to give it top priority.

The door opened and Manus came out. Remar nodded to him uneasily, then headed into the director's office. Maybe now the director would see that they had to change tactics. And understand that the situation was spiraling out of control.

He closed the door behind him and immediately said, "We just got an Insider Threat flag. On Gallagher."

The director practically jumped from his desk chair. "What?"

"Someone purchased a prepaid cell phone for cash this morning at a Columbia Walgreens. This was nine minutes after Gallagher's phone showed up at the store."

"Did the system confirm dual movement?"

"No, Gallagher's phone remained at the Walgreens for almost an hour. The prepaid was activated near Rockville, then shut off."

"What was it used for?"

"I don't know yet. I have a team looking into it."

"Do they know Gallagher is the focus?"

Jesus. He was going to do it again. First Aerial. And then Stiles? He'd wondered about the hanging, but had managed to persuade himself. But then Perkins . . . and now Gallagher? Where would it ever end?

He touched the scar tissue below the eye patch and shook his head. "Of course not. All they have is the phone number."

"Good. Need to know."

"There's more. Gallagher didn't buy anything in the store. At least not with a credit card."

There was no need to explain what that meant. It was possible Gallagher had bought something with cash. It was possible she had bought nothing at all. But most people used plastic. And why go to a Walgreens and buy nothing?

The director pulled at his chin. He'd been doing that a lot lately, Remar had noticed. Rubbing his hands together, patting his stomach, squeezing his thighs. Touching different parts of himself as though confirming he was still there, that he wasn't flying apart.

The director fell back in his chair and blew out a long breath. "How long was she in the store?"

"Her phone was there for over an hour."

"Could she have been someplace adjacent? A coffee shop, something like that?"

"No. It's a stand-alone store. Nothing else around. Unless she was sitting in the woods, or by the side of the road. And she was the first customer in the store. In fact, she arrived early and was waiting for it to open. The other cell phones belong to employees."

"No other customers in the store?"

"I'm having a geolocation team look into that. If there were other customers, we'll use their phones to find out who they are and what they were doing there. My guess? If there was anyone other than employees in that store during those ten minutes, they were locals, there to pick up prescriptions. And I'll bet they used plastic. No other anomalies. Only Gallagher."

The director nodded, more to himself than to Remar. "All right. This is good to know. I'll take it from here."

Neither needed to fill in the details of the picture the metadata painted. Gallagher had gone to the Walgreens and bought a prepaid, then left her own phone in the vicinity and activated the burner somewhere else to conceal her behavior. What Remar didn't know was why. But he sensed the director did—that he wasn't even surprised, in fact.

Remar knew it was probably useless to press, and maybe worse than useless. Still, he said, "Why are you so concerned about some analyst knowing the prepaid might belong to Gallagher?"

The director gave him a sharp look. "I told you. Need to know."

"No. Why really, Ted?"

There was a pause. Then the director said, "She's being dealt with."

That feeling of looseness, of things spiraling out of control, intensified. "Dealt with how?"

"Mike, there are things you don't want to know."

"You mean don't need to know."

"That, too."

"How is she a threat, Ted?"

225

Another long pause. Then: "She suspects the bombing near the White House was an inside job."

"Jesus," Remar said, unable to keep the disgust out of his tone.

"Yes, I know."

Remar suspected this was as close as the director would ever come to telling him. Still, he said, "Why?"

No answer.

"Because someone would figure out the phones associated with the attack belonged to Ergenekon people?"

"I told you, Mike, no one else knows about the Ergenekon connection."

"Why, then? Because it just looked too sloppy that the phones were also in touch with numbers at a local mosque? Someone was going to suspect it was engineered? A false flag? So what? Every bombing spawns conspiracy theories. Hell, that's our primary rebuttal when a conspiracy theory is true."

The director looked away, his fingers rubbing against his thumbs.

"I told you there were limits, Ted. I told you—"

The director slammed a hand down on his desk. "What limits, Mike? Really, tell me, I want to know. Where's the point you reach where you say, 'Okay, that's far enough, beyond this line we give up God's Eye and let the privacy freaks dismantle NSA'? Where do you decide you'd rather just drop all our defenses and leave the nation open to attack? You know what's out there, Mike. You know what'll happen if we can't see it coming anymore."

"We haven't always had God's Eye. If we had to shut it down, we could do without."

"Oh, for Christ's sake, of course we need God's Eye. If you want to run the world, you need to know what's going on in it. All of it. But you know what? Okay, fine, take it to the people. We can have a referendum. 'America's no longer going to be a great nation, yea or nay.' The people already voted for who we are in the world,

Mike. Again and again. Because you can't choose to rule without also choosing what ruling requires. So if you're asking me, in some chickenshit way, whether my conscience is clear? Yes, it's clear as water. I implement what the people want, even if they don't have the integrity and self-awareness to admit they want it. And I have no patience for anyone who enjoys meat but moans about slaughterhouses, who wears cheap clothes but deplores sweatshops, who weeps about climate change from behind the wheel of an SUV or from the window seat of an airplane. We're not sentimentalists, Mike. We're not children. We're not fools. And God knows, we're not politicians. We're the realists. The ones who do what needs to be done. So the sheep can be safe, and satisfied, and go on believing they're good and moral people in a fallen world."

Remar shook his head, not wanting to accept the director could be that far gone. "Come on, we've survived breaches before. We survived Snowden, we can—"

"Don't you get it? This is different! Every time some anarchist reveals our capabilities, our adversaries take countermeasures. Which means we need to develop new capabilities. And that gets harder and harder. Tell me, Mike, what's going to replace God's Eye when it's blown? Mind reading? Because that's all we'll have to turn to. So unless you're going to tell me you've suddenly become clairvoyant, don't try to convince me we can live without God's Eye. We can't. We're helpless without it. We can't see, we can't hear, we can't understand. We're a pitiable, helpless giant, blind, deaf, and dumb, stumbling and flailing while our enemies buzz around us at will, stinging us to death. Well, I won't let that happen. Ever."

Remar had seen the director under pressure before, but had never seen him this agitated. Well, enough strain, and cracks would begin to appear. More and more of them, wider and deeper, until they reached . . . he didn't know what. Didn't *want* to know what. He couldn't let it come to that. He wouldn't.

"What are you going to do about Gallagher?" he said.

The director rubbed his hands together. "You know what I'm going to do. It's already happening."

"I still don't understand."

"She knows too much, Ted, all right? Even if the Insider Threat flag you just received turns out to be a false alarm, and I doubt it will. She knows about the connection between Perkins and Hamilton. Which means she might know about God's Eye. Not just the program, but what we've used it for, too, okay?"

We? Remar thought. But this wasn't the moment to argue about who had been driving all these years and who had been in the passenger seat. In fact, it would be better not to have that argument at all. He needed to keep his own counsel now. In case. Just in case.

"How?" Remar said. "How could she know any of that?"

"I think she's seen things on the camera footage she hasn't told me about. An omission like that would be problematic under any circumstances, but with everything else going on? We'd have to be insane to take that chance."

Insane. That's certainly the word. "I still don't like it."

"You don't have to like it. You shouldn't even have asked. I told you, it's being handled. Hamilton and Perkins are both settled. Gallagher is about to be settled, too. And that's it. No more loose ends, no more insider threats. We can get back to protecting the country."

"You mean running it."

The director shook his head. "Mike. When are you going to learn it's one and the same?"

CHAPTER........
........31

The moment Remar was gone, Anders sent Delgado an encrypted text: *Need you in here immediately.*

While he waited, he accessed God's Eye. The system received an alert every time someone bought a cell phone, a smartphone, or any Internet-capable device for cash. Especially a prepaid phone. Because who bought things like that for cash, except people who were trying to remain anonymous, trying to prevent the government from knowing what they were up to? Which of course was tantamount to being up to no good.

Once the alert was received, the system attempted to match the purchaser via geolocation of known cell phones. The system had access to so much data it was almost impossible to evade. Most people who bought prepaids carried them alongside their legitimate phones as they moved from tower station to tower station, making identification of the purchaser almost comically easy. A few were a little smarter—careful to power up their legitimate units before powering down their burners. But one unit powering on again and again at about the same time another unit powered off was only marginally more difficult to correlate. A very few were smart—or paranoid—enough to not turn off their regular phones at all, but rather to leave them at home and power up the prepaid somewhere else. But even those people had patterns that could be uncovered. Some spent time with the same cohorts while carrying one phone and then the other, enabling God's Eye to map them indirectly, like backscatter imaging. Others frequented the same places while carrying one phone and then the other, enabling another kind of pattern matching. No matter what, it was almost always just a matter of time.

And that was just the cell phone geolocation system. God's Eye also had access to a DEA license-plate tracking program—a program powerful enough to capture clear photos of drivers and passengers in addition to vehicle information—along with various state and local equivalents; speed and other traffic enforcement cameras; records of credit card purchases; automatic toll booth collection points; and, of course, Gallagher's own camera network and biometric match system. The only way to avoid God's Eye was to disconnect so completely, to live in such total physical and electronic isolation, to neuter yourself so utterly, that no one could possibly have any interest in you anyway.

Whatever Gallagher might have known about God's Eye, he doubted she understood it was integrated with the Insider Threat Program. An NSA employee buying communication equipment for cash was almost certainly already, or about to become, a severe problem, and anytime the mobile phone or other movements of an NSA employee were correlated with a problematic cash purchase, the system sent out an immediate alert. Which was how Remar had been able to flag Gallagher's behavior that morning: the system had simply matched the cell phone and the purchase. The next step was closer scrutiny, through programs like PRISM and XKeyscore. Or, when even closer monitoring was required, by the deployment of special teams. Attempting to hide, paradoxically, was what brought the gaze of God's Eye upon you. Which was exactly the point.

He checked, and saw that Gallagher had arrived at work at 9:17 that morning. A few more keystrokes showed this was almost an hour later than her average. A divorced mother with a young son . . . the odd domestic emergency could explain periodic discrepancies in her schedule. But this morning didn't feel like a fluke.

An alert popped up on his monitor—the telephone analysis. The prepaid unit had been used to call a mailbox and shipping store in Rockville. He immediately thought of the store to which Hamilton had FedExed his package from Istanbul. That one had been in Adams Morgan. Was there a connection? A second package? It was a very uncomfortable thought.

He called the store and said, "Sorry to trouble you, but was my wife in your store this morning? Curvy brunette, about thirty-five? She would have arrived just as you opened."

There was a pause, then the person on the other end said, "Yeah, I guess she was, and you can tell her to not bother coming back. She was playing some kind of weird joke with one of my employees— stuffing her panties in the toilet or something. Or maybe she was trying to steal something. You know anything about that?"

Anders hung up. Gallagher, without a doubt. But her panties in the toilet?

Make it overflow. Distract the staff. Slip behind the mailboxes and steal—

There was a knock. The door opened and Delgado came in, dapper as usual in a navy suit and a neat row of hair plugs.

"Thomas," Anders said, rubbing his hands together. "I have something I need you to take care of right away."

CHAPTER . . . .
. . . . 32

Evie left work before six, frustrated and scared. She hadn't gotten anywhere with Hamilton's thumb drive. NSA had formidable decryption capabilities, she knew, but the people she asked to take a crack at the thumb drive told her it was protected with a robust, open-source program. No backdoors, no weakened standards, no shortcuts. Even brute force via NSA's full suite of supercomputers would be iffy at best, and that access was tightly controlled, not something just anyone could manage outside protocol, LOVEINT or otherwise. She wanted to make a duplicate for safekeeping, but even that turned out to be impossible—Hamilton had used a copy protection program she couldn't get around.

It was maddening, to feel she was in possession of exactly what she needed and yet unable to use it. Plan B looked like the *Intercept*, but she didn't know how to communicate with anyone there securely. She'd have to buy a computer for cash, download Tails from an anonymous location, set up encrypted chat . . . and then hope someone would get back to her quickly. Where she was going to find time—for all that, and probably for the face-to-face follow-up, too—she had no idea. But right now, it looked like her only option.

It had been a week since she'd visited her father, and she needed a few things from the Safeway, too, so she parked in the supermarket side lot, an easy walk to the back of the senior center. Her father was relatively lucid when she saw him, looking and sounding a bit like his old self, and so obviously glad to see her that she felt guilty for not staying longer. But Digne was waiting and Dash would be hungry, and she still had so much she needed to think through. Maybe she could visit the Apple or Microsoft store in the mall and buy a computer or tablet for cash. She wished she had spent more time thinking through security before she'd really needed to. But she'd always been comfortably on the inside. She'd never done anything wrong. She'd never expected NSA's penetrating gaze to turn on her.

She stopped in the women's room on her way out and used the toilet. And then, washing her hands, she was suddenly gripped by paranoia. All day long, she'd been carrying around the thumb drive in her purse. She'd even brought it into headquarters. How had she persuaded herself that was a safe thing to do? She realized that she had so few alternatives, she must have been rationalizing the danger. And now that the danger was past, she could see how reckless she'd been. True, no one else had any reason to know of the thumb drive's existence. But . . . she'd asked several colleagues to take a crack at decrypting it, hadn't she? And though of course she hadn't told them what the drive really was, allowing them to believe instead it was something from her personal life, if someone told someone else, and word got back to the director that she had a thumb drive and was trying to get it decrypted . . .

She looked around the restroom. She supposed she could just hide the thumb drive here. Temporarily, until she figured something out. It would feel safer than keeping it on her person. Assuming she could find the right spot.

Under the garbage can? No, the first time a cleaning person

picked up the can to empty it, they'd see it. Maybe get some tape and secure the drive to the underside? But no, it would still be visible if, say, someone knocked the can over or dropped it while emptying it. Behind one of the toilets? That could work, though again, still some danger of discovery by a cleaning person.

She looked at the sinks in front of her. Four of them, all in a row in some sort of faux granite countertop. The back of the countertop was secured to the wall under the mirror, but the front rested on four metal legs. She squatted and examined the leg furthest to the left. It was circular, with a finish of what, polished nickel? It must have been hollow—why would the facility spend for solid nickel fixtures in a public restroom?

She gripped the leg and rotated it counterclockwise. There was a moment of resistance, and then it turned ninety degrees. She tried turning it more, but it wouldn't budge. She pushed it. Nothing. She pulled—and it slid smoothly off its fastening. Suddenly she was holding a three-foot metal tube, open at the top end, closed with a rubber stopper at the bottom.

She glanced at the door, then reached into her purse and took out the thumb drive. She dropped it into the tube, hearing a slight ping as it hit the bottom. She upended the tube, and the drive slid right back out.

She dropped the drive in again, pushed the leg back into place, and rotated it clockwise until it was secure. Then she stepped back to examine her handiwork. Perfect. Technically, she wouldn't have access during nonvisiting hours, but she didn't expect anyone would deny her if she really pressed.

On the way back to the Safeway, she noticed a white Sprinter van parked next to her Prius. Which was a little odd, because the side lot was mostly empty. Someone else visiting the senior facility, maybe? Still, something about it was making her uneasy, and she started edging away as she went past, toward the opposite side of the lot.

"Evie," a voice called from behind her. She turned and saw Marvin. What was he doing here? Well, shopping, obviously, it was a supermarket and he lived in the area. But still, why was he parked around the side—

Something hit her hard in the back of the head. She staggered. An arm shot roughly across her throat and dragged her backward. She struggled but couldn't find her balance. She was choking, she couldn't breathe. Panic surged through her. She tried to bite the arm but it was too tight, she couldn't get her chin under it. She tried to scratch, but encountered a thick sleeve and a gloved hand. She felt herself jerked sharply up and back, her heels smacking into the edge of something. Then she was shoved facedown onto the floor, the floor of the van she'd seen. She turned her head to scream, but a knee landed on her back, knocking the wind out of her. A hand clamped over her mouth. She felt a sting in the side of her neck, a spread of heat. Suddenly everything was heavy, heavy, as though someone had covered her with a lead blanket. Her vision swam, and as the world faded out, she saw Marvin, standing outside, looking away and sliding the van door shut.

CHAPTER . . . .
. . . . 33

Delgado turned onto an access road near the Triadelphia Reservoir, following it into the woods to a chained access gate. He got out, cut the chain with bolt cutters, and continued on until he reached the water. He parked, cut the lights, and waited, making sure no one else was coming.

When he was satisfied they were alone, he got out and went back in through the side door. There was a metal partition between the seats in front and the cargo area behind, which was good because it meant no light could bleed from the cargo area through the front. The cargo area itself was entirely windowless and private. There was a wheel well along either side, but other than that the back was empty—just some folded padding for moving furniture. Lying on her side on top of the padding, her wrists handcuffed behind her back, was Evelyn Gallagher. She was moaning softly, and that was good. It had been over twenty minutes since Delgado had injected her with the propofol, and if she hadn't been stirring by now, it would mean either that he'd administered an overdose or that she was faking unconsciousness. But no, everything seemed normal. Good color in her cheeks; those sweet little moans; and now some movement, too, albeit impeded by the handcuffs.

Manus had taken her purse, and if she had what the director wanted, it was more likely there rather than directly on her person. Still, he needed to search her. He smiled, admitting he would have checked her out even if there had been nothing to look for.

He squatted next to her and removed one of the soft brown flats she was wearing. She'd lost the other on the way into the Sprinter, but Manus would have retrieved it. Couldn't afford to leave evidence in the Safeway parking lot, and besides, the director had surmised they were looking for a thumb drive, so a shoe was a possible hiding spot. The leather was soft and warm. He twisted it left, then right, feeling nothing out of place. He examined the sole and the lining. Nothing. He unclipped his knife and pried off the heel. Still nothing. Okay, the shoe was a negative. He tossed it and the heel aside, then slid the knife back in his pocket.

He ran his hands over her legs from ankle to thigh, feeling himself getting hard as he did so, then went up under her skirt and caressed her ass. Nothing but bare skin. He felt for a thong string and couldn't find one. Holy shit, the little slut was going commando? He ran his hand around to the front and felt a nice, wide landing strip, the shaved skin to either side smooth and soft. He lifted the skirt to take a look, then ran a finger along her slit, fully erect now. *You like that, sweetheart? God, I'll bet you do. Well, don't you worry, I'll take care of you soon. Such good care. I promise.*

He doubted she would have been walking around with anything in a cavity, though of course if nothing turned up anywhere else, he'd have to check. Check carefully. But he wanted her to be awake for that. So for now, he satisfied himself with her belly and back, then under her arms, and then her neck, her hair, behind her ears. Nothing. He saved her tits for last, rubbing, squeezing, pinching. Jesus, they were big. But nothing hidden under her bra. All right, she was clean. He wished he'd found something, that thumb drive or whatever, anything. Because he was really fucking aroused. But he had to stop for now. So he could question her. He sat on one of the wheel wells, breathing hard, just relishing the sight of her, so helpless like that. God, he loved this shit.

After a few minutes, her eyes opened. She blinked, then grimaced and squeezed them shut.

"Head hurt?" Delgado said. "I had to hit you. And that lip looks swollen—you must have smacked it on the floor. My bad. If you want, I can give you something for the pain."

She didn't answer. He gave her a minute, knowing the propofol was still in her system, but knowing too how quickly it dissipated.

She pulled in her knees and sat up. Delgado liked that. Sometimes they stayed helpless, supine, in whatever position he had chosen for them. But not this one. She made her own decisions, insofar as she could, anyway. A fighter. God, he liked the fighters.

She noticed her skirt was hiked up, and managed to pull it down a little. "Sorry about that," Delgado said. "I had to search you. Nothing personal. But . . . you're really not wearing panties? You must have been expecting me, right?"

She shifted a bit, lifting her ass by putting her hands on the floor behind her and doing a modified crabwalk, the buttons of her blouse straining across her tits as she moved. Jesus, the body on this one. He couldn't believe his luck. He was so fucking hard. He reminded himself it was business first, pleasure after.

She stopped when her back bumped up against the side opposite from where he was sitting. "What is this?" she said, looking at him, and doing a pretty good job, he had to admit, of keeping her voice even and otherwise hiding her fear.

He waited a moment, giving her time to stew, showing her he didn't have to answer her questions, letting her know he was completely in control. She glanced at his scalp and squinted as though trying to figure out what she saw.

"Yeah, the hair plugs," he said, smiling. "They're not working out so well. Shouldn't even have bothered. I mean, it's not like you care, right, Evie? You like me either way, don't you?"

She was looking at him closely, and it was weird, it felt almost like she had recognized him and was trying to place his face. But that didn't make sense. He knew she'd never seen him before. Probably she was just trying to figure out what kind of man was now holding her helpless.

Don't worry, honey. You're going to find out.

After a moment, she said, "Who are you? What do you want?"

He smiled. "Who I am . . . that depends. I guess I'm your best friend right now, if you want to be smart. Or your worst nightmare, if you want to be dumb. As for what I want, just what you took from the mailbox facility in Rockville this morning. Tell me where it is, and we're done. We can all forget this little misunderstanding ever even happened."

She shook her head. "I don't know what you're talking about."

Delgado couldn't help laughing. "You know they all say that, right? Every one of them, in your position. 'I don't know anything, I swear!' I wish I could place a big fat bet every time. I'd be rich."

He examined a cuticle, taking his time, letting it all sink in. "The thing is, we know you know. We know everything about you. We know where you live, we know what you drive, we know how much you have in the bank. We know about your father in the nursing home, we know about your son at the deaf school. Likes baseball, Dash, doesn't he? Evie, we know *everything*. And we don't care about any of it. We only want the one thing. Give it to me, and you can go home to your boy right now. Isn't he expecting you? Won't he be worried?"

She looked down and didn't answer. *Bitch is tough*, he thought, not unhappily. Not unhappily at all.

"Evie, if you don't give me what I've asked for, I have to start doing some really bad shit to you. Like . . . torture shit, not to put too fine a point on it. I don't think you're tough enough to endure that kind of shit. In fact, I haven't met anyone yet who was. So I think what'll happen is, you'll wind up telling me what I want to know and suffering for nothing. But you know what? Maybe I'm wrong. Maybe you can handle having your fingertips crushed with pliers, having your lips burned off with a cigarette lighter." He pulled a pliers and a lighter from his coat pocket to illustrate the point, set them on the floor, and continued. "But do you think you could watch me do all that to Dash? And worse? Because that's where this thing goes if you don't give me now what you're going to give me eventually."

A long moment went by. Delgado waited. He wasn't in a hurry. Fuck, on the contrary, he was savoring all of it.

"Marvin," she said, shaking her head. "He's part of this. God."

Delgado was surprised. "You mean Manus? You call him Marvin? How do you know him?"

"He's . . . God, he's been watching us. I'm so stupid."

The director must have had Manus surveilling her. Though if she knew him as "Marvin," the surveillance was pretty up close and personal. He wondered why the director hadn't told him, then almost laughed. What did the director tell anyone that he didn't absolutely need to?

He wondered for a moment whether that nice shaved bush, the lack of panties, could have been for Manus? Before the grab, Manus had told him the woman wasn't to suffer, which at the time had been a total non sequitur. But now . . . Jesus, had the big deaf freak been *fucking* this hottie? He couldn't imagine it. Well, even if he had been, so what? The thought of Manus's sloppy seconds wasn't exactly an aphrodisiac, but shit, there was still plenty of upside here to focus on.

He patted her arm, letting his hand linger for a moment before removing it. "Well, we all make mistakes, right? What matters is how we fix them. So fix your mistake, Evie. Tell me where it is."

"I can't tell you that," she said. "I have to take you there."

Delgado couldn't stop himself from laughing again. "Hey, you're right on schedule. Because that's the next thing everyone says. To buy themselves time, a little reprieve, maybe an opportunity to actually escape. And everyone who says it thinks it's original to them. No, Evie, you don't need to show me. If you hid what you took, you hid it somewhere you can find it. If you can find it, you can explain where it can be found. No one buries something in the middle of a field with no landmarks, see? Okay, maybe an idiot might do something like that, but I can tell you're no idiot. You're a careful woman. Not quite careful enough, it turns out, but careful."

He squatted in front of her and she looked down. He shot out a hand, gripped her chin hard, and raised her face until it was inches from his own. She tried to twist loose and he squeezed tighter.

"So let's stop fucking around here, okay? Unless you want me to start having some fun with you."

She tried to move back and he moved his face closer. "Would you like that, Evie? I think maybe you would."

Christ, the smell of her, and the way those buttons were straining on her blouse. He thought how easy it would be to reach down and squeeze one of those tits. Fucking twist it. *Think you'd tell me what I want to know then, bitch?*

Maybe. But going that fast would foreclose possibilities, too. For now, he needed her to believe she had two completely different options: give him what he was asking for and walk away clean, on the one hand; give him what he was asking for after being permanently disfigured, on the other. If he started hurting her too soon, it would muddy that framework, and might make her more stubborn.

No, now wasn't the time. Though soon it would be. One way or the other.

Her nostrils were flaring in and out with her breathing. He lifted her chin higher and she grimaced in pain. God, he wanted to hurt her. Not just a little like this. Not just to scare her. Really hurt her. Hurt her so she screamed.

"All right," she said, through clenched teeth. "Okay."

He eased off the pressure on her chin but didn't release it.

"But how do I know?" she said. "How do I know you'll let me go once I tell you?"

He laughed again. "Congratulations, sweetheart, you're officially three for three. That's the next thing everyone asks. And the answer's always the same, too. You don't know. Maybe I'm lying. And maybe I'm lying about torturing you and your boy Dash, too. Well, there's an easy way to test me. Just don't tell me what I want to know. See what happens. But you know what? I think you already know the answer. I think you're looking at me and you know perfectly well that I'm telling the truth. So. Where'd you hide it, Evie? Tell me so I can get you home. In one fucking piece."

There was a pause, then she said, "In the senior facility. Where I visited my father just before you grabbed me."

Delgado considered. If it was a lie, it was a clever one. Because how the fuck was Manus going to slip in and out of a nursing home without getting challenged?

On the other hand, the difficulty of someone like Manus retrieving it was exactly what would have made the nursing home a good spot for real.

He looked her up and down. "You fucking with me, Evie?"

She shook her head.

"Because I have 'Marvin' standing by, and he's going to go look wherever you tell me it is. And if he reports back that he couldn't find it, then I'm going to hurt you like you can't even imagine. Do you understand that?"

She glared at him. "I understand that."

"What media is it stored on? Do not fucking lie to me."

"It's a thumb drive."

"Where, precisely?"

"The women's room, on the left as you go in through the side entrance. Handicapped stall, taped to the back of the toilet near the floor."

Delgado released her chin. "All right, Evie. Good girl. I'll have Marvin go take a look. If it checks out, little Dash gets his mommy back, safe and sound. If not . . . well, let's not even think about that, right?"

God, he loved how much defiance he saw in her eyes. And how he was going to fuck every last bit out of her the moment he'd gotten confirmation they had what the director wanted. By the time he was through with her, all she'd have left was begging. And he'd let her, too. He'd let her beg for a long time. He wanted to be able to remember it for after.

CHAPTER . . . .
. . . . 34

Manus was pacing at the periphery of the giant Columbia Mall parking lot. The sun shone headache-bright in his eyes as it approached the horizon, then cast a lengthening shadow on the pavement in front of him as he headed the other way. He flexed his hands as he walked. Open. Closed. Open. Closed.

He hadn't liked it when Delgado hit the woman to stun her, but he understood it had to be done. Delgado had tossed Manus her purse, and Manus had done his part, picking up the shoe she'd lost, getting out her keys, driving her car away from the scene of the snatch. He was supposed to search the car and the purse and then text Delgado when he was done, regardless of whether he found anything. Well, he hadn't found anything, not even in her shoe. But he hadn't texted Delgado. He doubted the woman had on her person what the director wanted—the purse or the car were more likely. So if he told Delgado he hadn't found anything, Delgado would think the woman had hidden it somewhere else. At which point, he would make her tell. Manus didn't want to think about how. He didn't like the way Delgado had been looking at her in the Sprinter, when he was kneeling on her back. Manus knew what that look meant. He'd tried to tell himself he was wrong, but he knew Delgado. Knew what he was like.

You should never have left her alone with him. Never.

Stop it. It's what the director wanted. You had no choice.

He paced, the sun below the treetops now, their shadows overtaking his. With every other step, he smacked a fist into a thigh, harder and harder.

But you're supposed to tell him. You have to find what she took from the director. It's something she could hurt him with. That's why the director had to do this.

He'd told Delgado not to hurt her. Delgado had given him a strange look, as though Manus had asked him not to hurt a fly, an ant. He'd responded, "Why do you care?" And Manus hadn't answered. Couldn't.

He told himself he should have gone to her earlier, before any of this had happened, even before he had gone to the director. He could have explained, made her understand she had to give back the thumb drive. Maybe she would have listened.

Or maybe she wouldn't have. And what would he have done then?

But he could explain now. Now she would understand. Now she would listen. Because . . .

If the thumb drive is what the director wanted, once he has it why couldn't he just let her go?

Open, closed. Open. Closed.

But what if he's afraid she could still hurt him, somehow? Because of what she knows. And he must be afraid of that. He must be. That's why he's doing this. Not just to get the thumb drive back. To make sure she can never say anything to anyone afterward. That's why. She was going to do something bad and she still could and you had NO CHOICE.

He stopped and clutched the sides of his head.

Why did she have to do whatever she did? Why?

He thought of the way she had put her hands on his face, the way she had kissed him.

I'm sorry, Evie. I'm so sorry.

He sat on the curb, covered his face, and started to cry.

He didn't know what to do. He didn't want her to get hurt. He didn't want her to die. But it wasn't up to him. She'd done something, something to the director. But why? Why did she have to do that?

His phone vibrated and he yanked it out of his shirt pocket. A text from Delgado: *You checked the car and the purse? And that shoe?*

Manus's heart started pounding. He hesitated, then texted, *Yes.*

And?

He had to tell Delgado. It was what the director wanted. But if Delgado was asking, it meant he hadn't found it on her person. So if it wasn't in the car or the purse or the shoe, it meant she had hidden it. Which meant the next step was, Delgado would make her tell where.

He pressed his palms to his temples and squeezed. *What do I do what do I do WHAT DO I DO.*

You there, genius?

Manus looked at the text. Suddenly, he wanted to go to work on Delgado. Everything else was so confusing, but that was so clear.

Yes.

Did you check her shit?

Yes.

Holy shit, are you fucking mute now, too? Did you find anything?

Tears running down his face, Manus typed, *No.* And hit Send.

He blinked and looked at the text. Had he meant to send it? He hadn't thought. He'd just typed the two letters and then hit Send. And now it was done. Now he didn't have to think about it anymore. But he couldn't *stop* thinking.

He stood and began pacing again. A moment later, another text came in.

Yeah, that's what I was expecting. She says she hid it. Thumb drive, as expected. In the nursing home next to the supermarket. Ladies' room, on the left as you go in through the side entrance. Handicapped stall, taped to the back of the toilet near the floor.

Manus was so relieved his knees went rubbery. Delgado must have scared her into telling, but he wouldn't have hurt her. Not yet. Manus knew how it worked. It was better to hold the pain back, if you could.

But that didn't mean it wouldn't come later.

He texted, *Okay.*

Okay as in, you're going to check it out now?

Yes.

How long?

I don't know. I'm not there right now.

Wait a minute, didn't you bring the car back to the supermarket?

No. Why?

You have to bring it back.

Why?

So things look right.

Manus shook his head, not liking this at all.

What does that mean?

Do I have to spell it out for you, dummy? Her car just needs to be where she was last seen. So it looks right. Jesus, I hate this fucking texting. Can't you get a hearing aid or something?

Looks like what?

We're wasting time. Check the nursing home and let me know what you find.

You're not supposed to hurt her.

Yeah, I got that the first time, genius. It's cute that you like her but I didn't care then, either. This has to be taken care of a certain way. Director's orders.

He'd known, hadn't he? Even if he'd tried to hide from it. The thumb drive alone wasn't going to be enough. The director wanted her dead.

But . . . a certain way?

What way?

It's not your fucking concern, okay? You have one job. The nursing home. Now do it. Don't think about anything else. I'm doing what I was told to do. You need to do the same.

What were you told to do?

Hey fuck off, okay?

I'm not helping until you tell me.

Hey asshole you want me to tell the director you said that?

Manus didn't care. He wasn't going to back down.

Almost a minute went by. Then another text came in:

Make it look random, okay? Like a crime that could happen to anyone, not something targeted. You getting the picture now, idiot? Now, can you get to work, or do I have to call in backup?

Manus felt a cold fury settle behind his ears, in his chest. He held the phone at his side for a moment and flexed his free hand. Then he texted back.

No. I can go to work. Happy to.

CHAPTER . . . .
. . . . 35

M anus drove Evie's car back to the Safeway, trying to keep his mind clear, to force himself to focus.

One thing at a time. One thing at a time.

He circled the lot before moving in, looking for police, a crowd . . . any evidence that the snatch had been noticed. There was nothing. He parked the car where he had taken it and killed the engine, then placed her purse and shoe inside a plain canvas grocery bag, the same kind ecologically minded shoppers carried in and out of the supermarket every day. He got out, pulled off the work gloves he was wearing, and dropped those in the bag, as well.

He walked over to the nursing home and tried the side entrance. Locked. Well, slipping in and out unobserved was probably too much to hope for.

He circled around to the front and went in. Immediately he was struck by the smell of strong antiseptic. He suppressed a gag and kept moving.

A pretty black woman was sitting behind a large, circular receptionist's station just beyond the foyer. She smiled and raised her eyebrows as he approached, and he didn't need to be a lip reader to make out what she said: "Can I help you?"

He stopped in front of the station, smiled awkwardly, and said, "My father can't care for himself anymore and I think it's time. If you have some brochures I could show him, I think . . . it would make things easier."

She nodded sympathetically, eyeing him just a moment too long. He was accustomed to the reaction. It happened whenever he spoke in front of someone for the first time. She was wondering what was wrong with him. Deaf? Retarded? He didn't mind. He knew there was something about his presence that made people uncomfortable, edgy, even afraid. The strangeness of his voice gave them something to focus on, something to explain away a feeling produced by something else.

She gathered up a few forms and handed them over. He glanced through them for appearance's sake. Slick-looking materials depicting laughing, well-dressed, healthy-looking old people with perfect dentures and salon-coiffed white hair enjoying strolls and shuffleboard under brilliant blue skies, gourmet meals lit by chandelier. No one alone, everyone part of a pleasant, happy community. He'd never seen such bullshit.

He looked up and saw that she was speaking. Either she hadn't figured out he was deaf, or she didn't know how to talk to deaf people.

". . . and we strongly encourage residents to join in all the activities we offer. I'm sure your father would be very happy here, if you decide to enroll him."

Manus wondered whether he had read that right. *Enroll? Commit* would have been more honest.

"Thank you," Manus said. "I think he would."

"And your name is . . . ?"

"Miller," Manus said, wondering if the woman stood to receive a commission if she reeled him in. "Mark Miller."

"Well, Mr. Miller, the main office is closed now, so I can't offer a tour of our facilities. But if you'd like to come back . . . ?"

"I think I'll go through the brochures first. Thank you, you've been very helpful. Oh, is there a men's room I could use?"

"Of course." She gestured to her right. "Left at the end of the corridor, restroom's on the right. You can't miss it."

Manus nodded his thanks and headed off down the corridor. He turned the corner and saw a black man almost as large as himself sitting in a chair halfway down the hall, his elbows on his knees and a newspaper opened before him. The man was wearing green surgical scrubs, and Manus realized he was a nurse or something like it, stationed near the side entrance to make sure the "residents" didn't wander off.

Manus continued on. The man looked up, and Manus gave him a friendly nod. The man returned the nod and went back to his newspaper. He wasn't terribly interested in Manus, which was good. But as he got closer, Manus could see the man was positioned just beyond the restrooms. Manus wasn't going to be able to enter the women's room without the man noticing. He considered for a moment, weighing the pros and cons of various possibilities.

"Excuse me," he said, pausing in front of the restrooms. "Is anyone in the women's room?"

The man looked up and frowned. "I don't think so, no."

"My aunt thinks she left her glasses in there. Okay if I take a quick look?"

Plan B was to drop the man, check the bathroom, and head out the side exit. And Manus had gamed out other possibilities, too, depending on what the man did next. But there was no need. The man simply shrugged, said, "Be my guest," and went back to the newspaper.

Manus nodded his thanks and headed in. The bathroom was spotless, the tile almost glowing under the fluorescent lights. Surprisingly, the antiseptic smell was much less strong here, and Manus was momentarily grateful for it.

He ducked into the handicapped stall, got on his knees, and felt around behind the toilet near the floor. Nothing, just cold, smooth porcelain. He ran his hand up higher. Still nothing. He squeezed his head up against the wall and looked at the back of the toilet. Everywhere other than the tracks left by his hand was a slightly greasy covering of dust. Not a place anyone bothered to clean, even in a facility as apparently conscientious as this one. There was nothing taped there, and obviously there never had been.

He performed an identical examination of the other toilets. They were all the same.

She had lied to Delgado. Lied to buy herself time. Because she knew what Manus had tried to deny. That when they found the thumb drive, she was dead.

He headed out, ready to tell the man in the chair he'd been unsuccessful. But the man never even looked up from his paper.

He went out through the front entrance, being sure to thank the receptionist again on the way, then walked to the Safeway. Once outside the facility and no longer needing to be in character, he could feel panic closing in. He breathed deeply, in and out, willing it away. He had to decide what to do. He couldn't tell Delgado. He couldn't. If he did, Delgado was going to hurt Evie. Assuming he hadn't hurt her already. Assuming he wasn't hurting her right then.

And hurting her wouldn't even be the end of it. It would only be the start.

He walked to the edge of the parking lot and paced, examining options, weighing risks. After five minutes, he kept coming back to the same idea. It was dangerous and it was bad. But everything else seemed worse.

His phone vibrated and he pulled it out. It was Delgado. *What the fuck is going on?*

Manus didn't respond. He dropped the phone back in his pocket and went into the Safeway. Using cash, he bought a bottled water. A few granola bars. And a thumb drive.

Outside, he tore open and tossed the packaging and pocketed the thumb drive. The water and granola bars went into the canvas shopping bag, along with Evie's purse and shoe.

He walked to his pickup, which he had left in a nearby parking lot, opened the toolbox, put the canvas bag inside, and took out the StingRay. In less than a minute, he had the location of the cell phone Delgado had been texting from. It looked like he was in the middle of the woods around the Triadelphia Reservoir. Manus's stomach clenched at the thought of how dark it would be there, how private.

His phone vibrated again. Delgado: *Answer me, asshole. Did you find the drive?*

He texted back, *Waiting outside the bathroom. Need it to be empty.*

Okay. Just stop blowing me off. I want to know what's going on. I don't trust this bitch.

Manus closed the toolbox, touched the hilt of the Espada in his front pocket and the butt of the Force Pro in the holster, got in the pickup, and drove off.

CHAPTER........
........36

I t took Manus less than twenty minutes to pull onto a dirt road at the end of which the StingRay told him he would find Delgado. Delgado had texted him twice while he drove. The first time, Manus had texted back that he was still waiting. The second time, he didn't respond at all. Now he cut the headlights, driving slowly by the glow of the parking lights until he came to an access gate. He stopped and got out to examine it. Sure enough, the chain had been cut, then wrapped around one of the support posts to pass a casual inspection. Manus opened the gate and drove on. When the StingRay indicated he was a quarter mile away, he did a tight K-turn, cut the engine, and continued on foot.

The air was moist amid the trees, perfumed by wood and dirt. He could smell the reservoir just ahead, a clean smell like brass or ozone. He walked slowly, a new Defender Ultra set low and cupped in one hand, careful to avoid branches that might crack under the weight of his boots.

When he was close to the water, he spotted the contours of the Sprinter, the metal incongruous in the dim light against the trees around it. He clicked off the flashlight, returned it to his pocket, and positioned himself to the left of the sliding door. Delgado was right-handed, and by keeping to the left, Manus would force the man to emerge from cover to get off a shot, while at the same time making shooting itself maximally awkward. If it came to that.

He texted, *I'm here.*

A few seconds went by. Then: *What do you mean here?*

Outside the Sprinter. I have the drive.

A long moment spun out. Manus watched the Sprinter, his hand on the grip of the Force Pro.

The Sprinter door slid open. Manus saw Delgado, silhouetted from within. He was holding a pistol, but it was pointing down. Concerned about trouble, but not quite ready to make trouble of his own. Okay. Manus moved his hand off the Force Pro and let his shirt fall back over it.

Delgado was talking, but with the light coming from behind him, Manus couldn't make out what he was saying.

"I can't read your lips from here," Manus said. He moved closer, his arms loose at his sides, letting Delgado see his empty hands. There, that was better.

Delgado brought up the pistol and pointed it at Manus's chest. "Stop. How'd you know where to find me?"

Manus stopped. "StingRay. And you call me the dummy."

He knew Delgado was insecure. He hoped the insult would cause enough irritation to momentarily occlude clear thinking.

Delgado frowned and glanced around. Manus could tell he sensed something was off, but that he couldn't put his finger on what. The trick now was to deny his brain time to examine what his gut was trying to tell him.

Manus gestured to Delgado's gun. "Are you planning to shoot me, or can I come in?"

"Where's the drive?"

"There's too much light. We need to close that door."

Delgado raised the gun so the muzzle was pointing at Manus's face. "Where is the fucking drive?"

255

He was more suspicious than Manus had hoped. Nowhere to go but straight on.

"Let me see the woman."

"Why?"

"I need to know she's safe."

"You been fucking her?"

"I need to know she's safe."

Delgado held out his free hand. "Give me the drive."

"I don't have it. But it's close."

"Where?"

"The woman first."

Delgado put a second hand on the grip and adjusted his head so he was sighting down the barrel. "I will shoot you, Manus."

"Go ahead. Then you can explain to the director how you shot the only person in the world who knows where the drive is."

A long moment went by. Manus didn't think Delgado would do it. But he didn't know, either. It didn't matter. There was no other way to play this.

Delgado lowered the muzzle to chest level and stepped out of the Sprinter, giving Manus wide berth. "All right," he said. "You first."

The man's tactics were good. He wasn't going to let Manus get too close. Manus would have to make an opportunity.

Manus stepped into the Sprinter. Evie was sitting on the floor in one of the rear corners, her hands cuffed or tied behind her back. Her clothes were somewhat in disarray and her upper lip was swollen, but it didn't seem she'd otherwise been hurt. She glanced at Manus and said nothing. But the hate he saw in her eyes was awful.

Delgado climbed in and slid the door closed behind him. He kept the gun on Manus. "Move back," he said. "Give me room."

Manus stooped and moved further back. The opportunity wasn't there. Not yet.

Delgado looked at him. "Where's the drive, dummy?"

Manus glanced at Evie, then back to Delgado. "The director doesn't want you to harm her."

"Bullshit."

"I just texted with him."

Delgado sneered. "Yeah? Let me see your phone."

"I delete my texts. I hope you're smart enough to do the same. Dummy."

Delgado reddened. "Who the fuck—"

"Why don't you call him yourself? Afraid he might say you can't have your fun?"

Delgado's eyes narrowed. He swung the gun over to Evie. She flinched but didn't look away.

"Fun? You want to have fun? Here's what we do. I start counting. If I get to three before you tell me where the fuck that drive is, I shoot your girlfriend in the face. Sound good? Sound fun? Here we go. One. Two—"

"All right," Manus said bringing his hands up, palms open. "All right!"

Delgado kept the gun on Evie. "Where?"

"Right here. In my left pocket. I'm going to take it out. Slowly."

He reached into his left pocket, slowly as promised, removed the thumb drive, and held it out.

Delgado glanced at it, then back to Manus. The gun didn't waver. "This isn't the plan. You're supposed to take it to the director so he can confirm it's what he wanted. For all we know, that's just some random thumb drive this bitch picked up in a Walgreens."

Manus kept his arm extended, the hand holding the thumb drive less than a yard from Delgado. "Then take it to him. I'll watch the woman."

"No, you won't. You'll get the fuck out of this van."

"Call the director," Manus said. "You're not supposed to harm her."

Manus couldn't predict exactly what Delgado would do next.

Reach for the drive? Have Manus set it on the floor? Make Manus change to a less advantageous posture or position? Call the director? It was impossible to say. But whatever he did next, he'd gotten what he'd wanted. Meaning he no longer needed to threaten the woman. Meaning he was going to stop pointing the pistol at her, and point it at Manus again, instead. That moment would be Manus's best opportunity. Probably his *last* opportunity.

He sensed the move an instant before it happened. And as Delgado's arm swung left from the woman and back to Manus, Manus was already shooting in with a drop step, his extended left hand blurring in and slapping Delgado's gun hand up and back. The pistol discharged. Manus closed his hand around it, keeping it pointed away, and speared a forearm into Delgado's throat. The gun went off again. Delgado gagged and fumbled at his pants pocket with his free hand. Manus grabbed the hand, head-butted Delgado's face, then stepped back and shot a knee into his balls. Delgado folded forward and Manus yanked his arms wide, bringing his face in for another head-butt, then clubbed him in the neck with another forearm as he went down. Delgado pitched face-first onto the floor and Manus tore the gun from his hand.

Delgado lay still. For an instant, Manus imagined stomping his neck . . . stomping again and again until the man had been functionally decapitated. The urge was so strong his leg actually trembled. But with everything else he was doing, if he killed Delgado, who he knew the director valued . . . he just didn't know.

He drew in a huge breath and blew it out, forcing himself to focus. If he could just get Evie to tell him where she had hidden the drive. If she would promise she would never, ever say anything to anyone. Manus would guarantee her silence to the director, with his own life as collateral. She would never say anything if she knew he would die as a result, would she?

Yes, that was the better way, the surer way. He wanted to kill Delgado, but what he wanted wasn't the point.

He dropped to his knees and ran his hands up and down Delgado's legs and torso. He found a wallet, a knife, a cell phone, a pair of handcuff keys on a small ring, and the keys to the Sprinter. He tossed aside everything but the cell phone and the handcuff keys. Then he folded Delgado's hands across his back, put a knee across his wrists, and looked over at Evie, who had shrunk back into the corner, her eyes wide.

"Are you hurt?" he said.

She shook her head once, her shoulders rising and falling rapidly with her breathing.

"Are you handcuffed?" he said. "I can't see."

She nodded. A tear slid down her cheek.

"It's okay," he said. "It's okay now. I have the keys. Come closer so I can unlock the cuffs. I don't want to let him up."

She hesitated for a moment, then crab-walked forward, turning when she was close so Manus could access the cuffs. He popped one side free. She turned to face him, rubbing her free wrist. He handed her the key. She undid the other side, let the cuffs and keys drop to the floor, then pressed her fingers to her ears and grimaced. Manus realized the sound of the shots, magnified inside the Sprinter, had hurt her.

Delgado stirred under Manus's weight. "Hand me the cuffs," Manus said. "He's starting to wake up."

She crouched, staring at Delgado, seemingly paralyzed. Manus realized she was in a kind of shock. He leaned over, snatched up the cuffs, and got them around Delgado's wrists. Then he stood, stooping to avoid the roof. "We have to go."

Evie stood and backed away, rubbing her wrists. "What is this? Who are you?"

Manus shook his head. "We have to go."

She glanced at Delgado, then back to Manus. "Is this some kind of good cop / bad cop?"

Manus moved to the side door and slid it open. "We have to go. My truck is close by."

She glanced at Delgado again, then suddenly stepped forward and kicked him soccer style full in the face. Delgado's head rocketed back and blood shot from his nose. Evie grimaced and clutched her foot. Delgado rolled back and forth and bled.

Manus pulled Delgado out of the Sprinter and yanked him to his feet. The smaller man was choking and spitting. Blood ran freely from his crumpled nose.

Evie came to the door. Manus saw she had picked up her shoe. She started to step out, then paused and glanced around, obviously disoriented, holding the shoe in front of her as though it could somehow protect her from all this insanity. Manus realized she had no idea where she even was.

"The Triadelphia Reservoir," Manus said. "My truck is a quarter mile away. I should have thought to bring your other shoe. I'm sorry. But it's in the truck. So is your purse."

He switched on the Defender and shone it in Delgado's face. "Get in front," he said. "Driver's seat."

Delgado spat out a huge wad of phlegm and blood. "Do you know what the director is going to do when he hears about this?" he said.

Manus slid the Sprinter door closed and gave the handcuff keys to Evie. "Follow us around. I need to keep him here." He took Delgado by the collar and marched him to the front of the Sprinter, Evie just behind them. Manus pushed Delgado up into the driver's seat, then circled around to the other side. Delgado watched as he moved, his eyes dark with rage. Manus got in, gripped Delgado's collar again, and pressed the muzzle of the pistol just behind his right ear. "Turn toward the driver-side door," he said. "So your back is to the steering wheel."

Delgado glared at him. "Motherfucker, you can't just leave me here. This is bullshit."

"You want to be left cuffed to the wheel, or with a bullet in your head?"

Delgado said nothing.

Manus nodded to Evie. "Uncuff his hands, then cuff them back through the steering wheel." He let Delgado feel the tight grip on his collar, the muzzle behind his ear.

Her hands were shaking, but she managed, handing the keys to Manus when she was done. Manus double-locked and double-checked the cuffs, and then, satisfied, dropped the keys on the floor, slid out, and went around. When he made it to the driver-side door, he saw that Delgado was saying something to Evie.

". . . but first I'm going to make your little deaf prick son watch. Or maybe I'll make *you* watch me do *him*."

Manus looked at Evie to see her response. She didn't answer. Instead, a flatness crept into her eyes, an expressionlessness into her features. "Give me the gun," she said, her eyes never leaving Delgado.

Delgado recognized what had come over her. He looked at Manus and shook his head. "If that bitch kills me, the director will make you pay. And you know it."

"Give me the gun," Evie said again.

Manus shook his head. "We can't. We have to go. I'll explain on the way."

Delgado turned to her and smiled. "See you soon, sweetheart. Love that shaved bush."

The flatness in Evie's eyes was suddenly replaced by rage. She grabbed Delgado by the hair and bashed his face into the edge of the door. Twice. A third time. Delgado jerked his arms, but his wrists were secured and there was nothing he could do to defend himself.

Manus threw an arm around her and pulled her back. A bloody clump of hair plugs pulled free, and Delgado howled.

Evie tried to twist loose. Manus held her firmly, letting her understand it was useless. After a moment, she stopped struggling. Manus let her go and watched her warily.

She flung the hair clump away and looked at Delgado. "The next time I see you," she said, panting, "I'm going to kill you. So you better hope it's not soon."

Delgado was too busy coughing out blood to respond.

CHAPTER . . . .
. . . . 37

They moved as fast as they could, but it was slow going given the terrain and Evie's lack of shoes. Neither of them said anything—it was too dark to talk, and besides, Manus wanted to keep moving. He removed the magazine from Delgado's gun while they walked, ejected the round in the chamber, wiped everything down, and tossed it all in different directions into the woods.

When they reached his truck, he gave her the purse and shoe from the toolbox. They got in and he put the keys in the ignition. But Evie flipped on the dome light and held out a hand to indicate he should wait.

What was that thumb drive? she signed.

A decoy.

Why?

Manus hesitated, unsure of how to respond. *He was going to hurt you.*

Evie looked at him for a long moment. Then she signed, *Get me home to Dash.*

What about your car? It's still at the supermarket.

Just get me home.

Manus fired up the engine and pulled out. A hundred yards

down the dirt road, he glanced over at Evie. She had her cell phone to her ear. Horrified, Manus snatched it away and cut off the call. He looked at her and shook his head violently.

"What?" she said, her eyes wide. "What?"

"Were you calling home?"

She nodded.

"Your apartment," he said, looking back at the road. "I think it might be bugged."

He glanced over to see how she reacted to that. Her lips were pursed and she was pale.

He slowed for a curve, then accelerated again. "Were you calling the nanny?" he said. If she had been planning on talking rather than texting, it couldn't have been Dash.

He glanced over and caught her nod, then looked ahead again. "What did you say to her? They might have been listening."

He looked over just long enough to catch, "It was still ringing. She hadn't picked up."

He focused on driving again. "You have to be careful. They could hear what you say."

Delgado's phone vibrated in his pocket. Manus thought, *Shit.* He pulled out the phone and glanced down at it.

It was the director. *Status?*

The director must have been all over her phone. He'd seen the call go through and then get interrupted. He wanted to know what was going on.

Manus handed Evie the phone. "It's the director," he said, taking another curve in the road. "Text back exactly as I say. Do you understand?"

He glanced over and saw her say, "No, I don't—"

He looked back at the road. "I can't drive and read your lips. You have to listen to me and do exactly as I say. Don't argue, I'll explain as we go. Okay? Text him, 'She's taking us to it. Should know soon.'"

He glanced over and saw she was doing it. He gave her a moment, then said, "Do you understand?"

She shook her head.

He looked back to the road. "If he's geolocating, he thinks Delgado, you, and I are all together."

He saw her say, "Delgado?"

"The man in the van. The director thinks Delgado just told him you're taking us to the thumb drive. If that were true, we wouldn't let you out of our sight. So the phones have to stay together. And you can't say anything to the nanny that would be inconsistent with that."

He went back to driving, and a minute later they were back on paved road. He wanted to hit the gas but couldn't risk a traffic cop, so he kept it at just over the speed limit, his eyes going from the road to the speedometer and back because he didn't trust himself to keep it slow and steady.

Evie touched his arm. He glanced over and she held up Delgado's phone so he could read it. The director had texted, *What about the appearances we discussed? A random thing, yes?*

Manus felt a wave of anger ripple through him. He had hoped Delgado was lying about the director's orders. Now he knew better.

"Text him, 'Had to improvise. We needed her phone. But it's under control. Will check in soon.'"

He waited, then said, "Is it done?" He glanced over and saw her nod.

The light at Clarksburg Pike was red. He stopped and signed, *I know you're worried about Dash. You can call now. Just be careful of what you say. An emergency at work, you're on your way home now. Say . . . you're on your way to pick something up. If he's listening, that will make him feel better.*

She nodded, then input some numbers and put the phone to her ear. The conversation lasted only a few seconds. He couldn't read it well from the side. The light turned green and he turned left. When he looked over again, the phone was back in her lap. She was cry-ing—more from relief, he sensed, than from pain.

"Is Dash okay?"

She nodded and wiped her face.

"Evie," he said, his eyes going back and forth from her to the road. "Don't worry. It's going to be okay."

He wished he could believe it.

A minute later, she touched his arm. He glanced over. "It's ring-ing," she said. "It's him. The director."

Too much was happening. Manus couldn't think it all through. He needed more time. He said, "Text him, 'Can't talk now.'"

He kept driving. She touched his arm again and held up the phone. Another text from the director: *If she told you it's in her apart-ment, she's lying. She hasn't been there since retrieving it from Rockville this morning.*

"Fuck. Text, 'Got that. We're going to get the boy. She'll give it to us then.'"

He glanced over. She was staring at him, her eyes wide. He looked at the road again, then back at her.

"Text him."

She shook her head.

He shifted his gaze back to the road. "Evie, we have to respond." He waited, then glanced at her again. She was shaking her head and signing, *Stop the car.*

There was a turnout just ahead. He pulled over and looked at her.

Are you going to hurt me? she signed, tears welling up in her eyes. *Or Dash?*

Manus looked left, then right, feeling trapped, fighting panic. She leaned in and gripped his arm until he looked at her again.

Are you?

No, he signed, shaking his head emphatically.

The tears spilled down her cheeks. She covered her face with her hands and shook. Manus leaned forward and stroked her hair for a moment. Then he took hold of her hands and gently pulled them away so she could see him.

But someone will. If we don't figure out what to do first.

She nodded, then blew out a long breath and began inputting a message. Manus felt sick that he was piling new lies to the director upon the existing ones. He needed to think, to take control. But things were happening so fast, all he could do was react.

Five minutes later, he was circling her building. She touched his shoulder. He glanced over and she signed, *Stop.*

He shook his head and kept driving, his head swiveling, his eyes on every ambush position they passed. "We have to be careful," he said. He hoped she understood. He knew this was all new to her. She didn't understand how suddenly a mistake could happen, or what it would cost.

He did two complete circuits. He didn't see anything that rubbed him the wrong way. But he had a bad feeling. The kind he had learned to trust.

He backed into a space in the shadows of some trees, the front of the truck facing the entrance to her section of the complex. He cut the lights, but moved the gearshift to drive and left the engine running. Just in case. It was the same place he had parked when he'd come to build Dash's loft. But everything was different then.

She started to get out, but he took her arm.

I'll take you and Dash somewhere safe, he signed. *While I make things right with the director.*

She looked at him for a long moment, then signed, *He sent you to watch me.* No sign for a question. Just a statement.

Manus nodded.

To fuck me?

Manus couldn't meet her eyes. His hands floated helplessly for a moment. Then he managed, *No. I didn't tell him about that. Until . . .*

She tapped his leg to make him look at her. *Until what?*

When I realized he black-bagged your apartment. That he knew anyway. And knew that I'd been lying to him. I shouldn't have lied. But . . . but . . .

He couldn't finish. Didn't know how. He looked around, still seeing nothing, still feeling uneasy.

He wanted to tell her she needed to trust him, she needed his help. That he had to get her somewhere safe before he contacted the director, before this whole thing got any worse. That more than anything else, she needed to give him that thumb drive. Because as long as it was out there, the director would never stop.

But he didn't know how to say any of it. All he could manage was *I'm sorry. I'm so sorry. I didn't want any of this to happen. I'm going to fix it.*

How?

He shook his head, wishing he had an answer. *You need to go in. Make it fast. Apologize to the nanny and send her home. And only use sign with Dash. Tell him to grab whatever he needs for a hotel. I think the director is watching but he doesn't know much sign.*

What if he has an interpreter with him?

That's why you need to be in and out fast. Just grab some clothes, a pair of shoes, and some cash if you have it, that's all. I don't know how much time we have.

She nodded and turned to get out. He put a hand on her arm.

Wait. Take all three phones with you. And leave them inside when you go. He handed her his and Delgado's.

Why?

The director would expect all of us to be moving together. And . . . I don't know. Just a feeling.

What kind of feeling?

How could he explain something like that?

A bad one. Hurry.

CHAPTER........
........38

As soon as Evie was inside, Manus put the pickup in park, cut the engine, and got out. He wanted to believe the director would never hurt him, but his gut warned that if there were any opposition, they would be looking for his truck, and that he should therefore be somewhere else when they found it.

There was a long cluster of mulberry bushes on a grass berm ten feet behind the pickup. Good concealment. But if Manus was tempted to hide there, someone else would be, too. So he went past the bushes into the line of trees just behind them, crouching close to the thick trunk of an old maple. There was a slight breeze, but other than that the night was still. Manus mirrored that stillness, retracting, retreating, letting himself fade away as he had when his father would come home drunk, when being overlooked, remaining unseen, was the only way to survive.

A few minutes went by. A middle-aged woman came out through the entrance, about fifty yards from Manus's position. She looked Latina, but she was backlit by the building and Manus couldn't be sure. She walked to a dark Honda Civic near the front to the lot, got in, and drove off. Manus had a feeling she was the nanny.

Another minute ticked by. He saw headlights approaching along the access road to the complex. Big lights, high off the ground. A truck or SUV.

A moment later, a black Suburban turned into the parking lot. It passed several empty spaces, paused in front of Manus's pickup, and then continued slowly on. Manus tried to see inside it, but the windows were smoked and he couldn't make anything out.

The Suburban backed into a space at the end of the parking area, about thirty feet from Manus's position. The lights went out and the front doors opened. Two large men emerged, both wearing dark suits, neither of them remarkable but for a certain tension in their posture and gait, and for the sunglasses they wore despite the weak light of the parking lot lampposts. They strolled toward Manus's truck, their heads swiveling as they moved, each hitching up his pants as though adjusting for something heavy around the waistband.

Manus understood the director had sensed something was amiss. These men were here to keep things running smoothly. And what would that entail, when they realized Delgado had been side-lined and Manus was helping the woman?

You're looking for a thumb drive, he could imagine the director instructing them. *Retrieve it. Whatever it takes.*

Manus had always assumed the director relied entirely on Delgado and him for contract work, but realized now that was naïve and even narcissistic, a product of his need to believe the director was as devoted to him as he was to the director. He felt bitterness welling up in his chest and throat and willed it away. He didn't want to feel anything. Someone was here to hurt him. He would stop them, the way he always had. That was all this was. He would figure out the rest later.

One of them peeled off fifteen feet short of Manus's pickup and eased into the cluster of mulberry bushes at its far end. Manus nodded, knowing he'd been right not to use the spot himself. The other kept coming, taking up a mirror-image position at the other end of the bushes not ten feet in front of where Manus crouched.

They were watching the front entrance. The director must have told them he'd tracked Delgado, Manus, and the woman all going inside. They'd confirmed Manus's truck was empty, and now they were waiting for everyone to emerge from the building.

Maybe he was wrong about what they had come for. But it didn't matter. They weren't here to help. And when they saw Evie coming out alone with Dash, they were going to move in. She and the boy would be in the crossfire. Manus would have lost the element of surprise. He couldn't let that happen.

He knew he was making things worse. But maybe he could still explain. He hadn't killed Delgado, only disabled him. And only because Delgado was doing things the wrong way, and wasn't going to find the thumb drive. And these men . . . he didn't know who they were, or who sent them. Not really. If it turned out they were the director's men, then it was a misunderstanding, and Manus would apologize and explain. If he could just get Evie to give him the drive, and make her promise never to say anything, he could still make things right. He had to make things right.

He could have dropped the man in front of him with the Force Pro, but the sound would alert the man's partner, as well as all the neighbors. So instead, he eased the Espada out of his pocket and unfolded it with both hands, holding open the safety catch to prevent the blade from clicking when it locked into place. There was nothing between him and the man directly ahead other than soft, manicured grass. No branches, no gravel, not even any mulch. He moved forward, letting the heel of each boot slowly take his weight, then rolling along the outer sole as they'd taught him at the Farm. He kept the knife back along his thigh lest some stray light glint off the surface of the blade.

At the last moment, the man began to turn, whether by instinct or chance or because Manus had made some sound, Manus neither knew nor cared. He clamped his left hand around the man's mouth and nose, swept him back onto his heels, and plunged the point of the nearly eight-inch stainless steel blade into the right side of the man's neck, driving it all the way past the front of the cervical vertebrae and out the opposite side, then punched it edge-forward, transecting the man's larynx, both carotid arteries, both jugular veins, and pretty much everything else in the neighborhood, too.

A geyser of hot blood erupted from the wound. The man's hands came up, scrabbled spasmodically at Manus's forearm, and then fell away as oxygenated blood plummeted out of his brain. Manus waited until the pressurized spray had ebbed, then stepped back and carefully laid the man out on his back. He stayed down, watching to see if the other man offered any reaction. He saw nothing.

He wiped the knife and his wet hand on the grass, then eased back to the tree line. Once clear of the mulberry bushes, he could see the other man again. He was still focused on the entrance.

Manus moved laterally until he was directly behind the man, then began to ease forward. Something about the man's posture, his attention, sharpened. Manus froze. He looked to the entrance and saw Evie and Dash coming through it, Dash wearing a backpack, Evie holding an overnight bag. Fuck, he was out of time.

He moved more quickly, trading stealth for speed. The man must have heard him because he turned, turned and saw Manus. It was too dark for Manus to make out his expression, but there was recognition in his posture, in how quickly he was reaching inside his jacket, in the way he was moving offline to buy time and distance.

Manus charged forward, took hold of the man's right hand just as it closed over the butt of a side-holstered pistol, and speared the Espada straight up under his jawline, driving it with such force that the man's feet left the ground. For a moment, the man dangled and danced as though skewered on a pike, supported only by a blade buried in his brain and a fist in his throat, blood spraying from his neck, tongue protruding, eyes bulging and fixed on Manus's face. Then his body sagged, his eyes drifted skyward, and Manus could no longer hold him aloft. Manus lowered his arm and stepped back, and the man folded onto his knees. Manus took him by the hair, jerked out the knife, and let the body spill facedown onto the grass.

For a moment, his vision blurred and his eyes stung. Blood, he realized. He swiped an arm across his face and accomplished nothing—the sleeve was soaked. He used the other arm, and that worked better. He wiped the Espada on the dry sleeve, folded it, and clipped it back in place. Then he stripped off his shirt and used it to clean his face and arms. He could feel his tee shirt had gotten blood on it, too, but it was dark blue, and in the low light he didn't think the blood would show up right away. If it did, he'd think of something.

He looked through a break in the foliage and saw Evie and the boy. They were thirty yards away and hadn't seen anything—the bushes were too thick.

He balled up his shirt and crept along until he could see the Suburban. He didn't think there was anyone else inside, but it wasn't impossible, either, and he didn't want to take the chance. He considered slashing a tire, but if there were someone in there, they might feel that and emerge while he was out of position. So instead, he moved forward in a crouch until he was directly behind the vehicle.

He eased out the Force Pro, took a deep breath, stood, and hammer-fisted the butt into the rear window. Glass exploded inward and he saw two men in the middle seats flinch and start to turn. Muscle, waiting in the car to help secure whoever the other two brought back from the apartment. Manus shot the one on the left in the face. The other was quick, ducking down as Manus tracked back to him.

Manus adjusted and fired four times through the seatback. He saw blood and brain matter explode onto the back of the front seats, and knew the man was done.

Had anyone heard? The gun had been inside the vehicle, which might have muffled the sound at least somewhat. But he had no way of knowing.

He holstered the Force Pro and jogged back to the pickup. Evie and Dash were just walking up the passenger side. Dash waved hello and gave Manus a big smile. He looked around, wrinkled his nose, and signed, *What's that smell?*

The answer, of course, was blood, which Manus knew had a different scent by the liter than it did in whatever sorts of cuts and scrapes Dash might have experienced during a blessedly innocent childhood. Other than the question, the boy seemed untroubled, and Manus assumed Evie had dreamed up a comforting story about why they had to run out.

Someone hit a deer, he signed. *I tried to help, but there was nothing I could do.*

Can I see? Dash signed.

Manus shook his head. *You don't want to see that. Come on, we should go.* He opened the passenger door and Dash got in.

Evie looked in the direction of the Suburban and said, "Was that . . . shooting?" It wasn't easy to make out the words in the dim light, and Manus wondered why she hadn't signed. Then he realized: she didn't want Dash to know.

He opened the pickup's toolbox and tossed in the bloody shirt. *Later,* he signed. *Did you leave the phones?*

She nodded.

All right. Let's go.

Evie got in and he closed the door behind her. Manus moved toward the back of the truck, yanked off his tee shirt, tossed it on top of the other shirt, then grabbed a fistful of hospital bleach wipes from a canister and cleaned his hands and arms and face. The dirty wipes went on top of the dirty shirt. He'd get rid of it all somewhere safe, and bleach down the toolbox, too. But distance first. He pulled on a clean shirt and got in.

They sat three across, with Dash in the middle. As he drove, Manus caught snatches of the two of them signing. The boy wanted to know where they were going. Evie was telling him Mr. Manus was helping her fix a big problem at work and that she'd explain more just as soon as she could.

Manus drove northwest, keeping to secondary roads. He couldn't go north to his apartment, and while the urban density of Baltimore to the east and the District to the south were tempting, there were also too many license plate readers in the cities, too many cameras, too many cops. All of which rendered west or northwest a possibly predictable choice, but on the other hand, there were innumerable state and regional parks, forests, and campgrounds in the area. Not to mention cheap motels—the nearby Civil War battlefields were popular attractions. He'd always kept the toolbox well stocked as a bugout kit. He hadn't planned on using it for three people, but they'd manage. He'd get them somewhere safe, and then they'd figure out what to do.

He just hoped they could agree on what that might consist of.

CHAPTER . . . .
. . . . 39

They drove along dark roads in silence, their surroundings becoming more rural and remote as the night deepened, the headlights of the truck picking up nothing but trees and the odd grain silo and occasional modest houses. Dash was slumped against Evie, asleep. Evie wished she could nod off, too. But she was too terrified by everything that was happening, and everything that had happened before.

When she had awakened in the van, she'd first thought she'd been in some kind of accident and was now in an ambulance. Someone was asking her if her head hurt. But she couldn't move . . . had they strapped her to a gurney?

Then she had seen that man—Delgado—and the way he was looking at her, like she was something he was planning to cook and eat. And she remembered Marvin, outside the supermarket, and it all came back to her in a sickening rush.

The man had looked familiar, which somehow had made the whole thing even more disturbing and surreal. And then she'd realized why: the camera footage. The man who had planted the bomb and then disappeared in the cemetery. He'd been wearing a cap and glasses, but that sneer was unforgettable.

She had been sure she was going to die. And then Marvin had shown up, claiming to have the thumb drive, and she hadn't known what the hell to think. And then . . . had he *shot* someone in the parking lot of her building? She thought that was what she'd heard, and there was that story about a deer, but when she'd asked he hadn't answered. But had someone been waiting for her outside her building? Had Marvin *killed* someone there?

There was too much happening. She couldn't keep up. And now that the immediate danger had passed, she felt herself wanting to fall apart. But she couldn't. She had to stay strong for Dash. She just needed a little time to catch her breath. And more than anything, to think. *Think.*

Marvin had stopped to switch the truck's license plates just outside of Clarksville, explaining that he kept a spare pair in the truck toolbox just in case. She was glad he was well outfitted, but it made her uncomfortable, too. She had thought she knew who he was. She had taken him into her home, into her body. And now . . . she felt confused, and frightened, and violated. And also grateful, because he certainly seemed to know what he was doing in the current situation while she didn't have a clue. But how much could she really trust him?

Somewhere north of Gettysburg, she was finally beginning to nod off from nervousness and exhaustion—or was it the aftereffects of whatever drug they'd given her?—when she felt the pickup stop. She shook herself awake and looked around, seeing nothing but rolling fields and farmland. Marvin was gesturing to a poorly illuminated sign next to a driveway to their right: *Big Sky Motel.* Beneath the faded blue and red letters, flickering in pink neon, the word *Vacancy.*

Independent, he signed. *We can use cash.*

She stared down the driveway but couldn't see where it led. *How do you know?*

The corporate chains have policies. The independents are usually family run. They're getting harder to find, but they'll always take a cash deposit.

She decided to file his apparent experience with that sort of thing in the same place she had filed his spare license plates: as something better examined later.

Wait, she signed. *Cash is bad. They might be looking for that pattern. Someone registering at a hotel within a certain radius of my apartment tonight. For cash.*

They can do that?

I'm getting the feeling I don't know a fraction of what they can do.

I have some prepaid credit cards. Unused. Untraceable to me. In case of emergency.

She smiled faintly. *Well, I guess this is an emergency.*

I'll tell them to not even register us. It's just going to be a night clerk. For an extra fifty bucks, they'll give us a room key and forget to enter us into the system. Look at this place. I doubt it's part of Travelocity or whatever.

You sure?

He nodded and turned right into the driveway. A swimming pool was illuminated by the passing headlights, then disappeared again in the darkness. Then an old swing set, a lopsided picnic table, some chairs. He parked a little way past the office—just beyond where someone inside could see the pickup without getting up, she noted. He wasn't hiding them, but he wasn't making it easy for anyone, either.

She rolled down the window and heard only the sound of crickets. No distant traffic, no neighbors, nothing. She leaned her head out and looked up. The sky was studded with stars.

Marvin returned a few minutes later. He pulled the truck door closed behind him and showed her a key on a plastic fob. *Thirty-four dollars,* he signed. *Plus a fifty-dollar security deposit. And another fifty for not entering us into their computer system because I'm paranoid about my office finding out I'm playing hooky. Old guy, well into a bottle of Four Roses. He's not going to remember us.*

She nodded and gave him a small smile. He must have known how upset she was, and was trying to make her feel better. It wasn't much, but maybe it was something.

Their room was at the far end of the structure, which was shaped like a U around a central parking area. Marvin backed in directly in front of the door. She figured parking nose-out was for a quick getaway, but again decided not to ask.

He cut the engine and looked around. *Stay here for a minute.*

She glanced at Dash. He was still out cold. *Why?*

He removed the ashtray, and from behind it withdrew a small leather pouch, which he placed on his lap. *I'm going to let us into the room next to ours. I asked the owner to give us a room with unoccupied ones alongside it because my wife is a light sleeper. He said no problem, we're mostly empty tonight, I'll give you a room at the end of the complex.*

She glanced at the leather pouch. *Those are lock picks?*

He nodded.

She had to ask. *Marvin . . . who are you?*

He stared through the windshield, into the darkness.

Right now, I'm not really sure.

CHAPTER . . . .
. . . . 40

The room was clean and functional: two queen beds separated by a nightstand; a table and two chairs; pine-paneled walls and low-pile carpeting. It was deluxe compared to some of the places Manus had stayed, but he wasn't sure how the woman and the boy would like it. He knew Evie was scared and uncertain, though she was doing a good job of hiding it. Dash seemed all right, and Manus sensed he was picking up his emotional cues from his mother.

They all took turns in the small bathroom. Manus went last, and when he came out, Dash was in pajamas. Smart of Evie, to bring something of their home routine on the road with them, a small comfort for her son. Far back in his mind, Manus was aware of that feeling—a ghost, a vanished memory, a shadow from another life. He noticed Evie looking at him closely and pushed it away.

Dash went to the bathroom to brush his teeth. Manus pointed to the bed farthest from the exterior door, then signed, *You take that one. Better for me to be closer to the door.*

She looked frightened at that, and he realized the possibility of having to engage someone breaching the door was new and unnerving to her. Along with, presumably, everything else that was happening. He signed, *Just being careful.*

I've noticed that about you.

I'm sorry.

It's okay. I think we need it right now.

I mean . . . I'm sorry for everything.

Dash came out of the bathroom. He handed Evie his toothbrush and yawned.

She smiled at him. *Time for bed.*

He smiled back. *No school tomorrow?*

No school.

He walked over to Manus and looked up at him. *Thanks for helping my mom.*

Manus nodded, not knowing how to explain that he deserved no thanks for anything he had done.

When you're finished, will you help me build a desk under my loft? My mom said you might.

Manus glanced over at Evie. She looked discomfited, and he gathered she hadn't expected the boy to repeat that. And of course whenever she'd said it, things had been completely different.

Only if you help me carry the lumber.

The boy's face lit up in a big smile and he held out his hand. Manus shook it, and then the boy hugged him. As always, it made Manus feel strange—guilty, happy, sad.

And now, he realized, something else, as well. What? Maybe . . . protective. Not the way he always had with the director. That was different. This was . . . he didn't know. He'd think about it later.

Evie tucked the boy in and kissed his forehead. She held out the tee shirt the boy had been wearing and signed, *Mister Manus and I are going to talk for a few minutes. Put this over your eyes so the light won't disturb you, okay?*

The boy signed, *It's okay, it won't bother me,* and Manus knew he wanted to see what they were saying.

Evie smiled. *You go to sleep.*

Manus signed, *It's late. Probably better to turn the lights off anyway. We can just talk in the bathroom.*

Evie looked at him for a moment, then nodded in apparent understanding. No advantage to having light creeping under the door or through the edges of the drapes and drawing attention to the room, even though they were registered in the one adjacent to it.

They left the door open a crack. Evie sat on the edge of the tub; Manus took the closed toilet.

She glanced through the crack in the door as though at the world outside, then signed, *What are we supposed to do?*

He knew how it would sound, but he said it anyway. *You have to give the director the thumb drive.*

She looked at him for a long moment. *How do you know I have it?*

They told me you do.

How did they know? How did they know about the Rockville mail drop?

I don't know. The director told me you had stolen media, probably a thumb drive, and that we had to get it back.

Do you even know what this is about?

Manus was perplexed. He didn't know. Not really. He didn't need to. *He really just wants the thumb drive. That's why—*

She shook her head forcefully. *No. That's not just what he wants. Maybe it was at one point. But not anymore.*

Manus knew she might be right, probably *was* right. But his way at least offered a chance. He had to persuade her. *Then what?*

She hesitated. Manus knew she was gauging how much she should trust him. If he were in her shoes, he knew he wouldn't say anything. But maybe she decided she had no choice, because she signed, *I told you, I saw some things I wasn't supposed to. I guess that's what you were fishing for, weren't you?*

He nodded, ashamed.

I was talking about the bombing in DC, she continued. *The director was behind it.*

Manus didn't understand. *What do you mean, behind it?*

He did it. He ordered it.

Manus shook his head, certain she was mistaken. He had killed many people on the director's orders, of course. But those actions had always been discriminate, even surgical. They'd never involved innocents. Never a massacre.

No, he signed, not sure of who he was trying to convince. *He would never do that.*

Your friend Delgado planted the bomb.

What?

I saw him plant the bomb. On a food truck. I monitored him via video footage, and he knew exactly where to exploit the gaps in my coverage so I couldn't track where he came from before or where he went after. Who else could have told him about those gaps? I don't think anyone besides the director even knows about the camera networks.

No, the director would never—

What do you think, the director is some kind of nice guy? Delgado was going to kill me tonight. I think he was supposed to make it look like some random abduction and rape. You think the director didn't know about all that?

Manus didn't answer. Knowing the director would allow something like that was already almost unbearable. As for the bomb . . . for the first time, he allowed himself to wonder why the director had sent him back to Turkey to kill those men. And take their cell phones.

Did you know?

Manus shook his head violently.

Did you?

Not . . . at first. At first I thought it was just about the thumb drive. But then . . .

He couldn't finish.

Then what?

It was like his world had been shattered, and now someone was shattering even the pieces. *Why? Why would the director set off a bomb?*

He wanted an excuse to launch a drone strike on where they were holding that kidnapped journalist Ryan Hamilton. Hamilton was working with an NSA whistleblower, Daniel Perkins, the one who died in a car accident in Ankara the same day Hamilton was kidnapped. You think that's a coincidence?

How do you know Hamilton was working with Perkins?

There was a pause, then she signed, *Camera networks. That's my job. I hack the networks and I wrote the software that monitors them all with a biometric matching program.*

Manus struggled to keep up. *So . . . you saw Hamilton and Perkins together?*

She nodded. *In Istanbul. I'm the one who told the director about it. Which I think is part of the reason he went to such lengths to make what happened to Hamilton and Perkins look so . . . I don't know. Disconnected. Random. He knew I was going to suspect.*

But why kidnap Hamilton if he wanted him dead?

I think he was supposed to die. The kidnapping was intended to be a kind of circuit breaker. I mean, a journalist getting kidnapped by some ISIS-affiliated jihadist group . . . how would anyone connect something like that to the director? But something went wrong. Whoever kidnapped Hamilton didn't kill him the way they were supposed to. So the director had Delgado plant a bomb, and claimed it was the same terrorist group that was holding Hamilton, and convinced the president to launch a drone strike. All to kill Hamilton. All to cover up whatever Hamilton had gotten from Perkins.

Without thinking, Manus signed, *Hamilton is alive.*

She blinked. *What? How do you know?*

He didn't want her to know of his role in what had happened to Hamilton. He wondered why he'd told her. But he couldn't take it back now.

I saw him. In Turkey. He was hurt, but . . . he was alive when I saw him.

But all the networks said he was dead.

Maybe he is, but not in that drone strike. He was in Turkey when it happened.

Where is he now?

Manus hesitated, then signed, *I don't know.*

She stared at him for a moment. *What are you not telling me?*

Nothing.

Marvin, if he's alive, he might be my only hope.

Why?

Just tell me. Do you know anything about where he is?

Manus shook his head.

She put her hands on his face and looked in his eyes. "Please," she said. "Help me."

Her hands were warm and her face was beautiful. Manus was afraid she would hate him if she learned what he'd done, what he was. But it would be worse if something happened to her. Or to Dash. He closed his eyes and put his hands over hers so he could remember what it felt like when she touched him.

After a moment, he took his hands away. *If he's alive, I think he's somewhere near Lake Tuz.*

How do you know this?

I just do.

How?

I saw him there.

How?

He felt anger well up inside him. *It doesn't matter!*

She recoiled as though he had hit her. He held up his hands palms out in apology, then signed, *I'm sorry.*

She shook her head. *Why won't you tell me?*

He flexed his fingers, searching for words. *I don't . . . want you to know.*

Because I won't like it?

He looked down. *Because you won't like me.*

She touched his knee. When he looked up, she signed, *I do like you.*

You wouldn't if you knew.

Knew what?

He hesitated, then signed, *You and Dash are good.*

She gave him a faint smile. *Well, Dash is, anyway.*

No. You are, too. I see how you are with him. You're good.

I guess with Dash I am, yes.

I'm not good.

Because you've done bad things?

He nodded.

Did you do something bad to Hamilton?

He nodded again, unable to look at her.

She rested a hand on his knee. After a moment, he raised his eyes. She was looking at him with a gentleness and understanding he knew he didn't deserve, and never expected to have. It hurt like a stab wound. But . . . he so wanted to believe what he saw in her eyes could be true.

Whatever you did, she signed, *he's still alive.*

I think he is. I didn't do anything to him. But he was in bad shape. Some people hurt him.

What people?

It doesn't matter. They're gone. They can't hurt anyone anymore. And I don't know anything else. Not really. The men who hurt him are dead. He could have taken money from them, and the keys to their van.

Where would he go?

Manus imagined Hamilton, scared, hurt, disoriented. He gets out of that dress they'd put him in, and changes into the work clothes in the back of the van. He goes out and finds the bodies. He's terrified, horrified. But his survival instincts are strong, and he subdues his urge to vomit at the sight of all that gore. He forces himself to go through the dead men's pockets. He finds money, he finds the van keys. He drives off. He sees some tourists at one of the concession stands by the lake. He asks directions. He buys a map. And then . . .

He's a city guy, I could tell. He wouldn't know how to survive outdoors. Or how to get across a border. He might look for a youth hostel. But . . . the way he was hurt, he wouldn't want to share a room or bathroom. Or have to talk to a bunch of backpackers. Plus his face has been on television. Not so likely that he would be recognized, but the more people who see him, the more the risk. So I think . . . a hotel like this one. The kind that doesn't require credit cards. A place where he could bring in some food and pull the drapes and cry and hide and heal.

Where?

There's not much around Lake Tuz, so my guess is he would head to Ankara. Closer than anything else and he'd have the most options there.

Her eyes were excited, her expression intense. *What day and time did you see him? Be precise.*

The day before I built Dash his loft. Noon, local time.

He could see her calculating the elapsed time. *All right,* she signed, *it's morning there now. He would have been holed up for . . . four nights. Wherever he went, do you think he could still be there?*

He was traumatized. If he found a safe place, I think he'd be afraid to move. Until his money was close to running out. What are you thinking?

She pressed her fingertips against her forehead in concentration. *What I was saying before we took this room—about the way NSA could comb through hotel reservation systems? I can do that. Hamilton isn't as tactical as you, and he doesn't know as much as I do about NSA capabilities. Plus he wouldn't want to draw any more attention to himself than necessary. He wouldn't ask anyone to not register him in a computer system.*

He nodded, impressed. *That makes sense.*

If I could access something called XKeyscore, there's a chance I could locate him. The kind of hotel you're describing . . . it couldn't be more than, what, a dozen, two dozen? I just need the one that checked in someone with an American name for cash within, say, six hours after you last saw him. But they probably revoked my account privileges.

Why?

Are you joking? I'm supposed to be dead by now, remember? Abducted and raped.

The comment stung, but Manus tried to ignore it in favor of what was relevant. He reminded himself she was just an analyst. That she wasn't used to thinking operationally.

But that's the point, he signed. *If your death was supposed to look like a random thing, they wouldn't want to do anything out of the ordinary at work like directing some sysadmin to revoke your privileges.*

She looked at him, a glimmer of hope in her eyes. *That's true.* She paused as though considering, then added, *All right, I need a laptop.*

They'll trace the access back to the hotel.

Not if I use Tor.

But your search parameters will be logged. If they're monitoring your work searches and you find Hamilton, you'll lead them straight to him.

I'll warn him. Anyway, I'm going to have to take that chance. If he'll just tell me the passphrase, I can decrypt the drive and expose what's on it. There won't be anything for the director to cover up anymore.

Hamilton won't trust you.

She smacked her palms down on the edge of the tub. *Well, do you have any better ideas?*

As it happened, he did. *Give the drive to the director. Promise to never say anything.*

No! I know you think you know him, and can trust him. But you don't and you can't. He's not a good person, Marvin. He's sick and power-mad and terrified of being found out. He would never, ever trust me to keep my mouth shut. He'd say he would, and then he'd have me removed the first chance he could.

Manus felt something cold come over him. *I'd tell him if that happened, I would kill him.*

For a moment, she looked frightened. Then her expression softened and she touched his knee. *Then he would kill you, too. You must know that.*

Manus didn't answer. He could feel his mind trying to believe what it wanted, trying to push away logic and evidence. He felt so alone. It was like that first night in the juvenile facility. Everything he thought he knew and could count on, ripped away. No one he could rely on. Everyone an enemy, everyone trying to hurt him.

I need to get on the Internet, she signed.

Manus didn't like her plan. It was risky for Hamilton, and more important, it felt risky for them. But she'd been adamant about not trusting the director. And despite his reluctance to agree, he knew she might be right.

The guy who checked me in had a laptop, he signed. *He might let me borrow it. Or more like rent it. How long would you need it?*

If I'm lucky, ten minutes. But no more than a few hours.

Manus hesitated, then signed, *Double-lock the door behind me. I'll knock when I come back. One knock, on the window. If someone knocks on the door or more than once, it's not me.*

She nodded. They got up and walked to the door. Manus checked through the window and went out.

The old guy he'd negotiated with earlier was still there, the air still perfumed by bourbon. The guy was looking at his laptop, and closed it when Manus came in.

"Everything all right with the room?"

Manus nodded. "My wife didn't bring her laptop. Could we borrow yours? Just a little while, a few hours at most. I'd pay you, of course."

"Well, shoot, you don't have to pay me, but . . . how much?"

Manus noted that the bottle of Four Roses was a couple of inches lower than it had been earlier. He shrugged. "Another fifty?"

The man raised his eyebrows, and Manus realized he'd offered too much. "A work thing," he said quickly. "If she doesn't take care of it right away, we might as well kiss our little vacation good-bye. We can access the Internet from the room, right?"

"Sure, free Wi-Fi in every room. A few hours, you say?"

Manus nodded.

"Say, you're not fixing to make off with my laptop, are you? I mean, it's nothing new, but it's worth more than fifty bucks."

"How about a security deposit?"

The man rubbed his chin. "Ah, forget about the deposit. Give me an even hundred and it's yours for the night."

Manus pulled two fifties from his pocket and placed them on the counter. The man looked like he might salivate.

"All right, we got ourselves a deal. Give me just a minute, I need to take care of a few things."

The man opened the laptop and worked the trackpad. Manus assumed he was deleting records of visits to porn sites. Which was actually good. It suggested they kept no central records of anyone's browsing history.

He took the laptop back to the room and knocked once on the glass. Evie let him in and they went back to the bathroom. It took her only a minute to download the Tor browser. A minute more, and she signed excitedly, *You were right. They didn't revoke my privileges. I'm in.*

She hunched forward and worked the keyboard. Manus couldn't see what she was doing, but he had an idea. Accessing NSA's full take on worldwide hotel reservation systems. Screening out every hotel that was located outside a 150-mile radius from Lake Tuz. Screening out every transaction that occurred more than eight hours after Manus had seen Hamilton. Screening out every credit card transaction. Screening out everyone who had checked in with a passport. And leaving only . . .

I think I've got him, she signed. *The Sunaa Hotel, central Ankara. Registered as Bill Moore. No other hits.*

Manus nodded, trying to share her excitement. But what he felt instead was dread. He had never been afraid of a fight. But he preferred to avoid fights he thought were unwinnable. Or worse, unsurvivable. They'd been lucky to get this far. He was afraid she was going to push things until their luck ran out.

He stood. *You see if you can reach him*, he signed. *I'm going to keep watch.*

CHAPTER . . . .
. . . . 41

In less than five minutes, Evie had signed up for a secure VoIP account, using one of Manus's prepaid cards to pay for the access. She called the Sunaa and asked to be connected to Bill Moore. There was a pause, then an intermittent buzz as the call was put through. She waited, her heart pounding, trying not to hope. Would he be there? Would he answer? Did she even have the right person? She might have made a mistake. It could have been a coincidence—

"Hello?" A male voice, American accented, the tone uncertain, almost tremulous. It had to be him. It had to be.

"Ryan," she said, "I'm a friend. Please, don't hang up."

There was a pause. He said, "I . . . who is this?"

There was a little latency on the line, but nothing too terrible. This was going to work. It was going to be okay.

"I'm so sorry," she said, suddenly fighting tears. "I didn't know any of this was going to happen. I was just doing my job. I'm sorry."

"I don't know what you're talking about."

The fear in his voice had worsened. *Get it together, girl*, she thought. *Don't freak him out. Help him. Help him help you.*

"I'm sorry," she said again. "I'm just scared. I've learned some things I wasn't supposed to, about your meetings in Turkey, about the thumb drives you mailed. I have one of them. Earlier tonight I was abducted and barely got away. And now my little boy and I are on the run. I don't know anyone else who can help us."

There was another pause. Then: "What do you mean, you have one of the thumb drives?"

"You sent two. One by FedEx, I'm guessing to your news organization. The other by ordinary mail, to a mail drop in Rockville. The first one would have been intercepted. But I have the other."

"Who are you?"

She blew out a deep breath, feeling like what came next had a fifty-fifty chance of blowing up the whole thing. But if it didn't, if they could get past this point, maybe her plan could work.

"I'm an NSA analyst," she said. "But I'm not your enemy, I swear. They're trying to kill me, too."

"NSA? Oh, my God. You can't be fucking serious."

"Look, what can I offer as bona fides?"

"How do you know about any of this? How did you know—"

"—where to find you?"

He didn't answer. She imagined his terror at confirming his identity. But he must have realized they were already past that.

"That's a long story," she said. "The gist of it is, no one else is looking because everyone else thinks you're dead. In a drone strike."

Another pause. "They really think that? It's not just some official bullshit?"

"You know about it?"

"There's a TV in the room."

He was reluctant, of course he was, but he was talking. Probably because he was scared and desperate, but why didn't matter. What mattered was that she keep him going.

"No," she said, "it's not some official bullshit. At least as far as I know. They launched that strike because they thought you were there. They want you dead."

"Who is 'they'?"

"The director of NSA. He knows about your meeting with Perkins."

"Where's Perkins now? Can you get a message to him?"

She realized Perkins's accident hadn't made the international news. Of course not. His status was covert, and besides, it was just a car accident.

"Perkins is dead. A car accident in Ankara, the same day he met you in Istanbul. Except, not an accident. I'm pretty sure that was the director, too."

"Oh, Jesus. Oh, fuck."

"Listen. Whatever's on that thumb drive, it's so explosive the director of the National Security Agency has practically lost his mind over it. He kidnapped you, he killed Perkins, now he's trying to kill me. And that bombing in DC? A false flag. An excuse to bomb the jihadist camp where the director believed you were being held."

"How—"

"It doesn't matter how. I don't know what to do other than publish whatever's on the drive, right? Take away the director's ability to cover it up with murder? His reason for wanting you and me dead? Doesn't that make sense?"

"Of course, it makes perfect sense. But how?"

"I told you, I have the second thumb drive. But you encrypted it. Give me your passphrase and I'll decrypt it. And from there, I don't know, you're the journalist . . . I'll get it to your editor, or something."

"Stop right there. The fact that I'm still on the phone with you means that okay, I must at least halfway believe what you're telling me. But there is no way in the world I'm giving you the passphrase. For all I know, you're just some NSA operative trying to get into the thumb drive so you can ascertain how bad the damage is. And there's a CIA team outside my door, waiting to grab me the moment you've confirmed the passphrase is accurate."

She fought the urge to scream. All she needed was for this idiot to tell her the damned passphrase, and she could save all of them.

Think, Evie. He's scared. You have to be the calm one. So think. Think.

"Ryan, think about it. If there were a team, they could grab you right now. Why would I want the passphrase if I didn't have the thumb drive? And if I do have the thumb drive, that team could make you tell them the passphrase. If you tried to lie, they'd know because what you gave them wouldn't decrypt the drive. They'd torture you until you told them the truth."

"Forgive me, but you sound just a little too knowledgeable about how these things work for me to feel comfortable."

"Yeah?" she said, feeling her calm slipping. "You know where my knowledge comes from? From being hit over the head earlier this evening and held by some NSA contractor who enjoys his work just a little too much. I hid the thumb drive, and he explained how they were going to find it. By crushing my fingers and burning my lips off and torturing my little boy right in front of me until whatever I told him checked out with his people. So yeah, I'm kind of an expert now on what the CIA would be doing if they were really right outside your door!"

She squeezed her eyes shut and gritted her teeth, furious with herself for losing control. But God, that fucking Delgado, the terror she felt . . . it was all right there, just behind everything she was trying to focus on, bubbling like some horrible cauldron constantly on the verge of boiling over.

She opened her eyes and took a deep breath. "I'm sorry," she said. "It's just been . . . an unbelievable day."

"Yeah. Tell me about it."

She managed a weak laugh. "So what do we do, Ryan?"

There was a pause. Then he said, "If you can get the thumb drive to Betsy Leed, I'll give the passphrase to her."

"Betsy Leed?"

"My editor at the *Intercept*. I trust her. But I don't have any Internet access and I've been afraid to call her. She's monitored. We're all monitored. I've been afraid to call anyone. I know they're looking for me. I can't believe I'm talking to you."

She felt her spirits sag. "Ryan . . . I can't. That drive is all the leverage I have."

"Yeah, well, the passphrase is all the leverage I have. You ask me to trust you, but you won't trust me?"

"What about . . . before you left, you didn't tell anyone else at your organization the passphrase? Just in case. Leed? Anyone?"

"I'm the only one who knows it."

Maybe he was telling her the truth. Maybe not. No way to know, and in the end it didn't matter.

She closed her eyes again and tried to see another way. She couldn't.

"All right," she said after a moment. "How do I contact Leed?"

"Do you know about SecureDrop?"

"Of course. NSA hates it."

"That's good to hear. That's how you contact her. Buy a new computer. For cash. Download the Tails operating system. It comes with the Tor browser. You know what they are?"

He was sounding more confident than he had at the beginning of the call. She supposed that was good. It suggested he was beginning to trust her, at least a little.

"Of course. NSA spends half its time trying to subvert them."

"I'll bet they do. Well, that's the way you do it. You get a message to Leed and arrange a meeting. You're both going to have to be extremely careful about being followed. No cell phones, no personal vehicles, nothing. And watch out for foot surveillance. It's easy to forget about the old-fashioned stuff when you have to be so obsessive about electronic bread crumbs. Speaking of which, how the hell did you find out about Perkins and me? He was beyond paranoid, and

I'm no security slouch myself. You wouldn't believe the protocols we use at the *Intercept*."

She hesitated for a moment, the old reflex against sharing anything with outsiders, especially anything about a top-secret program, still strong. Then she thought, *Fuck it.*

"I run an initiative that pulls footage from Internet-linked camera networks all over the world and runs it through a biometric match program, including facial recognition. There's a list of top-secret-cleared personnel, on the one hand, and of known subversives, on the other."

"You include journalists among those subversives?"

"I don't know everyone who's on it. But there are reporters, yes."

"Well, that's something, anyway. Beats any other award I can imagine."

She gave him a weak laugh. "Yes, I suppose it does. Well, my system threw up a red flag when it spotted you and Perkins together in Istanbul. After that, we started looking more closely. And my system is also why I know the director was behind the DC bombing. The man who abducted me and threatened to do all those horrible things to me and my son? I saw him plant the bomb."

"Then you're in as much trouble as I am."

"Yes, that's what I've been trying to tell you."

"NSA is monitoring camera networks in Turkey? I mean, DC I might have imagined. But this thing is global?"

"I thought I knew how global it was. But apparently Perkins got a hold of something even bigger."

"Yeah, he did. You want to know what your director calls it?"

"Tell me."

"God's Eye. You guys sure have a knack for creepy names. Carnivore, Total Information Awareness, Boundless Informant . . ."

"What is it?"

"That I'm not telling you. Get that thumb drive to Leed and I'll give her the passphrase. You'll be able to read all about it in the *Intercept* for the next year at least. I'm telling you, it's bigger than Snowden."

For a moment, she wondered if he was exaggerating to reinforce her commitment to get his editor the thumb drive. Then she remembered what the director had done to try to contain this God's Eye, and she decided Hamilton was probably just being accurate.

"Listen," she said. "Not to be morbid, but if anything were to happen to you . . ."

"Or to you."

"Yes, or to me. The point is, maybe it would be safer for you to get the passphrase to your editor right away. So she'll already have it when I get her the thumb drive."

"All that would do is put her in danger. Besides, I don't have any secure means of getting it to her. I'm not going to say it over an open line where you people could just vacuum it up. Not until she confirms she has the drive."

She thought of Marvin, how he had switched drives with Delgado. "But if I weren't who I claim to be, what would stop me from just handing over any old thumb drive, then intercepting your transmission of the passphrase?"

"I don't know, okay? I don't know what the hell to do. At this point I'm just trying to stay alive."

All the stress and fear was back in his voice. She needed to get him to dial it down.

"I'm sorry for pushing," she said. "But we just . . . I want to make sure we have a plan that'll work, okay?"

He sighed. "You need to meet Leed. If she trusts you, I'll trust you. Contact her with SecureDrop and tell her I'm going to find a way to call her cell phone in twelve hours. I want to hear her voice. I want to hear her tell me she's got the thumb drive. And that she trusts you. When I hear that, I'll give her the passphrase."

"Okay. Okay, I'll contact her. But is she going to believe me?"

There was a pause. He said, "Tell her . . . tell her I said the first time I met her, her six-year-old daughter, Brett, hid behind her leg. We laughed about it. No one else was there. No one else would know."

"Okay. Good. But look, tell me something about this program. I told you about my camera networks. Is what I do part of God's Eye?"

"It's all part of it."

She waited, but he didn't go on.

"Give me some context," she said. "Isn't that why you and Perkins took a chance on a face-to-face meeting to begin with? So you could make better sense of whatever documents he was providing?"

"I told you, I'm not going to—"

"Why? I was abducted tonight, I have people trying to kill me, I would really, really like to know what the hell it's all about. All right? What fucking harm could come from telling me? We're probably both dead anyway!"

The moment it was out, she kicked herself for saying it. It was going to amp him up again. But there was no way to take it back.

There was a long pause. Then he chuckled and said, "That's a hell of a way of persuading me. But . . . okay. In case I don't make it out of here. At least someone will know some of it. And maybe you can help the *Intercept* make sense of it, if . . . if I'm not there to."

She didn't respond. She was too afraid he might change his mind.

"All right," he said. "What does the government want to listen to?"

She considered. "Well, everything."

"No. Not quite. It wants to be *able* to listen to everything. But what does it want to focus on?"

"I'm not following you."

"Let me put it another way. Does the government care what people write on postcards?"

"No. It's right out in the open."

"Exactly. People who send postcards aren't trying to hide anything.

It's the people who use envelopes, and especially the ones who use security envelopes, and put extra tape along the flap to make sure no one can steam it open, that the government is concerned about. Now extrapolate."

"You're saying . . . the government is focusing on, what, people who use encryption?"

"Yes, but that's only a tiny part of it. The focus is on every form of electronic and other behavior that could be considered an attempt to preserve privacy."

"What are we talking about specifically?"

"I don't want to get into it. I'll just say it started as an antiterror initiative, like every other example of government overreach these days. Terrorists need a way of communicating clandestinely, right? So someone had the insight that your organization could map every way terrorists might go about those clandestine communications. The behaviors involved. And then search for those behaviors wherever they occurred, applying something called Bayesian networks."

"Of course," she said, realizing. "It makes perfect sense."

"You know about it?"

"Bayesian inferences are a kind of probability theory. I'm a computer scientist."

"Yeah, I've got a background myself. Well, the problem—"

"—the problem is that terrorists aren't the only ones who try to safeguard their privacy."

"Bingo. Although as far as I'm concerned, whether the broader applications of God's Eye were a bug or a feature is absolutely an open question. Because one of the ways they use Bayesian inferences to filter data is by a matrix. What do you read? What sites do you visit? Who do you follow on Twitter? And I'll give you a hint: following the ACLU, or Jacob Appelbaum, or the Electronic Frontier Foundation, or the Freedom of the Press Foundation, or *WikiLeaks*, or donating to organizations like those, might be the kind of thing they like to know about. They don't like dissent. Whether from the powerless, or the powerful. Dissent is one of those things that's best nipped in the bud."

"So you're saying God's Eye—"

"God's Eye only looks at what people are trying to hide. It only listens when people are trying to whisper. Now think about what you would uncover with something like that, what it could be used for, and you're starting to get the idea."

"There would be . . . you'd know everything."

"Everything worth knowing, if your goal were to control a population. You NSA types must really groove on irony. Because hell yes, as long as you don't try to protect your privacy, you can still have privacy! Well, at least in theory. I mean, NSA still has access to everything about you. You'll still be one of the hundreds of millions of volumes in their limitless collection. They just won't take you down from the shelf to read you. At least until they want something. Or if you misbehave. Then you're fucked."

They were quiet for a moment. Her mind was racing with possibilities. The truth was, the concept was ingenious. She wondered who had thought of it. And how they would implement. She knew NSA already focused heavily on collecting encrypted communications, in the hope that at a minimum some decryption breakthrough would allow the communications to be read at a later date. And that they were exceptionally interested in lawyer-client privileged communications, as well. What else would they focus on? Social network accounts with only a pair or at most a handful of users. Email accounts with similarly restricted use. People who cleared their browsers regularly. People who purged emails from their online trash. Hell, you could even get more specific than that. You could focus on *which* messages got deleted. After all, those would be the interesting ones. The secrets you would uncover . . . it would be everything. Affairs. Closeted homosexuality. Financial improprieties. Perversions. The most personal aspects of people's lives. The most shameful secrets.

Look at the way the FBI had nailed General Petraeus when he was director of Central Intelligence, by focusing on the email account he was using with his lover. The two of them had been storing sexual messages as drafts, not sending them. That would be a giant red flag right there. And only one user on the account, logging in from different locations. Another dead giveaway. What if the account hadn't been uncovered in the course of an FBI investigation? What if instead it had been discovered by the director? In all likelihood, Petraeus would still be DCI. A lot of people had thought he was on the fast track to run for *president*, for God's sake. And the director would have owned him.

She suddenly wondered how many other people the director owned. Powerful people. Politicians. Regulators. Judges. Journalists. And how many organizations he had penetrated, subverted. It was almost too big to fathom.

She realized there was another thing they would focus on: prepaid phones. Bought for cash. Who pays cash for a prepaid phone? Poor people, but they don't matter to you and you quickly screen them out. Everyone else . . . would be someone trying to hide something. Something you've now uncovered.

"Could that be how they caught me?" she said. "I bought a prepaid phone for cash. Is that the kind of thing God's Eye looks for?"

"It's exactly the kind of thing."

It made a horrible kind of sense. She'd thought she was being so clever and careful. But it seemed clever and careful was exactly what drew the attention of God's Eye.

"I think you should change hotels," she said. "I'm taking every precaution, but obviously there are things they can do neither of us even knows about."

Weird to call NSA "they," and to refer to herself and this journalist as "us." But that was how it felt at the moment.

"Yeah, you're right. I've been wanting to move, but . . . I've been afraid to. They"—his voice cracked, but he went on—"they did some bad shit to me. Hey, how did you find me, anyway? You didn't really answer before."

"The man who saw you by Lake Tuz a few days ago. He—"

"Wait a minute. What man?"

She paused for a moment. What *had* Marvin been doing there? She'd asked, but he'd refused to say. But he'd looked so racked by guilt. And things were going so fast and it all felt so out of control, she'd barely paused to consider. Had he been sent to kill Hamilton, and then, for some reason, changed his mind? Was that what Manus was? Some kind of NSA assassin?

"I'm . . . not exactly sure who he is," she said. "But he told me he saw you at Lake Tuz."

"Big guy? Glasses? A beard?"

"He's big, yes, but no glasses or beard."

"It was a disguise, then. Is he deaf?"

Alarm bells went off in her mind and she was suddenly unsure how much to say. But if Hamilton knew something about Marvin, she wanted to hear it.

"Yes."

"You *know* him?"

"He's helping me."

"*Helping* you? Oh, fuck, are you serious? You're being played, lady. Assuming you're not the one playing me."

"What do you—"

"He's the guy who fucking abducted me! He's a sociopath, can't you see that? I begged him, seriously begged him, and he looked at me like I was, I don't know, a fly or something. And turned me over to . . . to . . ."

"To who?"

"I don't know. Three sick Turkish assholes straight out of *Deliverance*. What was the point of that? Why would he do that?"

"I think the Turks were a cutout. I think they were supposed to get you to some third party, a jihadist group, something like that."

"Yeah, well, I guess they were having too much fun to stick with the plan. But your friend got the party going, do you understand? You cannot trust that guy. Is he with you now?"

"No." She hadn't wanted to lie, but technically it was true—Marvin was in the other room. Besides, it was more important to calm Hamilton down.

"Jesus, I can't believe I'm talking to you. Oh, my God."

"It's okay. He's not here. It's just me. But . . . what happened by Lake Tuz?"

"Your friend happened. He killed those Turks—I mean, fucking butchered them, I think with this axe he carries, you should have seen their bodies—and then he just left me."

"Why didn't he kill you, too?"

"How the hell should I know? Maybe he thought it was funnier to just let me die of thirst next to that goddamned salt lake. The point is, if you think he's on your side, you're even stupider than I am."

She wondered whether he could be right about Marvin. Three men? With an *axe*? It sounded completely insane. On the other hand, *had* those been shots outside her apartment? Had Marvin killed someone there? But the details weren't what mattered. What mattered was . . . who was he, really? And how could she know?

"I don't think that," she said. "I'm being careful. I promise."

"Oh, man," Hamilton said. "Oh, man."

She needed to get him to refocus. "How long before Leed can publish?"

There was a pause, then, "A while. But that doesn't matter. Once the drive is decrypted, she'll upload copies to a dozen mirror sites.

I should have done exactly that from Turkey, but Perkins was afraid something could be intercepted and he would be exposed."

"I don't know that he was entirely wrong about that."

"Yeah, well, I don't think things could have gone a lot worse than they have."

"Fair point."

"Anyway. Once the contents of that thumb drive are uploaded to mirror sites, the game is over. The cover-up will be useless. It'll just be a question of spin. And I can't wait to see these assholes try to spin their way out of what I got from Perkins."

"Okay. I'll contact your editor. But twelve hours . . . can you make it sooner? I don't know how long I can stay ahead of the people coming after me."

"If you think you can make it happen faster, great. I'll call her in six hours. But if you haven't closed the loop with her by then, the call is wasted. And every time I get on the phone, it's exposure none of us wants. We need to make it count."

She thought about it. Six hours should be okay. As long as . . .

"Do your people monitor SecureDrop? Or is something going to sit in there unattended?"

"Right now? They're probably monitoring it in real time."

"Okay, then. Call her in six hours. I'll make it happen."

"God, I hope you are who you say you are."

"Well, you'll know soon enough. Hang in there, Ryan. I'll see you soon somehow, okay?"

"Yeah, let's hope."

She ended the call, signed out from the service, purged the browser, and closed the laptop. A partial success, she supposed. But it was hard to feel good about it. Their plan felt improvised and half-assed. And even if it worked, she wasn't sure Hamilton was right when he said the game would be over. She was about to make some very powerful people into very powerful angry people. Maybe this was all just business to them, and maybe they would all just stand down if the business were done. But Delgado wasn't like that, she knew. He wasn't about logic, or cost-benefit, or anything else that could be subject to reason and negotiation. Business for him was an excuse. An excuse for what he was going to do anyway.

But she didn't think she had another play. If this didn't work, she was out of options.

Marvin appeared in the door and signed, *How did it go?*

He must have been watching from the room. But the way she was sitting on the tub, he would have been able to see her only in profile. He couldn't have been reading her lips. And even if he had, she hadn't said anything he didn't already know.

Okay, I guess.

How is he?

She was a little surprised by the concern. Was it an act? Was he fishing, trying to learn whether Hamilton had told her about the deaf man who had abducted him?

Traumatized, I'd say. And scared.

He nodded and looked away. It was horrifying to know why he'd been so reluctant to tell her how he knew about Hamilton. Again, that feeling of violation, of an almost physical disgust, washed over her. Who was this man she had been so intimate with, so unguarded? Who had built her own son's bed, who had been inside her body and occupied her mind?

But she couldn't dwell on any of that here, while he was looking at her, watching her. She couldn't trust him, but she needed him.

For now.

She briefed him on the conversation, leaving out Hamilton's warnings.

He was still for a long moment after she was done. Then he signed, *So the plan is to get his editor the thumb drive?*

Yes.

Where is it?

She didn't like that he asked. *Somewhere safe.*

There are a lot of people looking for you now.

Yeah. I got that.

And if you hid it anywhere that's a known nexus, they could try to anticipate you there. You'd show up, you wouldn't see them, you'd retrieve the drive, and they'd take you then. Probably take you right back to Delgado.

If he was trying to scare her, it was working.

Then what?

Let me retrieve it. I know what surveillance looks like. And how to get around it.

She didn't like the way he was inserting himself into this.

No, she signed. *They're looking for you, too, remember? If you show up at a nexus for me, they'll spot you just as easily.*

They'll have a harder time taking that thumb drive from me than they would from you.

No, she didn't like the way he was inserting himself one bit. What if . . . what if this whole thing were an elaborate game of good cop / bad cop, the way she'd momentarily thought in the van? Marvin "rescues" her from Delgado, getting her to trust him enough to tell him where she'd hidden the thumb drive. He takes the drive, they grab Hamilton . . .

It didn't make sense. Why would Marvin have let Hamilton go? Was there some sort of tracking device, a way of picking up the journalist again once he'd served his function? But Delgado had been holding her, so what would be the point of letting her go? Delgado could have just tortured the thumb drive's location out of her; she knew he'd been right about that. So if this whole thing was a ruse, what kind of ruse? She couldn't see it.

You couldn't see how they tracked you to the Rockville mail drop, either, she thought. *And Hamilton couldn't see how you tracked him to that Ankara hotel. Just because you can't see it doesn't mean it isn't there.*

She hesitated, then signed, *Do you . . . do you carry a gun?*

He nodded.

Did you shoot someone before? Outside my building?

He looked down for a moment, then signed, *There are a lot of people after you. You should know how to use a gun.*

She didn't disagree. But he certainly hadn't answered her question. Or maybe he had.

All right, she signed. *Show me how.*

He reached behind his waist and came back with a huge, black pistol. He ejected the magazine and pulled back the slide. A bullet popped out and tumbled to the bed. He handed her the gun.

She hefted it, then set it down so she could sign. *It's heavy.*

Check that it's unloaded.

What? You just unloaded it.

Always check for yourself.

He showed her how. *The weight is good, by the way. It compensates for kick.*

She nodded. *Where's the safety?*

I keep it uncocked. The first trigger pull cocks the gun, which means a long pull. That itself is a kind of safety. After the first shot, the gun cocks automatically. So subsequent trigger pulls are short and easy. All you have to do to fire is aim and pull the trigger. The first pull will be long. After that, all it takes is a very light squeeze. But think of it as pressing more than pulling or squeezing. It'll keep your hand steadier.

He showed her how to hold it—two hands and a tight grip—and how to aim by lining up the sights.

I'll take you to the range sometime, he signed. *And Dash, if you like.*

She gave him a smile and nod she hoped looked real. *It's late. I need to send Hamilton's editor a message.*

He nodded. *I'll keep watch.*

I'll bet you will, she thought. And then signed, *No, why don't you sleep for a while? I'll keep watch, and when I get tired, I'll wake you.*

He looked at her for a long moment. She couldn't read his expression. Then he signed, *Are you sure?*

Yes. I'm too keyed up right now, anyway.

He reloaded and reholstered the gun, then went back to the bedroom.

She used Tor to go to the *Intercept* website, then accessed Secure-Drop and wrote out a long message to Betsy Leed. She hoped it sounded less crazy to the *Intercept* editor than it did to her.

CHAPTER . . . .
. . . . 42

Anders paced in his office, rubbing his hands, trying to manage his agitation. He was practically sleeping at Fort Meade these days. And just when he thought he'd gotten things under control, this. Some anomalies in his text communications with Delgado. Anomalies he'd tested, with results that made him even more suspicious. He'd geolocated on Delgado's phone, and then, on a hunch, on Manus's and Gallagher's, as well. The three of them appeared to be together, which made no sense, and heading toward Gallagher's apartment. He'd sent a team to investigate. The team had failed to check in. He'd sent another team, which reported that the first team had been annihilated. The second team cleaned up the mess and retrieved three cell phones from Gallagher's apartment. No sign of anyone. Anders had worked backward to last known locations, and saw Manus converging on the Triadelphia Reservoir, where geolocation records indicated Delgado had been holding Gallagher. Anders had sent Remar, and he'd found Delgado, handcuffed to the steering wheel of his van, bloody and raving. Anders had spoken to him briefly, and he said he had the thumb drive. So thank God for that. But the first drive, the one Manus had taken from Hamilton, had been a decoy. This one could be, too. Anders needed to examine the drive. And debrief Delgado. Remar was bringing him in now. But it felt like it was taking forever.

After fifteen long minutes, there was a knock on the door. Remar opened it and Delgado stormed past him into the office. Anders stopped and stared. Delgado's face was a mess—bruised, swollen, the nose obviously broken, a bloody scalp wound where the hair plugs had once rested, his mouth a crimson disaster. It looked like Remar had administered a certain degree of first aid—there were iodine stains on the cuts, and a dressing over one cheek—but he was going to need more than just that. He was going to need a plastic surgeon.

"What the hell happened?" Anders said. Remar started to ease out, and Anders said, "No, stay." Remar closed the door and stood next to it as though fearing Delgado might run.

Delgado started pacing. "That fucking Manus," he said, his speech slightly slurred from his injuries. "That's what happened. How many times have I told you you couldn't trust that guy? How many? Did you know he was fucking Gallagher? Did you?"

Somehow, Delgado's distress made Anders feel calmer. "I know a great many things, Thomas. I share them only when operationally necessary."

"Oh, really? Did you not think it might be operationally necessary to let me know Manus just might have a fucking thing for this chick? That he might not like the idea of her being, I don't know, abducted, raped, and murdered in an unsolved crime? Did you not realize any of that?"

"No. I didn't."

"Well, fuck me sideways, maybe you should have! The guy just shows up outside the Sprinter, totally violating the plan, what the hell am I supposed to do? I knew something was hinky, too, I knew it. I had my gun out and was going to call you. But that deaf cocksucker is fast."

Anders knew he ought to indulge the man, let him rant for a few minutes, but he couldn't wait. "Where is the thumb drive?"

"Right. That." Delgado reached into a pants pocket and handed it over.

Anders dashed around to the other side of his desk, not even trying to conceal his eagerness. It took less than ten seconds to confirm it wasn't encrypted.

And that there was nothing on it.

He stood there, arms crossed, squeezing his biceps, his head hanging, for a moment feeling completely defeated.

Remar said, "No go?"

Anders shook his head and looked at Delgado. "How did you get this? Be specific."

"That's what I was trying to tell you. The woman said she'd hidden it behind the toilet of the ladies' room in the nursing home where she keeps her father. Manus went to check it out while I held her. A little while later, he shows up at the Sprinter, says he found it just where she said it would be."

Remar said, "Hamilton might have sent two decoys, not just one. Although—"

"Yes," Anders said, "agreed it's not likely. The FedEx shipment felt like a head fake, intended to distract from the snail-mail shipment. If so, there would be nothing to gain by snail-mailing a second decoy. Meaning that, presumably, the snail-mail shipment was the real drive."

"All right," Remar said, "Gallagher herself might have planted a decoy. But—"

"Agreed again," Anders said, finding some small comfort in the familiar back-and-forth analysis that had long since become a kind of shorthand with Remar. "Thomas, you texted me that you and Manus took Gallagher easily outside the supermarket. No signs of surveillance consciousness, no indications of paranoia of any kind, is that correct?"

"Correct."

"Right," Remar said. "Difficult to imagine she'd be so sanguine, and yet have taken precautions elaborate enough to include planting a decoy drive. Okay, then, the third possibility. Manus took the real drive, or maybe he failed to find it, and provided this fake one, instead."

Anders nodded. Of course, there was a fourth possibility—that Delgado was the one providing the fake drives. But this seemed the most unlikely scenario of all. It was impossible to imagine a motive for Delgado, for one thing, while, as Delgado himself had pointed out, Manus's motive was obvious. Beyond which, there was the fact of Delgado's condition, and his unfortunate detention in the van. Not to mention the four bodies outside Gallagher's apartment.

No, the most likely explanation was that Manus was simply torn between his loyalty to Anders and his newfound infatuation with Gallagher. Anders had sensed this dynamic earlier, of course, when Manus had failed to fully report on what had happened with the woman. But he thought Manus had come to his senses. Well, either Anders had been played, or Manus was ambivalent and acting inconsistently as a result. It didn't really matter. The problem was the same either way. Manus had become unreliable.

But there was something . . . something that didn't quite fit.

"You said you had a gun on him," Anders said, thinking out loud.

"Yeah, that's right. I shouldn't have let him inside the Sprinter. Not enough space. And like I said, he's fast. He took it away from me."

"That's interesting."

"Interesting how?"

"Well, I've never known a man who pulled a gun on Marvin Manus and lived to tell about it. Indeed, after his run-in with you, Manus killed four men I sent to Gallagher's apartment."

"What? I told you. He's a complete psycho."

"What I'm wondering is, why didn't he kill you?"

"I don't know. But I'll tell you this. Not killing me? Worst mistake that freak ever made. Look at my fucking face. Jesus, it hurts. And his girlfriend, too. She got in a few cheap shots after I was handcuffed."

Anders considered. "I'm sure I don't need to remind you that Manus has no compunction about killing. Killing is practically a default setting for him. On top of which, as I'm sure you're aware, you've given him ample reason over time to feel some . . . animosity toward you. And yet he didn't kill you tonight. He could have, clearly, but he didn't."

Delgado touched a swollen lip and winced. "What are you saying, I was somehow in on this? You think I *let* Manus do this?"

"No. Not at all. I'm just trying to make sense of Manus's behavior."

"Yeah, well, good luck with that. You might as well try to figure out a rabid dog. What's the point? You just put the damn thing down."

Anders suspected that in fact Delgado would torture such a dog first, but saw nothing to be gained by pointing it out.

"No," he said after a moment. "Manus isn't a rabid dog. But"—he glanced at Remar—"I've heard him compared to an abused one. One who is exceptionally loyal to the only master who's ever been good to him."

"Honestly? My head feels like there's a brass band playing inside it and I don't know what the fuck you're talking about."

"What I'm saying is, Manus didn't refrain from killing you because he likes you. He refrained from killing you because he knows I like you. Well, value you."

"Thanks. I feel very appreciated."

"Manus knows how much I value your services, Thomas. Hurting you would be hurting me. And Manus would never hurt me. Which is why he didn't hurt you."

"Seriously? Look at me. You don't think this hurts?"

"I once saw Marvin Manus tear a man's ear off and tell him, 'This is the only warning you get.' Think about that. Tearing a man's ear off, a mere warning."

"Great. So you already knew he's a psycho."

"You see, from Manus's perspective, he didn't hurt you. He wanted to kill you, I have no doubt of that. But he didn't."

"What's the point?"

"He's doing what he has to right now, but also trying to minimize the damage. He doesn't want to burn bridges. Because . . . he wants the bridges to be intact. So he can cross back over. In fact . . . I believe in sparing your life, Manus was sending me a message."

"Yeah, well, I've got a message for him. He's a dead man."

Remar said, "What message?"

"He's telling us he's still on-side."

Delgado groaned. "You have got to be kidding."

"Think about it. What happened tonight? He rescued Gallagher. He beat you severely. He killed four men outside her apartment. And now he's on the run with her and her little boy. How could she do other than trust him now? He's telling us to give him a little space. He's still intent on that thumb drive. And he plans to give it to us— if we agree to his terms."

Remar said, "Which are?"

"Obviously that we leave Gallagher alone. Presumably in exchange for her promise to forget any of this ever happened."

Remar's expression was unreadable. "Do you think that could work?"

"No," Delgado said, "it couldn't work. Because I'm going to kill that bitch. And that psycho."

"What matters," Anders said, rubbing his hands, "isn't whether it could work. What matters is whether Manus believes it could work. Clearly he does."

"So you get him to turn over the drive . . ." Remar said.

Anders nodded. "In exchange for a promise. A promise we have no intention of honoring."

Delgado nodded. "That sounds more like it. Just tell me when and where."

"Thomas, respectfully, you're injured. And you've seen how formidable Manus is. We're not looking for a fair fight here. What we need is overwhelmingly superior firepower."

"Wait a minute—" Delgado started to say.

Remar cut him off. "We're shorthanded after what happened outside Gallagher's apartment, but I can get a detachment of contractors from Jones."

"Oh, come on," Delgado said. "Don't deal me out on this. This is bullshit."

"You can have Gallagher," Anders said. "But we can't take chances with Manus. Surely you can see that."

Anders glanced at Remar. If the man had a problem with what Anders had just promised Delgado, he wanted to hear about it now, rather than letting it fester. But Remar was impassive.

There was a long pause while Delgado gritted his teeth and rubbed his head. "All right. Fair enough. I want to watch, though, okay? I want to see him go down. You owe me that much."

Anders nodded. "Try to get some rest. General Remar and I are going to locate Manus and Gallagher. I'll contact you as soon as we have."

CHAPTER . . . .
. . . . 43

Manus lay on his back in one of the beds, one eye closed, the other open just a crack. Evie had been in the bathroom for almost an hour, presumably composing her message to Hamilton's editor. And then she had come out and sat on one of the chairs in the small room, keeping watch through the window as she had said. Now Manus was waiting for her to do what he thought she was planning next.

He knew they were already at cross-purposes. And while he respected her determination, he also thought confronting the director head-on was suicidal. They had no good options, but Manus was sure returning the thumb drive and a promise of silence would be the least worst of the realistic possibilities. If he could get the drive, he would do what he had to, and hope Evie would understand after that it was for her own good. And Dash's.

He thought about where she had told Delgado she had hidden the drive. There was no way to be sure, of course, but Manus sensed it was someplace she had in fact considered and then rejected. The best lies were generally the ones closest to the truth, and in the confusion and terror of the Sprinter, a smart person like Evie would have reached for something familiar, something real.

Besides, the director had said her cell phone geolocation records indicated she hadn't been home since retrieving the drive. Manus had searched her car—and, he thought with a jolt of fury and disgust, Delgado would have been no less comprehensive in searching her person. A good hiding place had to be both secure and accessible, with familiarity also a plus, and for Evie, the senior center would have been all three. If she had hidden the drive somewhere in the women's room, she had chosen an exceptionally clever spot, because Manus had searched the room carefully on just this kind of hunch. Or she'd chosen poorly, and the drive had been discovered by a third party. It was also possible she'd placed it somewhere in her father's room. Regardless of the exact location, Manus had a feeling the senior center was the place.

He waited another half hour, then deepened his breathing. He couldn't hear it himself, but he could feel it and knew it would be audible to Evie. A few minutes went by, and then he was gratified to see her walk over to Dash's bed. Manus couldn't see what she was doing without turning his head, but he thought he knew.

A minute later, he saw them heading to the door. The boy had on his backpack; Evie was holding her bag in one hand and the laptop under her arm. Manus imagined the conversation she must have had with the sleepy child: *We have to go, Dash. We're going to meet Mr. Manus later. For now he needs to sleep. No questions, okay? I'll explain everything soon.*

Something like that, anyway.

The moment they were gone, Manus got up and watched through the window as they headed into the front office.

She was on her way to get the thumb drive, as he'd expected. And he would be there waiting for her.

CHAPTER . . . .
. . . . 44

Evie and Dash walked into the front office. There was an old guy sitting behind the desk—the one Marvin had described, presumably—watching a small television that appeared not much newer than he did. He looked up and said, "Help you?"

"I just wanted to return the laptop," Evie said, trying to sound blasé.

"Oh," the man said, apparently realizing she must have been the person for whom Marvin borrowed it. "Sure."

"And if you could call us a cab."

"At this hour? You must have an early flight."

"That's right."

The man looked at her swollen lip and his expression darkened. "Say, how'd you get that lip?"

"Hmm? Oh, just a stupid accident."

"A stupid accident, huh? That big fella hit you? There was something about him, I could tell."

"What? No. No. Nothing like that."

"You protecting him? I've seen this kind of thing before. Now you're running off with your little boy to protect him, too. Sneaking out while the big bastard is sleeping off a drunk. And probably not for the first time, is my guess."

"Look, I appreciate your concern, but it's really not like that."

"The hell it isn't," the old guy said, picking up the receiver of a landline phone. "I'm calling the cops."

"No!" Evie said, alarmed at how quickly and weirdly her simple plan was being hijacked by this codger. "No, please, I promise you, it isn't what you think. Please."

The old guy paused, the receiver halfway to his ear. Then he shook his head as though doubting his own judgment, and put the receiver back in its cradle. "You sure you know what you're doing?"

The question was obviously pro forma, but nonetheless for an instant it caught Evie off guard because, good God, could she have any *less* an idea of what she was doing?

Then she got it together. She nodded and placed the laptop on the counter. "Quite sure. And really, thank you for your concern. Even though I promise you it's misplaced."

The old guy looked at Dash. "You all right, son?"

In his sleepiness and confusion, Dash hadn't managed to read the man's lips. He looked at Evie, and she signed a translation. Dash turned back to the old guy and gave him a tired thumbs-up.

"Oh," the old guy said, nodding as though this explained everything. "Deaf, is he? Like his father?"

Evie smiled. The smile felt overbright, but at this point she had no idea how else to react.

"That cab," she said. "If you could."

CHAPTER . . . .
. . . . 45

Remar closed the door behind Delgado and turned to the director. He tried to keep the concern—no, the outright distress—out of his expression, but he doubted he was notably successful.

"I know," the director said, pacing. "It's bad."

"Bad? We've got a thumb drive all about God's Eye floating around with no idea where. We've got your junkyard dog helping the woman who took it. Oh, and gutting our own operatives while he's at it. Have you ever thought about how much Manus knows? How badly he could incriminate us if he turns? Or make that, now that he has turned."

Of course, there was some nuance Remar was deliberately leaving out. Manus was the director's man, having done God knew what on the director's orders. The truth was, and as far as the world would be concerned, Remar had nothing to do with Manus. Everyone knew the director was a fanatic about operational security. It stood to reason that whatever existed between the director and his personal contractor was between them only.

The director stopped pacing and tugged at his chin. "I don't think he has turned, actually. As I said, I think he wants to get us that drive. But he doesn't want the woman harmed, either. I think he's going to cooperate. Possibly even contact us. At which point, we thank him for his troubles and have Jones's detachment put him down."

Remar didn't respond. There was something so cold about the matter-of-fact way the director had put it. Whatever else Manus was, his loyalty had always been exemplary. To hear the director so casually describe . . . euthanizing him was unnerving.

"Well," Remar said, "I'm glad we have a plan, anyway. There's just one thing missing. Where the hell are they? Gallagher is fundamentally a civilian, but Manus is CIA and Spec Ops trained. Between the two of them, they know a hell of a lot about our capabilities. Sure, eventually we'll find them, but I don't think 'eventually' is quite going to cut it here. Unless you're planning on just waiting for Manus to call in?"

The director started pacing again. Remar could sense the mental gears turning. But it was taking a long time for them to spit something out.

Finally, the director stopped. He looked at Remar and said, "What's the status of God's Ear?"

Remar shook his head, realizing just how desperate the director had become. "Ted, you can't be serious."

"What's the status?"

"It's not even close to being ready for—"

The director slammed a hand down on his desk and shouted, "Well, make it ready!"

Remar had about had enough. "How, Ted? You want me to suspend the laws of physics? It's too much data, too many false positives, requiring too much processing power to sift through. Maybe in a year, maybe six months, if we're lucky. But not now."

"Why? The data's there, Mike. Every cell phone has a microphone. If we're not going to listen in, why the hell did we develop WARRIOR PRIDE and NOSEY SMURF? We can even use the phone's gyroscopes like microphones—what was the point of that program if we're not going to use it? Every new car has Bluetooth, and voice recognition, and a microphone that gets activated when an airbag deploys, or when the driver wants to access some concierge service. Home entertainment systems are getting equipped with voice recognition. People are installing personal electronic assistants like that Amazon Echo in their homes. All voice-activated. And how many baby monitors are there? The whole world is being wired for sound, every vehicle, every room, every person. We need to access that. We need to use it."

"But we can't make sense of it yet. God's brain hasn't caught up to God's Ear."

"Damn it, you're not thinking. The parameters here are small. Only a certain radius from Gallagher's apartment. We can redeploy the sensors in the JLENS blimps—we were going to do that anyway. That is a huge multiplier on what we can perceive in the DC area."

The Joint Land Attack Cruise Missile Defense Elevated Netted Sensor System was a pair of surveillance blimps the army had managed to launch over Maryland, ostensibly to defend against cruise missiles. In Remar's view, the near-three-billion-dollar program was a giant white elephant. On the other hand, as the director said, it could be redeployed. But still.

"And the dirtboxes," the director went on. "That joint CIA/US Marshals cell phone tracking program. We'll repurpose that, too."

Remar thought that one might make a little more sense. The program involved the use of planes that mimicked cell phone towers, tricking phones into reporting unique registration information. CIA and the Marshals had most of the US population covered, but for Gallagher and Manus they would need coverage only of the DC area.

"Okay, fine," Remar said. "You're saying the data set is manageable because we'd only be listening for two voices."

"That's right. Gallagher's. And Manus's."

"Manus barely talks. He signs."

For a moment, the director looked crestfallen. Then he shook it off.

"It doesn't matter. We only need a snippet. We know that. It's been prototyped. And his voice is unusual, too, because of his deafness. When he does talk, we can pick it out from the background noise more easily than the norm. Anyway, they're together—we don't need both of them, just one or the other."

"Look, even within the parameters you're describing, the processing power we'd need would be massive. What do you want to do, shut down everything else?"

"Yes! Yes, if that's what it takes. Why not?"

Remar couldn't believe what he was hearing. "You're saying you want us to go dark on all the terrorist chatter, on the Kremlin's plans for Ukraine, on the launch of new Chinese spy satellites, on the cartels in Mexico, on the disposition of nukes in India and Pakistan . . . so we can try to listen in on Manus and Gallagher?"

"If we don't find Manus and Gallagher, if someone puts out God's Eye, we will be shut down. Game over. We'll be deaf and blind anyway. All I'm proposing is a short . . . hiatus. Probably no more than twenty-four hours, possibly a good deal less than that. Divert all the processing power we need to locate Manus and Gallagher, roll them up, and we're done. We save God's Eye. And who knows, maybe we learn from field-testing God's Ear how to bring it on line faster."

"How the hell are we even going to explain this? We can't divert that much processing power discreetly. Half the technical side of the organization is going to know."

"Intel on a second bomb threat. All need-to-know."

"A bomb threat? For something like what you're describing, they'll think we're under nuclear attack. There will be leaks. You'll cause a panic."

"Not if we clarify that the parameters are extremely tight and the time frame extremely limited. By the time anyone even has a chance to think too much about it, it'll already be over."

Remar didn't answer. He was no longer asking himself whether the director had lost it. That question had been answered, and there was no time to be emotional about it. He just needed to figure out what to do.

But the director seemed to take his silence as assent. "Don't you see? We need this. It's like I said, every time some civil liberties extremist leaks another one of our capabilities, we have to develop new ones. Well, God's Eye is at risk now. At a minimum, we have to have God's Ear to replace it. And Manus and Gallagher will have no idea it's out there. They'll walk right into it."

CHAPTER . . . .
. . . . 46

H ello, miss, hello, son, where may I take you this morning?"

The man had a sunny Maharashtra accent. For some reason, Evie found it reassuring.

"Is there a Walmart around here?"

"There is indeed, a twenty-four-hour facility on Route 30. Will that be your destination today?"

"I just need to stop there to pick up a few things. My destination is in Columbia. Is that all right?"

"Of course, as long as you don't mind the meter running."

"I don't mind at all. Thank you."

She and Dash were in and out of the Walmart in less than ten minutes—Evie with a new prepaid cell phone, Dash with some new comic books—and a little over an hour later, they were standing in front of the senior center, watching the cab drive off. Evie pulled on the door but it didn't open. Of course. They'd keep it locked at night.

She knocked on the glass. She didn't recognize the person behind the desk—a big man in scrubs, unlike the attractive women in business suits they seemed to favor during the day. An orderly, she supposed, more than a receptionist.

The man looked up, then stood and came to the door. "Can I help you?" he asked.

"Yes, thank you, my father lives here, and . . . well, would it be all right if I see him?"

"Ma'am, visiting hours don't start until seven."

"Yes, I know. And I know it's odd, but . . . look, could you at least open the door? It feels strange to have to talk to you through the glass."

The man looked dubious, but it was a retirement home, for God's sake, not a bank. He unlocked the door and opened it, but didn't step out of the way or invite her in.

"Thank you," she said. "The thing is, my son and I are going on a trip. On our way to the airport, in fact. And . . . I had this terrible dream, just before I woke up, that my father would be gone when we got back. I know it's silly, but it felt so much like a premonition. I just wanted to make sure we saw him before we left. In case. Would that be all right?"

The man was still wearing the dubious expression, but Evie thought she detected some softening in it. There was a pause, and he said, "What's your father's name?"

"Kevin Gallagher. Room 717. And I'm Evie, by the way." She extended her hand and the man shook it.

"And I'm Cooper. I know Mister Gallagher. Very nice man, very polite with the staff, though he doesn't always remember where he is."

She didn't know whether Cooper was a first name or a last. Either way, apparently it was what he wanted to be called. "I know. He's been . . . declining. But yes, he's the same nice man he always was. There's that, at least."

Cooper looked at Dash. "Here to see your grandfather, son?"

Dash nodded.

That seemed to seal the deal. Cooper nodded and held the door open. "Don't be too long, all right? It's not exactly the crime of the century, but I could get in trouble letting you in here after hours."

"Thank you so much, Cooper. I promise, we'll make it quick."

She and Dash went and looked in on her father, who was asleep and snoring loudly. She was actually afraid he might wake up—if he was lucid, it would make it hard to leave quickly, which they very much needed to do. She wondered about the story she had made up for Cooper. Was that her unconscious speaking up? Because she did have the dreadful sense that this really could be the last time she saw her father. She pushed the feeling away. She couldn't be emotional. She couldn't let herself be afraid, or it would just consume her. She had to focus.

On the way out, she asked Dash if he needed the bathroom. He shook his head.

For a second, she was afraid to leave him alone and considered bringing him in with her.

You're jumping at shadows now, she told herself. *No one's here. It's practically the middle of the night. The doors are locked.*

Okay, you wait here, she signed. *I'll be right out.*

She headed into the women's room and went straight to the hiding place. The thumb drive was exactly where she'd left it. Well, why wouldn't it be? But she was almost surprised. The director, and Delgado, and Marvin being involved with them . . . she realized she'd almost started to suspect they were omniscient, and that they would have gotten here ahead of her. But no, everything was fine. So far.

Back in the corridor, she signed, *You know what? I just need to use one of the computers in the rec center for a minute—a work thing. Want to play an online game?*

Dash loved his online baseball games, but for once his enthusiasm was muted. *I guess.*

What is it, hon?

I'm tired. What's going on? Why are we here?

It killed her that he was being such a trooper. And that he looked so zonked. *Just some things I need to take care of. And I wanted to see Grandpa. Only a little while longer, okay?*

They walked into the rec center. The rest of the facility was dead quiet, and she'd been expecting the same here. But there was a white-haired man at one of the two terminals. She recognized him—Mr. Bollinger, who she knew played checkers with her father when her father was able. *Shit.*

Mr. Bollinger looked up when they came in. "Oh, Evie, what are you doing here? Is your father all right?"

"Thank you, Mr. Bollinger. He's fine. Just checking up on him."

"At this hour?"

"It's a long story. And what are you doing up?"

"Oh, I don't sleep well since my wife passed. Sometimes I'll find a fellow insomniac in here and we'll chat. Otherwise, I read the news online."

"I see. Actually, I was just going to use one of the terminals myself. A work thing." She signed to Dash, *Okay if you wait on the baseball, good-looking? Only one terminal.*

Dash nodded. And though he couldn't have known what they were saying, Mr. Bollinger seemed to understand the gist. He said, "Oh, why don't you both have a go? I need to attend to a call of nature, anyway."

"You sure?" Evie said, wanting desperately to just say *thank you* instead.

"Oh, these days never surer of anything than that. Here, have at it." Mr. Bollinger got up and shuffled out, and suddenly, mercifully, they had the room, and the terminals, to themselves.

Dash sat and started working the keyboard. As soon as she saw he was engaged, Evie downloaded Tor—not exactly shocking that none of the residents seemed to have done so earlier—and checked the SecureDrop file she had established at the *Intercept.* There was a reply. Her heart kicked and she opened it.

Call me at the number below as soon as you can after getting this message. The number belongs to a burner phone, purchased for cash, never used before. To make the call, you should first purchase one of your own.

If after talking we decide to proceed, I propose we meet at the Pennyfield Lock boat launch on the C&O Canal. It is very important that we do NOT discuss the location on the phone. We can talk about a time, but not a place. Given the precautions we're already using, I doubt anyone could be listening, but we should also be extra careful and not take anything for granted.

The boat launch is easy to find. Don't search for it online—again, just an abundance of caution. Use paper maps if you have to, but the directions are actually quite simple: it's at one end of Pennyfield Lock Road, the other end of which is at River Road in Potomac. Turn onto Pennyfield and follow it to the water, at which point you have to turn either right or left. Turn right and you'll see the boat launch just ahead of you. There's a gravel parking area just above it. That's where we'll meet.

Do NOT use your own vehicle or one that could be associated with you. If you have a cell phone with you, make sure the battery has been removed. If it's a model where you can't remove the battery, you CAN-NOT bring it with you.

I'll be holding something, probably a newspaper or magazine in both hands. If either of my hands is empty, it means either that the person you're looking at is someone else, or that there's a problem and you have to abort. Do the same. Unless both your hands are occupied, I will NOT approach.

If I see you with both hands occupied, I'll ask you if there's a way to rent a kayak. You tell me you think they're closed for the season. At that point, we'll each know we're dealing with who we're supposed to be dealing with.

There was a phone number at the bottom. She wrote it on a piece of paper, double-checked, and closed and purged everything.

She touched Dash on the shoulder. He looked over and she signed, *Come on, hon, gotta go.*

Dash looked back to the screen, then to her again. *Just five more minutes? I'm at level four in—*

She laughed, glad he was distracted. *Later, okay? Got a lot to do this morning.*

They headed back to the front desk.

Cooper looked up as they approached. "Your old man doing okay?"

"He's fine. Thank you so much. I really appreciate it."

Cooper waved a hand. "Ah, it was nothing. Glad you got to see him. Nice man, like I said."

"Could I ask you one more small favor?"

Cooper raised his eyebrows. There was something about the man's face that lent itself to dubiousness.

"I, uh, forgot my cell phone—"

Cooper cocked his head as though this visit was getting less plausible by the minute. A suffocating sense of despair started to close in on her. Everything she was doing was so transparent. If a drunken motel clerk and a tired nursing home orderly could see right through her, what the hell chance did she have against NSA?

But she forced the feeling away. She had to stay focused. She had to get through this. For Dash. For Dash.

"I know," she said. "It's a long story and it's been pretty crazy. But . . . if I could use your phone to call a cab? I'd really, really appreciate it."

"It's no trouble. I just hope you're okay."

"We're fine. I just need that cab."

"Hang on." He leaned forward for a closer look at something behind his monitor—a list of frequently called numbers, she guessed—punched some digits into the desk phone, and handed her the receiver. She told the person who answered that she needed a cab from the senior center in Columbia to Baltimore/Washington International Airport. As soon as possible. Oh, there was one right in the area? Five minutes? That would be perfect.

She handed the receiver back to Cooper. "Thank you. We'll wait outside, okay? I don't want to cause you any more trouble than we already have."

"Hey now, listen, it's no trouble. You can—"

"No, no, it's really okay. It's starting to get light, and we don't get to see that many sunrises. Besides, they said it would be just a few minutes."

"All right, if you really don't mind waiting outside. If you change your mind, though, I'm right here at this desk. Just knock on the glass again."

Dash signed, *I need to use the bathroom after all.*

She nodded. *Okay, but hurry up. Cab's coming in five minutes.*

She made a little small talk with Cooper while Dash was gone. There were so many nice people around her. She didn't know why she'd never really appreciated that before. She was going to change that.

If she got through this.

Dash came back, and Cooper came around and let them out. The sky was pink in the east, she was pleased to see, and it really was lovely. It had been a long night. She was glad it was almost morning.

. . . .

Manus sat in the pickup, watching from a parking lot across the street as Evie and Dash emerged from the senior center. For a cab, no doubt, the same way they had arrived. She would know not to use Uber or Lyft; the services tracked user movements so closely it was hard to imagine NSA hadn't found a way into their systems, covertly or with their cooperation.

He'd thought she would go to the senior center, and it had been easy enough to take an alternate route and arrive before they had. He'd watched them go in, and now that they were out, he could tell from the relief in her expression that she'd retrieved the thumb drive. He hated what he had to do next, but there was no other way. He started to get out of the truck.

A cab pulled up. He paused, his hand on the door handle. Rush the cab? No, they were already getting in, it was too late. Damn, he should have waited somewhere closer to the entrance. But he hadn't wanted to take a chance on being seen, and he hadn't expected to have so little time to move in.

He considered running them off the road, but was concerned someone could be injured. Maybe a fender bender? The driver would stop to exchange information. But it would be a lot to manage: the woman, making a hell of a fuss; the driver, growing increasingly concerned, possibly intervening. Manus didn't want a scene in front of the boy. Didn't want to hurt him in any way. Better just to follow them for the moment.

He'd get another opportunity. And this time, he wouldn't wait.

CHAPTER . . . .
. . . . 47

Evie looked around as the cab pulled away, fighting the feeling they were being watched. It was true that the senior center was a "nexus," as Marvin had put it, and they might be able to connect her to it. But so what? Even if NSA was monitoring taxi dispatches—and at this point she assumed they were monitoring everything—they'd have to parse a lot of data if all they had to go on was that she had taken a cab to BWI. And tracking her in a new cab from the airport, where she planned to catch another one at the curb, would be even harder.

What about Marvin? Could he have followed you?

No. Marvin had been asleep when they'd left. And she'd checked behind them on the way to the senior center, more than once. There had been no one. All right, she was just feeling jumpy. Not exactly a surprise.

What about your camera network?

That might be more of a problem. She assumed they had made it a priority to get someone else up to speed on the network's operation so they had as many tools as possible devoted to running her down. She knew she couldn't stay ahead of them forever, or even for long. In the twenty-first century, people threw off data like dead skin cells. And sooner or later, some of those dead cells would get sucked into the maw of the colossal vacuum the director's "collect it all" fever dream had conjured into being. But "collect it all" entailed one weakness—one Achilles' heel amid all those torrents of raw data. And that weakness was latency.

You could collect it all, yes. But understanding what you'd collected took time. Maybe not a lot of time—look how fast she'd discovered Hamilton and Perkins, after all, and how fast the organization had acted on that discovery—but a little time was all she needed. The trick was to keep moving, and be careful, and most of all, to get the thumb drive to Leed as soon as possible. So that by the time the director's God's Eye saw what was happening, it would already be too late to do anything about it.

Fifteen minutes later, they were getting out of the cab in the BWI departures lane. She tipped the driver well, but not so well that the tip itself would make her memorable. She was starting to get low on cash, which wasn't good. It wasn't like she could go to an ATM, after all, or use a credit card. But with luck, this would be over very soon.

They went inside. Dash looked around and signed, *Mommy, I don't get it. Are we flying somewhere? Where's Mr. Manus?*

She ruffled his hair. *There's so much to explain, hon, and I don't have time right now. It's a kind of scavenger hunt. And Mr. Manus is helping.*

A scavenger hunt? I thought that was just a kid thing.

She smiled. *Grown-ups do different kinds of scavenger hunts. For this one, it's really important that I win. And if we hurry, I think I could.*

There's a prize?

A big one.

What is it?

Well, remember how happy you were when Mr. Manus gave you the game ball?

Dash nodded, smiling at the memory.

Well, it's worth at least that much.

What?

I need to make a call first. Tell you in just a little while, okay?

He nodded and looked around again. *Mommy, I'm tired.*

She kissed the top of his head. *I bet you are. You are doing so well and being such a big help.*

How am I helping you?

For a moment, she had to fight back tears. *Hon, you help me in ways I don't think I could ever explain. But you'll understand one day.*

He gave her an affectionate scowl. *You always say stuff like that.*

She kissed him again. *Only it's because it's true.*

They walked over to an unused baggage carousel. Dash sat on the floor and settled into one of the comics she had bought him. Keeping her back to the wall, Evie activated the prepaid phone and called the number Leed had given her via SecureDrop. One ring, then a woman's voice, slightly husky and reassuringly confident: "Hello?"

She suddenly realized she didn't know what to say. "I . . . got your message."

"Do you have the item we discussed?"

"Yes."

"And can you meet as we discussed?"

"Yes."

There was a pause. "I wish I had some way of knowing you are who you say you are."

"I gave you the bona fides in my message. About your daughter. Our friend told me that would be enough."

"I would describe those bona fides as necessary, but not sufficient. I have a whole team of smart lawyers here telling me not to take this meeting. Warning me this could be the government, trying to entrap me into accepting information it will then claim is stolen, so they can do a Julian Assange to me and the organization I work with."

"And what did you say to them?"

"That I owed it to our employee to take that chance. That I wouldn't be worth a damn as the head of the organization if I played it any other way."

"They probably told you the government would know you'd feel that way, and exploit it."

"That's exactly what they told me."

It was frightening. Could this woman really blow her off, when they were so close? "Look," she said, "if you won't meet me, if you won't take the item I have, your employee . . . I don't think he's going to make it. And I don't think I'm going to make it, either. And I have a child who depends on me. So, apologies for playing the guilt card, but I want you to know that when you read about my having been raped and murdered in some apparently 'random' crime, that's one of the things you could have prevented."

No response. Evie tried to wait, but couldn't. "You know," she said, "I'd really like to do this in whatever way most keeps me out of it. I never intended to get mixed up with any of this, and all I want to do right now is get you what your employee wanted to get you himself. But if you won't meet me securely, then fine, I'll take my chances marching into your damn offices."

"Don't you think I wish we could just bring you in? We can't. We're heavily watched. On any given day, we have one to three 'maintenance' vans parked in the area. Well, for the last forty-eight hours, it's more like six. Not to mention all the new gardeners, and telephone-line repair people, and delivery people. Maybe you could just pull up and try to sprint inside. And maybe they'd tackle you en route. Or just follow you in and arrest you on the premises. It's not a high-percentage option."

Evie felt a jolt of hope. "Then you believe me?"

Another pause. "I'm afraid I'm going to have to."

Evie blew out a long breath. "Okay. Good. Look, traffic is light right now. I can be at the meeting place in an hour."

"It'll take me a little longer. I have to take some pretty elaborate precautions to ensure I'm not being tailed. You need to do the same. There are some quiet neighborhoods not far from where we'll be meeting. Use them. It'll be hard for anyone to follow you when there isn't any traffic to hide in."

"We don't have that much time. Your guy is going to call you soon, remember? And you need to be able to tell him you have the item or he won't tell you what you need to use it."

"Okay then, let's meet in ninety minutes. That should give us a few minutes extra just in case. If you're followed, if you see anything or anyone that doesn't feel right, abort. We'll go back online and figure something else out."

"Okay," Evie said, feeling an odd combination of relief and nervousness. "Oh, and that child I mentioned? He'll be with me. Just don't want you to be surprised. I guess that'll make it easy for you to know who I am."

"Are you sure that's a good idea?"

"I'm not leaving him alone until this is done."

"Up to you. The phone you're on now . . . can you take out the battery?"

"I'm just going to leave it here. Probably someone will pick it up and carry it off. And hopefully take anyone who might be geolocating on a long, wild goose chase."

"Good idea. You won't be able to reach me at this number, either."

Evie felt a sudden surge of nervousness and blew out a long breath, trying to manage it. "Okay. See you in ninety minutes. Let's get this done."

. . . .

Manus kept the truck idling at the curb in the arrivals lane, at the end of a long row of incoming and outgoing cars and taxis. He hadn't anticipated that the woman would come to the airport. She had good instincts. He had no way to follow her in without abandoning his truck in the departures lane. And once she was inside the airport, she had a lot of options. There was Amtrak, the MARC train, and the light rail train. Not to mention numerous buses, sedans, and taxis.

He didn't expect her to fly anywhere—there was too much scrutiny of passengers for that to make sense. And a rental car would require identification, as well. So he was left to try to get in her head again, to anticipate her next move. She was smart, but not experienced. She was in a hurry. She was afraid of cameras. And he doubted she wanted to be around lots of other passengers—a woman with a small deaf boy would be too easy a description to follow.

She'd taken two cabs already. She was clearly comfortable with that mode of transport. His gut told him she was going to use it again. So he drove around to the arrivals area and waited, hoping his intuition was sound. If it wasn't, he'd lost her.

A traffic cop came by and knocked on the window. Manus rolled it down. The man said, "You can't park here, sir. Passenger pick-up only. No waiting."

Manus was prepared for this. He pulled out government-issued FBI identification. He'd used it many times in similar circumstances, and always to magic effect.

It worked this time, as well. "Oh, I'm sorry, sir," the traffic cop said, instantly deferential to the big, bad Bureau. "I didn't realize. I'll, uh, make sure you're not disturbed."

Manus nodded his thanks and the man went away. But as it happened, it made no difference. Because there they were, Evie and Dash, getting into a cab at the front of the line. Manus nodded grimly to himself and pulled out a moment after the cab did.

When they got out of that cab, Manus would move in. He hoped he wouldn't have to hurt anyone. But he was going to get that thumb drive. They were all dead if he didn't.

CHAPTER . . . .
. . . . 48

Remar felt like a man who'd stepped on a merry-go-round that was now spinning so fast and wobbling so hard he couldn't get off it. He and the director hadn't left the building all night. Hadn't slept. An aide was funneling in food and coffee while they ran the director's office like some kind of wartime command center.

They'd diverted just about every far-flung supercomputer, every bit of processing power they had, to God's Ear—already the biggest data take in the history of intelligence collection, and now substantially augmented by the feed from the JLENS blimps and the CIA/Marshals program. Amazingly, it seemed to be working. They had picked up Gallagher's voice calling from a landline located at the nursing home where her father was cared for. They'd looked more closely, and someone had accessed an online baseball game from the facility's IP address. It turned out Gallagher's son had an account—further confirmation that the voice they'd picked up had been Gallagher's. She had called a cab, and they were scrambling to track it when they'd picked up her voice again, calling from a prepaid unit at BWI, bought not twenty minutes earlier at the Walmart just outside the damned NSA campus. Remar had already sent units to BWI. He supposed they might get lucky, but he had a feeling Gallagher was too smart to stay there. Still, they were getting closer. The first intercepted call had taken nearly a half hour to process. But the confirmation had enabled them to filter out a lot of background noise, and they nailed the second call less than ten minutes after it had actually happened. A little more time, and just a little luck, Remar thought, and the next time they picked up Gallagher's voice, they'd be right on top of her.

The door to the inner office opened and the director strode out. "Manus," he said. "I told you."

He showed Remar his phone. There was a text message: *I'm on her. I'll get you the thumb drive. And make her promise never to tell. But you have to promise not to hurt her. Or the boy.*

There was a reply. It said, *If you can make her promise, then I promise. Yes.*

"Burner," the director said. "But it's Manus. Geolocated at BWI. He's following them."

"Are you tracking him now?"

"No. He pulled the battery."

"Why would he do that?"

"He isn't certain. He wants to do this on his own terms. But I told you. He still believes we're all on the same team."

Remar nodded, keeping his expression neutral. "A dangerous error in judgment."

"Yes, well, let's not make one of our own. Stay on the woman. If we can get to her before Manus does, so much the better. Eliminate the middleman."

He returned to his office, closing the door behind him.

Remar's secure line buzzed. He looked and saw it was Jones. He picked up and said, "Vernon. How are we doing on that local detachment?"

"I got four handpicked door kickers locked and loaded and waiting in your very parking lot. Hard men who will do as they are told with no questions. But you don't get to use them until you tell me what the hell is going on."

"What do you mean?"

"Come on, Mike, a bullshitter knows a bullshitter. What's this new bomb threat I'm hearing about?"

"Terrorist chatter. Just taking precautions."

"Terrorist chatter my ass. That horseshit is what we feed to the morons running the six o'clock nightly news to give the rubes a sense of meaning and make them think we're on top of things we in fact know nothing of. Are you trying to insult my intelligence?"

"No," Remar said. "Anyone who did that would have to be stupid himself."

"And you're not stupid, Mike."

"I've never thought so before."

There was a pause while Jones absorbed that. "Is something different now?"

Remar looked over at the closed door to the director's office. It was time. Past time.

He sighed and said, "You and I need to talk."

CHAPTER . . . .
. . . . 49

The closer they got to the meeting place, the more Evie struggled with her nervousness. It didn't help that the driver, a voluble Scots transplant, was intent on conversation the whole way there.

"I'm a particular fan of the C&O Canal," he assured her. "What takes you there today?"

"Just a walk with a friend."

"Lovely place for a walk. Especially this time of year. Are you a bird watcher?"

She looked over at Dash, who was absorbed in one of the comics she'd bought him. "Uh, no, not really. I mean, I think they're pretty, of course, but . . ."

"Well, today, if you're very lucky, you may spy a rare Carolina wren. Or perhaps even the truly elusive common grackle. Or even a white-breasted nuthatch."

All Evie could think about was Leed, and whether she was going to be there, and whether Hamilton would call in, and whether they would be able to decrypt the thumb drive, and when they would publish it. She wanted the man to stop talking. But she didn't want to be memorable for being rude. Or for any other reason.

"I'm afraid I won't even recognize them if I do," she said. "But they do sound lovely."

"Oh, they are. Some of the loveliest birds in the world, and right here in my own backyard. The truth is, blessings are all around us. The trick is to know the right things to focus on."

"I . . . hadn't thought of it that way," Evie said, remembering how she had felt as they'd left the senior center. About how she hadn't appreciated how many nice people there were.

"And what of your boy? A handsome lad, but very quiet."

She considered a lie, not wanting to fit a "woman with deaf boy" description, but decided it might backfire. So she simply said, "My son is hearing impaired. He's more comfortable signing than he is talking."

The man laughed. "If I did all this talking only with my own hands, I'd either be exhausted, or in better condition than an Olympic athlete. Or maybe both."

Evie chuckled politely but otherwise didn't respond. And the man, perhaps aware of just how chatty he'd been, decided to take a little rest.

Which turned out to be a mixed blessing. The chatter had at least been mildly distracting. Without it, she found herself worrying about what Marvin would think, when he woke to find them gone. Why did she feel guilty about that? Did it mean that deep down, she believed he was on her side, even though she also knew she couldn't afford to trust that feeling?

On top of which, there were all the ways she might have screwed up, all the ways somehow they might be on to her. And of course, even if she'd done everything right, she had to hope Leed had been equally cautious.

But no, the woman had sounded exceptionally confident, exceptionally . . . tactical. That would be a good combination. As for Evie herself, she couldn't think of anything that would have given her away. They were almost there. They were going to make it, she and Dash. Her beautiful boy. They were going to be okay.

. . . .

Remar rubbed the sleep from his eyes. It hadn't been an easy conversation with Jones. And the wily bastard certainly knew how to negotiate. But in the end, they were both pragmatists. And while they both had their own interests, it was true too that there was much they both wanted to preserve.

The director was on the phone, reassuring the White House chief of staff that "everything was under control." Remar had been forced to listen to a half dozen such conversations. To him, having to tell the chief of staff or the national security advisor or the secretary of defense that "everything was under control" was about as clear a sign of the opposite as he could imagine. But there wasn't much he could do about any of it.

For the moment.

His monitor flashed. The confirmation he'd been hoping for.

"Ted," he called out. "We've got her."

The director made his apologies and cut short the call, no doubt earning himself a permanent place on the chief of staff's shit list in the process. He hurried over to Remar's desk. "Where?"

"Heading southwest from BWI. We accessed the cell phone microphone of every driver heading in and out of the airport. And picked her up in a cab."

"I told you. God's Ear. I told you."

Remar wanted to shake his head in disgust. To hear one conversation, they'd deafened themselves to everything else. But remonstrating would be a waste of time. Instead, he just said, "Here, listen."

He pressed a key, and they were rewarded with a recording of

Gallagher conversing with someone who sounded straight out of an ad for the Macallan.

"The C&O Canal," Remar said. "A quiet place for an exchange."

"But where? The C&O Canal is 185 miles long. It goes all the way to Cumberland. We need to narrow it down. What's the latency on this conversation?"

"Less than five minutes. But we've got geolocation on the driver's phone now. Hang on, he's . . ." Remar worked the keyboard for a moment, and a map overlay appeared on his screen. "Two Hundred West—the toll road."

"My God, she's twenty minutes away from here."

"Yes."

"Is this application mobile?"

"Of course."

"The detachment's ready to go?"

"Waiting in the parking lot."

"Good. We're going with them."

Remar kept a poker face. "Is that necessary?"

"I'm not taking any chances on anyone screwing this up. One way or another, we finish this thing. Today. No matter what we have to do."

. . . .

Delgado watched the director and Remar climb into a black Suburban in front of the building and go screaming off. The Suburban was riding low on the shocks—either they were hauling some heavy cargo, or there was a full complement of large men inside.

He pulled out behind them, keeping a nice, safe distance. He'd followed the director before. Funny how clueless the superspooks could be. Like that former CIA and NSA director, giving an "off-the-record" phone interview on an Acela train while a nearby passenger live-tweeted the whole exchange. Or that other former NSA director, who didn't bother to cover his MacBook's webcam. Something about all that power seemed to make the assholes who wielded it believe they were invulnerable. Gave them the idea that they could sideline the little people who worked so hard for them.

He'd seen the director's expression when he was talking about how Manus was still on their side. How Manus just wanted to get them the thumb drive in exchange for a promise of the woman's safety. He could tell the director had been considering it. And that he'd sent Delgado to "get some rest" just to move him out of the way while he figured out how he wanted to handle things. While he considered the deal Manus seemed to want.

What the director didn't understand was that there was only one deal. Which was, the freak and the bitch were going to die. Today. Along with anyone who tried to get in the way of it.

CHAPTER . . . .
. . . . 50

E vie looked around as they drove. Once they were off the high-way, the streets grew increasingly quiet and residential, as Leed had said they would. They passed numerous speed cameras, which made her nervous. She knew that depending on angle, lighting, and speed, some of these cameras could return images of passengers sharp enough for her facial recognition system to process. She reminded herself that even if her face got picked up, and even if it were recognized, the director wouldn't be able to act on it quickly enough to make a difference. They were just a few minutes away now. Almost there.

Traffic had become sparse, but it wasn't nonexistent, either, and she was mindful of Leed's admonition about taking measures to ensure she wasn't tailed. But she didn't see how anyone could have followed her from the airport—or from earlier, for that matter. And besides, what was she going to do, tell the driver, *Hey, would you mind doubling back, and driving in circles, and zigzagging for a while? Just want to make sure we don't have any unwanted company.*

She saw a sign for Tobytown, and the driver made a left off River Road. This was it. Pennyfield Lock Road. She checked her watch—right on time. Okay.

They drove slowly along, passing nothing but trees and fields and a few modest houses, the road growing increasingly narrow and rutted as it curved left, then right, then left again, the ground to either side gradually sloping upward and the trees growing closer and closer, creating a canopy of leaves overhead. The area felt exceptionally quiet, even private. She could see why Leed had chosen it.

They came to a one-lane bridge. A sign announced that the park closed at dark. *Well*, Evie thought nervously, *we ought to be out of here before then, anyway.*

A sign on the other side of the bridge announced that they had arrived at Pennyfield Lock, of the Chesapeake & Ohio Canal National Historical Park. A moment later, she saw the canal. This was where she was supposed to turn right. But if Leed was already waiting, she didn't want the driver to see. So she let him follow the road left, and drive the short distance to a small parking area.

Dash had fallen asleep. She rubbed his leg until he moaned and opened his eyes. *Hey, good-looking*, she signed. *We're here. Almost done with our scavenger hunt.*

She paid the driver and they got out. "Enjoy the birds," he told them, then did a K-turn and drove off.

Hey, she signed to Dash. *We're almost done. This is where the scavenger hunt ends.*

He yawned. *You still haven't told me the prize.*

Soon. Let me carry those comic books for you, okay?

Dash handed them over. Evie made sure to keep a couple in each hand as they walked back the way they had come. As soon as they were past the road they had come in on, she saw the boat launch. There was a green minivan parked just above it—not a Sprinter, she was glad to see, about which she expected to suffer a permanent phobia. A blond woman, younger than Evie had been expecting, was standing near it. She was holding a rolled-up magazine with both hands.

Evie blew out a long breath and kept walking. This was it.

The woman looked around, then back at Evie. Evie did the same, trying not to be nervous. She didn't see anyone else.

She stopped a few feet away. The woman said, "Hey, do you know if there's a way to rent a kayak around here?"

"Uh, I think they're closed for the season."

The woman looked around again. "Okay. We're good. Do you have it?"

"Yes. Betsy?"

"Yes. We have to hurry. Ryan should be calling any minute."

Evie turned to Dash and handed him the comics. *Hon, hold these, okay?* Dash rolled them up and jammed them in a pocket. Evie started to reach for the thumb drive.

She heard tires on the gravel behind her. She glanced over. A white pickup. She felt a hot rush of adrenaline and her heart started thudding hard in her chest.

"Relax," Leed said. "Could be an early morning jogger. Just be cool."

The pickup paused at the water. She squinted, unsure. The driver looked left, then right.

Marvin.

"Fuck," Evie breathed.

"What is it?"

"NSA."

"Goddamn it, you were followed?"

"I don't know how," she said, trying not to panic. "I don't know how it could be possible."

Marvin saw them. He cut the wheel right, gunned the engine, and drove toward them.

What to do? Run? Where?

Dash signed, *Hey, it's Mr. Manus.*

Marvin stopped the truck and got out. He looked at Leed, then at Evie.

You can't give it to her, he signed. *Don't.*

Dash signed, *Hey, Mister Manus. Are you here for the scavenger hunt?*
Marvin looked at him, seemingly uncomprehending.

What are you going to do to stop me? Evie signed.

Just give it to me. It's the only way.

Leed looked at Marvin, then at Evie. "What is going on? What
are you signing?"

"Just give me a minute."

"We don't have a minute."

It's not the only way, she signed. *The director wants you to think
that, but it's not. You can't trust him.*

No. He's always been fair to me.

Did she sense some uncertainty in the way his hands formed the
words? She hoped so.

*He's not who you think he is, Marvin. Maybe he was once, I don't
know. But he's not anymore. I know you can see that. I know it.*

We'll promise him you won't tell.

*It'll never be enough. He'll make a bunch of promises in return, and
the first chance he gets, you know what will happen. To you. To me. To
Dash. You* know.

A dark-haired twenty-something guy with stubble and black
glasses got out of the minivan. Marvin's right hand moved toward
his hip.

No, Evie signed. *Marvin, no!*

The kid's hands were empty. Evie thought that was fortunate.
He looked around and said, "What's going on?"

Leed kept her eyes on Marvin. "Micah, give us a minute."

"Do we have what we came for?"

"I don't know."

I can't let you give it to them, Marvin signed. *I'm sorry.*

Then you have to stop me.

He shook his head. Every time he stopped signing, his right
hand went back to his hip.

351

Leed's cell phone rang. She pulled it out and looked. "It's him."

I'm not going to spend the rest of my life afraid, Evie signed. *I won't. Evie, please. Don't make me.*

Leed put the phone to her ear. "Are you all right?" she said. A pause, then, "Yes, I'm right here with her. But we have a slight problem. Stand by."

This isn't who you are, Evie signed. *This isn't who you have to be. You're not a bad person, Marvin. You're not.*

Yes, I am.

Not if you don't want to be.

Marvin's hand went behind his back. "Don't, Evie," he said, his voice loud, intimidating. "Don't."

She didn't think. She didn't consider. She just kept her eyes on his.

Pulled the drive from her pocket.

And handed it to Leed.

Marvin slumped. He put his fingers to his temples and slowly shook his head.

Leed said, "I have it. Text us the passphrase. Micah and me both. Hurry."

There were two incoming chimes. The guy named Micah looked at his phone. "Got it."

Leed tossed him the drive. Micah caught it one-handed. "Go!" she said. Micah turned and raced back to the van.

"We're sharing it," Leed said into her phone. "The *Guardian*, *McClatchy*, the *Nation*, *ProPublica*, *Rolling Stone*, *WikiLeaks*. Plus various individuals we trust. Micah's got a satellite link. He's decrypting and uploading right now. Everyone's ready. Everyone has their own passphrase. Can you stay on the phone with me? I want to know everything you learned directly from Perkins. The context. His impressions. The more you can tell me, the faster we'll get through the documents. And the faster we can publish. They can't put this genie back in the bottle. Not anymore. Give me a day, and we're going to get you home."

"Go," Evie said to her. "Now."

Leed looked at Marvin, then at Evie. "Look, why don't you come with Micah and me? It'll be safer for you. And we could really use your help to—"

"I'm fine. Just publish what's on that fucking thumb drive."

There was a pause, then Leed nodded. "Count on it." She ran to the van, got in the driver's side, and roared out of the parking area.

Dash tugged at her arm. *Mommy, what's going on? Who were those people?*

Journalists, hon. Helping us.

Is the scavenger hunt over?

She nodded.

Did we win?

She looked at Marvin. *Yes. I think we did.*

Marvin just stood there, his shoulders slumped, slowly shaking his head.

It's okay, she signed. *I told you. You're not a bad person.*

He let out a long sigh. *They won't ever stop.*

She heard tires on the gravel again. She looked up, alarmed. Marvin followed her gaze. A black Suburban came barreling down the road right toward them.

Evie looked at him, not understanding. *Did you do this?*

But she could see from his expression, his body language, that he hadn't. He looked to his pickup, and must have decided it was too far to get all three of them there in time. He moved so that he was between Evie and the Suburban, then put a hand on Dash's shoulder and eased the boy behind him, too. The hand stayed behind his back. Evie could see it was resting on the butt of his gun.

The Suburban stopped ten feet away, pointed straight at them. The doors opened. Four large men in shades got out. They had longish hair and were wearing casual clothes, but they looked fit. Military-serious. They kept behind the doors. Each of them pointed a gun at Marvin.

Dash turned to her, his eyes wide. She shook her head—*no questions*—and pulled him close.

Remar came out. And then—of course—the director.

"Marvin," he said. "What would I do without you? My most reliable aide. My most trusted."

Evie felt gut-punched. Had Marvin been working for the director the whole time? But then why had he positioned himself as though to protect them?

"You're too late," she said, surprising herself with her bravado. "The thumb drive's gone. The *Intercept* has it. And they've already uploaded it to a dozen mirror sites. Everyone's going to know what you've been up to. All your business, all your secrets. Let's see how you like it."

Did his face lose a little color? Yeah, she thought maybe it did.

He looked at Marvin. "Marvin, what's going on? Do you have it?"

Marvin shook his head. "No. It's gone. She's telling you the truth."

The color the director's face had lost a moment before was nothing. Because suddenly he looked practically bloodless.

Remar walked over and put a hand on the director's shoulder. "Ted. Listen."

The director shook off the hand. "How could you?" he said to Marvin. "Betray me? For what? A sweaty little romp? Don't you think I knew? Yes, even before you told me. I knew."

There was a long pause. Marvin said, "You only know what you see. You don't know what I feel."

"Really. Well, let's see about that." He turned to the men behind him. "Take care of them."

Evie dropped, spun around, and threw her arms around Dash to shield him with her body. But she heard a new voice, a deep Southern baritone: "No. You will not 'take care of them.'"

She turned and saw a tall black man in a blue army service uniform emerging from the Suburban. She recognized him from television—Vernon Jones, the chairman of the Joint Chiefs.

"What are you talking about?" the director said. "We need to finish this."

Jones shook his head. "It's already over. You need to listen to Mike."

The director looked at Remar. "All right," he said, massaging his shoulders, "what is going on here?"

Remar shook his head and looked down. "I'm sorry, Ted. It's time for new management. Long past time, in fact. You must see that."

The director's eyes narrowed and his lips thinned. "You scheming son of a bitch."

Remar nodded. "I guess you can't know everything after all."

"After what I've done for you? I *saved* you. I pulled you from the fires of hell, you ungrateful bastard, I promoted you and protected you. Without me, you'd be nothing. You'd be dead, ashes, a cinder!"

"I know. And I'll never be able to repay you for it. Although God knows I've tried. But this is bigger than that, Ted. Bigger than you and me. It can't keep going like this. The fact that you don't realize that . . . you're not fit anymore. I'm sorry."

"Are you insane? You're implicated in all of it."

"No. Not really. God's Eye was your baby. So were its uses. That audit you had me conduct? There was a lot Perkins could have gotten. But he didn't have everything. We'll rebuild. But we'll be more sensible this time. More discriminating. More discreet. Ted, don't make this harder than it needs to be. Please."

"Like hell you'll rebuild. You think I don't know? I know everything. *Everything!*"

Remar looked at Jones.

Jones nodded and said, "Take him."

Two of the men came forward and grabbed the director by the arms. He started to struggle, but the men barely seemed to notice. "Marvin!" he shouted. "Marvin, stop them!"

Marvin watched, his face as still as stone.

"Keep him in the car for a minute," Remar said to the men. "I need to talk to these people."

Jones walked back to the Suburban. The men followed him, dragging the director inside. He was shouting that he was going to burn them, burn them all. Evie was glad that, the way she was holding him, Dash couldn't see any of it. Still, he was gripping her tightly, obviously badly frightened.

The Suburban's doors closed, and the director's shouting was abruptly cut off. Remar walked over. "Marvin. Evie. I apologize for all of this. No one wanted any of it to happen."

Evie was afraid to respond. She looked up at Marvin, but his expression remained unreadable.

Remar smiled a little sadly. "Let's face it. The director went too far. He was at sea so long, he lost sight of land. Lost sight of the purpose, you understand?"

"No," Evie said cautiously, straightening and turning back to him. "Not exactly."

Dash clung to her leg. He might not have understood all the words, but he'd sure as hell picked up the gist.

Remar nodded. "Well, it doesn't really matter. I'm a realist, and so is Jones. We'll make things better. And I can tell you're a realist, too."

"What are you telling me?" Evie said. "That you expect me to keep my mouth shut? What difference does it make? The *Intercept* has the thumb drive."

"Yes, they do, and they'll publish what's on it. We'll ride it out. We've been through storms before."

"What about Hamilton? And Perkins? And Delgado, planting that bomb? How are you going to spin all that?"

"Conspiracy theories."

His confidence was unnerving. It made her want to shake him up, prove him wrong.

"There's camera footage," she said warily.

He nodded almost sadly. "You don't have to worry about that. It's being taken care of. So there's no proof of anything. Well, that's not entirely true. You could corroborate a lot. And if the director were in a position other than facedown in the back of that Suburban, you know how he would handle that possibility. But that's the old way. It isn't my way."

She waited, and he went on.

"It's true you know things, Evie, that we'd really rather not have publicly aired. And not just Perkins and Hamilton. Things like the director being behind the DC bombing. Of course, if you talk about any of it, it could implicate Manus."

He looked at Marvin, then back to Evie. "Had you considered that?"

She said nothing. It felt like he was circling her, boxing her in, tying her up. So he could deliver some sort of coup de grace.

"And not just Manus," he went on. "It could implicate you, as well."

There it was, then. "In what?"

"In criminal conduct. That camera network? Severe Fourth Amendment violations. Your work has been an integral part of God's Eye, an integral part of the files we assembled on various influential Americans. Senators. Judges. Those kinds of people. The same files I'm going to use to protect the system now. If your involvement came out—and please believe me when I assure you it would—you'd be investigated by the Justice Department. Could you afford that? Could your boy manage with you doing life in a federal prison, much of it in solitary?"

It was horrible. He had her. He knew exactly what buttons to press.

"Why not come back to work, instead?" he said. "I meant it when I said new management. No more cloak-and-dagger. No more killing. I'm going to run things differently."

"You think you're going to be the new director?"

He touched the scar tissue below his eye patch. "I think there's a chance."

"You must have something on the president." She'd meant it to be flip, but the moment it came out, it felt anything but.

"Evie, we have something on *everyone*. The problem isn't what we have. The problem is how the director was using it. We'll fix that, as I said."

"You call that democracy?"

He sighed. "Let's not be naïve. We're not subverting democracy; democracy was subverted a long time ago. I wish it weren't so, I really do. But you can't work in this town as long as I have and not see it. Not unless you're willfully blind. And all right, I may be missing an eye, but I'm not blind."

He shook his head and looked over at the Suburban, then back to Evie. "Sad as it is, it's really not complicated. We compete against various interests, mostly corporate interests, and if you look at it realistically, you'll see we're the better alternative. The choice here, the choice for realists, isn't NSA management versus democratic management. It's NSA management . . . or corporate management. And believe me, you don't want the corporations running the show all by themselves. We're not exactly Thomas Jefferson, okay, that ship has sailed, but we're not complete slaves of mammon, either."

He turned to Marvin. "I'm sorry about the director, Marvin. If you like, you'll always have a place with me. I hope you know that. Or, if you prefer, a generous severance. The same goes for you, Evie. I believe in live and let live. For people who believe the same about me."

Marvin said nothing. Remar looked at him, and Evie thought she saw something pained in his expression. Almost mournful.

"I have a feeling you'd like a moment alone with your former boss, Marvin. Am I correct?"

Marvin looked at the Suburban. "Yes. You're correct."

Remar nodded. "Take as much time as you need." He turned and walked back to the Suburban. "Let him out," he called.

A rear door opened, and two men dragged the director out and released him. "You think I'm done?" he shouted. "You think I don't know people? I don't know things? You can't do this to me. I know everything. And I'll spill all of it! I'll tear this city apart!"

Remar and Jones got back in the Suburban. Their men followed suit.

"Where are you going?" the director shouted. "You're not done with me! You'll see!"

The Suburban pulled away. Suddenly the area was very quiet.

Evie squatted and kissed Dash's cheeks. His eyes were closed. She stroked his hair and he looked at her.

It's okay, she signed. *It's okay, my beautiful boy.*

She saw Marvin, watching them. Tears were running down his face. He turned and looked at the director.

"Marvin," the director said, his voice unsteady. "I'm so sorry for all this. For all these . . . misunderstandings."

Marvin turned back to Evie. *I need a minute.*

It made her uneasy, but she didn't see that she had much choice. She signed to Dash, *Come on, hon. Let's give Mr. Manus some privacy.*

Dash started crying, too. He had sensed the danger, and had been keeping it together. Now that it was past, the tears were flooding through. She expected she would have a similar reaction. But not now. Later, when she could start getting her mind around everything that had happened.

She took Dash's hand and they walked to the canal. She hoped Marvin wouldn't be too long. She wanted to get the hell out of there.

CHAPTER . . . .
. . . . 51

M anus walked down to the boat launch. The director was alongside
him. Manus could see him gesticulating and knew he was talking,
but it was as though he had forgotten Manus couldn't hear.

Other than the night his mother had died, he thought he'd never
been so sad. He felt . . . amputated. Orphaned. Marooned. Like his
future had been extinguished by a sudden surge of the darkest parts
of his past.

He couldn't stop crying. He didn't care if the director could see
it. It didn't matter anymore.

They stopped at the edge of the water. A slight breeze had picked
up. It felt good on Manus's face. He looked out. There was a tunnel under a stone bridge, a tunnel that led to the canal, which led
to the Potomac, which led to the Chesapeake Bay . . . all the way to
the Atlantic Ocean. He imagined floating through that tunnel, and
on and on and on, nothing able to see him or touch him or hurt
him. Ever.

The director put a hand on Manus's shoulder. Manus turned
and looked at him.

". . . and I'm so sorry, Marvin. So sorry. Can you forgive me?"

Manus cried harder.

"It's all right," the director said again, rubbing his thighs. "We'll make it all right. We'll stop these people. You'll see." And then he shocked Manus by putting his arms around him, and cradling Manus's head against his shoulder.

Manus held him, a huge sob wracking his body, and then another, and another. He couldn't remember the last time he'd wept like this. Not since his mother. And his grief now was like a bridge to the grief of that earlier time, fusing all the grief, amplifying it, magnifying it. He held the director tighter, his eyes squeezed shut, crying out all the pent-up anguish of a lifetime alone. The director held him, too. And then stiffened. And tried to push him away. Manus squeezed tighter, crying harder. The director squirmed and kicked. Manus doubled over, bending the director back, squeezing as though if he could just squeeze hard enough, he would never lose what he had once had with the director, with his mother, with his long ago vanished life.

He felt a crack deep in the director's body, and suddenly the director wasn't squirming anymore, or kicking, or moving at all. His head lolled, and his legs settled, and his arms flopped open as gently as a butterfly's wings.

Still crying softly, Manus lay him down on his back, then rolled him into the water. He watched as the body began to drift toward the tunnel, the head tilted back slightly, the mouth open in mute incomprehension, the eyes staring sightlessly at the clear sky above. Manus wondered whether it would float all the way to the ocean.

He walked back up. Evie and Dash were by the canal. The boy was skimming stones. Evie was coaching him. It made Manus want to cry again, how good she was to the boy, how protective and loving. But he had no more tears inside him.

He walked over. Evie heard him coming and turned. *Where's the director?* she signed.

Manus shook his head. *There is no director.*

361

She nodded slowly, her eyes frightened, but seeming to understand. He was glad of that. He didn't want to have to explain.

The breeze shifted, carrying a slightly acrid odor along with it. Hair gel. Floral soap.

Manus glanced around casually, his eyes sweeping across the tree line to their right, upwind from their position. The smell was coming from there.

I have to tell you something, he signed.

Evie and Dash looked at him, their expressions open, questioning.

Manus squatted in front of Dash. *Can you promise not to act scared when I tell you?*

Dash looked at Evie, then back to Manus. He nodded.

Evie signed, *What is it?*

Delgado's here. I smell him. Smile now. Don't look afraid.

Evie managed a tight smile. Dash signed, *Who's Delgado?*

Manus eased his truck keys out and discreetly placed them in Dash's hand, who pocketed them. *He's a bad man. But he can't understand sign. So we can talk and he won't know what we're saying. You hold these keys until you're in my truck, okay? Then you give them to your mom.*

Dash nodded.

He doesn't even know we're talking about him right now. He doesn't know I know he's here. And that's good. That gives me a big advantage.

Dash signed, *How?*

I'll explain later. For now, I want us to walk back to the truck. I'll keep watch while you two get in. I want you to drive off. I'll make sure you're safe.

What? Evie signed. *No, I'm not going to just leave you with that sick—*

I'll be fine. Just get in the truck. I'll follow on foot, okay?

Evie didn't look quite persuaded.

If there's shooting, you have to run. That might be your only oppor-
tunity to make it to the truck. Do you understand? Because he'll try to
hit me first.

Dash signed, *I understand.*

Manus nodded. *Good boy. I want you to stay behind me.*

I'm not afraid.

I know you're not. You're brave. But I still want you behind me,
okay? Evie, you too.

They started walking to the pickup. Manus kept Evie and Dash
to his left and casually scanned the tree line while they moved. There
were a number of fat trees and some boulders, too. Delgado could
have been behind any of them.

Manus hoped he was playing it right. He didn't think Delgado
would be much of a shot. The man seemed to prefer knives, and
Manus had never known him to fire a gun. He'd received no military or intelligence training. Even if he'd managed to replace the gun
Manus had taken from him in the reservoir the night before, the new
one would be unfamiliar to him. So on balance, Manus's chances of
getting hit seemed low. But knowing all that wasn't quite the same
as wearing body armor, either.

He kept glancing over at the tree line. He knew what he'd smelled.
But he detected no movement. Where the hell—

All at once he realized his mistake. Stupid. So stupid. He was
so tired, so overwrought, that he'd missed the incredibly obvious.

His own truck.

The smell was coming from the right, from the tree line, that's
what had thrown him. What had stopped him from thinking clearly.

They were thirty feet away. He moved in front of Evie and Dash
and stopped. His hand swept to the Force Pro—

Too late. Delgado popped up from the truck bed, a pistol
extended. He was proned out, most of his body covered by one of the

long panels. Had Manus been alone, he would have instantly moved offline while laying down fire. With Evie and Dash behind him, that wasn't an option. He let his hand drift back to his side.

Delgado smiled. His face was a mess—swollen, bruised, a strip of angry red where the hair plugs had once been.

"Hello, sweetheart," he said, looking at Evie. "I told you I'd see you soon."

Manus felt Evie putting Dash behind her, then moving in closer herself. She put her left hand on his shoulder. For comfort, he thought—but then he felt her other hand on the butt of the Force Pro, easing it out of its holster.

"How'd you like the cologne?" Delgado said. "I sprinkled it in the trees. Just for you. I knew you'd smell it, you fucking freak."

Manus held up his hands as though in surrender and started walking forward. "I like the new hairline," he said. "More handsome than ever. Thomas Delgado, ladies' man."

Twenty feet. Still too far for an inexperienced shooter juiced on adrenaline to reliably hit the mark. He kept moving slowly forward.

Delgado laughed. "Yeah, that's it. Get it all out now. I want to hear everything you have to say in that goofy voice of yours. Christ, you have no idea how stupid you sound when you talk. Like a lobotomy case or something."

Twelve feet. "Really? Have you known a lot of lobotomy cases?" *Just keep him talking*, he thought. *Engaged.*

"None like you, freak, I'll say that. That's close enough, by the way. And keep those hands up."

He stopped. They were ten feet away. They weren't going to get any closer.

"What's the problem?" Delgado said, looking at Evie. "You scared, sweetheart? About what I'm going to do to you and your little boy as soon as I'm done splattering your boyfriend's brains all over both of you? Hmm?"

Manus felt Evie tensing. Delgado seemed to sense it, too. Manus needed to distract him somehow, with something.

An image came to him. It was funny. He started laughing.

Delgado looked at him suspiciously. Manus laughed harder.

"Okay, dimwit. What's the joke? Make it good, it's going to be your last."

"Those hair plugs Evie ripped out of your head. Do you think they're growing on the forest floor?"

Delgado's face darkened. It was now or never.

Evie stepped to the right and brought up the Force Pro in a two-handed grip, just as Manus had showed her. Manus heard a faint *pop* as she fired. The round caught Delgado in the shoulder and spun him back. Evie walked forward and kept firing, too rapidly to place her shots. A few went high, a few went low, and the rest hit the truck panel, which probably stopped the rounds. The *pop pop pop* Manus could hear abruptly ended, and he realized she had emptied the magazine.

He sprinted in and vaulted onto the truck bed. Delgado brought up his gun and Manus swatted it aside so hard he felt Delgado's wrist crack. The gun flew past Manus's field of vision. Delgado tried to stand and Manus blasted a knee into his face. Delgado was knocked back and slammed his head against the edge of the panel. Manus saw his eyes lose focus. He grabbed him by the lapels, hauled him up, and hurled him into the air.

Delgado hit the ground with a thud Manus could feel all the way through the truck tires. He unlatched the toolbox and pulled free the Berserker, then leaped out of the truck bed alongside Delgado. But Evie was already there, one hand gripping the back of Delgado's collar and hauling his limp upper torso off the ground, the other holding the muzzle of Delgado's gun against the side of his head. Her face was a mask of fury and determination.

"I told you," she panted. "The next time I saw you. I told you."

Dash was watching, his fists curled against his cheeks, his eyes wide with horror. Manus said, "Evie, no. No! Take care of Dash."

She blinked and looked up at him.

"Not in front of your boy. Give me the gun. Walk out of here. Walk out. I'll pick you up along the way."

She blinked again, then looked at the gun as though not understanding how it had wound up in her hand. She released Delgado's collar and he collapsed. Then she handed the gun to Manus.

"The keys," he said.

Evie gently removed them from Dash's pocket and gave them to Manus.

"My gun?"

She glanced around, her expression confused, then pointed. "There. I . . . must have dropped it."

Delgado managed to get to his knees. He was panting and snorting. Blood ran from the ruination that had once been his nose.

Evie looked at the Berserker as though noticing it for the first time. "You did kill those Turks," she said. "It was you."

Manus didn't answer. He wasn't sure what connection she was making. He would think about it later.

Evie took Dash by the hand and they started jogging up the road. Manus circled around Delgado so he could keep him in his field of vision while he watched them go. Within a minute, they were over the bridge and he could no longer see them.

Delgado looked up at him. "It doesn't matter," he said. "You'll always be a freak."

Manus smiled. "You know what, Delgado? There's something I always wanted to say to you."

"Yeah? And what's that?"

The smile widened. "This."

He stretched and brought his arm high, as though the Berserker were a tennis racket about to deliver a blistering serve, then brought it down with all his strength. The blade cleaved Delgado's head in two. A fountain of blood erupted from within his riven skull, and Manus leaped back to avoid the spray. Delgado's body twitched and jerked for an instant, and then folded up and collapsed, all useless joints and truncated nerve endings.

Manus retrieved the Force Pro, swapped in a fresh magazine, and reholstered the weapon. He wiped the Berserker in the grass, placed it and Delgado's gun in the truck toolbox, and headed out. A moment later, he pulled up alongside Evie and Dash. They got in, Dash in the middle. The boy was crying hard. Manus extended an arm and rubbed his back as he drove. He didn't know where he was going, and Evie didn't ask him. He supposed she was in shock. Maybe he was, too.

Twenty minutes later, he started to get the shakes. He couldn't remember the last time that had happened to him. He pulled into the parking area at Black Hill Regional Park and waited for it to pass.

Dash had stopped crying. *You okay, Mr. Manus?* he signed.

Manus nodded. *I will be. How about you?*

I don't know. Who was that man?

He was a bad man. He was going to hurt your mother. And maybe you, too.

And you stopped him?

Yes. We don't have to worry about him anymore. Ever.

Was there really a scavenger hunt?

Evie stroked his hair. *Not a real one, honey. But . . . a kind of one. It's a long story.*

I want to hear it.

I'll tell you. But only if Mr. Manus promises to help. He knows parts I don't.

Dash looked at Manus, his eyes questioning. Manus raised his hands, but found no words. He looked at Evie for help. But all she signed was *Well?*

That feeling of being amputated, marooned, seemed to slacken. Only a little, but a little was enough.

I'll try, he found himself signing.

Dash gave him a hesitant smile and a thumbs-up. Then he turned to Evie. *Can we go home?*

Evie nodded and looked at Manus. *Yes. Let's do that. I'm ready.*

Manus drove slowly and carefully. He didn't think anyone was watching. But he knew he could never be sure.

EPILOGUE . . . .
. . . .

Remar and two aides strode down the corridor of the Hart Senate Office Building, flanked by a four-man security detail, their footfalls along the long carpeted floor the muffled drumbeat of a large and purposeful group of visitors. Remar had never needed, or wanted, an entourage before, but apparently being appointed by the president to the office of director of the National Security Agency had its rewards. Or its burdens. Regardless of his personal feelings, today he knew it was important to look the part. He would be testifying before the Senate Intelligence Committee, which in turn would recommend to the full Senate that his appointment either be confirmed or shot down. He was reasonably confident things would go smoothly, but saw no reason to leave anything to chance, either.

From beyond the railing to their left, one floor down on the ground level of the eight-story atrium, came the muted cacophony of platoons of cynical lobbyists, exhausted staffers, high school field trippers craning their necks to better take in the wonder of finding themselves surrounded by the marble-clad walls of the World's Greatest Deliberative Body. They passed the flag-draped entrance to the Senate Committee on Ethics and a long line of ceiling security cameras, then stopped outside 219, the secure room where the committee met to discuss classified matters. Remar checked his watch. Perfect. There was another hearing in 219 that morning, scheduled to finish just before Remar's began, and Remar wanted to be there when it ended.

After a few minutes, the doors opened with a slight hiss of escaping, pressurized air. Ryan Hamilton walked out beside Betsy Leed, the editor of the *Intercept*. A second woman, older than either, was in tow. Remar recognized the second woman as the paper's lawyer. He was struck by the irony that the reporters felt they needed a lawyer while he didn't. And by how the committee was willing to hear Hamilton's testimony only in secret.

They saw Remar and pulled up short. The two women looked at him with cold implacability; Hamilton, with hatred.

For a moment, they all stood and eyed each other, like a scene from the OK Corral. Hamilton was wearing a cheap-looking gray suit that hung loosely from his shoulders. Under it, a white shirt too large for his neck and swallowing the knot of a blue tie. He'd lost weight following his abduction, and hadn't yet managed to gain it back. Well, according to the transcripts Remar had seen of Hamilton's sessions with his therapist, loss of appetite was common after an ordeal like his. So were Hamilton's vivid nightmares—nightmares involving details of his abduction he preferred not be made public. Understandably so.

"Ryan," Remar said. "You're looking well. I'm glad."

"Fuck you," Hamilton shot back. The lawyer touched his arm, but he shook it off.

"I'm sorry there hasn't been more progress in locating the deaf man you say abducted you. I can assure you, NSA has been offering all its resources to the FBI and Interpol."

Hamilton drew back his lips as though to spit. "You people make me sick."

Remar nodded gravely. "I understand how you feel. For what it's worth, I want to personally thank you for helping to expose the abuses former director Anders was committing. As well as I thought I knew him, in the end I was as shocked as you must have been."

"Really?" Hamilton said. "You think we're shocked to learn the government is lying? And worse?"

"No, you're right. Of course not. But speaking as a citizen, I'm glad the press has been doing its part in maintaining the vital balance between our nation's liberty and its security. In fact, I think your coverage of this God's Eye program former director Anders was running has been superb, and I'm grateful for it."

"Ah, the former director," Leed said. "I'm guessing you haven't been any more successful in finding his killers than you have been in finding Mr. Hamilton's kidnapper?"

Remar dipped his head and touched the eye patch. He'd sensed how Manus would handle the knowledge of the director's betrayal. And while he hadn't told Manus what to do, he hadn't told him not to, either. The outcome was good, he knew. Cleaner. Simpler. But still.

"I wish I had better news in that regard," he said, after a moment. "But no. The working theory is that it was a revenge operation, carried out by elements of the terror cell responsible for the DC bombing."

"That was an inside job," Hamilton said. "And you know it."

"I know there are people who believe that. There are also people who say the same about 9/11. Of course, if you have proof—an unimpeachable source, that kind of thing—I'm sure you'll be covering it."

He waited for a moment, watching them closely.

"You're right about that," Leed said. "There's lots more to come."

She said it with confidence, but Remar knew it was a bluff. If they'd had anything, Hamilton, who was running hotter than the other two, would have blurted it out then and there.

371

Besides, Gallagher had taken the severance Remar had offered. He wasn't even bothering to have her watched. He knew she would do nothing to put her son at risk. And even if she did, so what? The word of a disgruntled former employee against a decorated war hero and soon-to-be four-star general? And Manus would never say anything, either. He was even more implicated than Gallagher. And, it was plain, was as intent on protecting her as she was on protecting her son. He hadn't checked in since the C&O Canal, but that was okay. Remar had no desire to press him. Live and let live.

"I'll look forward to your continued reporting," he said. "And now, if you'll excuse me, it seems I have a confirmation hearing to attend."

Hamilton frowned as though getting ready to say something, but Leed touched his arm. "Ryan. Why don't we write another of those articles the general seems to enjoy so much?"

Hamilton nodded and allowed himself to be led off, his eyes still glowing with fury.

Remar's men looked at him for guidance. He nodded sympathetically and said, "He's been through a lot."

He patted the fruit salad on the breast of his army service uniform, gave the jacket tails a brisk tug, and strode into the hearing.

The nineteen members of the committee were waiting for him, arrayed around a red, velvet-draped, U-shaped platform raised several feet above the long wooden table where he and his aides took their seats.

"General," Senator McQueen said, after the room had been secured. His amplified voice echoed off the high ceiling, giving it a disembodied feel, and not for the first time in a setting like this one, Remar imagined the Wizard of Oz. "Welcome. I'm sure the rest of the committee is looking forward to this hearing as much as I am. Despite all the conspiracy theories we've been hearing about lately, I'm confident the entire process of your confirmation will be a smooth one."

Remar dipped his head modestly. "Thank you, Senator. I'm looking forward to answering all your questions and dispelling what myths I can."

The remainder of the hearing was as scripted as its opening. A lot of talk about more oversight, a beefed-up FISA court, maybe a "privacy advocate," whatever the hell that would be. Though as a marketing concept, Remar had to admit, the idea had its merits. The president himself would appoint whomever he wanted in the role, but people would hear the nomenclature, believe their privacy was being advocated, and tune out all the troubling details.

"And we'll need proof that this 'God's Eye' has been dismantled," one of the more liberal members of the committee opined.

"Of course, Senator. As you know, that's already under way."

"Now just one minute," Senator McQueen interjected. "We all know former director Anders was abusing God's Eye. But we also know the program prevented numerous terror attacks. Saved countless lives. Were there excesses? Of course there were. But those were Anders's excesses. We'll fix the program. Ensure there's better oversight. But let's not throw out the baby with the bathwater."

There were murmurs of disagreement and assent. The liberal senator spoke up again. "This kind of program is too dangerous to exist. I want it dismantled, not cleaned up."

Remar thought about the "privacy advocate" and was struck by sudden inspiration.

"Well, Senator," he said, "there is a successor program. Much less intrusive, much greater oversight. I expect it to be equally effective against the terrorist threat."

"Yes?" the senator said. "And what is this program called?"

Remar smiled. "We're calling it Guardian Angel."

The senators collectively leaned back in their plush chairs, nodding sagely, and a low purr of contentment echoed in the room.

That was the way it worked in the modern world. Remar hadn't designed the machine; his job now was simply to run it, and he intended to do his job sensibly and well. Because, in the end, God's Eye was more than just a name. It was a way of life, and people had gotten used to it.

"Guardian Angel, then?" Remar said.

Senator McQueen nodded. "And I can't think of a better man to run it than you, General. You know you will have my full support. Thank you for your service, and for your lifelong dedication to keeping the American people safe."

Remar offered a single, crisp nod. "Thank you, Senator. I'll continue to do what I can. In fact, I know we all will."

AUTHOR'S NOTE........

I couldn't have written this book without the benefit of what the public has learned from whistleblower Edward Snowden. Though if I *had* written it before Snowden's revelations, I'm confident substantial portions would have sounded like tinfoil-hatted crazy talk.

What we know instead is that most of what I've described in these pages is real. And while God's Eye itself is speculative, anyone familiar with the record of J. Edgar Hoover, the history of COINTELPRO, the allegations of NSA analyst Russell Tice, or the workings of human nature generally will know that even God's Eye is unlikely to be entirely imaginary.

That said, I know here and there I've taken some minor institutional and technical liberties, mostly in the service of moving the plot along more crisply. Apologies for this to the experts (thanked below) who were kind enough to read and correct the manuscript before publication. As for the unintentional errors I'm sure I've made despite a fair amount of research and fact-checking, I'll look forward to hearing from readers, and to posting corrections on my website at http://www.barryeisler.com/mistakes.php.

For more on the facts behind my fiction, I recommend the following:

PROLOGUE

Timeline of NSA revelations
> http://america.aljazeera.com/articles/multimedia/timeline-edward-snowden-revelations.html

"13 Ways the NSA Has Spied on Us"
> http://www.vox.com/2014/7/9/5880403/13-ways-the-nsa-spies-on-us

One of the NSA's least known and most potent surveillance tools: EO 12333
> http://www.washingtonpost.com/opinions/meet-executive-order-12333-the-reagan-rule-that-lets-the-nsa-spy-on-americans/2014/07/18/93d2ac22-0b93-11e4-b8e5-d0de80767fc2_story.html

The false and propagandistic notion of an American "oath" of secrecy
> http://barryeisler.blogspot.com/2013/06/memo-to-authoritarians-oath-is-to.html

Not so many burning Humvees in Desert Storm, true, but see Day 15 and Day 41
> http://armylive.dodlive.mil/index.php/2013/02/operation-desert-storm/

How an undersea oil eruption became a "leak"
> http://barryeisler.blogspot.com/2010/07/its-just-leak.html

"Enhanced Interrogation" sounds better in the original German
http://www.theatlantic.com/daily-dish/archive/2007/05/-
versch-auml-rfte-vernehmung/228158/

It's almost as though all these "narcissist" hacks were working off
the same set of talking points
https://www.google.com/search?client=safari&rls=en&q=snow
den+a+narcissist&ie=UTF-8&oe=UTF-8

Speaking of the "narcissism" talking points/projection, don't miss
Jay Rosen on the "Toobin Principle"
http://pressthink.org/2013/08/the-toobin-principle/

"They are using the exact same deny, degrade, distract, disrupt,
destroy playbook against [Snowden] that his own revelations show
are being used against every other activist."
https://occupysavvy.wordpress.com/2015/07/07/occupy-
independence-forever/

Our august lawmakers solicit the Defense Intelligence Agency for
dirt they can use to undermine Snowden's credibility
https://news.vice.com/article/exclusive-inside-washingtons-
quest-to-bring-down-edward-snowden

1.2 million people on US government watch list
http://www.theguardian.com/us-news/2014/oct/11/second-
leaker-in-us-intelligence-says-glenn greenwald

CHAPTER 1

US/Turkish intelligence cooperation
https://firstlook.org/theintercept/2014/08/31/
nsaturkeyspiegel/

More on NSA Special Liaison Advisors
https://firstlook.org/theintercept/document/2014/08/31/
foreign-relations-mission-titles/

Webcam hacking
http://arstechnica.com/tech-policy/2013/08/webcam-spying-
goes-mainstream-as-miss-teen-usa-describes-hack/

Mesh network CCTV surveillance systems are trivial to hack
http://www.forbes.com/sites/kashmirhill/2014/08/11/
surveillance-cameras-for-all/

Harvard secretly installs cameras in its classrooms
http://www.nytimes.com/2014/11/07/us/secret-cameras-
rekindle-privacy-debate-at-harvard.html

Gunshot-detecting microphones
http://www.economist.com/news/united-states/21617018-
how-gunshot-detecting-microphones-help-police-curb-crime-
calling-shots?fsrc=scn/tw/te/pe/callingtheshots

Identifying people via biometric data like height, stride length,
and walking speed
http://arstechnica.com/tech-policy/2014/12/4-seconds-of-
body-cam-video-can-reveal-a-biometric-fingerprint-study-
says/

"New Surveillance Technology Can Track Everyone in an Area for
Several Hours at a Time"
http://www.washingtonpost.com/business/technology/
new-surveillance-technology-can-track-everyone-in-an-area-
for-several-hours-at-a-time/2014/02/05/82f1556e-876f-11e3-
a5bd-844629433ba3_story.html

Facial recognition technology is everywhere, even in churches
http://fusion.net/story/154199/facial-recognition-no-rules/

Who is this Marcy Wheeler?!
https://www.emptywheel.net

CHAPTER 2

Intelligence agencies achieve greater openness by prohibiting officials from talking to media
http://www.wsj.com/articles/SB10001424052702304049904
579516103606857772

Those damn subversives the director is so upset about
Barrett Brown—http://frontburner.dmagazine.com/author/barrettbrown/

Sarah Harrison—https://wikileaks.org/Profile-Sarah-Harrison.html

Murtaza Hussain—https://firstlook.org/theintercept/staff/murtaza-hussain/

Angela Keaton—https://twitter.com/antiwar2

Jason Leopold—https://news.vice.com/contributor/jason-leopold

Janet Reitman—http://www.rollingstone.com/contributor/janet-reitman

Trevor Timm—https://freedom.press/about/board-staff/trevor-timm

Marcy Wheeler—https://www.emptywheel.net

How the NSA tracks cell phone locations
https://www.eff.org/deeplinks/2013/10/nsa-tracked-americans-cell-locations-two-years-senator-hints-theres-more

A lost dog identified three thousand miles from home via a microchip implant. Coming soon to babies everywhere, no doubt
http://www.aol.com/article/2014/09/18/lost-dog-found-3-000-miles-away/20964319/

Amazingly, about a day after I wrote the scene where the director ruminates about using a kidnapping to persuade Americans to have microchips implanted in their children, this was published (and quickly debunked)
http://www.washingtonpost.com/posteverything/wp/2014/09/23/i-helped-save-a-kidnapped-man-from-murder-with-apples-new-encryption-rules-we-never-wouldve-found-him/

Another place the government used the all-seeing eye of providence was as part of the design for the Total Information Awareness program. The Latin means "knowledge is power"
https://en.wikipedia.org/wiki/Scientia_potentia_est#/media/File:IAO-logo.png

The brilliant cartoonist Tom Tomorrow summed up Total Information Awareness perfectly . . . all the way back in 2002
https://twitter.com/tomtomorrow/status/613187965737660416/photo/1

Inventing ever scarier-sounding terrorist groups to justify more bombings. Heard of the Khorasan group lately?
https://firstlook.org/theintercept/2014/09/28/u-s-officials-invented-terror-group-justify-bombing-syria/

https://firstlook.org/theintercept/2015/05/28/called-khorasan-group-doesnt-exist/

CHAPTER 6

United Nations Special Rapporteur on Torture finds Chelsea Manning's treatment cruel and inhuman

    http://www.theguardian.com/world/2012/mar/12/bradley-manning-cruel-inhuman-treatment-un

Yemenis seek justice in wedding drone strike

    http://www.aljazeera.com/indepth/features/2014/01/yemenis-seek-justice-wedding-drone-strike-201418135352298935.html

The best coverage of America's drone wars ever is courtesy of comedian John Oliver

    http://www.motherjones.com/mixed-media/2014/09/john-oliver-drones-obama-harvey-keitel

Detaining someone assisting in journalism under the pretext of antiterrorism

    http://barryeisler.blogspot.com/2013/08/david-miranda-and-preclusion-of-privacy.html

Hacking a car and turning it into a drone

    http://www.youtube.com/watch?v=3D6jxBDy8k8&feature=youtu.be

    http://www.nytimes.com/2011/03/10/business/10hack.html?_r=1&

    http://www.huffingtonpost.com/2013/06/24/michael-hastings-car-hacked_n_3492339.html

    http://www.forbes.com/sites/andygreenberg/2013/07/24/hackers-reveal-nasty-new-car-attacks-with-me-behind-the-wheel-video/

http://www.economist.com/news/science-and-technology/21654954-computer-networks-cars-are-now-targets-hackers-deus-ex-vehiculum

https://www.techdirt.com/articles/20150721/08391831712/newsflash-car-network-security-is-still-horrible-very-dangerous-joke.shtml

Airplanes are vulnerable to cyberhacking, too
http://www.foxnews.com/us/2015/04/17/security-expert-pulled-off-flight-by-fbi-after-exposing-airline-tech/

Everything in a high-end car is microprocessor-controlled—even the steering
http://auto.howstuffworks.com/car-driving-safety/safety-regulatory-devices/self-parking-car1.htm

Hertz puts cameras inside some of its rental cars
http://arstechnica.com/cars/2015/03/hertz-puts-cameras-in-some-of-its-rental-cars-but-it-never-meant-to-be-creepy/

CHAPTER 7

It's possible Manus has seen this video on concealing a handgun inside a vehicle
https://www.youtube.com/watch?v=odT-CfS7lQs

CHAPTER 8

How Western media is manipulated by ISIS into spreading jihadist propaganda
http://www.juancole.com/2014/09/media-politicians-should-stop-letting-isil-manipulated-them.html

The real starship *Enterprise*-like "Information Dominance Center," used by former NSA chief Keith Alexander, is at Fort Belvoir, not Fort Meade. But I couldn't resist moving it

http://www.theguardian.com/commentisfree/2013/sep/15/
nsa-mind-keith-alexander-star-trek

See how excited Brian Williams gets when the government permits him a peek inside the (gasp) Situation Room!

http://rockcenter.nbcnews.com/_
news/2012/05/04/11539949-inside-the-situation-room-a-
guided-tour

CHAPTER 9

If you think Brian's interview of the director was deferential to the point of parody, you probably haven't seen Wolf Blitzer's version, with FBI director James Comey

https://twitter.com/ggreenwald/status/624612963064807428/
photo/1

https://www.youtube.com/watch?t=204&v=7RyVXLKO0DM

Pakistani government forces cell phone users to turn over fingerprints or lose their service

http://www.washingtonpost.com/world/asia_pacific/
pakistanis-face-a-deadline-surrender-fingerprints-or-give-
up-cellphone/2015/02/23/de995a88-b932-11e4-bc30-
a4e75503948a_story.html

CHAPTER 10

ACLU rendition of just how powerful a tool location data can be

https://www.aclu.org/meet-jack-or-what-government-could-
do-all-location-data

Leaving your cell phone at home when you go out? Using encryption? The NSA might think you're a terrorist
http://www.theguardian.com/world/2014/nov/09/berlins-digital-exiles-tech-activists-escape-nsa

NSA spied on US senators
http://foreignpolicy.com/2013/09/25/secret-cold-war-documents-reveal-nsa-spied-on-senators/

"We Kill People Based on Metadata"
http://www.nybooks.com/blogs/nyrblog/2014/may/10/we-kill-people-based-metadata/

CHAPTER 11

ISIS waterboarded journalist James Foley
http://www.ibtimes.com/james-foley-waterboarding-us-journalist-was-tortured-isis-using-same-techniques-cia-used-1673268

CHAPTER 12

Obama prosecutes whistleblowers under the 1917 Espionage Act more than twice as many times as all administrations in history combined
http://theweek.com/article/index/246029/is-obama-abusing-the-espionage-act

Here's what the Constitutional law professor and Nobel Peace laureate did to whistleblower Jeffrey Sterling
https://firstlook.org/theintercept/2015/01/27/torture-must-circumstances-call-new-york-times/
https://firstlook.org/theintercept/2015/06/18/jeffrey-sterling-took-on-the-cia-and-lost-everything/

Secret FISA "court" is nothing but an administrative rubber stamp
http://www.thedailybeast.com/articles/2013/07/24/the-secret-fisa-court-must-go.html

FISA "court" approves 99.97 percent of government surveillance requests
http://www.motherjones.com/mojo/2013/06/fisa-court-nsa-spying-opinion-reject-request

CHAPTER 13

Journalists relying on face-to-face meetings and human couriers
http://barryeisler.blogspot.com/2013/08/david-miranda-and-preclusion-of-privacy.html

NSA spends billions to weaken international standards, install backdoors, and otherwise subvert encryption
http://www.nytimes.com/2013/09/07/us/politics/legislation-seeks-to-bar-nsa-tactic-in-encryption.html?smid=tw-share&_r=0

NSA intercepts shipments of Internet-ordered computers; infects them with malware
http://www.spiegel.de/international/world/the-nsa-uses-powerful-toolbox-in-effort-to-spy-on-global-networks-a-940969.html

"Secret Documents Reveal NSA Campaign Against Encryption"
http://www.nytimes.com/interactive/2013/09/05/us/documents-reveal-nsa-campaign-against-encryption.html?_r=0

"A Few Thoughts on Cryptographic Engineering"
http://blog.cryptographyengineering.com/2013/09/on-nsa.html

The menace of "insider threats"
http://www.mcclatchydc.com/2013/06/20/194513/obamas-crackdown-views-leaks-as.html

Over 700,000,000 people changing their online behavior to evade NSA surveillance
https://www.schneier.com/blog/archives/2014/12/over_700_millio.html

US Postal Service logs all mail for law enforcement
http://www.nytimes.com/2013/07/04/us/monitoring-of-snail-mail.html?_r=0

CHAPTER 14

Over 1.5 million people with top-secret clearances (more than the population of Norway)
http://www.washingtonpost.com/blogs/the-switch/wp/2014/03/24/5-1-million-americans-have-security-clearances-thats-more-than-the-entire-population-of-norway/

CHAPTER 16

"New Hi-Tech Police Surveillance: The 'StingRay' Cell Phone Spying Device"
http://www.globalresearch.ca/new-hi-tech-police-surveillance-the-stingray-cell-phone-spying-device/5331165

CHAPTER 17

In case you're wondering how the director can come up with spare grenade launchers to trade like playing cards

http://www.washingtonpost.com/world/national-security/
pentagon-loses-sight-of-500-million-in-counterterrorism-
aid-given-to-yemen/2015/03/17/f4ca25ce-cbf9-11e4-8a46-
b1dc9be5a8ff_story.html

NSA's AURORAGOLD cell phone eavesdropping and encryption
subversion program
https://firstlook.org/theintercept/2014/12/04/nsa-auroragold-
hack-cellphones/

CHAPTER 18

NASA's SHARAD technology
http://mars.nasa.gov/mer/technology/si_remote_
instrumentation.html

And other existing and coming means of peering through brick
and concrete
https://www.documentcloud.org/documents/1505138-00-
wallsensorreport-508.html#document/p20/a198024

CHAPTER 20

Mobile IMSI-catcher cell phone trackers
http://arstechnica.com/tech-policy/2013/09/meet-the-
machines-that-steal-your-phones-data/

CHAPTER 22

Pakistani government forces cell phone users to turn over
fingerprints or lose their service

http://www.washingtonpost.com/world/asia_pacific/
pakistanis-face-a-deadline-surrender-fingerprints-or-give-
up-cellphone/2015/02/23/de995a88-b932-11e4-bc30-
a4e75503948a_story.html

"We don't know if it was terrorism" means "We don't know if it
was Muslims," and other aspects of the "terrorism expert" industry
http://www.democracynow.org/2015/1/13/glenn_greenwald_
on_how_to_be

If you think Barbara Stirr's exchange with the director was
deferential to the point of parody, you probably haven't seen Wolf
Blitzer's version, with FBI director James Comey
https://twitter.com/ggreenwald/status/624612963064807428/
photo/1
https://www.youtube.com/watch?t=204&v=7RyVXLKO0DM

CHAPTER 23

No one uses words like "homeland" accidentally
http://intercepts.defensenews.com/2013/08/auvsi-dont-say-
drone-no-really-dont-say-drone/

http://www.huffingtonpost.com/barry-eisler/its-just-a-
leak_b_635570.html

"US Military Drone Network in the Middle East and Africa"
http://apps.washingtonpost.com/g/page/world/us-military-
drone-network-in-the-middle-east-and-africa/325/

US automatically counts all military-age males killed as terrorists
http://www.nytimes.com/2012/05/29/world/obamas-
leadership-in-war-on-al-qaeda.html?_r=0

ISIS claims US hostage killed in coalition air strike in Syria
http://www.theguardian.com/world/2015/feb/06/us-hostage-isis-coalition-air-strike-killed-syria

On the CIA choosing its own pet reporters, by two great journalists for whom I've named characters in other books—Dan Froomkin and Scott Horton
https://firstlook.org/theintercept/2015/01/09/democracy-people-dont-know-government/

Wolf Blitzer is a particularly compliant tool
https://firstlook.org/theintercept/2015/07/23/nbc-news-releases-long-awaited-trailer-summer-horror-film-isis/

The *New York Times* helpfully publishes the government's side of the story: Sure, American hostages were killed, but counterterrorism officials and analysts say the drone program overall is effective . . .
http://www.nytimes.com/2015/04/25/world/asia/cia-qaeda-drone-strikes-warren-weinstein-giovanni-lo-porto-deaths.html

Establishment "journalists" detest whistleblowers
http://antiwar.com/blog/2015/03/24/whistleblowers-and-the-press-heavyweights/

The surveillance state never stops looking for excuses to increase its powers
http://www.nytimes.com/2015/01/10/world/europe/britains-domestic-intelligence-chief-calls-for-greater-authority-for-spies.html?smid=tw-share&_r=0

"Former FBI Assistant Director: To Keep Budgets High, We Must 'Keep Fear Alive'"
https://www.privacysos.org/node/1660

CHAPTER 24

The FBI's tendency to create, then take credit for dismantling, terror plots that could never have existed without the FBI's assistance

> https://firstlook.org/theintercept/2015/01/16/latest-fbi-boast-disrupting-terror-u-s-plot-deserves-scrutiny-skepticism/

> http://www.salon.com/2015/01/29/feds_make_fed_up_friends_how_the_fbi_encourages_people_to_act_their_worst/

> https://firstlook.org/theintercept/2015/02/26/fbi-manufacture-plots-terrorism-isis-grave-threats/

> https://firstlook.org/theintercept/2015/03/16/howthefbicreatedaterrorist/

TED talk by Trevor Aaronson on how the FBI's tactics create domestic terrorists

> http://www.ted.com/talks/trevor_aaronson_how_this_fbi_strategy_is_actually_creating_us_based_terrorists

To get what you want it's good to "scare hell" out of the American people

> http://www.whale.to/b/mullins6.html

New eavesdropping equipment sucks all the data off your cell phone

> http://www.newsweek.com/2014/07/04/your-phone-just-got-sucked-255790.html

CHAPTER 25

"A Decade After 9/11, Police Departments Are Increasingly Militarized"

> http://www.huffingtonpost.com/2011/09/12/police-militarization-9-11-september-11_n_955508.html

Domestic drones
https://www.aclu.org/blog/tag/domestic-drones

FBI behind mysterious surveillance aircraft over US cities
http://bigstory.ap.org/urn:publicid:ap.org:4b3f220e33b64123
a3909c60845da045

More on domestic surveillance aircraft
https://medium.com/@MinneapoliSam/fleet-of-government-
aircraft-flying-secret-missions-over-u-s-cities-84cbdf57dfbb

This ACLU domestic drone "nightmare scenario" from 2012
doesn't sound so far-fetched now, does it?
https://www.aclu.org/blog/drones-nightmare-
scenario?redirect=blog/technology-and-liberty-national-
security/drones-nightmare-scenario

Spy organizations routinely monitor email accounts of journalists,
assessing investigative journalists as a threat comparable to
terrorists and hackers
http://www.theguardian.com/uk-news/2015/jan/19/gchq-
intercepted-emails-journalists-ny-times-bbc-guardian-le-
monde-reuters-nbc-washington-post

More on the NSA spying on journalists
http://www.spiegel.de/international/germany/the-nsa-and-
american-spies-targeted-spiegel-a-1042023.html

FBI's instructions to police: "Do not advise this individual that
they [*sic*] may be on a terrorist watchlist"
http://www.dailydot.com/politics/jeremy-hammond-terrorist-
watchlist-fbi/

White House: "It is with tremendous sorrow that we recently concluded that a US Government counterterrorism operation in January killed two innocent hostages held by al-Qaeda"

> https://www.whitehouse.gov/the-press-office/2015/04/23/statement-press-secretary

> http://www.nytimes.com/2015/04/24/world/asia/2-qaeda-hostages-were-accidentally-killed-in-us-raid-white-house-says.html?smid=tw-share&_r=0

One day after the news that US drones killed American hostages, the PR counteroffensive kicks into gear: "Counterterrorism officials and analysts say . . ."

> http://www.nytimes.com/2015/04/25/world/asia/cia-qaeda-drone-strikes-warren-weinstein-giovanni-lo-porto-deaths.html

CHAPTER 26

"5 NSA Whistleblowers Who Came Before Snowden"

> http://capitalismisfreedom.com/top-nsa-whistleblowers-came-snowden/

More on what happened to every NSA whistleblower who tried to work through the system can be found in chapter 9 of James Risen's excellent book, *Pay Any Price: Greed, Power, and Endless War* (New York: Houghton Mifflin Harcourt, 2014)

> http://www.amazon.com/Pay-Any-Price-Greed-Endless-ebook/dp/B00J76JPYK/ref=sr_1_1_twi_2_kin?ie=UTF8&qid=1427299672&sr=8-1&keywords=james+risen

More on Jesselyn Radack, whistleblower and lawyer to whistleblowers http://www.theverge.com/2014/6/24/5818594/edward-snowdens-lawyer-jesselyn-radack-will-keep-your-secrets

And Diane Roark and Thomas Tamm, who also tried to go through the system
http://cryptome.org/2014/10/roark-risen.htm
http://www.pbs.org/wgbh/pages/frontline/government-elections-politics/united-states-of-secrets/the-frontline-interview-diane-roark/

http://www.pbs.org/wgbh/pages/frontline/government-elections-politics/united-states-of-secrets/the-frontline-interview-thomas-tamm/

CHAPTER 27

Peyton Quinn's Five Rules for Managing Impending Violence
http://www.nononsenseselfdefense.com/get_attacked.htm

CHAPTER 28

HUMINT, SIGINT . . . and now, LOVEINT
http://crookedtimber.org/2013/08/24/loveint/

CHAPTER 31

The National License Plate Reader (LPR) Initiative—the DEA's massive license plate tracking system, open to other federal agencies
http://dissenter.firedoglake.com/2015/01/27/deas-massive-license-plate-tracking-program-spies-on-millions-of-americans-helps-agents-seize-property

Using license plate trackers to monitor gun shows . . . and what else?
http://www.theguardian.com/us-news/2015/jan/29/us-plan-track-car-drivers-documents

License plate readers are being paired with facial recognition technology, just like Evie's camera network
http://www.theguardian.com/world/2015/feb/05/aclu-dea-documents-spy-program-millions-drivers-passengers

The NSA targets the privacy-conscious
http://daserste.ndr.de/panorama/aktuell/nsa230_page-1.html

XKeyscore: NSA's Google for the World's Private Communications
https://firstlook.org/theintercept/2015/07/01/nsas-google-worlds-private-communications/

How XKeyscore works
https://firstlook.org/theintercept/2015/07/02/look-under-hood-xkeyscore/

How the FBI caught Petraeus: cross-referencing metadata, all without a warrant
http://www.aclu.org/blog/technology-and-liberty-national-security/surveillance-and-security-lessons-petraeus-scandal

MIT researchers report they don't need an individual's name, address, or credit card number to identify people
http://www.zdnet.com/article/credit-card-metadata-study-easily-identifies-individuals/

Don't worry; it's just metadata!
http://www.wired.com/2013/06/phew-it-was-just-metadata-not-think-again/

The CIA intercepts whistleblower communications

http://www.mcclatchydc.com/2014/07/25/234484/after-cia-gets-secret-whistleblower.html

How a surveillance system ostensibly targeted at terrorists in fact sucks in massive amounts of unrelated people and data: Canada's download dragnet
https://firstlook.org/theintercept/2015/01/28/canada-cse-levitation-mass-surveillance/

CHAPTER 32

How to leak securely using SecureDrop
https://firstlook.org/theintercept/2015/01/28/how-to-leak-to-the-intercept/

CHAPTER 41

CIA director's attempt to conceal emails by saving them as drafts, not sending
http://www.washingtonpost.com/blogs/worldviews/wp/2012/11/12/heres-the-e-mail-trick-petraeus-and-broadwell-used-to-communicate/

If you're using encryption, the NSA is watching extra closely
https://www.techdirt.com/articles/20130620/15390323549/nsa-has-convinced-fisa-court-that-if-your-data-is-encrypted-you-might-be-terrorist-so-itll-hang-onto-your-data.shtml

Lawyer-client privileged communications are of particular interest
http://www.theguardian.com/uk-news/2015/feb/18/uk-admits-unlawfully-monitoring-legally-privileged-communications

Governments monitor WikiLeaks website, collect IP addresses of visitors
> https://firstlook.org/theintercept/2014/02/18/snowden-docs-reveal-covert-surveillance-and-pressure-tactics-aimed-at-wikileaks-and-its-supporters/

Thinking about searching for privacy-enhancing tools? The NSA is watching for that
> http://daserste.ndr.de/panorama/aktuell/nsa230_page-1.html

UK Parliamentary Committee: "GCHQ's bulk interception capability is used primarily to find patterns in, or characteristics of, online communications which indicate involvement in threats to national security"—aka God's Eye
> https://firstlook.org/theintercept/2015/03/12/uk-parliament-finally-offers-evidence-mass-surveillance-stops-terror-attacks/

NSA spies on journalists
> http://www.spiegel.de/international/germany/the-nsa-and-american-spies-targeted-spiegel-a-1042023.html

"Surveillance Forces Journalists to Think and Act Like Spies"
> https://cpj.org/2015/04/attacks-on-the-press-surveillance-forces-journalists-to-think-act-like-spies.php

This is by design: "When journalists must compete with spies and surveillance, even if they win, society loses."
> http://inthesetimes.com/article/18035/a-spys-guide-to-protecting-whistleblowers

Another example of God's Eye-type pattern recognition: the NSA's SKYNET program https://firstlook.org/theintercept/2015/05/08/u-s-government-designated-prominent-al-jazeera-journalist-al-qaeda-member-put-watch-list/

Israel's Unit 8200 uses compromising information gathered from captured emails to coerce key Palestinians. Unthinkable NSA does anything similar?

http://blogs.reuters.com/great-debate/2015/05/11/if-youre-not-outraged-about-the-nsa-surveillance-heres-why-you-should-be/

CHAPTER 45

Turning a phone into a listening device via WARRIOR PRIDE and NOSEY SMURF (yes, they really have names like that—your tax dollars at work)

https://firstlook.org/theintercept/2015/03/10/ispy-cia-campaign-steal-apples-secrets/

New exploit turns Samsung Galaxy phones into remote bugging devices

https://twitter.com/rj_gallagher/status/618543070884315136/photo/1

Using a cell phone's gyroscopes like a microphone

http://www.wired.com/2014/08/gyroscope-listening-hack/

The $2.8 billion JLENS blimps floating over Maryland

https://firstlook.org/theintercept/2014/12/17/billion-dollar-surveillance-blimp-launch-maryland/

The CIA/US Marshals joint cell phone tracking initiative

http://www.wsj.com/articles/cia-gave-justice-department-secret-phone-scanning-technology-1426009924

Accessing baby monitors and other listening devices
http://www.forbes.com/sites/kashmirhill/2013/09/04/shodan-terrifying-search-engine/

Entertainment systems listening in on your living room conversations
http://www.bbc.com/news/technology-31296188

The NSA converts spoken words into searchable text so surveillance of conversations can be conducted at huge scale
https://firstlook.org/theintercept/2015/05/05/nsa-speech-recognition-snowden-searchable-text/

I wish I were inventing the phrase "civil liberties extremist," as clear a sign of our authoritarian times as any. Alas, I'm not. Pity Barry Goldwater
http://www.theguardian.com/us-news/live/2015/may/18/obama-clinton-christie-politics-live

CHAPTER 46

Uber tracks user movements with a program called God View (aka Creepy Stalker View)
http://www.forbes.com/sites/kashmirhill/2014/10/03/god-view-uber-allegedly-stalked-users-for-party-goers-viewing-pleasure/

http://www.engadget.com/2014/11/19/uber-godview-tracking/

CHAPTER 47

"When you collect it all, when you monitor everyone, you understand nothing."

http://www.theguardian.com/us-news/2015/may/22/edward-snowden-nsa-reform

"We are drowning in information. And yet we know nothing." https://firstlook.org/theintercept/2015/05/28/nsa-officials-privately-criticize-collect-it-all-surveillance/

CHAPTER 49

Former CIA and NSA director Michael Hayden's "off-the-record" interview gets live-tweeted
    http://www.theguardian.com/world/2013/oct/24/former-spy-chief-overheard-acela-twitter

Former NSA director Keith Alexander doesn't cover his laptop webcam
    http://www.theguardian.com/world/2015/feb/03/do-webcams-watch-the-watchmen-ex-nsa-head-no-sticker

EPILOGUE

Not quite the "privacy advocate" position imagined in the book, but close enough: the president's blue ribbon intelligence reform panel recommends "public interest advocate"
    http://www.theatlantic.com/politics/archive/2014/12/civil-libertarians-need-to-infiltrate-the-nsa/383932/

    http://www.nybooks.com/articles/archives/2015/jan/08/must-counterterrorism-cancel-democracy/

Names change; programs continue
    http://en.wikipedia.org/wiki/Information_Awareness_Office#Components_of_TIA_projects_that_continue_to_be_developed

GENERAL READING

For more on the real-world events depicted in the prologue and in the novel generally, I recommend Glenn Greenwald's *No Place to Hide: Edward Snowden, the NSA, and the U.S. Surveillance State* (New York: Metropolitan Books, 2014)

> http://www.amazon.com/No-Place-Hide-Snowden-Surveillance-ebook/dp/B00E0CZX0G/ref=tmm_kin_swatch_0?_encoding=UTF8&sr=&qid=

And Laura Poitras's Oscar- and other award-winning documentary, *Citizenfour*

> https://citizenfourfilm.com

A brief history of the US surveillance state

> http://www.tomdispatch.com/post/175724

Julian Assange's *When Google Met WikiLeaks* (New York: OR Books, 2014)

> http://www.amazon.com/When-Google-WikiLeaks-Julian-Assange-ebook/dp/B00PYZONM2/ref=sr_1_2_twi_1_kin?s=books&ie=UTF8&qid=1427299771&sr=1-2&keywords=when+google+met+wikileaks

Scott Horton's *Lords of Secrecy: The National Security Elite and America's Stealth Warfare* (New York: Nation Books, 2015)

> http://www.amazon.com/Lords-Secrecy-National-Security-Americas-ebook/dp/B00N02RCCE/ref=sr_1_1_twi_2_kin?ie=UTF8&qid=1427299720&sr=8-1&keywords=lords+of+secrecy

For an overview of the ever-metastasizing international surveillance state, I recommend two great books:

Julia Angwin's *Dragnet Nation: A Quest for Privacy, Security, and Freedom In a World of Relentless Surveillance* (Times Books, 2014)

> http://www.amazon.com/Dragnet-Nation-Security-Relentless-Surveillance-ebook/dp/B00FCQW7HG/ref=tmm_kin_swatch_0?_encoding=UTF8&sr=1-1&qid=1434757525

Bruce Schneier's *Data and Goliath: The Hidden Battles to Collect Your Data and Control Your World* (W. W. Norton & Company, 2015)

> http://www.amazon.com/Data-Goliath-Battles-Collect-Control-ebook/dp/B00L3KQ1LI/ref=la_B000AP7EVS_1_1_title_1_kin?s=books&ie=UTF8&qid=1434757502&sr=1-1

If you'd like some historical context for Edward Snowden's actions and what the government has been trying to do to him, Judith Ehrlich's and Rick Goldsmith's Academy Award–nominated *The Most Dangerous Man in America: Daniel Ellsberg and the Pentagon Papers* is as illuminating as it is riveting

> http://www.amazon.com/Most-Dangerous-Man-America-Ellsberg/dp/B00329PYGQ/ref=sr_1_1?s=movies-tv&ie=UTF8&qid=1434862283&sr=1-1&keywords=the+most+dangerous+man+in+amcrica

ACKNOWLEDGMENTS........

Although I'm sure I came up short in various ways, I tried hard to accurately convey the experience of being hearing impaired. In this regard, I'm indebted to two authors:

Andrew Solomon, for *Far from the Tree: Parents, Children, and the Search for Identity* (New York: Scribner, 2012)

http://www.amazon.com/Far-Tree-Parents-Children-Identity/dp/0743236726/ref=sr_1_1?s=books&ie=UTF8&qid=142569651 7&sr=1-1&keywords=far+from+the+tree

And Cece Bell, for her wonderfully evocative and moving graphic novel, *El Deafo* (New York: Amulet Books, 2014)

http://www.amazon.com/El-Deafo-Cece-Bell/dp/1419712179/ref=sr_1_1?s=books&ie=UTF8&qid=1425696451&sr=1-1&keywords=el+deafo+by+cece+bell

If you don't think someone deaf could be as deadly as Manus, you must have missed Andrew Vachss's Burke books, featuring Max the Silent, the last courier you would ever want to cross. Now you know . . .

http://www.amazon.com/Andrew-Vachss/e/B000APBFC2

I'm not as technologically savvy as I'd like, which means this article by Micah Lee for the Freedom of the Press Foundation, "Encryption Works: How to Protect Your Privacy in the Age of NSA Surveillance," was perfect for me. Thorough, understandable, and useful.

https://freedom.press/encryption-works

Another great Micah primer on how to keep your online communications private.

https://firstlook.org/theintercept/2015/07/14/communicating-secret-watched/

And from BeYourOwnReason: "Tightening your Security, Safeguarding Your Right to Privacy"

https://medium.com/@beyourownreason/tightening-your-security-safeguarding-your-right-to-privacy-29af5b7a31c

To the extent I get violence right in my fiction, I have many great instructors to thank, including Massad Ayoob, Tony Blauer, Wim Demeere, Dave Grossman, Tim Larkin, Marc MacYoung, Rory Miller, and Peyton Quinn. I highly recommend their superb books and courses for anyone who wants to be safer in the world, or just to create more realistic violence on the page:

http://www.massadayoobgroup.com

http://www.tonyblauer.com

http://www.wimsblog.com

http://www.killology.com

http://www.targetfocustraining.com

http://www.nononsenseselfdefense.com

http://www.chirontraining.com

http://www.rmcat.com

Rex Bonomelli presented so many knockout design concepts it made me sad a book can only have one cover. But what a cover!

I like to listen to music while I write, and sometimes a certain band or album gets especially associated with what I'm working on.

This time around, the band was Royal Jelly Jive. Listen to lead singer Lauren Michelle Bjelde belt out *Pterygophora*—the elegance of Nina Simone and the rough grit of Tom Waits, indeed.

http://www.royaljellyjive.com

Ali Watkins, Huffington Post political reporter, helped me better understand the arcane workings of the Senate while the two of us happened to be lurking outside the Room 219 SCIF (Sensitive Compartmented Information Facility) in the Hart Senate Office Building. And Mark Fallon and Steve Kleinman were also generous in sharing their experience from inside the SCIF (experience they've gained through tireless efforts to persuade American legislators that torture is a bad idea).

Thanks to Naomi Andrews, Judith Eisler, Blake Crouch, Barton Gellman, Dan Gillmor, Montie Guthrie, Mona Holland, Mike Killman, Lori Kupfer, Daniel Levin, Mark Steven Long, Genevieve Nine, Laura Rennert, Ken Rosenberg, Ted Schlein, Laura Schoeffel, Jennifer Soloway, Derek Thomas, Trevor Timm, and Alan Turkus for helpful comments on the manuscript.

Most of all, thanks to my wife, Laura, also mentioned above, for her help with the manuscript, who I really can't thank enough. But I'm going to keep trying.

ABOUT THE AUTHOR.......

Photo © 2007 Naomi Brookner

Barry Eisler spent three years in a covert position with the CIA's Directorate of Operations, then worked as a technology lawyer and startup executive in Silicon Valley and Japan, earning his black belt at the Kodokan International Judo Center along the way. Eisler's award-winning thrillers have been included in numerous "Best Of" lists, have been translated into nearly twenty languages, and include the #1 bestseller *The Detachment*. Eisler lives in the San Francisco Bay Area and, when he's not writing novels, blogs about torture, civil liberties, and the rule of law. Learn more at http://www.barryeisler.com.

22398SBV00003B/17/P

Breinigsville, PA USA
13 September 2009

The Custom
of the Country

Francis Beaumont and John Fletcher

Persons Represented in the Play.

Count Clodio, *Governour and a dishonourable pursuer of* Zenocia.
Manuel du Sosa, *Governour of* Lisbon, *and Brother to* Guiomar.
Arnoldo, *A Gentleman contracted to* Zenocia.
Rutilio, *A merry Gentleman Brother to* Arnoldo.
Charino, *Father to* Zenocia.
Duarte, *Son to* Guiomar, *a Gentleman well qualified but vain glorious.*
Alonzo, *a young* Portugal *Gentleman, enemy to* Duarte.
Leopold, *a Sea Captain Enamour'd on* Hippolyta.
Zabulon, *a* Jew, *servant to* Hippolyta.
Jaques, *servant to* Sulpitia.
Doctor.
Chirurgion.
Officers.
Guard.
Page.
Bravo.
Knaves, *of the Male Stewes.*
Servants.

WOMEN.

Zenocia, *Mistress to* Arnoldo, *and a chaste Wife.*
Guiomar, *a vertuous Lady, Mother to* Duarte.
Hippolyta, *a rich Lady, wantonly in Love with* Arnoldo.
Sulpitia, *a Bawd, Mistress of the Male Stewes.*

*   *   *   *   *

The Scene sometimes Lisbon, *sometimes* Italy.

*   *   *   *   *

The principal Actors were

Joseph Taylor.   Robert Benfeild.
John Lowin.   William Eglestone.
Nicholas Toolie. Richard Sharpe.
John Underwood. Thomas Holcomb.

The Custom of the Country

The Prologue.

So free this work is, Gentlemen, from offence,
That we are confident, it needs no defence
From us, or from the Poets—we dare look
On any man, that brings his Table-book
To write down, what again he may repeat
At some great Table, to deserve his meat.
Let such come swell'd with malice, to apply
What is mirth here, there for an injurie.
Nor Lord, nor Lady we have tax'd; nor State,
Nor any private person, their poor hate
Will be starved here, for envy shall not finde
One touch that may be wrested to her minde.
And yet despair not, Gentlemen, The play
Is quick and witty; so the Poets say,
And we believe them; the plot neat, and new,
Fashion'd like those, that are approv'd by you.
Only 'twill crave attention, in the most;
Because one point unmarked, the whole is lost.
Hear first then, and judge after, and be free,
And as our cause is, let our censure be.

Another Prologue for the Custom of the Country.

We wish, if it were possible, you knew
  What we would give for this nights look, if new.
It being our ambition to delight
  Our kind spectators with what's good, and right.
Yet so far know, and credit me, 'twas made
  By such, as were held work-men in their Trade,
At a time too, when they as I divine,
  Were truly merrie, and drank lusty wine,
The nectar of the Muses; Some are here
  I dare presume, to whom it did appear
A well-drawn piece, which gave a lawfull birth
  To passionate Scenes mixt with no vulgar mirth.
But unto such to whom 'tis known by fame
  From others, perhaps only by the name,
I am a suitor, that they would prepare
  Sound palats, and then judge their bill of fare.
It were injustice to decry this now
  For being like'd before, you may allow
(Your candor safe) what's taught in the old schools,
  All such as liv'd before you, were not fools.

The Custom of the Country

Actus primus. Scena prima.

Enter Rutilio, *and* Arnold[o].

Rut. Why do you grieve thus still?

Arn. 'Twould melt a Marble,
And tame a Savage man, to feel my fortune.

Rut. What fortune? I have liv'd this thirty years,
And run through all these follies you call fortunes,
Yet never fixt on any good and constant,
But what I made myself: why should I grieve then
At that I may mould any way?

Arn. You are wide still.

Rut. You love a Gentlewoman, a young handsom woman,
I have lov'd a thosand, not so few.

Arn. You are dispos'd.

Rut. You hope to Marry her; 'tis a lawful calling
And prettily esteem'd of, but take heed then,
Take heed dear Brother of a stranger fortune
Than e're you felt yet; fortune my foe is a friend to it.

Arn. 'Tis true I love, dearly, and truly love,
A noble, vertuous, and most beauteous Maid,
And am belov'd again.

Rut. That's too much o' Conscience,
To love all these would run me out o' my wits.

Arn. Prethee give ear, I am to Marry her.

Rut. Dispatch it then, and I'le go call the Piper.

Arn. But O the wicked Custom of this Country,
The barbarous, most inhumane, damned Custom.

Rut. 'Tis true, to marry is a Custom

I' the world; for look you Brother,
Wou'd any man stand plucking for the Ace of Harts,
With one pack of Cards all dayes on's life?

Arn. You do not
Or else you purpose not to understand me.

Rut. Proceed, I will give ear.

Arn. They have a Custom
In this most beastly Country, out upon't.

Rut. Let's hear it first.

Arn. That when a Maid is contracted
And ready for the tye o'th' Church, the Governour,
He that commands in chief, must have her Maiden-head,
Or Ransom it for mony at his pleasure.

Rut. How might a man atchieve that place? a rare Custom!
An admirable rare Custom: and none excepted?

Arn. None, none.

Rut. The rarer still: how could I lay about me,
In this rare Office? are they born to it, or chosen?

Arn. Both equal damnable.

Rut. Me thinks both excellent,
Would I were the next heir.

Arn. To this mad fortune
Am I now come, my Marriage is proclaim'd,
And nothing can redeem me from this mischief.

Rut. She's very young.

Arn. Yes.

Rut. And fair I dare proclaim her,
Else mine eyes fail.

4

Arn. Fair as the bud unblasted.

Rut. I cannot blame him then, if 'twere mine own case,
I would not go an Ace less.

Arn. Fye *Rutilio*,
Why do you make your brothers misery
Your sport and game?

Rut. There is no pastime like it.

Arn. I look'd for your advice, your timely Counsel,
How to avoid this blow, not to be mockt at,
And my afflictions jeer'd.

Rut. I tell thee *Arnoldo*,
An thou wert my Father, as thou art but my Brother,
My younger Brother too, I must be merry.
And where there is a wench yet can, a young wench,
A handsome wench, and sooner a good turn too,
An I were to be hang'd, thus must I handle it.
But you shall see Sir, I can change this habit
To do you any service; advise what you please,
And see with what Devotion I'le attend it?
But yet me thinks, I am taken with this Custom,

[*Enter* Charino *and* Zenocia.

And could pretend to th' place.

Arn. Draw off a little;
Here comes my Mistress and her Father.

Rut. A dainty wench!
Wou'd I might farm his Custom.

Char. My dear Daughter,
Now to bethink your self of new advice
Will be too late, later this timeless sorrow,
No price, nor prayers, can infringe the fate
Your beauty hath cast on yo[u], my best *Zenocia*,
Be rul'd by me, a Fathers care directs ye,
Look on the Count, look chearfully and sweetly;

The Custom of the Country

What though he have the power to possess ye,
To pluck your Maiden honour, and then slight ye
By Custom unresistible to enjoy you;
Yet my sweet Child, so much your youth and goodness,
The beauty of your soul, and Saint-like Modesty,
Have won upon his mild mind, so much charm'd him,
That all power laid aside, what Law allows him,
Or sudden fires, kindled from those bright eyes,
He sues to be your servant, fairly, nobly
For ever to be tyed your faithful Husband:
Consider my best child.

Zeno. I have considered.

Char. The blessedness that this breeds too, consider
Besides your Fathers Honour, your own peace,
The banishment for ever of this Custom,
This base and barbarous use, for after once
He has found the happiness of holy Marriage,
And what it is to grow up with one Beauty,
How he will scorn and kick at such an heritage
Left him by lust and lewd progenitors.
All Virgins too, shall bless your name, shall Saint it,
And like so many Pilgrims go to your shrine,
When time has turn'd your beauty into ashes,
Fill'd with your pious memory.

Zeno. Good Father
Hide not that bitter Pill I loath to swallow
In such sweet words.

Char. The Count's a handsome Gentleman,
And having him, y'are certain of a fortune,
A high and noble fortune to attend you:
Where if you fling your Love upon this stranger
This young *Arnoldo*, not knowing from what place
Or honourable strain of blood he is sprung, you venture
All your own sweets, and my long cares to nothing,
Nor are you certain of his faith; why may not that
Wander as he does, every where?

Zen. No more Sir;
I must not hear, I dare not hear him wrong'd thus,

6

Vertue is never wounded, but I suffer.
'Tis an ill Office in your age, a poor one,
To judge thus weakly: and believe your self too,
A weaker, to betray your innocent Daughter,
To his intemp'rate, rude, and wild embraces,
She hates as Heaven hates falshood.

Rut. A good wench,
She sticks close to you Sir.

Zeno. His faith uncertain?
The nobleness his vertue springs from, doubted?
D'ye doubt it is day now? or when your body's perfect,
Your stomach's well dispos'd, your pulse's temperate,
D'ye doubt you are in health? I tell you Father,
One hour of this mans goodness, this mans Nobleness
Put in the Scale, against the Counts whole being,
Forgive his lusts too, which are half his life,
He could no more endure to hold weight with him;
Arnoldo's very looks, are fair examples;
His common and indifferent actions,
Rules and strong ties of vertue: he has my first love,
To him in sacred vow I have given this body,
In him my mind inhabits.

Rut. Good wench still.

Zeno. And till he fling me off, as undeserving,
Which I confess I am, of such a blessing,
But would be loth to find it so—

Arn. O never;
Never my happy Mistress, never, never,
When your poor servant lives but in your favour,
One foot i'th' grave the other shall not linger.
What sacrifice of thanks, what age of service,
What danger, of more dreadful look than death,
What willing Martyrdom to crown me constant
May merit such a goodness, such a sweetness?
A love so Nobly great, no power can ruine;
Most blessed Maid go on, the Gods that gave this,
This pure unspotted love, the Child of Heaven,
In their own goodness, must preserve and save it,

7

And raise you a reward beyond our recompence.

Zeno. I ask but you, a pure Maid to possess,
And then they have crown'd my wishes: If I fall then
Go seek some better love, mine will debase you.

Rut. A pretty innocent fool; well, Governour,
Though I think well of your custom, and could wish my self
For this night in your place, heartily wish it:
Yet if you play not fair play and above board too,
I have a foolish gin here, I say no more;
I'le tell you what, and if your honours guts are not inchanted.

Arn. I should now chide you Sir, for so declining
The goodness and the grace you have ever shew'd me,
And your own vertue too, in seeking rashly
To violate that love Heaven has appointed,
To wrest your Daughters thoughts, part that affection
That both our hearts have tyed, and seek to give it.

Rut. To a wild fellow, that would weary her;
A Cannibal, that feeds on the heads of Maids,
Then flings their bones and bodies to the Devil,
Would any man of discretion venture such a gristle,
To the rude clawes of such a *Cat-a-mountain*?
You had better tear her between two Oaks, a Town Bull
Is a meer *Stoick* to this fellow, a grave Philosopher,
And a *Spanish* Jennet, a most vertuous Gentleman.

Arn. Does this seem handsome Sir?

Rut. Though I confess
Any man would desire to have her, and by any means,
At any rate too, yet that this common Hangman,
That hath whipt off the heads of a thousand maids already,
That he should glean the Harvest, sticks in my stomach:
This Rogue breaks young wenches to the Saddle,
And teaches them to stumble ever after;
That he should have her? for my Brother now
That is a handsome young fellow; and well thought on,
And will deal tenderly in the business;
Or for my self that have a reputation,
And have studied the conclusions of these causes,

8

And know the perfect manage, I'le tell you old Sir,
If I should call you wise Sir, I should bely you,
This thing, you study to betray your child to,
This Maiden-monger. When you have done your best,
And think you have fixt her in the point of honour,
Who do you think you have tyed her to? a Surgeon,
I must confess an excellent dissector,
One that has cut up more young tender Lamb-pies—

Char. What I spake Gentlemen, was meer compulsion,
No Fathers free-will, nor did I touch your person
With any edge of spight; or strain your loves
With any base, or hir'd perswasions;
Witness these tears, how well I wisht your fortunes.   [*Exit.*

Rut. There's some grace in thee yet, you are determined
To marry this Count, Lady.

Zen. Marry him *Rutilio?*

Rut. Marry him, and lye with him I mean.

Zen. You cannot mean that,
If you be a true Gentleman, you dare not,
The Brother to this man, and one that loves him;
I'le marry the Devil first.

Rut. A better choice
And lay his horns by, a handsomer bed-fellow,
A cooler o' my conscience.

Arn. Pray let me ask you;
And my dear Mistris, be not angry with me
For what I shall propound, I am confident,
No promise, nor no power, can force your love,
I mean in way of marriage, never stir you,
Nor to forget my faith, no state can wound you.
But for this Custom, which this wretched country
Hath wrought into a law, and must be satisfied;
Where all the pleas of honour are but laught at,
And modesty regarded as a may-game,
What shall be here considered? power we have none,
To make resistance, nor policie to cross it:

9

'Tis held Religion too, to pay this duty.

Zeno. I'le dye an *Atheist* then.

Arn. My noblest Mistris,
Not that I wish it so, but say it were so,
Say you did render up part of your honour,
For whilst your will is clear, all cannot perish;
Say for one night you entertain'd this monster,
Should I esteem you worse, forc'd to this render?
Your mind I know is pure, and full as beauteous;
After this short eclipse, you would rise again,
And shaking off that cloud, spread all your lustre.

Zeno. Who made you witty, to undoe your self, Sir?
Or are you loaden, with the love I bring you,
And fain would fling that burthen on another?
Am I grown common in your eyes *Arnoldo*?
Old, or unworthy of your fellowship?
D'ye think because a woman, I must err,
And therefore rather wish that fall before-hand
Coloured with Custom, not to be resisted?
D'ye love as painters doe, only some pieces,
Some certain handsome touches of your Mistris,
And let the mind pass by you, unexamined?
Be not abus'd; with what the maiden vessel
Is seasoned first, you understand the proverb.

Rut. I am afraid, this thing will make me vertuous.

Zeno. Should you lay by the least part of that love
Y'ave sworn is mine, your youth and faith has given me,
To entertain another, nay a fairer,
And make the case thus desp'rate, she must dy else;
D'ye think I would give way, or count this honest?
Be not deceiv'd, these eyes should never see you more,
This tongue forget to name you, and this heart
Hate you, as if you were born, my full *Antipathie.*
Empire and more imperious love, alone
Rule, and admit no rivals: the purest springs
When they are courted by lascivious land-floods,
Their maiden pureness, and their coolness perish.
And though they purge again to their first beauty,

The Custom of the Country

The sweetness of their taste is clean departed.
I must have all or none; and am not worthy
Longer the noble name of wife, *Arnoldo*,
Than I can bring a whole heart pure and handsom.

Arnol. I never shall deserve you: not to thank you;
You are so heavenly good, no man can reach you:
I am sorrie I spake so rashly, 'twas but to try you.

Rut. You might have tryed a thousand women so,
And 900, fourscore and 19 should ha' followed your counsel.
Take heed o' clapping spurrs to such free cattell.

Arn. We must bethink us suddenly and constantly,
And wisely too, we expect no common danger.

Zen. Be most assur'd, I'le dye first.

Enter Clodio, *and* Guard.

Rut. An't come to that once,
The Devil pick his bones, that dyes a coward,
I'le jog along with you, here comes the Stallion,
How smug he looks upon the imagination
Of what he hopes to act! pox on your kidneys;
How they begin to melt! how big he bears,
Sure he will leap before us all: what a sweet company
Of rogues and panders wait upon his lewdness!
Plague of your chops, you ha' more handsome bitts,
Than a hundred honester men, and more deserving.
How the dogg leers.

Clod. You need not now be jealous,
I speak at distance to your wife, but when the Priest has done,
We shall grow nearer, and more familiar.

Rut. I'le watch you for that trick, baboon, I'le
Smoke you: the rogue sweats, as if he had eaten
Grains, he broyles, if I do come to the
Basting of you.

Arno. Your Lordship
May happily speak this, to fright a stranger,

But 'tis not in your honour, to perform it;
The Custom of this place, if such there be,
At best most damnable, may urge you to it,
But if you be an honest man you hate it,
How ever I will presently prepare
To make her mine, and most undoubtedly
Believe you are abus'd, this custome feign'd too,
And what you now pretend, most fair and vertuous.

Clod. Go and believe, a good belief does well Sir;
And you Sir, clear the place, but leave her here.

Arn. Your Lordships pleasure.

Clod. That anon *Arnoldo,*
This is but talk.

Rut. Shall we goe off?

Arn. By any means,
I know she has pious thoughts enough to guard her:
Besides, here's nothing due to him till the tye be done,
Nor dare he offer.

Rut. Now do I long to worry him:
Pray have a care to the main chance.

Zen. Pray Sir, fear not.   [*Exit* Ar. *and* Rut.

Clod. Now, what say you to me?

Zen. Sir it becomes
The modestie, that maids are ever born with,
To use few words.

Clod. Do you see nothing in me?
Nothing to catch your eyes, nothing of wonder
The common mould of men, come short, and want in?
Do you read no future fortune for your self here?
And what a happiness it may be to you,
To have him honour you, all women aim at?
To have him love you Lady, that man love you,
The best, and the most beauteous have run mad for?

12

The Custom of the Country

Look and be wise, you have a favour offer'd you
I do not every day propound to women;
You are a prettie one; and though each hour
I am glutted with the sacrifice of beautie,
I may be brought, as you may handle it,
To cast so good a grace and liking on you.
You understand, come kiss me, and be joyfull,
I give you leave.

Zen. Faith Sir, 'twill not shew handsome;
Our sex is blushing, full of fear, unskil'd too
In these alarms.

Clod. Learn then and be perfect.

Zen. I do beseech your honour pardon me,
And take some skilfull one can hold you play,
I am a fool.

Clod. I tell thee maid I love thee,
Let that word make thee happie, so far love thee,
That though I may enjoy thee without ceremony,
I will descend so low, to marry thee,
Me thinks I see the race that shall spring from us,
Some Princes, some great Souldiers.

Zen. I am afraid
Your honour's couzen'd in this calculation;
For certain, I shall ne're have a child by you.

Clod. Why?

Zen. Because I must not think to marry you,
I dare not Sir, the step betwixt your honour,
And my poor humble State.

Clod. I will descend to thee,
And buoy thee up.

Zen. I'le sink to th' Center first.
Why would your Lordship marry, and confine that pleasure
You ever have had freely cast upon you?
Take heed my Lord, this marrying is a mad matter,

The Custom of the Country

Lighter a pair of shackles will hang on you,
And quieter a quartane feaver find you.
If you wed me I must enjoy you only,
Your eyes must be called home, your thoughts in cages,
To sing to no ears then but mine; your heart bound,
The custom, that your youth was ever nurst in,
Must be forgot, I shall forget my duty else,
And how that will appear—

Clod. Wee'l talk of that more.

Zen. Besides I tell ye, I am naturally,
As all young women are, that shew like handsome,
Exceeding proud, being commended, monstrous.
Of an unquiet temper, seldom pleas'd,
Unless it be with infinite observance,
Which you were never bred to; once well angred,
As every cross in us, provokes that passion,
And like a Sea, I roule, toss, and chafe a week after.
And then all mischief I can think upon,
Abusing of your bed the least and poorest,
I tell you what you'le finde, and in these fitts,
This little beauty you are pleased to honour,
Will be so chang'd, so alter'd to an ugliness,
To such a vizard, ten to one, I dye too,
Take't then upon my death you murder'd me.

Clod. Away, away fool, why dost thou proclame these
To prevent that in me, thou hast chosen in another?

Zen. Him I have chosen, I can rule and master,
Temper to what I please, you are a great one
Of a strong will to bend, I dare not venture.
Be wise my Lord, and say you were well counsel'd,
Take mony for my ransom, and forget me,
'Twill be both safe, and noble for your honour,
And wheresoever my fortunes shall conduct me,
So worthy mentions I shall render of you,
So vertuous and so fair.

Clod. You will not marrie me?

Zen. I do beseech your honour, be not angry
At what I say, I cannot love ye, dare not;
But set a ransom, for the flowr you covet.

Clod. No mony, nor no prayers, shall redeem that,
Not all the art you have.

Zen. Set your own price Sir.

Clod. Goe to your wedding, never kneel to me,
When that's done, you are mine, I will enjoy you:
Your tears do nothing, I will not lose my custom
To cast upon my self an Empires fortune.

Zen. My mind shall not pay this custom, cruel man.   [*Ex.*

Clod. Your body will content me: I'le look for you.   [*Ex.*

Enter Charino, *and servants in blacks. Covering the place with blacks.*

Char. Strew all your withered flowers, your Autumn sweets
By the hot Sun ravisht of bud and beauty
Thus round about her Bride-bed, hang those blacks there
The emblemes of her honour lost; all joy
That leads a Virgin to receive her lover,
Keep from this place, all fellow-maids that bless her,
And blushing do unloose her Zone, keep from her:
No merry noise nor lusty songs be heard here,
Nor full cups crown'd with wine make the rooms giddy,
This is no masque of mirth, but murdered honour.
Sing mournfully that sad Epithalamion
I gave thee now: and prethee let thy lute weep.

Song, Dance. *Enter* Rutilio.

Rut. How now, what livery's this? do you call this a wedding?
This is more like a funeral.

Char. It is one,
And my poor Daughter going to her grave,
To his most loath'd embraces that gapes for her.
Make the Earles bed readie, is the marriage done Sir?

Rut. Yes they are knit; but must this slubberdegullion
Have her maiden-head now?

[*Char.*] There's no avoiding it.

Rut. And there's the scaffold where she must lose it.

[*Char.*] The bed Sir.

Rut. No way to wipe his mouldy chaps?

Char. That we know.

Rut. To any honest well-deserving fellow,
And 'twere but to a merry Cobbler, I could sit still now,
I love the game so well; but that this puckfist,
This universal rutter—fare ye well Sir;
And if you have any good prayers, put 'em forward,
There may be yet a remedie.

Char. I wish it, [*Exit* Rut.
And all my best devotions offer to it.

Enter Clodio, *and* Guard.

Clod. Now is this tye dispatch'd?

Char. I think it be Sir.

Clod. And my bed ready?

Char. There you may quickly find Sir,
Such a loath'd preparation.

Clod. Never grumble,
Nor fling a discontent upon my pleasure,
It must and shall be done: give me some wine,
And fill it till it leap upon my lips: [*wine*
Here's to the foolish maidenhead you wot of,
The toy I must take pains for.

Char. I beseech your Lordship
Load not a Fathers love.

16

Clod. Pledge it *Charino,*
Or by my life I'le make thee pledge thy last,
And be sure she be a maid, a perfect Virgin,
(I will not have my expectation dull'd)
Or your old pate goes off. I am hot and fiery,
And my bloud beats alarms through my body,
And fancie high. You of my guard retire,
And let me hear no noise about the lodging
But musick and sweet ayres, now fetch your Daughter,
And bid the coy wench put on all her beauties,
All her enticements, out-blush damask Roses,
And dim the breaking East with her bright Crystals.
I am all on fire, away.

Char. And I am frozen.   [*Exit.*

Enter Zenocia *with Bow and Quiver, an Arrow bent,*
Arnoldo *and* Rutilio *after her, arm'd.*

Zen. Come fearless on.

Rut. Nay an I budge from thee
Beat me with durty sticks.

Clod. What Masque is this?
What pretty fancy to provoke me high?
The beauteous Huntress, fairer far, and sweeter;
Diana shewes an Ethiop to this beauty
Protected by two Virgin Knights.

Rut. That's a lye,
A loud one, if you knew as much as I do,
The Guard's dispers'd.

Arn. Fortune I hope invites us.

Clod. I can no longer hold, she pulls my heart from me.

Zen. Stand, and stand fixt, move not a foot, nor speak not,
For if thou doest, upon this point thy death sits.
Thou miserable, base, and sordid lecher,
Thou scum of noble blood, repent and speedily,
Repent thy thousand thefts, from helpless Virgins,

17

Their innocence betrayed to thy embraces.

Arn. The base dishonour, that thou doest to strangers,
In glorying to abuse the Laws of Marriage,
Thy Infamy thou hast flung upon thy Country,
In nourishing this black and barbarous Custom.

Clod. My Guard.

Arn. One word more, and thou diest.

Rut. One syllable
That tends to any thing, but I beseech you,
And as y'are Gentlemen tender my case,
And I'le thrust my Javeling down thy throat.
Thou Dog-whelp, thou, pox upon thee, what
Should I call thee, Pompion,
Thou kiss my Lady? thou scour her Chamber-pot:
Thou have a Maiden-head? a mottly Coat,
You great blind fool, farewel and be hang'd to ye,
Lose no time Lady.

Arn. Pray take your pleasure Sir,
And so we'l take our leaves.

Zen. We are determined,
Dye, before yield.

Arn. Honour, and a fair grave.

Zen. Before a lustful Bed, so for our fortunes.

Rut. Du cat awhee, good Count, cry, prethee cry,
O what a wench hast thou lost! cry you great booby.   [*Exe.*

Enter Charino.

Clod. And is she gone then, am I dishonoured thus,
Cozened and baffl'd? my Guard there, no man answer?
My Guard I say, sirrah you knew of this plot;
Where are my Guard? I'le have your life you villain,
You politick old Thief.

Char. Heaven send her far enough,

Enter Guard.

And let me pay the ransom.

Guard. Did your honour call us?

Clod. Post every way, and presently recover
The two strange Gentlemen, and the fair Lady.

Guard. This day was Married Sir?

Clod. The same.

Guard. We saw 'em.
Making with all main speed to th' Port.

Clod. Away villains.   [*Exit Guard.*
Recover her, or I shall dye; deal truly,
Didst not thou know?

Char. By all that's good I did not.
If your honour mean their flight, to say I grieve for that,
Will be to lye; you may handle me as you please.

Clod. Be sure, with all the cruelty, with all the rigor,
For thou hast rob'd me villain of a treasure.

Enter Guard.

How now?

Guard. They're all aboard, a Bark rode ready for 'em,
And now are under Sail, and past recovery.

Clod. Rig me a Ship with all the speed that may be,
I will not lose her: thou her most false Father,
Shalt go along; and if I miss her, hear me,
A whole day will I study to destroy thee.

Char. I shall be joyful of it; and so you'l find me.

[*Exeunt omnes.*

19

The Custom of the Country

Actus Secundus. Scena Prima.

Enter Manuel du Sosa, *and* Guiomar.

Man. I Hear and see too much of him, and that
Compels me Madam, though unwillingly,
To wish I had no Uncles part in him,
And much I fear, the comfort of a Son
You will not long enjoy.

Gui. 'Tis not my fault,
And therefore from his guilt my innocence
Cannot be tainted, since his Fathers death,
(Peace to his soul) a Mothers prayers and care
Were never wanting, in his education.
His Child-hood I pass o're, as being brought up
Under my wing; and growing ripe for study,
I overcame the tenderness, and joy
I had to look upon him, and provided
The choicest Masters, and of greatest name
Of *Salamanca,* in all liberal Arts.

Man. To train his youth up.
I must witness that.

Gui. How there he prospered to the admiration
Of all that knew him, for a general Scholar,
Being one of note, before he was a man,
Is still remembred in that *Academy,*
From thence I sent him to the Emperours Court,
Attended like his Fathers Son, and there
Maintain'd him, in such bravery and height,
As did become a Courtier.

Man. 'Twas that spoil'd him, my Nephew had been happy.
The Court's a School indeed, in which some few
Learn vertuous principles, but most forget
What ever they brought thither good and honest.
Trifling is there in practice, serious actions
Are obsolete and out of use, my Nephew
Had been a happy man, had he ne're known
What's there in grace and fashion.

Gui. I have heard yet,
That while he liv'd in Court, the Emperour
Took notice of his carriage and good parts,
The Grandees did not scorn his company,
And of the greatest Ladies he was held
A compleat Gentleman.

Man. He indeed Daunc'd well;
A turn o'th' Toe, with a lofty trick or two,
To argue nimbleness, and a strong back,
Will go far with a Madam: 'tis most true,
That he's an excellent Scholar, and he knows it;
An exact Courtier, and he knows that too;
He has fought thrice, and come off still with honour,
Which he forgets not.

Gui. Nor have I much reason,
To grieve his fortune that way.

Man. You are mistaken,
Prosperity does search a Gentlemans temper,
More than his adverse fortune: I have known
Many, and of rare parts from their success
In private Duels, rais'd up to such a pride,
And so transform'd from what they were, that all
That lov'd them truly, wish'd they had fallen in them.
I need not write examples, in your Son
'Tis too apparent; for e're *Don Duarte*
Made tryal of his valour, he indeed was
Admired for civil courtesie, but now
He's swoln so high, out of his own assurance,
Of what he dares do, that he seeks occasions,
Unjust occasions, grounded on blind passion,
Ever to be in quarrels, and this makes him
Shunn'd of all fair Societies.

Gui. Would it were
In my weak power to help it: I will use
With my entreaties th' Authority of a Mother,
As you may of an Uncle, and enlarge it
With your command, as being a Governour
To the great King in *Lisbon.*

Enter Duarte *and his Page.*

Man. Here he comes.
We are unseen, observe him.

Dua. Boy.

Page. My Lord.

Dua. What saith the *Spanish* Captain that I struck,
To my bold challenge?

Page. He refus'd to read it.

Dua. Why didst not leave it there?

Page. I did my Lord,
But to no purpose, for he seems more willing
To sit down with the wrongs, than to repair
His honour by the sword; he knows too well,
That from your Lordship nothing can be got
But more blows, and disgraces.

Dua. He's a wretch,
A miserable wretch, and all my fury
Is lost upon him; holds the Mask, appointed
I'th' honour of *Hippolyta*?

Page. 'Tis broke off.

Dua. The reason?

Page. This was one, they heard your Lordship
Was by the Ladies choice to lead the Dance,
And therefore they, too well assur'd how far
You would outshine 'em, gave it o're and said,
They would not serve for foiles to set you off.

Dua. They at their best are such, and ever shall be
Where I appear.

Man. Do you note his modesty?

Dua. But was there nothing else pretended?

Page. Yes,
Young Don *Alonzo*, the great Captains Nephew,
Stood on comparisons.

Dua. With whom?

Page. With you,
And openly profess'd that all precedence,
His birth and state consider'd, was due to him,
Nor were your Lordship to contend with one
So far above you.

Dua. I look down upon him
With such contempt and scorn, as on my slave,
He's a name only, and all good in him
He must derive from his great grandsires Ashes,
For had not their victorious acts bequeath'd
His titles to him, and wrote on his forehead,
This is a Lord, he had liv'd unobserv'd
By any man of mark, and died as one
Amongst the common route. Compare with me?
'Tis Gyant-like ambition; I know him,
And know my self, that man is truly noble,
And he may justly call that worth his own,
Which his deserts have purchas'd, I could wish
My birth were more obscure, my friends and kinsmen
Of lesser power, or that my provident Father
Had been like to that riotous Emperour
That chose his belly for his only heir;
For being of no family then, and poor
My vertues wheresoe'r I liv'd, should make
That kingdom my inheritance.

Gui. Strange self Love!

Dua. For if I studied the Countries Laws,
I should so easily sound all their depth,
And rise up such a wonder, that the pleaders,
That now are in most practice and esteem,
Should starve for want of Clients: if I travell'd,
Like wise *Ulysses* to see men and manners,

I would return in act, more knowing, than
Homer could fancy him; if a Physician,
So oft I would restore death-wounded men,
That where I liv'd, *Galen* should not be nam'd,
And he that joyn'd again the scatter'd limbs
Of torn *Hippolytus* should be forgotten.
I could teach *Ovid* courtship, how to win
A *Julia*, and enjoy her, though her Dower
Were all the Sun gives light to: and for arms
Were the *Persian* host that drank up Rivers, added
To the *Turks* present powers, I could direct,
Command, and Marshal them.

Man. And yet you know not
To rule your self, you would not to a boy else
Like *Plautus* Braggart boast thus.

Dua. All I speak,
In act I can make good.

Gui. Why then being Master
Of such and so good parts do you destroy them,
With self opinion, or like a rich miser,
Hoard up the treasures you possess, imparting
Nor to your self nor others, the use of them?
They are to you but like inchanted viands,
On which you seem to feed, yet pine with hunger;
And those so rare perfections in my Son
Which would make others happy, render me
A wretched Mother.

Man. You are too insolent.
And those too many excellencies, that feed
Your pride, turn to a Pleurisie, and kill
That which should nourish vertue; dare you think
All blessings are confer'd on you alone?
Y'are grosly cousen'd; there's no good in you,
Which others have not: are you a Scholar? so
Are many, and as knowing: are you valiant?
Waste not that courage then in braules, but spend it
In the Wars, in service of your King and Country.

Dua. Yes, so I might be General, no man lives

24

That's worthy to command me.

Man. Sir, in *Lisbon*
I am: and you shall know it; every hour
I am troubled with complaints of your behaviour
From men of all conditions, and all sexes.
And my authority, which you presume
Will bear you out, in that you are my Nephew,
No longer shall protect you, for I vow
Though all that's past I pardon, I will punish
The next fault with as much severity
As if you were a stranger, rest assur'd on't.

Gui. And by that love you should bear, or that duty
You owe a Mother, once more I command you
To cast this haughtiness off; which if you do,
All that is mine, is yours, if not, expect
My prayers, and vows, for your conversion only,
But never means nor favour.   [*Ex.* Manuel *and* Guiomar.

Dua. I am Tutor'd
As if I were a child still, the base Peasants
That fear, and envy my great worth, have done this;
But I will find them out, I will o'boord
Get my disguise; I have too long been idle,
Nor will I curb my spirit, I was born free,
And will pursue the course best liketh me.   [*Exeunt.*

Enter Leopold, Sailers, *and* Zenocia.

Leop. Divide the spoil amongst you, this fair Captive
I only challenge for my self.

Sail. You have won her
And well deserve her: twenty years I have liv'd
A Burgess of the Sea, and have been present
At many a desperate fight, but never saw
So small a Bark with such incredible valour
So long defended, and against such odds,
And by two men scarce arm'd too.

Leop. 'Twas a wonder.
And yet the courage they exprest being taken,

25

And their contempt of death wan more upon me
Than all they did, when they were free: me thinks
I see them yet when they were brought aboard us,
Disarm'd and ready to be put in fetters
How on the suddain, as if they had sworn
Never to taste the bread of servitude,
Both snatching up their swords, and from this Virgin,
Taking a farewel only with their eyes,
They leapt into the Sea.

Sail. Indeed 'twas rare.

Leop. It wrought so much on me, that but I fear'd
The great ship that pursued us, our own safety
Hindring my charitable purpose to 'em,
I would have took 'em up, and with their lives
They should have had their liberties.

Zen. O too late,
For they are lost, for ever lost.

Leop. Take comfort
'Tis not impossible, but that they live yet,
For when they left the ships, they were within
A League o'th' shore, and with such strength and cunning
They swimming, did delude the rising Billows,
With one hand making way, and with the other,
Their bloudy swords advanced, threatning the Sea-gods
With war, unless they brought them safely off,
That I am almost confident they live,
And you again may see them.

Zen. In that hope
I brook a wretched being, till I am
Made certain of their fortunes; but they dead,
Death hath so many doors to let out life,
I will not long survive them.

Leop. Hope the best,
And let the courteous usage you have found,
Not usual in men of War perswade you
To tell me your condition.

The Custom of the Country

Zen. You know it,
A Captive, my fate and your power have made me,
Such I am now, but what I was it skills not:
For they being dead, in whom I only live,
I dare not challenge Family, or Country,
And therefore Sir enquire not, let it suffice,
I am your servant, and a thankful servant
(If you will call that so, which is but duty)
I ever will be, and my honour safe,
Which nobly hitherto ye have preserv'd,
No slavery can appear in such a form,
Which with a <u>masculine constancy</u> I will not
Boldly look on and suffer.

Leop. You mistake me:
That you are made my prisoner, may prove
The birth of your good fortune. I do find
A winning language in your tongue and looks;
Nor can a suit by you mov'd be deni'd,
And therefore of a prisoner you must be
The Victors advocate.

Zen. To whom?

Leap. A Lady:
In whom all graces that can perfect beauty
Are friendly met. I grant that you are fair:
And had I not seen her before, perhaps
I might have sought to you.

Zen. This I hear gladly.

Leap. To this incomparable Lady I will give you,
(Yet being mine, you are already hers)
And to serve her is more than to be free,
At least I think so; and when you live with her,
If you will please to think on him that brought you
To such a happiness, for so her bounty
Will make you think her service, you shall ever
Make me at your devotion.

Zen. All I can do,
Rest you assur'd of.

[handwritten margin note: She will adopt this → play is preoccupied w/ the trials of women]

Leap. At night I'le present you,
Till when I am your Guard.

Zen. Ever your servant.   [*Exeunt.*

    Enter Arnoldo *and* Rutilio.

Arn. To what are we reserv'd?

Rut. Troth 'tis uncertain,
Drowning we have scap'd miraculously, and
Stand fair for ought I know for hanging; mony
We have none, nor e're are like to have,
'Tis to be doubted: besides we are strangers,
Wondrous hungry strangers; and charity
Growing cold, and miracles ceasing,
Without a Conjurers help, cannot find
When we shall eat again.

Arn. These are no wants
If put in ballance with *Zenocias* loss;
In that alone all miseries are spoken:
O my *Rutilio*, when I think on her,
And that which she may suffer, being a Captive,
Then I could curse my self, almost those powers
That send me from the fury of the Ocean.

Rut. You have lost a wife indeed, a fair and chast one,
Two blessings, not found often in one woman;
But she may be recovered, questionless
The ship that took us was of *Portugal,*
And here in *Lisbon,* by some means or other
We may hear of her.

Arn. In that hope I live.

Rut. And so do I, but hope is a poor Sallad
To dine and sup with, after a two dayes fast too,
Have you no mony left?

Arn. Not a Denier.

Rut. Nor any thing to pawn? 'tis now in fashion,

Having a Mistress, sure you should not be
Without a neat Historical shirt.

Arn. For shame
Talk not so poorly.

Rut. I must talk of that
Necessity prompts us to, for beg I cannot,
Nor am I made to creep in at a window,
To filch to feed me, something must be done,
And suddenly resolve on't.

Enter Zabulon *and a Servant.*

Arn. What are these?

Rut. One by his habit is a *Jew.*

Zab. No more:
Thou art sure that's he.

Ser. Most certain.

Zab. How long is it
Since first she saw him?

Ser. Some two hours.

Zab. Be gone—let me alone to work him.   [*Exit* Ser.

Rut. How he eyes you!
Now he moves towards us, in the Devils name
What would he with us?

Arn. Innocence is bold:
Nor can I fear.

Zab. That you are poor and strangers,
I easily perceive.

Rut. But that you'l help us,
Or any of your tribe, we dare not hope Sir.

Zab. Why think you so?

Rut. Because you are a *Jew* Sir,
And courtesies come sooner from the Devil
Than any of your Nation.

Zab. We are men,
And have like you, compassion when we find
Fit subjects for our bounty, and for proof
That we dare give, and freely, not to you Sir,
Pray spare your pains, there's gold, stand not amaz'd,
'Tis current I assure you.

Rut. Take it man,
Sure thy good Angel is a *Jew*, and comes
In his own shape to help thee: I could wish now
Mine would appear too like a *Turk.*

Arn. I thank you,
But yet must tell you, if this be the Prologue
To any bad act, you would have me practise,
I must not take it.

Zab. This is but the earnest
Of [t]hat which is to follow, and the bond
Which you must seal to for't, is your advancement,
Fortune with all that's in her power to give,
Offers her self up to you: entertain her,
And that which Princes have kneel'd for in vain
Presents it self to you.

Arn. 'Tis above wonder.

Zab. But far beneath the truth, in my relation
Of what you shall possess, if you emb[r]ace it.
There is an hour in each mans life appointed
To make his happiness if then he seize it,
And this, (in which, beyond all expectation,
You are invited to your good) is yours,
If you dare follow me, so, if not, hereafter
Expect not the like offer.   [*Exit.*

Arn. 'Tis no vision.

Rut. 'Tis gold I'm sure.

Arn. We must like brothers share;
There's for you.

Rut. By this light I'm glad I have it:
There are few Gallants, (for men may be such
And yet want gold, yea and sometimes silver)
But would receive such favours from the Devil,
Though he appear'd like a Broker, and demanded
Sixty i'th' hundred.

Arn. Wherefore should I fear
Some plot upon my life? 'tis now to me
Not worth the keeping. I will follow him,
Farewel, wish me good fortune, we shall meet
Again I doubt not.

Rut. Or I'le ne're trust *Jew* more,   [*Exit* Arnoldo.
Nor Christian for his sake—plague o' my stars,
How long might I have walkt without a Cloak,
Before I should have met with such a fortune?
We elder Brothers, though we are proper men,
Ha' not the luck, ha' too much beard, that spoils us;
The smooth Chin carries all: what's here to do now?
[*Manet* Rutilio.

Enter Duarte, Alonzo, *and a* Page.

Dua. I'le take you as I find you.

Alon. That were base—you see I am unarm'd.

Dua. Out with your Bodkin
Your Pocket-dagger, your Steletto, out with it,
Or by this hand I'le kill you: such as you are
Have studied the undoing of poor Cutlers,
And made all manly weapons out of fashion:
You carry Poniards to murder men,
Yet dare not wear a sword to guard your Honour.

31

Rut. That's true indeed: upon my life this gallant
Is brib'd to repeal banisht swords.

Dua. I'le shew you
The difference now between a *Spanish* Rapier
And your pure Pisa.

Alon. Let me fetch a sword,
Upon mine honour I'le return.

Dua. Not so Sir.

Alon. Or lend me yours I pray you, and take this.

Rut. To be disgrac'd as you are, no I thank you
Spight of the fashion, while I live, I am
Instructed to go arm'd: what folly 'tis
For you that are a man, to put your self
Into your enemies mercy.

Dua. Yield it quickly
Or I'le cut off your hand, and now disgrace you,
Thus kick and baffle you: as you like this,
You may again prefer complaints against me
To my Uncle and my Mother, and then think
To make it good with a Poniard.

Alon. I am paid
For being of the fashion.

Dua. Get a sword,
Then if you dare redeem your reputation:
You know I am easily found: I'le add this to it
To put you in mind.

Rut. You are too insolent,
And do insult too much on the advantage
Of that which your unequal weapon gave you,
More than your valour.

Dua. This to me, you Peasant?
Thou art not worthy of my foot poor fellow,
'Tis scorn, not pity, makes me give thee life:

Kneel down and thank me for't: how, do you stare?

Rut. I have a sword Sir, you shall find, a good one;
This is no stabbing guard.

Dua. Wert thou thrice arm'd,
Thus yet I durst attempt thee.

Rut. Then have at you, [*Fight.*
I scorn to take blows.

Dua. O I am slain. [*Falls.*

Page. Help! murther, murther!

Alon. Shift for your self you are dead else,
You have kill'd the Governou[r]s Nephew.

Page. Raise the streets there.

Alon. If once you are beset you cannot scape,
Will you betray your self?

Rut. Undone for ever.   [*Exit* Rut. *and* Alonzo.

Enter Officers.

1 Off. Who makes this out-cry?

Page. O my Lord is murdered;
This way he took, make after him,
Help help there.   [*Exit* Page.

2 Offi. 'Tis *Don Duarte.*

1 Offi. Pride has got a fall,
He was still in quarrels, scorn'd us Peace-makers,
And all our Bill-authority, now h'as paid for't.
You ha' met with your match Sir now, bring off his body
And bear it to the Governour. Some pursue
The murderer; yet if he scape, it skills not;
Were I a Prince, I would reward him for't,
He has rid the City of a turbulent beast,

There's few will pity him: but for his Mother
I truly grieve indeed, she's a good Lady.   [*Exeunt.*

Enter Guiomar *and* Servants.

Gui. He's not i'th' house?

Ser. No Madam.

Gui. Haste and seek him,
Go all and every where, Pie not to bed
Till you return him, take away the lights too,
The Moon lends me too much, to find my fears
And those devotions I am to pay
Are written in my heart, not in this book,   [*Kneel.*
And I shall read them there without a Taper.   [*Ex.* Ser.

Enter Rutilio.

Rut. I am pursued; all the Ports are stopt too;
Not any hope to escape, behind, before me,
On either side I am beset, cursed fortune
My enemie on the Sea, and on the Land too,
Redeem'd from one affliction to another:
Would I had made the greedy waves my tomb
And dyed obscure, and innocent, not as Nero
Smear'd o're with blood. Whither have my fears brought me?
I am got into a house, the doors all open,
This, by the largeness of the room, the hangings,
And other rich adornments, glistring through
The sable masque of night, sayes it belongs
To one of means and rank: no servant stirring?
Murmur nor whisper?

Guio. Who's that?

Rut. By the voice,
This is a woman.

Guio. Stephana, Jaspe, Julia,
Who waits there?

Rut. 'Tis the Lady of the house,

34

I'le flie to her protection.

Guio. Speak, what are you?

Rut. Of all that ever breath'd, a man most wretched.

Guio. I am sure you are a man of most ill manners,
You could not with so little reverence else
Press to my private chamber. Whither would you,
Or what do you seek for?

Rut. Gracious woman hear me;
I am a stranger, and in that I answer
All your demands, a most unfortunate stranger,
That call'd unto it by my enemies pride,
Have left him dead i'th' streets, Justice pursues me,
And for that life I took unwillingly,
And in a fair defence, I must lose mine,
Unless you in your charity protect me.
Your house is now my sanctuary, and the Altar,
I gladly would take hold of your sweet mercy.
By all that's dear unto you, by your vertues,
And by your innocence, that needs no forgiveness,
Take pity on me.

Guio. Are you a *Castillian*?

Rut. No Madam, *Italy* claims my birth.

Guio. I ask not
With purpose to betray you, if you were
Ten thousand times a Spaniard, the nation
We Portugals most hate, I yet would save you
If it lay in my power: lift up these hangings;
Behind my Beds head there's a hollow place,
Into which enter; so, but from this stir not
If the Officers come, as you expect they will doe,
I know they owe such reverence to my lodgings,
That they will easily give credit to me
And search no further.

Rut. The blest Saints pay for me
The infinite debt I owe you.

Guio. How he quakes!
Thus far I feel his heart beat, be of comfort,
Once more I give my promise for your safety,
All men are subject to such accidents,
Especially the valiant; and who knows not,
But that the charity I afford this stranger
My only Son else where may stand in need of?

Enter Officers, and Servants, with the body of Duarte—Page.

1 Ser. Now Madam, if your wisedom ever could
Raise up defences against floods of sorrow
That haste to overwhelm you, make true use of
Your great discretion.

2 Ser. Your only son
My Lord *Duart's* slain.

1 Off. His murtherer, pursued by us
Was by a boy discovered
Entring your house, and that induced us
To press into it for his apprehension.

Guio. Oh!

1 Ser. Sure her heart is broke.

Off. Madam.

Guio. Stand off.
My sorrow is so dear and pretious to me,
That you must not partake it, suffer it
Like wounds that do breed inward to dispatch me.
O my *Duart*, such an end as this
Thy pride long since did prophesie; thou art dead,
And to encrease my misery, thy sad Mother
Must make a wilfull shipwrack of her vow
Or thou fall unreveng'd. My Soul's divided,
And piety to a son, and true performance
Of hospitable duties to my guest,
That are to others Angels, are my furies.
Vengeance knocks at my heart, but my word given
Denies the entrance, is no *Medium* left,

But that I must protect the murderer,
Or suffer in that faith he made his altar?
Motherly love give place, the fault made this way,
To keep a vow, to which high Heaven is witness,
Heaven may be pleas'd to pardon.

Enter Manuel, Doctors, Surgeons.

Man. 'Tis too late,
Hee's gone, past all recovery: now reproof
Were but unseasonable when I should give comfort,
And yet remember Sister.

Guio. O forbear,
Search for the murtherer, and remove the body,
And as you think fit, give it burial.
Wretch that I am, uncapable of all comfort,
And therefore I intreat my friends and kinsfolk,
And you my Lord, for some space to forbear
Your courteous visitations.

Man. We obey you.   [*Exeunt omnes with the body.*
Manet Guiomar.

Rut. My Spirits come back, and now despair resigns
Her place again to hope.

Guio. What ere thou art
To whom I have given means of life, to witness
With what Religion I have kept my promise,
Come fearless forth, but let thy face be cover'd,
That I hereafter be not forc't to know thee,
For motherly affection may return
My vow once paid to heaven. Thou hast taken from me
The respiration of my heart, the light
Of my swoln eyes, in his life that sustain'd me:
Yet my word given to save you, I make good,
Because what you did, was not done with malice,
You are not known, there is no mark about you
That can discover you; let not fear betray you.
With all convenient speed you can, flie from me
That I may never see you; and that want
Of means may be no let unto your journie,

There are a hundred Crownes: you are at the door now,
And so Farewell for ever.

Rut. Let me first fall
Before your feet, and on them pay the duty
I owe your goodness; next all blessings to you,
And Heaven restore the joyes I have bereft you,
With full increase hereafter, living be
The Goddess stil'd of Hospitalitie.

Actus Tertius. Scena Prima.

Enter Leopold, and Zenocia.

Leo. Fling off these sullen clouds, you are enter'd now
Into a house of joy and happiness,
I have prepar'd a blessing for ye.

Zen. Thank ye, my state would rather ask a curse.

Leo. You are peevish
And know not when ye are friended, I have us'd those means,
The Lady of this house, the noble Lady,
Will take ye as her own, and use ye graciously:
Make much of what you are, Mistris of that beautie,
And expose it not to such betraying sorrows,
When ye are old, and all those sweets hang wither'd,

Enter Servant.

Then sit and sigh.

Zen. My *Autumn* is not far off.

Leo. Have you told your Lady?

Ser. Yes Sir, I have told her
Both of your noble service, and your present,
Which she accepts.

Leo. I should be blest to see her.

Ser. That now you cannot doe: she keeps the Chamber
Not well dispos'd; and has denied all visits,
The maid I have in charge to receive from ye,
So please you render her.

Leo. With all my service,
But fain I would have seen.

Ser. 'Tis but your patience;
No doubt she cannot but remember nobly.

39

Leo. These three years I have lov'd this scornfull Lady,
And follow'd her with all the truth of service,
In all which time, but twice she has honour'd me
With sight of her blest beauty: when you please Sir,
You may receive your charge, and tell your Lady;
A Gentleman whose life is only dedicated
To her commands, kisses her beauteous hands;
And Faire-one, now your help, you may remember
The honest courtesies, since you are mine,
I ever did your modestie: you shall be near her,
And if sometimes you name my service to her,
And tell her with what nobleness I love her,
'Twill be a gratitude I shall remember.

Zen. What in my poor power lyes, so it be honest.

Leo. I ask no more.

Ser. You must along with me (Fair.)

Leo. And so I leave you two: but a fortune
Too happy for my fate: you shall enjoy her.

Scena Secunda.

Enter Zabulon and Servants.

Zab. Be quick, be quick, out with the banquet there,
These scents are dull; cast richer on, and fuller;
Scent every place, where have you plac'd the musick?

Ser. Here they stand ready Sir.

Zab. 'Tis well, be sure
The wines be lusty, high, and full of Spirit,
And Amber'd all.

Ser. They are.

Zab. Give fair attendance.
In the best trim, and state, make ready all.
I shall come presently again.   [*Banquet set forth. Exit.*

2 Ser. We shall Sir,
What preparation's this?
Some new device
My Lady has in hand.

1 Ser. O, prosper it
As long as it carries good wine in the mouth,
And good meat with it, where are all the rest?

2 Ser. They are ready to attend.   [*Musick.*

1 Ser. Sure some great person,
They would not make this hurry else.

2 Ser. Hark the Musick.

Enter Zabulon, *and* Arnoldo.

It will appear now certain, here it comes.
Now to our places.

Arn. Whither will he lead me?

41

What invitation's this? to what new end
Are these fair preparations? a rich Banquet,
Musick, and every place stuck with adornment,
Fit for a Princes welcome; what new game
Has Fortune now prepar'd to shew me happy?
And then again to sink me? 'tis no illusion,
Mine eyes are not deceiv'd, all these are reall;
What wealth and state!

Zab. Will you sit down and eat Sir?
These carry little wonder, they are usual;
But you shall see, if you be wise to observe it,
That that will strike dead, strike with amazement,
Then if you be a man: this fair health to you.

Ar. What shall I see? I pledge ye Sir, I was never
So buried in amazement—

Zab. You are so still:
Drink freely.

Ar. The very wines are admirable:
Good Sir, give me leave to ask this question,
For what great worthy man are these prepar'd?
And why do you bring me hither?

Zab. They are for you, Sir;
And under-value not the worth you carry,
You are that worthy man: think well of these,
They shall be more, and greater.

Ar. Well, blind fortune
Thou hast the prettiest changes when thou art pleas'd,
To play thy game out wantonly—

Zab. Come be lusty,
And awake your Spirits.   [*Cease Musick.*

Ar. Good Sir, do not wake me.
For willingly I would dye in this dream, pray whose Servants
Are all these that attend here?

Zab. They are yours;

42

They wait on you.

Ar. I never yet remember
I kept such faces, nor that I was ever able
To maintain so many.

Zab. Now you are, and shall be.

Ar. You'l say this house is mine too?

Zab. Say it? swear it.

Ar. And all this wealth?

Zab. This is the least you see Sir.

Ar. Why, where has this been hid these thirtie years?
For certainly I never found I was wealthie
Till this hour, never dream'd of house, and Servants.
I had thought I had been a younger Brother, a poor Gent.
I may eat boldly then.

Zab. 'Tis prepar'd for ye.

Ar. The taste is perfect, and most delicate:
But why for me? give me some wine, I do drink;
I feel it sensibly, and I am here,
Here in this glorious place: I am bravely us'd too,
Good Gentle Sir, give me leave to think a little,
For either I am much abus'd—

Zab. Strike Musick
And sing that lusty Song.   [*Musick. Song.*

Ar. Bewitching harmony!
Sure I am turn'd into another Creature.

Enter Hippolyta.

Happy and blest, *Arnoldo* was unfortunate;
Ha! bless mine eyes; what pretious piece of nature
To pose the world?

43

Zab. I told you, you would see that
Would darken these poor preparations;
What think ye now? nay rise not, 'tis no vision.

Ar. 'Tis more: 'tis miracle.

Hip. You are welcom Sir.

Ar. It speaks, and entertains me still more glorious;
She is warm, and this is flesh here: how she stirs me!
Bless me what stars are there?

Hip. May I sit near ye?

Ar. No, you are too pure an object to behold,
Too excellent to look upon, and live;
I must remove.

Zab. She is a woman Sir,
Fy, what faint heart is this?

Arn. The house of wonder.

Zab. Do not you think your self now truly happy?
You have the abstract of all sweetness by ye,
The precious wealth youth labours to arrive at;
Nor is she less in honour, than in beauty,
Ferrara's Royal Duke is proud to call her
His best, his Noblest, and most happy Sister,
Fortune has made her Mistress of herself,
Wealthy, and wise, without a power to sway her,
Wonder of *Italy*, of all hearts Mistress.

Arn. And all this is—

Zab. Hippolyta the beauteous.

Hip. You are a poor relator of my fortunes,
Too weak a Chronicle to speak my blessings,
And leave out that essential part of story
I am most high and happy in, most fortunate,
The acquaintance, and the noble fellowship
Of this fair Gentleman: pray ye do not wonder,

Nor hold it strange to hear a handsome Lady
Speak freely to ye: with your fair leave and courtesie
I will sit by ye.

Arn. I know not what to answer,
Nor where I am, nor to what end consider;
Why do you use me thus?

Hip. Are ye angry Sir,
Because ye are entertain'd with all humanity?
Freely and nobly us'd?

Arn. No gentle Lady,
That were uncivil, but it much amazes me
A stranger, and a man of no desert
Should find such floods of courtesie.

Hip. I love ye,
I honour ye, the first and best of all men,
And where that fair opinion leads, 'tis usual
These trifles that but serve to set off, follow.
I would not have you proud now, nor disdainful
Because I say I love ye, though I swear it,
Nor think it a stale favour I fling on ye,
Though ye be handsome, and the only man
I must confess I ever fixt mine eye on,
And bring along all promises that please us,
Yet I should hate ye then, despise ye, scorn ye,
And with as much contempt pursue your person,
As now I do with love. But you are wiser,
At least I think, more master of your fortune,
And so I drink your health.

Arn. Hold fast good honesty,
I am a lost man else.

Hip. Now you may kiss me,
'Tis the first kiss, I ever askt, I swear to ye.

Arn. That I dare do sweet Lady.

Hip. You do it well too;
You are a Master Sir, that makes you coy.

The Custom of the Country

Arn. Would you would send your people off.

Hip. Well thought on.
Wait all without.   [*Exit* Zab. *and Servants.*

Zab. I hope she is pleas'd throughly.

Hip. Why stand ye still? here's no man to detect ye,
My people are gone off: come, come, leave conjuring,
The Spirit you would raise, is here already,
Look boldly on me.

Arn. What would you have me do?

Hip. O most unmanly question! have you do?
Is't possible your years should want a Tutor?
I'le teach ye: come, embrace me.

Arn. Fye stand off;
And give me leave, more now than e're, to wonder,
A building of so goodly a proportion,
Outwardly all exact, the frame of Heaven,
Should hide within so base inhabitants?
You are as fair, as if the morning bare ye,
Imagination never made a sweeter;
Can it be possible this frame should suffer,
And built on slight affections, fright the viewer?
Be excellent in all, as you are outward,
The worthy Mistress of those many blessings
Heaven has bestowed, make 'em appear still nobler,
Because they are trusted to a weaker keeper.
Would ye have me love ye?

Hip. Yes.

Arn. Not for your beauty;
Though I confess, it blowes the first fire in us,
Time as he passes by, puts out that sparkle;
Nor for your wealth, although the world kneel to it,
And make it all addition to a woman,
Fortune that ruines all, makes that his conquest;
Be honest, and be vertuous, I'le admire ye,
At least be wise, and where ye lay these nets,

46

Strow over 'em a little modesty,
'Twill well become your cause, and catch more Fools.

Hip. Could any one that lov'd this wholesome counsel
But love the giver more? you make me fonder:
You have a vertuous mind, I want that ornament;
Is it a sin I covet to enjoy ye?
If ye imagine I am too free a Lover,
And act that part belongs to you, I am silent:
Mine eyes shall speak my blushes, parly with ye;
I will not touch your hand, but with a tremble
Fitting a Vestal Nun; not long to kiss ye,
But gently as the Air, and undiscern'd too,
I'le steal it thus: I'le walk your shadow by ye,
So still and silent that it shall be equal,
To put me off, as that, and when I covet,
To give such toyes as these—

Arn. A new temptation—

Hip. Thus like the lazie minutes will I drop 'em,
Which past once are forgotten.

Arn. Excellent vice!

Hip. Will ye be won? look stedfastly upon me,
Look manly, take a mans affections to you;
Young women, in the old world were not wont, Sir,
To hang out gaudy bushes for their beauties,
To talk themselves into young mens affections;
How cold and dull you are!

Arn. How I stagger!
She is wise, as fair; but 'tis a wicked wisdom;
I'le choak before I yield.

Hip. Who waits within there?   [Zabulon *within.*
Make ready the green Chamber.

Zab. It shall be Madam.

Arn. I am afraid she will injoy me indeed.

Hip. What Musick do ye love?

Arn. A modest tongue.

Hip. We'l have enough of that: fye, fye, how lumpish!
In a young Ladyes arms thus dull?

Arn. For Heaven sake
Profess a little goodness.

Hip. Of what Country?

Arn. I am of *Rome.*

Hip. Nay then I know you mock me,
The *Italians* are not frighted with such bug-bears,
Prethee go in.

Arn. I am not well.

Hip. I'le make thee,
I'le kiss thee well.

Arn. I am not sick of that sore.

Hip. Upon my Conscience, I must ravish thee,
I shall be famous for the first example:
With this I'le tye ye first, then try your strength Sir.

Arn. My strength? away base woman, I abhor thee.
I am not caught with stales, disease dwell with thee.   [*Exit.*

Hip. Are ye so quick? and have I lost my wishes?
Hoe, *Zabulon;* my servants.

Enter Zabulon *and* Servants.

Zab. Call'd ye Madam?

Hip. Is all that beauty scorned, so many su'd for;
So many Princes? by a stranger too?
Must I endure this?

Zab. Where's the Gentleman?

Hip. Go presently, pursue the stranger, *Zabulon*.
He has broke from me, Jewels I have given him:
Charge him with theft: he has stoln my love, my freedome,
Draw him before the Governour, imprison him,
Why dost thou stay?

Zab. I'le teach him a new dance,
For playing fast and loose with such a Lady.
Come fellows, come: I'le execute your anger,
And to the full.

Hip. His scorn shall feel my vengeance. —   [*Exeunt.*

The Custom of the Country

Scena Tertia.

Enter Sulpicia *and* Jaques.

Sul. Shall I never see a lusty man again?

Ja. Faith Mistress
You do so over-labour 'em when you have 'em,
And so dry-founder 'em, they cannot last.

Sul. Where's the *French*-man?

Ja. Alas, he's all to fitters,
and lyes, taking the height of his fortune with a Syringe.
He's chin'd, he's chin'd good man, he is a mourner.

Sul. What's become of the *Dane*?

Ja. Who? goldy-locks?
He's foul i'th' touch-hole; and recoils again,
The main Spring's weaken'd that holds up his cock,
He lies at the sign of the *Sun*, to be new breech'd.

Sul. The Rutter too, is gone.

Ja. O that was a brave Rascal,
He would labour like a Thrasher: but alas
What thing can ever last? he has been ill mew'd,
And drawn too soon; I have seen him in the Hospital.

Sul. There was an *English*-man.

Ja. I there was an *English*-man;
You'l scant find any now, to make that name good:
There were those *English* that were men indeed,
And would perform like men, but now they are vanisht:
They are so taken up in their own Country,
And so beaten of their speed by their own women,
When they come here, they draw their legs like Hackneys:
Drink, and their own devices have undone 'em.

Sul. I must have one that's strong, no life in *Lisbon* else,

The Custom of the Country

Perfect and young: my Custom with young Ladies,
And high fed City dames, will fall, and break else.
I want my self too, in mine age to nourish me:
They are all sunk I mantain'd: now what's this business,
What goodly fellow's that?

Enter Rutilio *and* Officers.

Rut. Why do you drag me?
Pox o' your justice; let me loose.

1 Offi. Not so Sir.

Rut. Cannot a man fall into one of your drunken Cellars,
And venture the breaking on's neck, your trap-doors open,
But he must be us'd thus rascally?

1 Offi. What made you wandring
So late i'th' night? you know that is imprisonment.

Rut. May be I walk in my sleep.

2 Offi. May be we'l walk ye.
What made you wandring Sir, into that vault
Where all the City store, and the Munition lay?

Rut. I fell into it by chance, I broke my shins for't:
Your worships feel not that: I knockt my head
Against a hundred posts, would you had had it.
Cannot I break my neck in my own defence?

2 Offi. This will not serve: you cannot put it off so,
Your coming thither was to play the villain,
To fire the Powder, to blow up that part o'th' City.

Rut. Yes, with my nose: why were the trap-doors open?
Might not you fall, or you, had you gone that way?
I thought your City had sunk.

1 Offi. You did your best Sir,
We must presume, to help it into th' Air,
If you call that sinking: we have told you what's the law,
He that is taken there, unless a Magistrate,

51

And have command in that place, presently
If there be nothing found apparent near him
Worthy his torture, or his present death,
Must either pay his fine for his presumption,
(Which is six hundred Duckets) or for six years
Tug at an Oar i'th' Gallies: will ye walk Sir,
For we presume you cannot pay the penalty.

Rut. Row in the Gallies, after all this mischief?

2 Offi. May be you were drunk, they'l keep you sober there.

Rut. Tug at an Oar? you are not arrant rascals,
To catch me in a pit-fall, and betray me?

Sul. A lusty minded man.

Ja. A wondrous able.

Sul. Pray Gentlemen, allow me but that liberty
To speak a few words with your prisoner,
And I shall thank you.

1 Offi. Take your pleasure Lady.

Sul. What would you give that woman should redeem ye,
Redeem ye from this slavery?

Rut. Besides my service
I would give her my whole self, I would be her vassal.

Sul. She has reason to expect as much, considering
The great sum she pays for't, yet take comfort,
What ye shall do to merit this, is easie,
And I will be the woman shall befriend ye,
'Tis but to entertain some handsome Ladies,
And young fair Gentlewomen: you guess the way:
But giving of your mind—

Rut. I am excellent at it:
You cannot pick out such another living.
I understand ye: is't not thus?

52

Sul. Ye have it.

Rut. Bring me a hundred of 'em: I'le dispatch 'em.
I will be none but yours: should another offer
Another way to redeem me, I should scorn it.
What women you shall please: I am monstrous lusty:
Not to be taken down: would you have Children?
I'le get you those as fast, and thick as flie-blows.

Sul. I admire him: wonder at him!

Rut. Hark ye Lady,
You may require sometimes—

Sul. I by my faith.

Rut. And you shall have it by my faith, and handsomly:
This old Cat will suck shrewdly: you have no Daughters?
I flye at all: now am I in my Kingdom.
Tug at an Oar? no, tug in a Feather-bed,
With good warm Caudles; hang your bread and water,
I'le make you young again, believe that Lady.
I will so frubbish you.

Sul. Come, follow Officers,
This Gentleman is free: I'le pay the Duckets.

Rut. And when you catch me in your City-powdring-tub
Again, boil me with Cabbidge.

1 Offi. You are both warn'd and arm'd Sir.   [*Exeunt.*

53

The Custom of the Country

Scena Quarta.

Enter Leopold, Hippolyta, Zenocia.

Zen. Will your Ladyship wear this Dressing?

Hip. Leave thy prating:
I care not what I wear.

Zen. Yet 'tis my duty
To know your pleasure, and my worst affliction
To see you discontented.

Hip. Weeping too?
Prethee forgive me: I am much distemper'd,
And speak I know not what: to make thee amends
The Gown that I wore yesterday, is thine;
Let it alone awhile.

Leo. Now you perceive,
And taste her bounty.

Zen. Much above my merit.

Leo. But have you not yet found a happy time
To move for me.

Zen. I have watched all occasions,
But hitherto, without success: yet doubt not
But I'le embrace the first means.

Leo. Do, and prosper:
Excellent creature, whose perfections make
Even sorrow lovely, if your frowns thus take me,
What would your smiles doe?

Hip. Pox o' this stale Courtship:
If I have any power.

Leo. I am commanded,
Obedience is the Lovers sacrifice
Which I pay gladly.

54

Hip. To be forc'd to wooe,
Being a woman, could not but torment me,
But bringing for my advocates, youth and beauty,
Set off with wealth, and then to be deni'd too
Do's comprehend all tortures. They flatter'd me,
That said my looks were charms, my touches fetters,
My locks soft chains, to bind the arms of Princes,
And make them in that wish'd for bondage, happy.
I am like others of a coarser feature,
As weak to allure, but in my dotage, stronger:
I am no *Circe*; he, more than *Ulysses*,
Scorns all my offer'd bounties, slights my favours,
And, as I were some new Egyptian, flyes me,
Leaving no pawn, but my own shame behind him.
But he shall finde, that in my fell revenge,
I am a woman: one that never pardons
The rude contemner of her proffered sweetness.

Enter Zabulon.

Zab. Madam, 'tis done.

Hip. What's done?

Zab. The uncivill stranger
Is at your suite arrested.

Hip. 'Tis well handled.

Zab. And under guard sent to the Governour,
With whom my testimony, and the favour
He bears your Ladiship, have so prevail'd
That he is sentenc'd.

Hip. How?

Zab. To lose his head.

Hip. Is that the means to quench the scorching heat
Of my inrag'd desires? must innocence suffer,
'Cause I am faulty? or is my Love so fatall
That of necessity it must destroy
The object it most longs for? dull *Hippolyta*,

55

To think that injuries could make way for love,
When courtesies were despis'd: that by his death
Thou shouldst gain that, which only thou canst hope for
While he is living: My honour's at the stake now,
And cannot be preserv'd, unless he perish,
The enjoying of the thing I love, I ever
Have priz'd above my fame: why doubt I now then?
One only way is left me, to redeem all:
Make ready my Caroch.

Leo. What will you Madam?

Hip. And yet I am impatient of such stay:
Bind up my hair: fye, fye, while that is doing
The Law may seise his life: thus as I am then,
Not like *Hippolyta*, but a *Bacchanal*
My frantique Love transports me.   [*Exit.*

Leo. Sure she's distracted.

Zab. Pray you follow her: I will along with you:
I more than ghess the cause: women that love
Are most uncertain, and one minute crave,
What in another they refuse to have.   [*Exit.*

Scena Quinta.

Enter Clodio, Charino.

Clo. Assure thy self *Charino*, I am alter'd
From what I was; the tempests we have met with
In our uncertain voyage, were smooth gales
Compar'd to those, the memory of my lusts
Rais'd in my Conscience: and if ere again
I live to see *Zenocia*, I will sue,
And seek to her as a Lover, and a Servant,
And not command affection, like a Tyrant.

Char. In hearing this, you make me young again,
And Heaven, it seems, favouring this good change in you
In setting of a period to our dangers
Gives us fair hopes to find that here in *Lisbon*
Which hitherto in vain we long have sought for.
I have receiv'd assur'd intelligence,
Such strangers have been seen here: and though yet
I cannot learn their fortunes, nor the place
Of their abode, I have a Soul presages
A fortunate event here.

Clo. There have pass'd
A mutual enterchange of courtesies
Between me, and the Governour; therefore boldly
We may presume of him, and of his power
If we finde cause to use them, otherwise
I would not be known here, and these disguises
Will keep us from discovery.

Enter Manuel, Doctor, Arnoldo, Guard.

Char. What are these?

Clo. The Governour: with him my Rival, bound.

Char. For certain 'tis *Arnoldo*.

Clo. Let's attend
What the success will be.

Mar. Is't possible
There should be hope of his recovery,
His wounds so many and so deadly?

Doct. So they appear'd at first, but the blood stop'd,
His trance forsook him, and on better search
We found they were not mortal.

Man. Use all care
To perfect this unhop'd for cure: that done
Propose your own rewards: and till you shall
Hear farther from me, for some ends I have,
Conceal it from his Mother.

Doct. Wee'l not fail Sir.   [*Exit.*

Man. You still stand confident on your innocence.

Arn. It is my best and last guard, which I will not
Leave, to relye on your uncertain mercy.

Enter Hippolyta, Zabulon, Leopold, Zenocia, 2 Servants.

Hip. Who bad you follow me! Goe home, and you Sir,
As you respect me, goe with her.

Arn. Zenocia!
And in her house a Servant!

Char. 'Tis my Daughter.

Clo. My love? Contain your joy, observe the sequel.   [*Zen. passes.*

Man. Fye Madam, how undecent 'tis for you,
So far unlike your self to bee seen thus
In th' open streets? why do you kneel? pray you rise,
I am acquainted with the wrong, and loss
You have sustain'd, and the Delinquent now
Stands ready for his punishment.

Hip. Let it fall, Sir,
On the offender: he is innocent,
And most unworthy of these bonds he wears,

58

But I made up of guilt.

Man. What strange turn's this?

Leo. This was my prisoner once.

Hip. If chastity
In a young man, and tempted to the height too
Did ere deserve reward, or admiration,
He justly may claim both. Love to his person
(Or if you please give it a fouler name)
Compel'd me first to train him to my house,
All engines I rais'd there to shake his vertue,
Which in the assault were useless; he unmov'd still
As if he had no part of humane frailty.
Against the nature of my Sex, almost
I plaid the Ravisher. You might have seen
In our contention, young *Apollo* fly
And love-sick *Daphne* follow, all arts failing,
By flight he wan the victory, breaking from
My scorn'd embraces: the repulse (in women
Unsufferable) invited me to practise
A means to be reveng'd: and from this grew
His Accusation, and the abuse
Of your still equall justice: My rage ever
Thanks heaven, though wanton, I found not my self
So far engag'd to Hell, to prosecute
To the death what I had plotted, for that love
That made me first desire him, then accuse him,
Commands me with the hazard of my self
First to entreat his pardon, then acquit him.

Man. What ere you are, so much I love your vertue,
That I desire your friendship: do you unloose him
From those bonds, you are worthy of: your repentance
Makes part of satisfaction; yet I must
Severely reprehend you.

Leo. I am made
A stale on all parts: But this fellow shall
Pay dearly for her favour.

The Custom of the Country

Arn. My life's so full
Of various changes, that I now despair
Of any certain port; one trouble ending,
A new, and worse succeeds it: what should *Zenocia*
Do in this womans house? Can chastity
And hot Lust dwell together without infection?
I would not be or jealous, or secure,
Yet something must be done, to sound the depth on't:
That she lives is my bliss, but living there,
A hell of torments; there's no way to her
In whom I live, but by this door, through which
To me 'tis death to enter, yet I must,
And will make tryal.

Man. Let me hear no more
Of these devices, Lady: this I pardon,
And at your intercession I forgive
Your instrument the Jew too: get you home.
The hundred thousand crowns you lent the City
Towards the setting forth of the last Navy
Bound for the Islands, was a good then, which
I ballance with your ill now.

Char. Now Sir, to him,
You know my Daughter needs it.

Hip. Let me take
A farewell with mine eye, Sir, though my lip
Be barr'd the Ceremonie, courtesie
And Custom too allows of.

Arn. Gentle Madam,
I neither am so cold, nor so ill bred
But that I dare receive it: you are unguarded,
And let me tell you that I am asham'd
Of my late rudeness, and would gladly therefore
If you please to accept my ready service
Wait on you to your house.

Hip. Above my hope:
Sir, if an Angel were to be my convoy,
He should not be more welcom.—   [*Ex.* Arn. *and* Hip.

Clo. Now you know me.

Man. Yes Sir, and honour you: ever remembring
Your many bounties, being ambitious only
To give you cause to say by some one service
That I am not ungratefull.

Clod. 'Tis now offer'd:
I have a suit to you, and an easie one,
Which e're long you shall know.

Man. When you think fit Sir,
And then as a command I will receive it,
Till when, most welcom: you are welcom too Sir,
'Tis spoken from the heart, and therefore needs not
Much protestation: at your better leisure
I will enquire the cause that brought you hither:
In the mean time serve you.

Clod. You out-doe me Sir.   [*Exeunt.*

The Custom of the Country

Actus Quartus. Scena Prima.

Enter Duarte, Doctor.

Dua. You have bestow'd on me a second life,
For which I live your creature, and have better'd
What nature fram'd unperfect, my first being
Insolent pride made monstrous; but this later
In learning me to know my self, hath taught me
Not to wrong others.

Doct. Then we live indeed,
When we can goe to rest without alarm
Given every minute to a guilt-sick conscience
To keep us waking, and rise in the morning
Secure in being innocent: but when
In the remembrance of our worser actions
We ever bear about us whips and furies,
To make the day a night of sorrow to us,
Even life's a burthen.

Dua. I have found and felt it;
But will endeavour having first made peace
With those intestine enemies my rude passions,
To be so with man-kind: but worthy Doctor,
Pray if you can resolve me; was the Gentleman
That left me dead, ere brought unto his tryal?

Doct. Not known, nor apprehended.

Dua. That's my grief.

Doct. Why, do you wish he had been punished?

Dua. No,
The stream of my swoln sorrow runs not that way:
For could I find him, as I vow to Heaven
It shall be my first care to seek him out,
I would with thanks acknowledge that his sword,
In opening my veins, which proud bloud poison'd,
Gave the first symptoms of true health.

Doct. 'Tis in you
A Christian resolution: that you live
Is by the Governours, your Uncles charge
As yet conceal'd. And though a sons loss never
Was solemniz'd with more tears of true sorrow
Than have been paid by your unequal'd Mother
For your supposed death, she's not acquainted
With your recovery.

Dua. For some few dayes
Pray let her so continue: thus disguis'd
I may abroad unknown.

Doct. Without suspicion
Of being discovered.

Dua. I am confident
No moisture sooner dies than womens tears,
And therefore though I know my Mother vertuous,
Yet being one of that frail sex I purpose
Her farther tryal.

Doct. That as you think fit—I'le not betray you.

Dua. To find out this stranger
This true Physician of my mind and manners
Were such a blessing. He seem'd poor, and may
Perhaps be now in want; would I could find him.
The Innes I'le search first, then the publick Stewes;
He was of *Italy*, and that Country breeds not
Precisians that way, but hot Libertines;
And such the most are: 'tis but a little travail:
I am unfurnisht too, pray Mr. Doctor,
Can you supply me?

Doct. With what summ you please.

Dua. I will not be long absent.

Doct. That I wish too;
For till you have more strength, I would not have you
To be too bold.

Dua. Fear not, I will be carefull.   [*Exeunt.*

Enter Leopold, Zabulon, Bravo.

Zab. I have brought him Sir, a fellow that will do it
Though Hell stood in his way, ever provided
You pay him for't.

Leop. He has a strange aspect,
And looks much like the figure of a hang-man
In a table of the Passion.

Zab. He transcends
All precedents, believe it, a flesh'd ruffian,
That hath so often taken the Strappado,
That 'tis to him but as a lofty trick
Is to a tumbler: he hath perused too
All Dungeons in *Portu[g]al*, thrice seven years
Rowed in the Galleys for three several murthers,
Though I presume that he has done a hundred,
And scap't unpunisht.

Leop. He is much in debt to you,
You set him off so well. What will you take Sir
To beat a fellow for me, that thus wrong'd me?

Bra. To beat him say you?

Leop. Yes, beat him to lameness,
To cut his lips or nose off; any thing,
That may disfigure him.

Bra. Let me consider?
Five hundred pistolets for such a service
I think were no dear penniworth.

Zab. Five hundred!
Why there are of your Brother-hood in the City,
I'le undertake, shall kill a man for twenty.

Bra. Kill him? I think so; I'le kill any man
For half the mony.

Leop. And will you ask more
For a sound beating than a murther?

Bra. I Sir,
And with good reason, for a dog that's dead,
The Spanish proverb says, will never bite:
But should I beat or hurt him only, he may
Recover, and kill me.

Leo. A good conclusion,
The obduracie of this rascal makes me tender.
I'le run some other course, there's your reward
Without the employment.

Bra. For that as you please Sir;
When you have need to kill a man, pray use me,
But I am out at beating.   [*Exit.*

Zab. What's to be done then?

Leop. I'le tell thee *Zabulon,* and make thee privy
To my most near designs: this stranger, which
Hippolyta so dotes on, was my prisoner
When the last Virgin, I bestowed upon her,
Was made my prize; how he escaped, hereafter
I'le let thee know; and it may be the love
He bears the servant, makes him scorn the Mistris.

Zab. 'Tis not unlike; for the first time he saw her
His looks exprest so much, and for more proof
Since he came to my Ladys house, though yet
He never knew her, he hath practis'd with me
To help him to a conference, without
The knowledge of *Hippolyta;* which I promis'd.

Leop. And by all means perform it for their meeting,
But work it so, that my disdainful Mistris
(Whom, notwithstanding all her injuries,
'Tis my hard fate to love) may see and hear them.

Zab. To what end Sir?

Leop. This *Zabulon:* when she sees

Who is her rival, and her Lovers baseness
To leave a Princess for her bondwoman,
The sight will make her scorn, what now she dotes on,
I'le double thy reward.

Zab. You are like to speed then:
For I confess what you will soon believe,
We serve them best that are most apt to give,
For you, I'le place you where you shall see all, and yet be
unobserv'd.

Leop. That I desire too.   [*Exeunt.*

Enter Arnoldo.

Arn. I cannot see her yet, how it afflicts me
The poyson of this place should mix it self
With her pure thoughts? 'Twas she that was commanded,
Or my eyes failed me grosly; that youth, that face
And all that noble sweetness. May she not live here,
And yet be honest still?

Enter Zenocia.

Zen. It is *Arnoldo,*
From all his dangers free; fortune I bless thee.
My noble husband! how my joy swells in me,
But why in this place? what business hath he here?
He cannot hear of me, I am not known here.
I left him vertuous; how I shake to think now!
And how that joy I had, cools, and forsakes me!

Enter above Hippolyta *and* Zabulon.

This Lady is but fair, I have been thought so
Without compare admired; She has bewitched him
And he forgot—

Arn. 'Tis she again, the same—the same *Zenocia.*

Zab. There they are together.—Now you may mark.

66

The Custom of the Country

Hip. Peace, let 'em parly.

Arn. That you are well *Zenocia,* and once more
Bless my despairing eyes, with your wisht presence,
I thank the gods; but that I meet you here—

Hip. They are acquainted.

Zab. I found that secret Madam,
When you co[m]manded her go home: pray hear 'em.

Zen. That you meet me here, ne're blush at that *Arnoldo.*
Your coming comes too late: I am a woman,
And one woman with another may be trusted;
Do you fear the house?

Arn. More than a fear, I know it,
Know it not good, not honest.

Zen. What do you here then?
I'th' name of vertue why do you approach it?
Will you confess the doubt and yet pursue it?
Where have your eyes been wandring, my *Arnoldo?*
What constancy, what faith do you call this? Fie,
Aim at one wanton mark, and wound another?
I do confess, the Lady fair, most beauteous,
And able to betray a strong mans liberty,
        [Leopold *places himself unseen below.*
But you that have a love, a wife—you do well
To deal thus wisely with me: yet *Arnoldo,*
Since you are pleas'd to study a new beauty,
And think this old and ill, beaten with misery,
Study a nobler way for shame to love me,
Wrong not her honesty.

Arn. You have confirm'd me.

Zen. Who though she be your wife, will never hinder you,
So much I rest a servant to your wishes,
And love your Loves, though they be my destructions,
No man shall know me, nor the share I have in thee,
No eye suspect I am able to prevent you,
For since I am a slave to this great Lady,

67

The Custom of the Country

Whom I perceive you follow,

Arn. Be not blinded.

Zen. Fortune shall make me useful to your service,
I will speak for you.

Arn. Speak for me? you wrong me.

Zen. I will endeavour all the wayes I am able
To make her think well of you; will that please?
To make her dote upon you, dote to madness,
So far against my self I will obey you.
But when that's done, and I have shewed this duty,
This great obedience, few will buy it at my price,
Thus will I shake hands with you, wish you well,
But never see you more, nor receive comfort
From any thing, *Arnoldo.*

Arn. You are too tender;
I neither doubt you, nor desire longer
To be a man, and live, than I am honest
And only yours; our infinite affections
Abus'd us both.

Zab. Where are your favours now?
The courtesies you shew'd this stranger, Madam?

Hip. Have I now found the cause?

Zab. Attend it further.

Zen. Did she invite you, do you say?

Arn. Most cunningly,
And with a preparation of that state
I was brought in and welcom'd.

Zen. Seem'd to love you?

Arn. Most infinitely, at first sight, most dotingly.

The Custom of the Country

Zen. She is a goodly Lady.

Arn. Wondrous handsom:
At first view, being taken unprepar'd,
Your memory not present then to assist me,
She seem'd so glorious sweet, and so far stir'd me,
Nay be not jealous, there's no harm done.

Zen. Prethee—didst thou not kiss, *Arnoldo?*

Arn. Yes faith did I.

Zen. And then—

Arn. I durst not, did not—

Zen. I forgive you,
Come tell the truth.

Arn. May be I lay with her.

Hip. He mocks me too, most basely.

Zen. Did ye faith? did ye forget so far?

Arn. Come, come, no weeping;
I would have lyen first in my grave, believe that.
Why will you ask those things you would not hear?
She is too untemperate to betray my vertues,
Too openly lascivious: had she dealt
But with that seeming modesty she might,
And flung a little Art upon her ardor,
But 'twas forgot, and I forgot to like her,
And glad I was deceiv'd. No my *Zenocia,*
My first love here begun, rests here unreapt yet,
And here for ever.

Zen. You have made me happy,
Even in the midst of bondage blest.

Zab. You see now
What rubs are in your way.

Hip. And quickly *Zabulon*
I'le root 'em out.—Be sure you do this presently.

Zab. Do not you alter then.

Hip. I am resolute.   [*Exit Zabulon.*

Arn. To see you only I came hither last,
Drawn by no love of hers, nor base allurements,
For by this holy light I hate her heartily.

Leop. I am glad of that, you have sav'd me so much vengeance
And so much fear,
From this hour fair befal you.

Arn. Some means I shall make shortly to redeem you,
Till when, observe her well, and fit her temper,
Only her lust contemn.

Zen. When shall I see you?

Arn. I will live hereabouts, and bear her fair still,
Till I can find a fit hour to redeem you.

Hip. Shut all the doors.

Arn. Who's that?

Zen. We are betray'd,
The Lady of the house has heard our parly,
Seen us, and seen our Loves.

Hip. You courteous Gallant,
You that scorn all I can bestow, that laugh at
The afflictions, and the groans I suffer for you,
That slight and jeer my love, contemn the fortune
My favours can fling on you, have I caught you?
Have I now found the cause? ye fool my wishes;
Is mine own slave, my bane? I nourish that
That sucks up my content. I'le pray no more,
Nor wooe no more; thou shalt see foolish man,
And to thy bitter pain and anguish, look on
The vengeance I shall take, provok'd and slighted;

70

The Custom of the Country

Redeem her then, and steal her hence: ho *Zabulon*
Now to your work.

Enter Zabulon, *and* Servants, *some holding* Arnoldo,
some ready with a cord to strangle Zenocia.

Arn. Lady, but hear me speak first,
As you have pity.

Hip. I have none. You taught me,
When I even hung about your neck, you scorn'd me.

Zab. Shall we pluck yet?

Hip. No, hold a little *Zabulon,*
I'le pluck his heart-strings first: now am I worthy
A little of your love?

Arn. I'le be your Servant,
Command me through what danger you shall aime at,
Let it be death.

Hip. Be sure Sir, I shall fit you.

Arn. But spare this Virgin.

Hip. I would spare that villain first,
Had cut my Fathers throat.

Arn. Bounteous Lady,
If in your sex there be that noble softness,
That tenderness of heart, women are crown'd for—

Zen. Kneel not *Arnoldo,* doe her not that honour,
She is not worthy such submission,
I scorn a life depends upon her pity.
Proud woman do thy worst, and arm thy anger
With thoughts as black as Hell, as hot and bloody,
I bring a patience here, shall make 'em blush,
An innocence, shall outlook thee, and death too.

Arn. Make me your slave, I give my freedom to ye,
For ever to be fetter'd to your service;

The Custom of the Country

'Twas I offended, be not so unjust then,
To strike the innocent, this gentle maid
Never intended fear and doubt against you:
She is your Servant, pay not her observance
With cruel looks, her duteous faith with death.

Hip. Am I fair now? now am I worth your liking?

Zen. Not fair, not to be liked, thou glorious Devil,
Thou vernisht piece of lust, thou painted fury.

Arn. Speak gently sweet, speak gently.

Zen. I'le speak nobly.
'Tis not the saving of a life I aim at,
Mark me lascivious woman, mark me truly,
And then consider, how I weigh thy anger.
Life is no longer mine, nor dear unto me,
Than usefull to his honour I preserve it.
If thou hadst studied all the courtesies
Humanity and noble blood are linkt to,
Thou couldst not have propounded such a benefit,
Nor heapt upon me such unlookt for honour
As dying for his sake, to be his Martyr,
'Tis such a grace.

Hip. You shall not want that favour,
Let your bones work miracles.

Arn. Dear Lady
By those fair eyes—

Hip. There is but this way left ye
To save her life.—

Arn. Speak it, and I embrace it.

Hip. Come to my private chamber presently,
And there, what love and I command—

Arn. I'le doe it,
Be comforted *Zenocia.*

Zen. Do not do this
To save me, do not lose your self I charge you,
I charge you by your love, that love [you] bear me;
That love, that constant love you have twin'd to me,
By all your promises, take heed you keep 'em,
Now is your constant tryal. If thou dost this,
Or mov'st one foot, to guide thee to her lust,
My curses and eternal hate pursue thee.
Redeem me at the base price of dis-loyalty?
Must my undoubted honesty be thy Bawd too?
Go and intwine thy self about that body;
Tell her, for my life thou hast lost thine honour,
Pull'd all thy vows from heaven, basely, most basely
Stoop'd to the servile flames of that foul woman,
To add an hour to me that hate thee for it,
Know thee not again, nor name thee for a Husband.

Arn. What shall I do to save her?

Hip. How now, what hast there?

Enter a Servant.

Ser. The Governour, attended with some Gentlemen,
Are newly entred, to speak with your Ladiship.

Hip. Pox o' their business, reprieve her for this hour,
I shall have other time.

Arn. Now fortune help us.

Hip. I'le meet 'em presently: retire awhile all.   [*Exeunt.*

Zab. You rise to day upon your right side Lady;
You know the danger too, and may prevent it,
And if you suffer her to perish thus,
As she must do, and suddenly, believe it,
Unless you stand her friend; you know the way on't,
I guess you poorly love her, less your fortune.
Let her know nothing, and perform this matter,
There are hours ordained for several businesses,
You understand.

Arn. I understand you Bawd Sir,
And such a Counsellour I never car'd for.

Enter the Governour, Clodio, Leopold, Charino *and*
Attendants *at one door,* Hippolyta *at the other.*

Hip. Your Lordship does me honour.

Gover. Fair *Hippolyta,*
I am come to ease you of a charge.

Hip. I keep none
I count a burthen Sir: and yet I lye too.

Gover. Which is the Maid; is she here?

Clod. Yes Sir,
This is she, this is *Zenocia,*
The very same I sued to your Lordship for.

Zen. Clodio again? more misery? more ruin?
Under what angry star is my life govern'd?

Gov. Come hither Maid, you are once more a free woman,
Here I discharge your bonds.

Arn. Another smile,
Another trick of fortune to betray us!

Hip. Why does your Lordship use me so unnobly?
Against my will to take away my bond-woman?

Gov. She was no lawful prize, therefore no bond-woman:
She's of that Country we hold friendship with,
And ever did, and therefore to be used
With entertainment, fair and courteous.
The breach of League in us gives foul example,
Therefore you must be pleas'd to think this honest;
Did you know what she was?

Leop. Not till this instant;
For had I known her, she had been no prisoner.

74

The Custom of the Country

Gov. There, take the Maid, she is at her own dispose now,
And if there be ought else to do your honour
Any poor service in—

Clod. I am vowed your servant.

Arn. Your Father's here too, that's our only comfort,
And in a Country now, we stand free people,
Where *Clodio* has no power, be comforted.

Zen. I fear some trick yet.

Arn. Be not so dejected.

Gover. You must not be displeas'd; so farewel Lady.
Come Gentlemen; Captain, you must with me too,
I have a little business.

Leop. I attend your Lordship:
Now my way's free, and my hope's Lord again.
             [*Exeunt all but* Hip. *and* Zab.

Hip. D'ye jeer me now ye are going?
I may live yet—to make you howl both.

Zab. You might have done; you had power then,
But now the chains are off, the command lost,
And such a story they will make of this
To laugh out lazie time.

Hip. No means yet left me?
For now I burst with anger: none to satisfie me?
No comfort? no revenge?

Zab. You speak too late;
You might have had all these, your useful servants,
Had you been wise, and suddain: what power, or will
Over her beauty, have you now? by violence
To constrain his love; she is as free as you are,
And no law can impeach her liberty,
And whilst she is so, *Arnoldo* will despise you.

75

Hip. Either my love or anger must be satisfied,
Or I must dye.

Zab. I have a way wou'd do it,
Wou'd do it yet, protect me from the Law.

Hip. From any thing; thou knowest what power I have,
What mony, and what friends.

Zab. 'Tis a devilish one:
But such must now be us'd: walk in, I'le tell you;
And if you like it, if the Devil can do any thing—

Hip. Devil, or what thou wilt, so I be satisfied.   [*Ex.*

Enter Sulpitia, *and* Jaques.

Sulp. This is the rarest and the lustiest fellow,
And so bestirs himself—

Jaq. Give him breath Mistress,
You'l melt him else.

Sulp. He does perform such wonders—
The women are mad on him.

Jaq. Give him breath I say;
The man is but a man, he must have breath.

Sulp. How many had he yesterday?
And they paid bravely too.

Jaq. About fourteen,
But still I cry give breath, spare him and have him.

Sulp. Five Dames to day; this was a small stage,
He may endure five more.

Jaq. Breath, breath I cry still;
Body o' me give breath, the man's a lost man else.
Feed him and give him breath.

The Custom of the Country

Enter 2 Gentlewomen.

Sulp. Welcome Gentlewomen,
Y'are very welcome.

1 Gen. We hear you have a lusty and well complexion'd fellow
That does rare tricks; my Sister and my self here,
Would trifle out an hour or two, so please you.

Sulp. Jaques, conduct 'em in.

Both. There's for your courtesie.   [*Ex.* Jaq. *and* Gent.

Sulp. Good pay still, good round pay, this happy fellow
Will set me up again; he brings in gold
Faster than I have leisure to receive it.
O that his body were not flesh and fading;
But I'le so pap him up—nothing too dear for him;
What a sweet scent he has?—Now what news *Jaques?*

Jaq. He cannot last, I pity the poor man,
I suffer for him; two Coaches of young City dames,
And they drive as the Devil were in the wheels,
Are ready now to enter: and behind these
An old dead-palsied Lady in a Litter,
And she makes all the haste she can: the man's lost,
You may gather up his dry bones to make Nine-pins,
But for his flesh.

Sulp. These are but easie labours
Yet, for I know he must have rest.

Ja. He must—you'll beat him off his legs else presently.

Sul. Go in, and bid him please himself, I am pleas'd too:
To morrow's a new day; but if he can
I would have him take pity o' the old Lady.
Alas 'tis charity.

Jaq. I'le tell him all this,
And if he be not too fool-hardy.

Enter Zabulon.

Sulp. How now?
What news with you?

Zab. You must presently
Shew all the art you have, and for my Lady.

Sulp. She may command.

Zab. You must not dream nor trifle.

Sulp. Which way?

Zab. A spell you must prepare, a powerful one,
Peruse but these directions, you shall find all;
There is the picture too, be quick, and faithful,
And do it with that strength—when 'tis perform'd,
Pitch your reward at what you please, you have it.

Sul. I'le do my best, and suddenly: but hark ye,
Will you never lye at home again?

Zab. Excuse me,
I have too much business yet.

Sulp. I am right glad on't.

Zab. Think on your business, so farewel.

Sulp. I'le do it.

Zab. Within this hour I'le visit you again
And give you greater lights.

Sulp. I shall observe ye;
This brings a brave reward, bravely I'le do it,
And all the hidden art I have, express in't.   [*Exeunt at both doors.*

Enter Rutilio *with a Night-cap.*

Rut. Now do I look as if I were Crow-trodden,
Fye, how my hams shrink under me! O me,

I am broken-winded too; is this a life?
Is this the recreation I have aim'd at?
I had a body once, a handsome body,
And wholesome too. Now I appear like a rascal,
That had been hung a year or two in Gibbets.
Fye how I faint! women? keep me from women;
Place me before a Cannon, 'tis a pleasure;
Stretch me upon a Rack, a recreation;
But women? women? O the Devil! women?
Curtius Gulf was never half so dangerous.
Is there no way to find the Trap-door again,
And fall into the Cellar, and be taken?
No lucky fortune to direct me that way?
No Gallies to be got, nor yet no Gallows?
For I fear nothing now, no earthly thing
But these unsatisfied Men-leeches, women.
How devilishly my bones ake! O the old Lady!
I have a kind of waiting-woman lyes cross my back too,
O how she stings! no treason to deliver me?
Now what are you? do you mock me?

Enter 3. with Night-caps very faintly.

1 No Sir, no;
We were your Predecessors in this place.

2 And come to see you bear up.

Rut. Good Gentlemen;
You seem to have a snuffing in your head Sir,
A parlous snuffing, but this same dampish air—

2 A dampish air indeed.

Rut. Blow your face tenderly,
Your nose will ne're endure it: mercy o' me,
What are men chang'd to here? is my nose fast yet?
Me thinks it shakes i'th' hilts: pray tell me gentlemen,
How long is't since you flourisht here?

3 Not long since.

Rut. Move your self easily, I see you are tender,
Nor long endured.

2 The labour was so much Sir,
And so few to perform it—

Rut. Must I come to this?
And draw my legs after me like a lame Dog?
I cannot run away, I am too feeble:
Will you sue for this place again Gentlemen?

1 No truly Sir, the place has been too warm for our complexions.
We have enough on't, rest you merry Sir,
We came but to congratulate your fortune,
You have abundance.

3 Bear your fortune soberly,
And so we leave you to the next fair Lady.   [*Ex. the* 3.

Rut. Stay but a little, and I'le meet you Gentlemen,
At the next Hospital: there's no living thus,
Nor am I able to endure it longer,
With all the helps and heats that can be given me,
I am at my trot already: they are fair and young
Most of the women that repair unto me,
But they stick on like Burs, shake me like Feathers.

Enter Sulpitia.

More Women yet?
Would I were honestly married
To any thing that had but half a face,
And not a groat to keep her, nor a smock,
That I might be civilly merry when I pleased,
Rather than labouring in these Fulling-mills.

Sul. By this the spell begins to work: you are lusty,
I see you bear up bravely yet.

Rut. Do you hear Lady,
Do not make a game-bear of me, to play me hourly,
And fling on all your whelps; it would not hold;
Play me with some discretion; to day one course,

80

And two dayes hence another.

Sulp. If you be so angry
Pay back the mony I redeem'd you at
And take your course, I can have men enough:
You have cost me a hundred crowns since you came hither,
In Broths and strength[n]ing Caudles; till you do pay me,
If you will eat and live, you shall endeavour,
I'le chain you to't else.

Rut. Make me a Dog-kennel,
I'le keep your house and bark, and feed on bare bones,
And be whipt out o' doors,
Do you mark me Lady? whipt,
I'le eat old shoes.

Enter Duarte.

Dua. In this house I am told
There is a stranger, of a goodly person,
And such a one there was; if I could see him,
I yet remember him.

Sulp. Your business Sir,
If it be for a woman, ye are couzen'd,
I keep none here.   [*Exit.*

Dua. Certain this is the Gentleman;
The very same.

Rut. Death, if I had but mony,
Or any friend to bring me from this bondage,
I would Thresh, set up a Cobler's shop, keep Hogs,
And feed with 'em, sell Tinder-boxes,
And Knights of Ginger-bread, Thatch for three
Half pence a day, and think it Lordly,
From this base Stallion trade: why does he eye me,
Eye me so narrowly?

Dua. It seems you are troubled Sir,
I heard you speak of want.

Rut. 'Tis better hearing

Far, than relieving Sir.

Dua. I do not think so, you know me not.

Rut. Not yet that I remember.

Dua. You shall, and for your friend: I am beholding to ye,
Greatly beholding Sir; if you remember,
You fought with such a man, they call'd *Duarte,*
A proud distemper'd man: he was my enemy,
My mortal foe, you slew him fairly, nobly.

Rut. Speak softly Sir, you do not mean to betray me,
I wisht the Gallows, now th'are coming fairly.

Dua. Be confident, for as I live, I love you,
And now you shall perceive it: for that service,
Me, and my purse command: there, take it to ye,
'Tis gold, and no small sum, a thousand Duckets,
Supply your want.

Rut. But do you do this faithfully?

Dua. If I mean ill, spit in my face and kick me:
In what else I may serve you, Sir—

Rut. I thank you,
This is as strange to me as Knights adventures.
I have a project, 'tis an honest one,
And now I'le tempt my fortune.

Dua. Trust me with it.

Rut. You are so good and honest I must trust ye,
'Tis but to carry a letter to a Lady
That sav'd my life once.

Dua. That will be most thankful,
I will do't with all care.

Rut. Where are you, white-broth?
Now lusty blood,
Come in, and tell your mony:

'Tis ready here, no threats, nor no orations,
Nor prayers now.

Sulp. You do not mean to leave me.

Rut. I'le live in Hell sooner than here, and cooler.
Come quickly come, dispatch, this air's unwho[l]som:
Quickly good Lady, quickly to't.

Sulp. Well, since it must be,
The next I'le fetter faster sure, and closer.

Rut. And pick his bones, as y'have done mine, pox take ye.

Dua. At my lodging for a while, you shall be quartered,
And there take Physick for your health.

Rut. I thank ye,
I have found my angel now too, if I can keep him.
                              [*Exeunt omnes.*

The Custom of the Country

Actus Quintus. Scena Prima.

Enter Rutilio and Duarte.

Rut. You like the Letter?

Dua. Yes, but I must tell you
You tempt a desperate hazard, to sollicite
The mother, (and the grieved one too, 'tis rumor'd)
Of him you slew so lately.

Rut. I have told you
Some proofs of her affection, and I know not
A nearer way to make her satisfaction
For a lost Son, than speedily to help her
To a good Husband; one that will beget
Both Sons and Daughters, if she be not barren.
I have had a breathing now, and have recovered
What I lost in my late service, 'twas a hot one:
It fired and fired me; but all thanks to you Sir,
You have both freed and cool'd me.

Dua. What is done Sir,
I thought well done, and was in that rewarded,
And therefore spare your thanks.

Rut. I'le no more Whoring:
This fencing 'twixt a pair of sheets, more wears one
Than all the exercise in the world besides.
To be drunk with good Canary, a meer Julip
Or like gourd-water to't; twenty Surfeits
Come short of one nights work there. If I get this Lady
As ten to one I shall, I was ne're denied yet,
I will live wondrous honestly; walk before her
Gravely and demurely
And then instruct my family; you are sad,
What do you muse on Sir?

Dua. Truth I was thinking
What course to take for the delivery of your letter,
And now I have it: but faith did this Lady
(For do not gull your self) for certain know,

You kill'd her Son?

Rut. Give me a Book I'le swear't;
Denyed me to the Officers, that pursued me,
Brought me her self to th' door, then gave me gold
To bear my charges, and shall I make doubt then
But that she lov'd me? I am confident
Time having ta'ne her grief off, that I shall be
Most welcome to her: for then to have wooed her
Had been unseasonable.

Dua. Well Sir, there's more mony,
To ma[ke] you handsome; I'le about your business:
You know where you must stay?

Rut. There you shall find me:
Would I could meet my Brother now, to know,
Whether the Jew, his Genius, or my Christian,
Has prov'd the better friend.   [*Exit.*

Dua. O who would trust
Deceiving woman! or believe that one
The best, and most Canoniz'd ever was
More than a seeming goodness? I could rail now
Against the sex, and curse it; but the theam
And way's too common: yet that *Guiomar*
My Mother; (nor let that forbid her to be
The wonder of our nation) she that was
Mark'd out the great example, for all Matrons
Both Wife and Widow; she that in my breeding
Exprest the utmost of a Mothers care,
And tenderness to a Son; she that yet feigns
Such sorrow for me; good God, that this mother,
After all this, should give up to a stranger,
The wreak she ow'd her Son; I fear her honour.
That he was sav'd, much joyes me, and grieve only
That she was his preserver. I'le try further,
And by this Engine, find whether the tears,
Of which she is so prodigal, are for me,
Or us'd to cloak her base hypocrisie.   [*Exit.*

Enter Hippolyta *and* Sulpitia.

85

Hip. Are you assur'd the charm prevails?

Sulp. Do I live?
Or do you speak to me? Now this very instant
Health takes its last leave of her; meager paleness
Like winter, nips the Roses and the Lilies,
The Spring that youth, and love adorn'd her face with.
To force affection, is beyond our art,
For I have prov'd all means that hell has taught me,
Or the malice of a woman, which exceeds it,
To change *Arnoldo's* love, but to no purpose:
But for your bond-woman—

Hip. Let her pine and dye;
She remov'd, which like a brighter Sun,
Obscures my beams, I may shine out again,
And as I have been, be admir'd and sought to:
How long has she to live?

Sulp. Lady, before
The Sun twice rise and set, be confident,
She is but dead; I know my Charm hath found her.
Nor can the Governours Guard; her lovers tears;
Her Fathers sorrow, or his power that freed her,
Defend her from it.

Enter Zabulon.

Zab. All things have succeeded,
As you could wish; I saw her brought sick home;
The image of pale death, stampt on her fore-head.
Let me adore this second Hecate,
This great Commandress, of the fatal Sisters,
That as she pleases, can cut short, or lengthen
The thread of life.

Hip. Where was she when the inchantment
First seis'd upon her?

Zab. Taking the fresh air,
In the company of the Governour, and Count *Clodio*,
Arnoldo too, was present with her Father,
When, in a moment (so the servants told me)

As she was giving thanks to the Governour,
And *Clodio,* for her unexpected freedom,
As if she had been blasted, she sunk down,
To their amazement.

Hip. 'Tis thy master-piece
Which I will so reward, that thou shalt fix here,
And with the hazard of thy life, no more
Make tryal of thy powerful Art; which known
Our Laws call death: off with this Magical Robe,
And be thy self.

Enter Governour, Clodio, *and* Charino.

Sulp. Stand close, you shall hear more.

Man. You must have patience; all rage is vain now,
And piety forbids, that we should question
What is decreed above, or ask a reason
Why heaven determines this or that way of us.

Clod. Heaven has no hand in't; 'tis a work of hell.
Her life hath been so innocent, all her actions
So free from the suspicion of crime,
As rather she deserves a Saints place here,
Than to endure, what now her sweetness suffers.

Char. Not for her fault, but mine Sir, *Zenocia* suffers:
The sin I made, when I sought to rase down
Arnoldo's love, built on a Rock of truth,
Now to the height is punish'd. I profess,
Had he no birth, nor parts, the present sorrow
He now expresses for her, does deserve her
Above all Kings, though such had been his rivals.

Clod. All ancient stories, of the love of Husbands
To vertuous Wives, be now no more remembred.

Char. The tales of *Turtles,* ever be forgotten,
Or, for his sake believ'd.

Man. I have heard, there has been
Between some married pairs, such sympathy,

That th' Husband has felt really the throws
His Wife then teeming suffers, this true grief
Confirms, 'tis not impossible.

Clod. We shall find
Fit time for this hereafter; let's use now
All possible means to help her.

Man. Care, nor cost,
Nor what Physicians can do, shall be wanting;
Make use of any means or men.

Char. You are noble.
          [*Exeunt* Man. Clod, *and* Char.

Sulp. Ten Colledges of Doctors shall not save her.
Her fate is in your hand.

Hip. Can I restore her?

Sulp. If you command my Art.

Hip. I'le dye my self first.
And yet I'le go visit her, and see
This miracle of sorrow in *Arnoldo*:
And 'twere for me, I should change places with her,
And dye most happy, such a lovers tears
Were a rich monument, but too good for her,
Whose misery I glory in: come *Sulpitia*,
You shall along with me, good *Zabulon*
Be not far off.

Zab. I will attend you Madam.   [*Exeunt.*

Enter Duarte, *and a* Servant.

Ser. I have serv'd you from my youth, and ever
You have found me faithful: that you live's a treasure
I'le lock up here; nor shall it be let forth,
But when you give me warrant.

Dua. I rely
Upon thy faith; nay, no more protestations,

88

Too many of them will call that in question,
Which now I doubt not: she is there?

Ser. Alone too,
But take it on my life, your entertainment,
Appearing as you are, will be but course,
For the displeasure I shall undergo
I am prepar'd.

Dua. Leave me, I'le stand the hazard.   [*Exit* Servant.
The silence that's observ'd, her close retirements,
No visitants admitted, not the day;
These sable colours, all signs of true sorrow,
Or hers is deeply counterfeit. I'le look nearer,
Manners give leave — she sits upon the ground;
By heaven she weeps; my picture in her hand too;
She kisses it and weeps again.

Enter Guiomar.

Gui. Who's there?

Dua. There is no starting back now Madam.

Gui. Ha, another murderer! I'le not protect thee,
Though I have no more Sons.

Dua. Your pardon Lady,
There's no such foul fact taints me.

Gui. What makes thou here then?
Where are my servants, do none but my sorrows
Attend upon me? speak, what brought thee hither?

Dua. A will to give you comfort.

Gui. Thou art but a man.
And 'tis beyond a humane reach to do it,
If thou could raise the dead out of their graves,
Bid time run back, make me now what I was,
A happy Mother; gladly I would hear thee,
But that's impossible.

Dua. Please you but read this;
You shall know better there, why I am sent,
Than if I should deliver it.

Gui. From whom comes it?

Dua. That will instruct you. I suspect this stranger,
Yet she spake something that holds such alliance
With his reports; I know not what to think on't;
What a frown was there? she looks me through, & through,
Now reads again, now pauses, and now smiles;
And yet there's more of anger in't than mirth,
These are strange changes; oh I understand it,
She's full of serious thoughts.

Gui. You are just, you Heavens,
And never do forget to hear their prayers,
That truly pay their vows, the defer'd vengeance,
For you, and my words sake so long defer'd,
Under which as a mountain my heart groans yet
When 'twas despair'd of, now is offer'd to me;
And if I lose it, I am both wayes guilty.
The womans mask, dissimulation help me.
Come hither friend, I am sure you know the Gentleman,
That sent these charms.

Dua. Charms Lady?

Gui. These charms;
I well may call them so, they've won upon me,
More than ere letter did; thou art his friend,
(The confidence he has in thee, confirms it)
And therefore I'le be open breasted to thee;
To hear of him, though yet I never saw him,
Was most desir'd of all men; let me blush,
And then I'le say I love him.

Dua. All men see,
In this a womans vertue.

Gui. I expected
For the courtesie I did, long since to have seen him,
And though I then forbad it, you men know,

Between our hearts and tongues there's a large distance;
But I'le excuse him, may be hitherto
He has forborn it, in respect my Son
Fell by his hand.

Dua. And reason Lady.

Gui. No, he did me a pleasure in't, a riotous fellow,
And with that insolent, not worth the owning;
I have indeed kept a long solemn sorrow,
For my friends sake partly; but especially
For his long absence.

Dua. O the Devil.

Guio. Therefore
Bid him be speedy; a Priest shall be ready
To tye the holy knot; this kiss I send him,
Deliver that and bring him.

Dua. I am dumb:
A good cause I have now, and a good sword,
And something I shall do, I wait upon you.   [*Exeunt.*

Enter Manuel, Charino, Arnoldo, Zenocia, *born in a chair.* 2 Doctors,
Clodio.

Doct. Give her more air, she dyes else.

Arn. O thou dread power,
That mad'st this all, and of thy workmanship
This virgin wife, the Master piece, look down on her;
Let her minds virtues, cloth'd in this fair garment,
That worthily deserves a better name
Than flesh and bloud, now sue, and prevail for her.
Or if those are denyed, let innocence,
To which all passages in Heaven stand open,
Appear in her white robe, before thy throne;
And mediate for her: or if this age of sin
Be worthy of a miracle, the Sun
In his diurnal progress never saw
So sweet a subject to imploy it on.

The Custom of the Country

Man. Wonders are ceas'd Sir, we must work by means.

Arno. 'Tis true, and such reverend Physicians are;
To you thus low I fall then; so may you ever
Be stil'd the hands of Heaven, natures restorers;
Get wealth and honours; and by your success,
In all your undertakings, propagate
Your great opinion in the world, as now
You use your saving art; for know good Gentlemen,
Besides the fame, and all that I possess,
For a reward, posterity shall stand
Indebted to you, for (as Heaven forbid it)
Should my *Zenocia* dye, robbing this age
Of all that's good or gracefull, times succeeding,
The story of her pure life not yet perfect,
Will suffer in the want of her example.

Doct. Were all the world to perish with her, we
Can do no more, than what art and experience
Give us assurance of, we have us'd all means
To find the cause of her disease, yet cannot;
How should we then, promise the cure?

Arn. Away,
I did bely you, when I charg'd you with
The power of doing, ye are meer names only,
And even your best perfection, accidental;
What ever malady thou art, or Spirit,
As some hold all diseases that afflict us,
As love already makes me sensible
Of half her sufferings, ease her of her part,
And let me stand the butt of thy fell malice,
And I will swear th'art mercifull.

Doct. Your hand Lady;
What a strange heat is here! bring some warm water.

Arn. She shall use nothing that is yours; my sorrow
Provides her of a better bath, my tears
Shall do that office.

Zeno. O my best *Arnoldo*!
The truest of all lovers! I would live

92

Were heaven so pleas'd, but to reward your sorrow
With my true service; but since that's denied me,
May you live long and happy: do not suffer
(By your affection to me I conjure you)
My sickness to infect you; though much love
Makes you too subject to it.

Arn. In this only

Zenocia wrongs her servant; can the body
Subsist, the Soul departed? 'tis as easie
As I to live without you; I am your husband,
And long have been so, though our adverse fortune,
Bandying us from one hazard to another,
Would never grant me so much happiness,
As to pay a husbands debt; despite of fortune,
In death I'le follow you, and guard mine own;
And there enjoy what here my fate forbids me.

Clod. So true a sorrow, and so feelingly
Exprest, I never read of.

Man. I am struck
With wonder to behold it, as with pity.

Char. If you that are a stranger, suffer for them,
Being tied no further than humanity
Leads you to soft compassion; think great Sir,
What of necessity I must endure,
That am a Father?

Hippolyta, Zabulon, *and* Sulpitia *at the door.*

Zab. Wait me there, I hold it
Unfit to have you seen; as I find cause,
You shall proceed.

Man. You are welcom Lady.

Hip. Sir, I come to do a charitable office,
How does the patient?

Clod. You may enquire

Of more than one; for two are sick, and deadly,
He languishes in her, her health's despair'd of,
And in hers, his.

Hip. 'Tis a strange spectacle,
With what a patience they sit unmov'd!
Are they not dead already?

Doct. By her pulse,
She cannot last a day.

Arn. Oh by that summons,
I know my time too!

Hip. Look to the man.

Clod. Apply
Your Art, to save the Lady, preserve her,
A town is your reward.

Hip. I'le treble it,
In ready gold, if you restore *Arnoldo*;
For in his death I dye too.

Clod. Without her
I am no more.

Arn. Are you there Madam? now
You may feast on my miseries; my coldness
In answering your affections, or hardness,
Give it what name you please, you are reveng'd of,
For now you may perceive, our thred of life
Was spun together, and the poor *Arnoldo*
Made only to enjoy the best *Zenocia*,
And not to serve the use of any other;
And in that she may equal; my Lord *Clodio*
Had long since else enjoyed her, nor could I
Have been so blind, as not to see your great
And many excellencies far, far beyond
Or my deservings, or my hopes; we are now
Going our latest journey, and together,
Our only comfort we desire, pray give it,
Your charity to our ashes, such we must be,

And not to curse our memories.

Hip. I am much mov'd.

Clod. I am wholly overcome, all love to women
Farewell for ever; ere you dye, your pardon;
And yours Sir; had she many years to live,
Perhaps I might look on her, as a Brother,
But as a lover never; and since all
Your sad misfortunes had original
From the barbarous Custom practis'd in my Country,
Heaven witness, for your sake I here release it;
So to your memory, chaste Wives and Virgins
Shall ever pay their vowes. I give her to you;
And wish, she were so now, as when my lust
Forc'd you to quit the Country.

Hip. It is in vain
To strive with destiny, here my dotage ends,
Look up *Zenocia*, health in me speaks to you;
She gives him to you, that by divers ways,
So long has kept him from you: and repent not,
That you were once my servant, for which health
In recompence of what I made you suffer,
The hundred thousand Crowns, the City owes me,
Shall be your dower.

Man. 'Tis a magnificent gift,
Had it been timely given.

Hip. It is believe it, *Sulpitia*.

Enter a Servant, *and* Sulpitia.

Sulp. Madam.

Hip. Quick, undoe the charm;
Ask not a reason why; let it suffice,
It is my will.

Sulp. Which I obey and gladly.   [*Exit.*

Man. Is to be married, sayest thou?

95

Ser. So she sayes Sir,
And does desire your presence.   [*They are born off in chairs.*

Man. And tell her I'le come.

Hip. Pray carry them to their rest; for though already,
They do appear as dead, let my life pay for't,
If they recover not.

Man. What you have warranted,
Assure your self, will be expected from you;
Look to them carefully; and till the tryal, —

Hip. Which shall not be above four hours.

Man. Let me
Intreat your companies: there is something
Of weight invites me hence.

All. We'll wait upon you.   [*Exeunt.*

Enter Guiomar, *and* Servants.

Guio. You understand what my directions are,
And what they guide you to; the faithfull promise
You have made me all.

All. We do and will perform it.

Guio. The Governour will not fail to be here presently;
Retire a while, till you shall find occasion,
And bring me word, when they arrive.

All. Wee shall Madam.

Guio. Only stay you to entertain.

1 Ser. I am ready.

Guio. I wonder at the bold, and practis'd malice,
Men ever have o' foot against our honours,
That nothing we can do, never so vertuous,
No shape put on so pious, no not think

96

What a good is, be that good ne're so noble,
Never so laden with admir'd example,
But still we end in lust; our aims, our actions,
Nay, even our charities, with lust are branded;
Why should this stranger else, this wretched stranger,
Whose life I sav'd at what dear price sticks here yet,
Why should he hope? he was not here an hour,
And certainly in that time, I may swear it
I gave him no loose look, I had no reason;
Unless my tears were flames, my curses courtships;
The killing of my Son, a kindness to me.
Why should he send to me, or with what safety
(Examining the ruine he had wrought me)
Though at that time, my pious pity found him,
And my word fixt; I am troubled, strongly troubled.

Enter a Servant.

Ser. The Gentlemen are come.

Guio. Then bid 'em welcome—I must retire.   [*Exit.*

Enter Rutilio, *and* Duarte.

Ser. You are welcom Gentlemen.

Rut. I thank you friend, I would speak with your Lady.

Ser. I'le let her understand.

Rut. It shall befit you.
How do I look Sir, in this handsome trim?   [*Exit* Servant.
Me thinks I am wondrous brave.

Duar. You are very decent.

Rut. These by themselves, without more helps of nature,
Would set a woman hard; I know 'em all,
And where their first aims light; I'le lay my head on't,
I'le take her eye, as soon as she looks on me,
And if I come to speak once, woe be to her,
I have her in a nooze, she cannot scape me;
I have their several lasts.

Dua. You are throughly studied,
But tell me Sir, being unacquainted with her,
As you confess you are —

Rut. That's not an hours work,
I'le make a Nun forget her beads in two hours.

Dua. She being set in years, next none of those lusters
Appearing in her eye, that warm the fancy;
Nor nothing in her face, but handsom ruines.

Rut. I love old stories: those live believ'd, Authentique,
When 20. of your modern faces are call'd in,
For new opinion, paintings, and corruptions;
Give me an old confirm'd face; besides she sav'd me,
She sav'd my life, have I not cause to love her?
She's rich and of a constant state, a fair one,
Have I not cause to wooe her? I have tryed sufficient
All your young Phillies, I think this back has try'd 'em,
And smarted for it too: they run away with me,
Take bitt between the teeth, and play the Devils;
A staied pace now becomes my years; a sure one,
Where I may sit and crack no girths.

Dua. How miserable,
If my Mother should confirm, what I suspect now,
Beyond all humane cure were my condition!
Then I shall wish, this body had been so too.
Here comes the Lady Sir.

Enter Guiomar.

Rut. Excellent Lady,
To shew I am a creature, bound to your service,
And only yours —

Guio. Keep at that distance Sir;
For if you stir —

Rut. I am obedient.
She has found already, I am for her turn;
With what a greedy hawks eye she beholds me!
Mark how she musters all my parts.

Guio. A goodly Gentleman,
Of a more manly set, I never look'd on.

Rut. Mark, mark her eyes still; mark but the carriage of 'em.

Guio. How happy am I now, since my Son fell,
He fell not by a base unnoble hand!
As that still troubled me; how far more happy
Shall my revenge be, since the Sacrifice,
I offer to his grave, shall be both worthy
A Sons untimely loss, and a Mothers sorrow!

Rut. Sir, I am made believe it; she is mine own,
I told you what a spell I carried with me,
All this time does she spend in contemplation
Of that unmatch'd delight: I shall be thankfull to ye;
And if you please to know my house, to use it;
To take it for your own.

Guio. Who waits without there?

Enter Guard, *and* Servants, *they seize upon* Rut. *and bind him.*

Rut. How now? what means this, Lady?

Guio. Bind him fast.

Rut. Are these the bride-laces you prepare for me?
The colours that you give?

Dua. Fye Gentle Lady,
This is not noble dealing.

Guio. Be you satisfied,
I[t] seems you are a stranger to this meaning,
You shall not be so long.

Rut. Do you call this wooing—Is there no end of womens persecutions?
Must I needs fool into mine own destruction?
Have I not had fair warnings, and enough too?
Still pick the Devils teeth? you are not mad Lady;
Do I come fairly, and like a Gentleman,

To offer you that honour?

Guio. You are deceiv'd Sir,
You come besotted, to your own destruction:
I sent not for you; what honour can ye add to me,
That brake that staff of honour, my age lean'd on?
That rob'd me of that right, made me a Mother?
Hear me thou wretched man, hear me with terrour,
And let thine own bold folly shake thy Soul,
Hear me pronounce thy death, that now hangs o're thee,
Thou desperate fool; who bad thee seek this ruine?
What mad unmanly fate, made thee discover
Thy cursed face to me again? was't not enough
To have the fair protection of my house,
When misery and justice close pursued thee?
When thine own bloudy sword, cryed out against thee,
Hatcht in the life of him? yet I forgave thee.
My hospitable word, even when I saw
The goodliest branch of all my blood lopt from me,
Did I not seal still to thee?

Rut. I am gone.

Guio. And when thou went'st, to Imp thy miserie,
Did I not give thee means? but hark ungratefull,
Was it not thus? to hide thy face and fly me?
To keep thy name for ever from my memory?
Thy cursed blood and kindred? did I not swear then,
If ever, (in this wretched life thou hast left me,
Short and unfortunate,) I saw thee again,
Or came but to the knowledge, where thou wandredst,
To call my vow back, and pursue with vengeance
With all the miseries a Mother suffers?

Rut. I was born to be hang'd, there's no avoiding it.

Guio. And dar'st thou with this impudence appear here?
Walk like the winding sheet my Son was put in,
Stand with those wounds?

Dua. I am happy now again;
Happy the hour I fell, to find a Mother,
So pious, good, and excellent in sorrows.

100

Enter a Servant.

Ser. The Governour's come in.

Guio. O let him enter.

Rut. I have fool'd my self a fair thred of all my fortunes,
This strikes me most; not that I fear to perish,
But that this unmannerly boldness has brought me to it.

Enter Governour, Clodio, Charino.

Gov. Are these fit preparations for a wedding Lady?
I came prepar'd a guest.

Guio. O give me justice;
As ever you will leave a vertuous name,
Do justice, justice, Sir.

Gove. You need not ask it,
I am bound to it.

Guio. Justice upon this man
That kill'd my Son.

Gove. Do you confess the act?

Rut. Yes Sir.

Clod. Rutilio?

Char. 'Tis the same.

Clod. How fell he thus?
Here will be sorrow for the good *Arnoldo.*

Gove. Take heed Sir what you say.

Rut. I have weigh'd it well,
I am the man, nor is it life I start at;
Only I am unhappy I am poor,
Poor in expence of lives, there I am wretched,
That I have not two lives lent me for his sacrifice;

One for her Son, another for her sorrows.
Excellent Lady, now rejoyce again,
For though I cannot think, y'are pleas'd in blood,
Nor with that greedy thirst pursue your vengeance;
The tenderness, even in those tears denies that;
Yet let the world believe, you lov'd *Duarte*;
The unmatcht courtesies you have done my miseries;
Without this forfeit to the law, would charge me
To tender you this life, and proud 'twould please you.

Guio. Shall I have justice?

Gover. Yes.

Rut. I'le ask it for ye,
I'le follow it my self, against my self.
Sir, 'Tis most fit I dye; dispatch it quickly,
The monstrous burthen of that grief she labours with
Will kill her else, then blood on blood lyes on me;
Had I a thousand lives, I'd give 'em all,
Before I would draw one tear more from that vertue.

Guio. Be not too cruel Sir, and yet his bold sword—
But his life cannot restore that, he's a man too—
Of a fair promise, but alas my Son's dead;
If I have justice, must it kill him?

Gov. Yes.

Guio. If I have not, it kills me, strong and goodly!
Why should he perish too?

Gover. It lies in your power,
You only may accuse him, or may quit him.

Clod. Be there no other witnesses?

Guio. Not any.
And if I save him, will not the world proclaim,
I have forgot a Son, to save a murderer?
And yet he looks not like one, he looks manly.

Hip. Pity so brave a Gentleman should perish.

102

The Custom of the Country

She cannot be so hard, so cruel hearted.

Guio. Will you pronounce? yet stay a little Sir.

Rut. Rid your self, Lady, of this misery;
And let me go, I do but breed more tempests,
With which you are already too much shaken.

Guio. Do now, pronounce; I will not hear.

Dua. You shall not,
Yet turn and see good Madam.

Gove. Do not wonder.
'Tis he, restor'd again, thank the good Doctor,
Pray do not stand amaz'd, it is *Duarte*;
Is well, is safe again.

Guio. O my sweet Son,
I will not press my wonder now with questions—
Sir, I am sorry for that cruelty,
I urg'd against you.

Rut. Madam, it was but justice.

Dua. 'Tis [t]rue, the Doctor heal'd this body again,
But this man heal'd my soul, made my minde perfect,
The good sharp lessons his sword read to me, sav'd me;
For which, if you lov'd me, dear Mother,
Honour and love this man.

Guio. You sent this letter?

Rut. My boldness makes me blush now.

Guio. I'le wipe off that,
And with this kiss, I take you for my husband,
Your wooing's done Sir; I believe you love me,
And that's the wealth I look for now.

Rut. You have it.

Dua. You have ended my desire to all my wishes.

Gov. Now 'tis a wedding again. And if *Hippolyta*
Make good, what with the hazard of her life,
She undertook, the evening will set clear

Enter Hippolyta, *leading* Leopold, Arnoldo, Zenocia, *in either hand*,
Zabulon, Sulpitia.

After a stormy day.

Char. Here comes the Lady.

Clod. With fair *Zenocia*,
Health with life again
Restor'd unto her.

Zen. The gift of her goodness.

Rut. Let us embrace, I am of your order too,
And though I once despair'd of women, now
I find they relish much of Scorpions,
For both have stings, and both can hurt, and cure too;
But what have been your fortunes?

Arn. Wee'l defer
Our story, and at time more fit, relate it.
Now all that reverence vertue, and in that
Zenocias constancy, and perfect love,
Or for her sake *Arnoldo*, join with us
In th' honour of this Lady.

Char. She deserves it.

Hip. *Hippolytas* life shall make that good hereafter,
Nor will I alone better my self but others:
For these whose wants perhaps have made their actions
Not altogether innocent, shall from me
Be so supplied, that need shall not compel them,
To any course of life, but what the law
Shall give allowance to.

Zab. *Sulpitia*, Your Ladiships creatures.

Rut. Be so, and no more you man-huckster.

The Custom of the Country

Hip. And worthy *Leopold*, you that with such fervour,
So long have sought me, and in that deserv'd me,
Shall now find full reward for all your travels,
Which you have made more dear by patient sufferance.
And though my violent dotage did transport me,
Beyond those bounds, my modesty should have kept in,
Though my desires were loose, from unchast art
Heaven knows I am free.

Leop. The thought of that's dead to me;
I gladly take your offer.

Rut. Do so Sir,
A piece of crackt gold ever will weigh down
Silver that's whole.

Gov. You shall be all my guests,
I must not be denied.

Arn. Come my *Zenocia*.
Our bark at length has found a quiet harbour;
And the unspotted progress of our loves
Ends not alone in safety, but reward,
To instruct others, by our fair example;
That though good purposes are long withstood,
The hand of Heaven still guides such as are good.

[*Ex. omnes.*

Epilogue.

Why there should be an Epilogue to a play,
I know no cause: the old and usuall way,
For which they were made, was to entreat the grace
Of such as were spectators in this place,
And time, 'tis to no purpose; for I know
What you resolve already to bestow,
Will not be alter'd, what so e're I say,
In the behalf of us, and of the Play;
Only to quit our doubts, if you think fit,
You may, or cry it up, or silence it.

The Epilogue.

I spake much in the Prologue for the Play,
  To its desert I hope, yet you might say
Should I change now from that, which then was meant,
  Or in a syllable grow less confident,
I were weak-hearted. I am still the same
  In my opinion, and forbear to frame
Qualification, or excuse: If you
  Concur with me, and hold my judgement true,
Shew it with any sign, and from this place,
  Or send me off exploded, or with grace.